Michael Coulson (1936–75) was Senior Lecturer in Sanskrit at Edinburgh University. He was educated at St Paul's School, London, and Trinity College, Oxford. His doctoral thesis was a critical edition of the *Mālatīmādhava*, a Sanskrit play translated in this volume. A passionate admirer of Sanskrit literature, and concerned to make it better known in the West, he also wrote *Teach Yourself Sanskrit*.

THREE SANSKRIT PLAYS

Śakuntalā
by Kālidāsa

Rākshasa's Ring
by Viśākhadatta

Mālatī and Mādhava
by Bhavabhūti

TRANSLATED
WITH AN INTRODUCTION BY
MICHAEL COULSON

PENGUIN BOOKS

Penguin Books Ltd, Harmondsworth,
Middlesex, England
Penguin Books, 625 Madison Avenue,
New York, New York 10022, U.S.A.
Penguin Books Australia Ltd, Ringwood,
Victoria, Australia
Penguin Books Canada Ltd, 2801 John Street,
Markham, Ontario, Canada L3R 1B4
Penguin Books (N.Z.) Ltd, 182–190 Wairau Road,
Auckland 10, New Zealand

This translation first published 1981

Made and printed in Great Britain by
Richard Clay (The Chaucer Press) Ltd,
Bungay, Suffolk
Set in Monotype Ehrhardt

Contents

To Pat

advaitaṃ …

Approximate Guide to Pronunciation

(The transcription of Sanskrit names is the standard one, with the exceptions that *ṛ* is represented by *ri*, *c* by *ch*, *ṣ* by *sh*, *ṅ/ñ* by *n* and *ṃ* by *m*.)

SHORT VOWELS

a like *u* in b*u*t
i like *i* in p*i*t
u like *u* in p*u*t

LONG VOWELS AND DIPHTHONGS

ā like *a* in f*a*ther
ī like *ee* in f*ee*t
ū like *oo* in m*oo*n
e like *ei* in r*ei*ns (N.B., never short as in p*e*t)
o like *oa* in m*oa*n (N.B., never short as in p*o*t)
ai like *ie* in l*ie*
au like *ou* in s*ou*nd

CONSONANTS

ś and *sh* are both like *sh* in *sh*ip, and *ch* like *ch* in *ch*ip. With these exceptions, *h* simply indicates aspiration. For instance, *ph* is pronounced rather like the *ph* in u*ph*eaval (not as in 'philosophy').

APPROXIMATE GUIDE TO PRONUNCIATION

The dot under *ṭ*, *ḍ* and *ṇ* indicates that the tongue is curled further back (retroflex). To English ears this distinction is a fine one, and can be ignored.

Note that *g* is always as in *g*et, *j* as in *j*et, *s* as in *s*et and *y* as in *y*et.

STRESS

Stress the last 'heavy' syllable other than the last syllable of the word. Failing a heavy syllable put the stress as far back as possible, up to four syllables from the end. A syllable is heavy if the vowel in it is long or a diphthong or followed by more than one consonant. So Durvā́sas, Aśóka, Dushyánta, Mā́latī, Víjayā, Saudā́manī, Śā́rngarava.

GENDER OF NAMES

It should be assumed that Sanskrit names ending in *ā* or *ī* are feminine, while all those ending in *a* together with most others are masculine.

Introduction

The three plays here translated are among the leading examples of Classical Sanskrit drama, and were probably all written within the period A.D. 350–750. This period represents the summit of Sanskrit literary achievement – though the earliest surviving Sanskrit texts, the hymns of the *Ṛg Veda*, go back some three thousand years, and work of considerable literary merit continued to be produced up to the tenth century A.D. and beyond. (The chronology of Sanskrit literature, as of Classical India in general, is extremely tentative, since the keeping of accurate historical records was never a culturally important activity.)

Sanskrit is a highly inflected language, historically cognate with Latin, Greek and most of the other languages of Europe. Its grammar was codified for all time in the fourth century B.C. by the grammarian Pāṇini. Thereafter the standards of correct Sanskrit (at least in the externals of inflexion and pronunciation) never altered, though the way people spoke informally naturally continued to change. As a result Sanskrit ceased to be a natural, spoken language and became the language of the educated, learnt at school and indispensable as the medium of administrative and cultural communication. Its position in Classical India is comparable with that of Latin in Medieval Europe.

In Sanskrit drama not all the dialogue is in Sanskrit. While men of high social status speak Sanskrit, the uneducated – men of inferior status, young children and almost all women – speak in varieties of Prakrit, the language which evolved from Sanskrit (rather as Italian evolved from Latin). Originally this must have been at least in part a reflection of social realities. But as time passed the Prakrit dialects used in the drama became no more than a rigid literary convention, and likely to be less comprehensible to people of ordinary education than Sanskrit itself. The medieval commentator Harihara, in undertaking to explain the Prakrit used in *Mālatī and Mādhava*, describes it as *vitrāsakāri kudhiyām adhunātanānām*, 'a source of terror to the dimwits of today'.

All Classical Sanskrit literature, in fact, was written for a highly educated, highly sophisticated audience. It was recognized that drama had a greater breadth of appeal than other literary genres because it incorporated the elements of spectacle, music and dance. But on the literary side the dramatist made no compromise with popular taste. Dramatic verse is fully as complex as that of any other genre, and if the audience numbered some who could make little of it, they are clearly not the ones at whom the poet was directing his work. There were no vast amphitheatres with mass audiences as in the Greek tradition. The typical performance would have been held either under private patronage (in a palace, for example) or as a contribution to a religious festival, and given in a hall of comparatively modest size, though preferably one specially constructed for the performance of plays. The style of performance was intimate and suited to a small audience, with attention paid to subtleties of gesture and expression.

We know in outline the conditions of stage presentation, though many questions remain unanswered. No curtain separated the stage from the audience. There was no scenery, and props were very little used: the ancient handbook on the theatre, the *Nāṭya Śāstra*, cursorily dismisses any suggestion that realism is desirable, for example when someone is represented as riding in a chariot or sailing in a boat, by observing that no one expects an actor to die when the character he is playing does so. However, importance is attached to costume and adornment, and in general the focus of attention is on the actor rather than on his physical environment.

A curtain did separate the back of the stage from the *nepathya*, or actors' changing-room. Normally when an actor came on stage, part of this curtain was drawn aside for him by attendants. Occasionally a sudden and dramatic entry was marked by the actor's pushing through the curtain for himself. The stage was divided (in the minds, that is, of spectators and actors) into zones, so that an actor could indicate a change of locality, such as a visit to a friend's house, by moving from one part of the stage to another: this is the significance of the frequent stage-direction '*he walks about*'. By means of this convention different groups of actors could occupy the stage simultaneously without supposedly being visible to each other. The action can switch in turn from one group to another in a way that might well be aided on the modern stage by the use of a spotlight.

A character often speaks '*to himself*', i.e. voices his thoughts for the benefit of the audience without any of the other characters hearing. The frequency with which this device is employed in the course of ordinary dialogue goes well beyond the normal use of soliloquy and asides in the Western theatre, and gives Sanskrit drama a flexibility in representing the private thoughts and attitudes of its characters which rivals a modern 'multiple-viewpoint' novel. Someone may also speak privately to a companion, while remaining unheard by others who are present. In addition, characters in one zone may speak without being heard by those in another zone, but this convention is not indicated by any special instruction in the text.

The stage-directions form an integral part of the original text of the plays, and I have been careful to preserve them exactly as written.* Again, they are entirely actor-oriented and never include a direct indication of setting. In other words the written text consists of two sets of instructions to the actors: what to say ('Who is that coming this way?') and how to behave ('*he peers anxiously*'). This fact emphasizes the integral part played by mime in Sanskrit drama. The actor communicated not merely by words but by the controlled use of his body and facial expressions. It was the elaboration of this art which made it possible to dispense with material props: actions such as riding in a chariot, flying through the air, watering flowers, being pestered by a bee, were all conveyed clearly by the actor's skill alone. The language of these stage-directions is terse and conventional, and the modern reader is left to fill out the picture from his own imagination. One stage-direction may sound rather puzzling, the not infrequent '*enter seated*'. The meaning of this in dramatic terms is not in doubt: it corresponds to the '*is discovered seated*' of a stage with a front curtain or a spotlighting system. But how this particular direction was realized in practice is less clear – perhaps simply by entering and then assuming a seated posture.

It is evident that music contributed significantly to the performance. The *Nāṭya Śāstra* compares a play without

*But with one minor exception: the original never identifies the source of a 'VOICE OFF-STAGE' – so that specific attribution, such as 'KING'S VOICE OFF-STAGE', merely represents my own inference from the context.

music to an unpainted building, and in another passage says that song, instrumental music and acting should be blended into one, like the circle of a whirling firebrand. Among the more important instruments were the *vīnā* or lute, the flute, drums and cymbals; while on the vocal side, female singers were more highly admired than male. Before the play began the musicians, including the singers, would take up their position at the back of the stage and embark on a series of elaborate preliminaries which served the dual purpose of 'tuning up' and of setting the mood for the coming performance. And throughout the play music was used to reinforce the action – thus a drunkard's staggering gait would be underlined on the drum. Particularly intriguing are the descriptions of the Prakrit mood-songs, called *dhruvā*, which it seems frequently accompanied the entrances and exits of the characters, and could be used at other points also to attune the expectations of the audience (one useful variety, the *antarā dhruvā*, was available to cover up any hitch in an actor's performance) Typically the language of such a song would take the form of a symbolic description of nature: thus a song about a mighty elephant crashing through the jungle would mark the appearance of the hero roaming desperately in search of his beloved.

Responsibility for the composition and performance of these songs seems to have rested essentially with the musicians rather than with the playwright and actors, and it is difficult to say how prominently they would have figured in a performance of a Classical drama. In one recension of Kālidāsa's play *Vikramorvaśī* which has come down to us, the fourth act incorporates material of this kind: but it is generally agreed that, in the form in which we have it, this version is late; and we cannot be sure how accurately it reflects the ordinary tradition of stage performance even of this particular piece, let alone of Classical drama in general. Clearly tact would have been needed to avoid a clash between such material and the subtle heightenings of mood conveyed by the dramatist's own poetry – just as, in the modern cinema, banal and over-obvious background music can ruin the artistic impact of a film.

Many of the features which give Sanskrit drama its distinctive nature will be apparent from the translations in this volume. One of the most fundamental is the blending of prose and verse. The word 'poetry' has no direct equivalent in Sanskrit: because a vast quantity of scientific writing is in metrical form, verse has no special association with belles-lettres. The nearest term, *kāvya*, embraces every variety of creative literature. Within it, the three major forms of extended creative writing are: narrative poems, entirely metrical, prose romances, entirely non-metrical, and dramas. The prose of the romances ('novels' would be a rather misleading term for this, the least important of the three genres) is often highly ornate. By contrast the prose of the dramas, which forms a counterpart of the verse, is generally clear and simple. The exception provided in the present volume by *Mālatī and Mādhava* really proves the rule. The beautifully complex verse-forms of Sanskrit are not well adapted to the Prakrit language, and Bhavabhūti (unlike Kālidāsa and Viśākhadatta) never writes Prakrit verse – very artificially, Mālatī's verses in Act II and those of Lavangikā in Act VII are in Sanskrit. Instead he allows his Prakrit-speaking characters to take wing from time to time into a more elaborate and descriptive prose, the consolations of verse being denied them.

The distinction between prose and verse in the plays is again something I have been careful to keep. In general I have aimed at a fairly close translation, and the preservation rather than naturalization of culturally unfamiliar images and ideas, except perhaps where these are wholly incidental to what is being said and might therefore be distracting. By keeping the four-line structure of Sanskrit stanzas, I have hoped to suggest something of the variety of long and short metres used in the original. It will be obvious enough that my translations are often extremely low-key, and they are not intended to be an addition to the corpus of English poetry. But I would resist the suggestion that I might just as well have used prose. Free-verse translations can serve a useful function in suggesting a metrical original, and this is particularly important where the work translated alternates between verse and prose. Undoubtedly it can be claimed that the formal beauty of Sanskrit verse can only adequately be represented by a highly melodious and formally patterned, perhaps therefore rhymed, English equivalent. But this calls both for considerable poetic talent and for an appreciably greater degree of freedom in adapting the original, and in practice the results seldom seem to justify the liberties taken. Even when it is reasonably successful, the final effect of a rhymed English translation is usually to suggest a minor English poet rather than a great Indian one, and one wonders uneasily whether it is right to turn someone like Kālidāsa into raw material for the exercise of frustrated poetic ambitions.

Translators from all languages have a difficult and thankless task: in the end there are no degrees of success, only degrees of failure. But translators of Sanskrit *kāvya* have more to complain about than most. To translate a

Sanskrit stanza so that it merely bores rather than bewilders the reader can be an achievement in itself. The chief reason is a syntactical one, and lies in the way in which the Classical poets exploited the structural possibilities of the language. In Classical Sanskrit subordinate phrases and clauses are largely replaced by compound noun formations. Not infrequently a stanza of verse is wholly organized around a small nucleus of subject–verb–object. Here is a piece of English verse which has something of the pace and cadence of a Sanskrit stanza:

For the clear voice suddenly singing, high up in the convent
  wall,
The scent of elder bushes, the sporting prints in the hall,
The croquet matches in summer, the handshake, the cough,
  the kiss,
There is always a wicked secret, a private reason for this.

W. H. AUDEN

And here is a literal English rendering of the grammatical structure such a verse might have in Sanskrit (one should perhaps caution the linguistically unsophisticated against importing into Sanskrit the English notion that long compounds have a comic flavour to them):

Convent-wall-height-sudden-clearsinging-voice-signalled,
Elderbush-scent-hinted, hall-hung-sportingprints-lurking,
Summer-held-croquetmatch-implicit, handshake-cough-kiss-
  betrayed,
Everywhere are found wicked private-reason-based secrets.

This is a straightforward example: factors such as the existence of a type of compound called *bahuvrīhi* and the highly inflected nature of Sanskrit would make similar renderings of other stanzas quite incomprehensible. The function a compound plays in a sentence depends on its grammatical ending, and many stanzas are tightly organized mosaics that defy literal translation. The baffled translator resorts to breaking up and rearranging this carefully constructed artefact, and two features of the original, order of ideas and syntactical unity, tend to be regarded as particularly expendable. No one would really find it necessary to resort to such rearrangement in the above example, but the following is a parody of the kind of thing that can happen:

Everywhere one finds wicked secrets based on private reasons: they are signalled by the sudden clear-singing voice in the heights of a convent wall; the scent of elder bushes hints at them, and they lurk among the sporting prints hung in the hall; croquet matches in summer imply t..em; handshakes, coughs and kisses betray them.

Faced with standard 'literal' versions of this kind, which are prosaic for a far more fundamental reason than the lack of rhyme and metre, it is difficult for the Western reader to guess at Sanskrit originals as tuneful and evocative as the verse by Auden.

I stress the tunefulness of Sanskrit verse, since it is relevant to the complementary roles of verse and prose in the theatrical idiom. The distinction is almost one of 'recitative and aria'. The perpetual alternation between the directness of the prose and the lyricism of the verse is fundamental to the dramatic rhythm. Except occasionally for motives of stylistic variety, verse is not used as a way of carrying the story forward. Its function is rather one of crystallization, of commenting on the situation and developing its implications. Even when characters talk to each other directly in verse, the verse tends to be preceded by a short remark in prose, a headline as it were for the following story ('I am disappointed in you', 'your eyes are so beautiful', 'who is that figure standing beside you?'). Deictic references ('look at this', 'here is the person who') are often kept out of the stanza even if they are grammatically part of it – one of the reaons why stanzas from Sanskrit plays can often appear in anthologies without their dramatic origin being apparent. The suggestion that Sanskrit drama is generally 'undramatic', while it no doubt has an element of truth, is in my view rather exaggerated, and perhaps stems from an over-preoccupation with the verse and a certain failure to recognize the important complementary role played by the prose. (One critical edition of the *Śakuntalā* actually quotes variant readings only for the verses!)

Of the three plays in this volume, *Śakuntalā* and *Rākshasa's Ring* are classified as *nāṭaka* or heroic drama, while *Mālatī and Mādhava* is a *prakaraṇa* or invented drama. The plot of the *nāṭaka*, the most highly regarded dramatic form, is taken from tradition, whereas the *prakaraṇa* has a plot devised by the playwright himself, and is nearer to being a play of everyday life in featuring the activities of such people as ministers, merchants and courtesans rather than kings and gods. Neither *nāṭaka* in this volume is entirely typical in the source of its plot. *Śakuntalā* is based not on one of the great Indian myths but on a threadbare minor legend recounted in the *Mahābhārata* and radically reshaped by Kālidāsa; while *Rākshasa's Ring* is not based on legend at all but on historical fact, though to its audience the exploits of Chandra Gupta were probably more remote than those of Rāma or Duryodhana.

But whether they derive from tradition or the writer's imagination, the characters in these dramas are types rather than individuals. The method of the Indian poet was not to elevate particular people to universal status but to take universal types and then infuse them with individual human life. The atmosphere of Sanskrit drama is of the fairy story taken to an ultimate pitch of sophistication. It is often said that the nearest parallel in Western tradition to plays such as *Śakuntalā* is Shakespearian comedy. There is the same blend of gentleness, grace and fantasy with a calm maturity and wisdom. Tragedy in the Greek sense does not occur, and unhappy endings of any kind are as foreign to the conventions of Sanskrit drama as they are for instance to the novels of Jane Austen. Even a play such as Bhavabhūti's *Later Story of Rāma*, in which the Sorrowful *rasa* (for which see below) predominates, modulates into serenity and reconciliation at the end.

A Western reader, of course, cannot hope to come to a Sanskrit play in the same state of preparedness as its original audience. There is not merely the question of cultural references (some of which at least can be explained in footnotes) and of the general context of life shared by the poet and his public. There is also the question of the literary tradition itself. A work of art as well as being a reflection of the culture that produces it is more specifically a comment on the works of art that have preceded it. This is particularly true where, as in India, the tradition has been a long, articulate and self-conscious one. When the poet embroiders on what has gone before, his work may seem strained and far-fetched to the outsider unfamiliar with what has gone before – a consideration which applies particularly to the use of figures of speech in Sanskrit poetry, which were elaborated and refined over a long period.

It is where cultural differences and literary tradition reinforce each other that the Western reader is likely to feel least at home. The Indian varieties of the lotus and the waterlily, for example, have a degree of symbolic value more than comparable with that of the rose in Western poetry. To select one aspect, the lotus, opening out at dawn and folding its petals again towards evening, is regarded as having a particular affinity with the sun, while the night-blossoming waterlily is regarded as being under the tutelage of the moon: these relationships, as part of the natural order of things, may be taken for granted or seen as mysterious and paradoxical (as in *Mālatī and Mādhava* – 'the searing sun makes the lotus bloom'), but either way they serve as a paradigm of many other such affinities in the world about us. Again, the comparison between the human eye and the deep colour of the dark blue variety of waterlily was so familiar that two people gazing long and deep into each other's eyes could be described as 'linked by a garland of dark waterlilies' (also relevant to this image is the fact that the process of seeing was conceived in terms of an outgoing radiation from the eye).

When in Act IX of *Mālatī and Mādhava* Mādhava is overcome with grief at the signs of the approach of the monsoon, this is because the season of the rains, being unsuitable for travelling, is a time symbolizing domestic tranquillity and the reunion of loved ones, when separation is especially bitter (a period comparable in this respect with Christmastide). As in the West, the season of spring is believed to inflame amorous feeling: but when lovers grow tormented by the intensity of their passion and their doubts as to its being reciprocated, they attain a state of such hypersensitivity that even the cool rays of the moon can burn them like fire. However, the pallor and emaciation brought on by love-fever are felt to heighten their physical attractiveness.

The ideal of female beauty is one of extreme shapeliness.

The waist must be slim and the breasts youthfully firm, but if these conditions are met, every pound of flesh on breasts and hips augments a woman's attractions. For this reason we are often told that her breasts are too heavy for her slender waist to bear, or that when she walks the exertion of moving her bulky hips causes her to break out in a fine sweat. (Conveniently, the wasting effect of love sickness usually seems to manifest itself less strikingly on the breasts and hips than on other parts of the body – most particularly the arms, on which bracelets in consequence grow loose.) The mention of sweating has pleasant associations, for in other amorous contexts it may give a lover a clue to his sweetheart's emotional state. Sweating, like other involuntary physical reactions such as tears or trembling, is valued by poets as a means whereby ideals of self-discipline can suffer an honourable defeat at the hands of invincible nature. One such involuntary reaction features far more prominently in Indian than in Western literature – horripilation ('gooseflesh'), frequently seen as a sign of sexual excitement.

While the depiction of these involuntary physical reactions is common to all Sanskrit literature, the need for them to be realized in concrete visual terms on the stage gives them prominence of a particular sort in the drama; and formalized into eight *involuntary states*, they provide one element in an ancient and important tradition of dramatic analysis, the theory of *rasa*. Critics divided the effect a drama, or a passage in a drama, might have on its audience into eight possible different flavours (flavour is the literal meaning of the term *rasa*) – Romantic, Comic, Sorrowful, Violent, Heroic, Terrifying, Repulsive and Marvellous. Later critics, who extended the theory to non-dramatic literature, added the Peaceful *rasa*. But how does the audience's experience ('tasting') of such a *rasa* relate to what is going on on stage? To describe this, the elements of *determinants*, *states* and *consequents* were distinguished. In the Terrifying *rasa*, determinants might include a deserted house at night, the sudden hooting of an owl, the apparition of a ghostly figure. States might include apprehensiveness, shock and fear. Consequents might include bulging eyes, trembling, a cry of alarm, an agitated attempt to get away. The states (other than the involuntary states, which became a special sub-class within the general category of consequents) are divided between thirty-three *transitory* or *subsidiary* states and eight/nine *permanent* or *predominant* states. These latter are each tied to a particular *rasa*, and they are in order Love, Mirth, Grief, Fury, Resoluteness, Fear, Revulsion, Wonder and Peace.

The expectations of an Indian audience were schooled to a significant extent by this way of looking at a play. A dramatist was judged largely by the effectiveness with which he evoked the *rasa* he was aiming at, and every detail of play and performance was expected to contribute directly or indirectly to the evocation of *rasa*. The description of setting and especially of natural phenomena, the selection of imagery in simile and metaphor were consciously guided by a search for harmony and the heightening of a particular mood. To take just one example, at the beginning of Act VI of *Rākshasa's Ring* (stanza 11 ff.), the Transitory state of Despair, established by Rākshasa's direct expression of his hurt and frustration, is reinforced by the natural images of blight and decay which surround him. The audience would take such reinforcement for granted, and be alert to notice not whether it was done, but only how well.

In this system of dramatic analysis, clearly the states are in broad terms the states of mind represented as belonging to the characters of the drama, and communicated to the audience both by the determinants, i.e. the dramatic situation, and by the consequents, i.e. above all the actor's performance. But the question of the relationship between *rasa* and corresponding permanent state was one which fascinated Indian thinkers. If in ordinary life we seek to avoid grief, why should tasting the Sorrowful *rasa* be a pleasant and even ennobling experience? – one comparable in fact with the exalted state of consciousness of the mystic. But if on the other hand the *rasa* is the permanent state not personally undergone but merely observed, why should someone who is moved by the sight of two lovers on the stage be quite likely to respond with such feelings as embarrassment, jealousy or indifference on seeing two lovers together in real life? In fact, since the emotion in a play is merely fictitious, why should one not *a fortiori* go through life tasting *rasa* at every true instance of strong emotion that one comes across?

The answer, in its finally accepted form, was that the Sorrowful *rasa* is grief experienced as it never is or can be in ordinary life, as directly and vividly as if it were one's own response to real circumstances (not at all as if it were the observed grief of some other person), yet with such complete detachment that one feels no anxiety, no wish to assert oneself in any way. It is the grief neither of oneself in a particular situation nor of any other person distinct from oneself: in other words it is grief *generalized.* The function of literature is to generalize emotion so that it can be tasted in this way. We can only respond insofar as the emotion evoked already lies within our experience. The tasting of *rasa* is nothing more nor less than the re-experience (*anuvyavasāya*) of our own emotions. That is why it is pleasant. Consciousness resents the intrusion of anything distinct from itself which wrests it from its state of repose. But the emotion awoken by art is a calm, unthreatening, recreative ordering of what is already within us.

This is the formulation arrived at by the great critic and philosopher Abhinavagupta, writing some three hundred years later than the last play in this volume. I mention his account both because it represents a drawing out within the Indian tradition of the implications of the original theory and because it is an analysis by a man of intelligence and sensibility of his own response to just such works as those here translated. The determinants will often seem strange to the Western reader, and the ancient actors are not here to help evoke the consequents. But I hope that, even through the thick veil of translation into an alien tongue, something of the essential *rasa* of these plays does still survive.

A Note on Editions

My translation of the *Śakuntalā* is based on Pischel's 'critical edition of the Bengali recension', always regarded as the best edition of the play. I must confess that I used it with increasing dissatisfaction, and have departed from it in several places. It is of course extremely artificial to base a supposedly 'critical' edition solely on the readings of one recension (though the practice is not uncommon in Sanskrit studies, and is certainly very labour-saving), since it involves the supposition not merely that the recension stems from the author and is the only one to do so, but that *all* divergences found in the other recensions are due to error or interpolation on the part of the latter. Among Pischel's more egregious readings, vines shed leaves like *limbs* rather than like *tears* in verse 14 of Act IV, and the chariot betrays its whereabouts by cloud-cuckoos flying out from fissures in *mountains* rather than from the interstices of the *spokes* of its wheels in verse 7 of Act VII.

I should mention with gratitude my indebtedness to Professor M. B. Emeneau's painstaking literal translation of Pischel's text, though it will be seen that I have ventured to disagree with his interpretation in a number of instances.

In the *Mudrārākṣasa*, the problem of markedly different recensions does not arise. In general I have followed Hillebrandt's edition, while taking some readings from his apparatus rather than from his text.

For the *Mālatīmādhava* I have translated the text of my own as yet unpublished edition. Since I am sure that this text bristles with many more mistakes than the other two,

I find it rather galling that the translator is not in a position to point out a single one of them to the editor. I am grateful to Dr Wendy O'Flaherty and Mr Jeremiah Losty for making many valuable comments on my translation of this play.

NUMBERING OF STANZAS

It is standard practice to refer to Sanskrit plays by quoting the number of the act followed by the number of the stanza, or of the nearest preceding stanza in the case of prose, as numbered from the beginning of the act. (For this purpose all forms of prologue or interlude count as part of the following act.) In *Śakuntalā* the numbering of the stanzas normally coincides with that of Pischel's edition, and in *Rākshasa's Ring* with that of Hillebrandt.

Śakuntalā
by Kālidāsa

Kālidasa

We have no firm facts about the life of India's most celebrated poet. Even the question of his date has to be determined on the sparsest of evidence, though Western scholars generally accept that he belongs to the period of the Gupta empire, and associate him in particular with the reign of Chandra Gupta II, *c.* A.D. 376–415. This conclusion harmonizes not merely with the meagre factual data but also with the spirit and style of Kālidāsa's poetry. The period in question (often declared to be the 'Golden Age' of Hindu India) was a time of prosperity and imperial greatness, and one which marked the culmination of the brahminical renaissance. Buddhist influence had declined in India, the land of its origin, and orthodox Hinduism, with its foundations in the Vedic scriptures, in the cultural hegemony of the brahmin caste and in the Sanskrit language, had reasserted itself. It is frequently observed (though such a judgement is inevitably somewhat subjective in character) that Kālidāsa's poetry breathes a sense of the ease and largeness of vision appropriate to a time of great political and cultural self-confidence.

Śakuntalā easily eclipses Kālidāsa's other two plays in scale and importance. But his contribution to narrative poetry is every bit as distinguished as his contribution to drama, though perhaps his achievement in this field is even less accessible through the medium of translation. Indeed he stands more clearly head and shoulders above other narrative poets than above other playwrights, and he is the only writer of the first rank to produce work in both genres. He wrote two great narrative poems: *The Birth of Kumāra* (*The War God*), the title of which has been seen as a compliment on the birth of Chandra Gupta II's heir Kumāra Gupta; and *The Dynasty of Raghu*. Smaller in scale but scarcely less celebrated is *The Cloud Messenger*, a work of metrical virtuosity and great lyrical power. Some of its stanzas picture with striking vividness the landscape of India as it would appear from above to a passing cloud, and it has often been remarked that Kālidāsa's imagination was able to anticipate the aeroplane. There is a similar vividness in the picture of the descending aerial chariot in Act VII of the present play.

Śakuntalā has a very special place in Western appreciation of Sanskrit literature. It was one of the first Sanskrit works ever to be translated into English – in 1789, only five years after Charles Wilkins's pioneering translation of the *Bhagavad Gītā*. The translation was by the brilliant orientalist Sir William Jones, the man who effectively founded the science of comparative philology by his observation that the resemblances linking Sanskrit with Latin and Greek were too strong to be accidental, and must point to 'some common source, which perhaps no longer exists'. In his introduction to the play, Jones describes how after his arrival in Bengal (as a judge of the Supreme Court) he investigated reports of a type of book called *Nátac* (i.e. *nātaka*), supposedly consisting of historical records. But on enquiry he was assured by brahmins that these works in fact abounded with fables, and 'consisted of conversations in prose and verse, held before ancient Rájás in their publick assemblies, on an infinite variety of subjects, and in various dialects of India'. Jones was still at a loss, until 'a very sensible Bráhmen' told him that the English presented similar compositions at Calcutta in the cold season under the name of 'plays'. Equally surprised and delighted, Jones ascertained that the most universally esteemed play was *Śakuntalā*, and set about studying it with the aid of a *paṇḍit*. He made a word-for-word translation, and then 'disengaged it from the stiffness of a foreign idiom'. The result is a very fine example of muscular eighteenth-century English, though sadly too full of misunderstandings of the original to be of more than historical interest today.

When he asked which Sanskrit play was most admired Jones had had quoted to him a verse which said:

> Of literary forms drama is the most pleasing,
> And of dramas 'Śakuntalā',
> And in 'Śakuntalā' the Fourth Act,
> And in that Act four verses.

It is no great matter if many Western readers find some other portion of the play more immediately striking – the graceful love-making of Act III, the dramatic confrontation of Act V, the depth of human feeling expressed in Act VII. The judgement quoted is clearly less concerned with isolating the most powerful examples of Kālidāsa's literary skill than with identifying those parts which most convey the essence of the whole. In Act IV Śakuntalā takes her leave of the heritage where she has spent her life, and at this pivotal moment in the play many underlying themes and ideals of Indian society come to the surface – the need for each individual to live in harmony with his allotted place in the scheme of things; the search for harmony also in the relationship between human beings and the rest of nature; recognition of the grief which all human ties bring, even those of love; and the aspiration to escape from such bondage, at least when one's worldly duties are at an end. The four verses specified (which are not among those normally anthologized from the play) are concerned with just such themes. They are verse 8 ('Śakuntalā leaves today . . .'), in which Kaṇva says that even he is not immune to some of the natural grief of fatherhood; verses 21 ('Obey your elders . . .') and 22 ('When you are honoured . . .'), which describes the duties and fulfilments of marriage, and verse 23 ('When you have long been . . .'), in which Śakuntalā is promised that she will return to end her days in peace in the hermitage.

Only *Śakuntalā* of the three plays in this volume contains that stock character of Sanskrit drama, the Clown. The Sanskrit term, *vidūṣaka*, seems literally to mean 'the Disgracer'. And the Clown (who is *not* a jester or intentionally funny person) does indeed disgrace the accepted ideals of Indian society. He is a brahmin, and yet, unique among brahmin men, he cannot speak Sanskrit – evidently because he was too lazy ever to acquire a proper education. Lacking the learning of a brahmin, he equally has nothing of the heroism of the warrior or the industry of the merchant. His vision of the perfect life encompasses nothing higher than finding a comfortable spot and eating sweets. But he is good-natured, and the boon companion and loyal friend of the hero, whose chivalrous duty it is to shield him from harm. And uneducated though he may be, and of severely limited mental horizons, he is no idiot: his comments can be both shrewd (Act V, 'tell a bull he's lord of the herd and his tiredness vanishes') and earthy (Act II, 'Were you expecting her to jump on your lap the moment she saw you?'). It is in his lack of idealism (a lack so total that it could only be contemplated under the guise of humour) that he furnishes the dramatic foil for the high ideals of the King; and in Act VI in particular the contrast between his crass insensitivity and Dushyanta's grief produces an ironical and almost Shakespearian counterpoint.

When Sir William Jones's translation was published, it caused a great stir. It went into five editions within twenty years, and was in turn translated into other European languages – into German in 1791, and into French in 1803. Goethe (who also paid homage of a practical sort, when he imitated in his *Faust* the Indian custom of beginning a play with a dialogue between the actors) greeted Georg Forster's German translation with praise which has been quoted countless times but which is so striking that it still bears repeating:

Willst du die Blüthe des frühen, die Früchte des späteren Jahres,
Willst du, was reizt und entzückt, willst du was sättigt und nährt,
Willst du den Himmel, die Erde, mit einem Namen begreifen;
Nenn' ich, Sakuntala, Dich, und so ist Alles gesagt.

Wouldst thou the young year's blossoms and the fruits of its decline,
And all by which the soul is charmed, enraptured, feasted, fed,
Wouldst thou the earth and heaven itself in one sole name combine?
I name thee, O Shakuntala, and all at once is said.
(trans. Eastwich)

Such praise is fully supported by the esteem in which Kālidāsa has always been held in India. In the reckoning of both East and West, he is the greatest of Sanskrit poets. Perhaps the reason lies more than anywhere in the fact that his poetry exemplifies so notably the literary quality known to Sanskrit critics as *prasāda*, 'limpidity'. This concept never received the degree of analytical attention given to other concepts such as *rasa*; but it refers essentially to a perfect matching of word and vision. Kālidāsa steers effortlessly (or rather, of course, with the art which conceals effort) between the Scylla of empty and slack phraseology that characterizes the second-hand poet with nothing new to say, and the Charybdis of strained expression which we find in the poet who has something to say but has been surprised in the middle of his search for a way of saying it. The latter often indulges in a sort of verbal overkill, piling detail upon detail in the effort to get his message across, and his audience has to pick over his words to extract their essence. Kālidāsa knows how to pare away this unnecessary, clogging detail, until there is nothing left for us to gaze on except what he intended us to see. And he knows (in fact it is another aspect of the same process) how to use large and simple words in such a way that they are defined by their context and made precise and vivid. It is this total control of his own particular linguistic medium which can make Kālidāsa's often deceptively simple Sanskrit the despair of any translator.

Śakuntalā

CHARACTERS IN THE PLAY

**Sanskrit speakers are marked with an asterisk.*

*KAṆVA, head of a community of ascetics
ŚAKUNTALĀ, his adopted daughter
ANUSŪYĀ, PRIYAMVADĀ — her close friends
GAUTAMĪ, a senior woman ascetic
*ŚĀRNGARAVA, *ŚĀRADVATA — ascetics, pupils of Kaṇva
*DURVĀSAS, a powerful sage (*heard off-stage*)

*THE KING, Dushyanta
*HIS CHARIOTEER
*HIS GENERAL, Bhadrasena
THE CLOWN, Mādhavya, his lazy and unscholarly brahmin friend
*CHAMBERLAIN in the royal household, Pārvatāyana
*CHAPLAIN in the royal household, Somarāta
FEMALE GUARD, Vetravatī
MAIDSERVANT, Chaturikā
QUEEN HAMSAVATĪ, one of Dushyanta's consorts (*heard off-stage*)

POLICE SUPERINTENDENT
TWO GUARDS, his subordinates
FISHERMAN

MIŚRAKEŚĪ, a celestial nymph, friend of the nymph Menakā (Śakuntalā's mother)
*MĀTALI, charioteer of Indra, chief of the gods

CHARACTERS IN THE PLAY

*KAŚYAPA, a primeval sage, head of a divine community
ADITI, his wife
A BOY, Sarvadamana or Bharata, the son of Dushyanta and Śakuntalā

Also other *ASCETICS (or *HERMITS) and *PUPILS, DOORKEEPER, MESSENGER, *COURT BARDS, SERVANT GIRLS

The action of the play takes place in Northern India – in or near Kaṇva's hermitage, in Dushyanta's capital Hastināpura (on the Ganges, north-east of modern Delhi), and in Kaśyapa's hermitage on Golden Peak mountain.

Benediction

1 Through the first work of the Creator, through the conveyer of the sacrifice, and through the sacrificer,
Through the twin apportioners of time, through the all-pervading element whose attribute is sound,
Through the source of all that germinates, through that whereby the breathing draw their breath –
Through these* his eight incarnate forms the Lord in his mercy grant you protection.

*The eight forms of Śiva here referred to are, in order, water, fire, the sacrificial priest, sun and moon, ether, earth and air.

PROLOGUE

[*After the Benediction, enter the Director.*]

DIRECTOR Enough, enough! [*Looking off-stage*] My wife, if you are ready back there, join me on stage.

[*Enter an actress.*]

ACTRESS Here I am, sir. Command me.

DIRECTOR This is no mean audience, dear wife, and we have a new play by Kālidāsa to present to them, 'Śakuntalā and the Love Token'. Every one of the players must do his very best.

ACTRESS You have directed us all so well, sir, that nothing can go wrong.

DIRECTOR [*smiling*] Truth to tell, my dear,

Till the critics applaud 2
I despise my skill as a director.
However expert he may be
A man can't trust his own judgement.

ACTRESS That is so, sir. But what were you going to ask me to do?

DIRECTOR What else but to charm our audience with a song?

ACTRESS What season shall my song be about?

DIRECTOR About this season just begun – summer, the time of relaxation. This is the time

When plunging into water is a joy, 3
When the woodland breeze is fragrant with trumpet-
  flower,

When every shadow lures one into slumber
And every day is loveliest at its close.

ACTRESS [*sings*]

4 Acacia flowers whose filaments
With trembling lips
The bee has known,
Plucked now with careful fingertips,
For ornaments
To women's ears are gone.

DIRECTOR Beautifully sung, dearest. The audience is sitting entranced, like people in a painting. Now what play can we perform to keep them happy?

ACTRESS But you've already announced that we're to do a new play called 'Śakuntalā and the Love Token'!

DIRECTOR My goodness, so I had. For the moment I'd quite forgotten. In fact

5 I was as swept away
By the enchantment of your song
As King Dushyanta here
Drawn on and on by the swift-fleeing deer.

[*They withdraw.*]

Act I

[*Enter on a chariot*, *bow and arrow in hand*, *in pursuit of a deer*, *the King*, *together with his charioteer*.]

CHARIOTEER [*gazing at both King and deer*] Sire,

When I look upon the deer 6
And on yourself with weapon poised,
I seem to see intent upon the chase
The Great Bowman * himself in human form.

KING He's drawn us a long way, this deer. Look at him! –

Gracefully arching his neck to throw a glance at our pursuing chariot, 7
Then drawing his hindquarters into his forepart in terror of our arrows,
Strewing his track with half-chewed grass from a mouth slackened in weariness,
In his bounds he travels the sky and hardly touches earth.

[*In surprise*] What's happened? I can hardly see him.

CHARIOTEER We've slowed down, sire. I had to rein in because of the rough ground, and he's drawn away. But now he's taken to level ground you'll easily come up with him.

KING Loose the reins, then.

CHARIOTEER Yes, Your Majesty. [*Acting movement of the chariot*] Look, sire.

* Śiva.

8 With the reins loosed, your horses stretch forward
And outstrip even the swirl of their own dust.
Ears flattened and plumes unstirring,
They are less galloping than floating.

KING [*exultantly*] They're catching up on him! See –

9 Tiny things suddenly loom,
Things split unite behind us,
Crooked things stream into straight lines –
Nothing stays distant at this speed, and nothing stays near.

A VOICE OFF-STAGE No, no, Your Majesty! Don't kill him, he's a deer of the hermitage.

CHARIOTEER [*listening and looking*] Sire, two ascetics have put themselves in front of the deer, just as you've got within range of him!

KING [*urgently*] Rein in, then!

CHARIOTEER Yes, sire. [*He does so.*]

[*Enter a hermit and a pupil.*]

ASCETIC [*lifting his hand*] Sire, sire! This is a deer of the hermitage:

10 Never, never discharge that weapon
Into this soft body, like fire into flowers.
What has the fragile life of deers to do
With your strong-shafted, sharply falling arrows?

11 At once remove
The arrow from your bow:
Your weapon is meant to help the weak
Not smite the innocent.

KING [*with a bow*] I do so remove it. [*He does as he says.*]

ASCETIC [*with pleasure*] You are a true scion of Puru's race, a true light among kings. May you gain a son to be emperor of heaven and earth.

KING [*with a bow*] I accept a brahmin's blessing.

BOTH ASCETICS We came out to collect firewood, Your Majesty. There along the bank of the Mālinī you can see the hermitage of our teacher Kaṇva, where Śakuntalā dwells like a guardian deity. If you have no urgent business, enter and accept our hospitality.

By seeing how the ascetics' holy rites 12
Are free of all hindrance,
You will realize how much
Your bow-scarred arm protects.

KING Is he at home, then, the head of your community?

ASCETICS For the moment he has charged his daughter with the duties of hospitality and gone to Somatīrtha to avert an ill fate that threatens her.

KING Then I will see her instead, and he can learn from her that I have done what is proper.

ASCETICS We will be on our way, then.

[*The hermit and his pupil withdraw.*]

KING Start the horses, driver – and let me purify myself with a sight of the hermitage.

CHARIOTEER Yes, sire. [*He again acts movement of the chariot.*]

KING [*looking about him*] No need to ask whether these are the outskirts of the holy grove.

CHARIOTEER Why so?

KING Don't you see? Look –

Those grains of wild rice beneath the trees must have 13
dropped from fledgling mouths in parrots' nests,

While the oily stones here and there must have been used for crushing ingudī * nuts.
The deer are so trustful their pace doesn't alter at the noise of our approach,
And on the paths from the pool clothes made of bark † have dripped long trails of water.

Besides which

14 Watering-channels, rippling in the wind, wash the trees at their roots.
Smoke from the sacrificial butter has discoloured the leaf-buds.
And here in the grove, where the sharp darbha shoots have been cut,‡
Come dawdling fawns, cropping the soft grass in safety.

CHARIOTEER Yes, it all fits.

KING [*when they have gone a little further*] We mustn't create a disturbance. Stop the chariot here and I'll dismount.

CHARIOTEER I've reined in. Dismount, sire.

KING [*dismounting and looking down at himself*] One must be respectfully dressed for a holy grove. Here, take my insignia and my bow. [*He hands them to the charioteer.*] While I am visiting the hermitage, wet down the backs of the horses.

CHARIOTEER Yes, sire. [*He withdraws.*]

KING [*walking about and looking*] Here is the hermitage –

* The oil thus obtained was used by hermits for their hair.

† Hermits dressed themselves in a kind of bark, which would have been far less absorbent than material such as cotton.

‡ For use in the sacrifice.

I'll enter. [*Indicating an omen as he enters*] Ha!

A peaceful hermitage, and yet my arm throbs! 15
What could such a thing mean in such a setting?
But then the doors of Fate
Lie open in all places.

A VOICE OFF-STAGE Come on, dear friends, this way!

KING [*listening*] Ah, I think I can hear voices to the right of the grove of trees. Let me go and see. [*Walking about and looking*] Why, there are some girls of the hermitage, with watering pots that match their own small size, coming to water the young trees. What a charming sight!

When looks so rare in palace women 16
Can be found in hermitage-dwellers,
Then our cultivated vines, it seems,
Must yield in excellence to the wild woodland kind.

I think I'll wait for them here in the shade. [*He stands watching.*]

[*Enter, occupied as stated, Śakuntalā and two companions Anusūyā and Priyamvadā.*]

ANUSŪYĀ Śakuntalā, my dear, if you ask me, Father Kaṇva must dote on his trees even more than he does on you, the way he makes you water all the tree basins like this, when you're as delicate as a jasmine flower yourself.

ŚAKUNTALĀ But Anusūyā, it's not just that Father makes me do it – I love our trees like a sister. [*She acts watering the trees.*]

PRIYAMVADĀ Śakuntalā dearest, we've watered all the summer-flowering trees. Let's water the ones that have finished flowering, and store up merit for ourselves by a disinterested action.

ŚAKUNTALĀ Priyamvadā, that's a lovely idea. [*Again she acts watering the trees.*]

KING [*to himself*] So this is Kaṇva's daughter Śakuntalā! [*In wonder*] How misguided of the revered Kaṇva to make her wear a dress of bark!

17 In trying to make this artlessly charming form
Endure the fatigue of pious austerities,
The sage has set himself the task of cutting hardwood
With a lotus-petal saw.

I'll stay hidden in the trees, where I can watch without alarming her. [*He keeps himself concealed from them.*]

ŚAKUNTALĀ Anusūyā, Priyamvadā has tied this dress so tight it's pinching me. Could you loosen it?

[*Anusūyā loosens it.*]

PRIYAMVADĀ [*in amusement*] Don't blame me – blame adolescence for making your breasts swell!

KING It's quite true what she says:

18 With its knot drawn tight against the shoulder
That dress of bark hides the roundness of her breasts,
And traps the radiance of her young form
Like a sallow leaf imprisoning a bud.

And yet the dress of bark, for all that it's quite unsuited to her youth, doesn't entirely lack an ornamental charm. For

19 Common duckweed can set off the lotus's beauty,
And black specks heighten the loveliness of the moon.
So her dress of bark makes this fair creature still more enchanting:
For what is not an ornament to a graceful form?

ŚAKUNTALĀ [*looking ahead of her*] Oh look, that mango-tree with its shoots beckoning in the breeze seems to want to tell me something. I'll just go and say hello. [*She does so.*]

PRIYAMVADĀ Hold still for a moment, Śakuntalā.

ŚAKUNTALĀ What for?

PRIYAMVADĀ With you beside it, the tree looks as if it's found a vine to love and cherish.

ŚAKUNTALĀ Your name means Flatterer, Priyamvadā – now I know how you got it!

KING Priyamvadā isn't flattering her.

Her lips are as red as the shoots of a vine,
Her arms are as delicate as its tendrils,
And the youthful bloom on her limbs
Is like a mass of blossom.

ANUSŪYĀ Look, Śakuntalā, there is the real bride of the mango-tree – the jasmine you call Forest Moonlight.

ŚAKUNTALĀ [*approaching and looking, in delight*] And the marriage of the two trees has turned out well, Anūsūyā – for the jasmine is covered in fresh blossom, and the mango has expressed its love in fruitfulness. [*She stays lost in contemplation.*]

PRIYAMVADĀ [*with a smile*] Anusūyā, do you realize why Śakuntalā can't stop looking at her jasmine plant?

ANUSŪYĀ I can't imagine: tell me.

PRIYAMVADĀ She's thinking, if only she can find a worthy husband just as Forest Moonlight has found itself a worthy tree!

ŚAKUNTALĀ You're just saying what you want for yourself. [*She pours water from the pot.*]

ANUSŪYĀ Śakuntalā dearest, what about the spring creeper here that Father Kaṇva tended with his own hands the way he did you? You've forgotten it.

ŚAKUNTALĀ Not till I forget myself. [*Going up and looking at the creeper, in delight*] Heavens, Priyamvadā, here's some good news!

PRIYAMVADĀ Dearest Śakuntalā, what is it?

ŚAKUNTALĀ This spring creeper is covered in late buds, right down to the root.

BOTH [*hurrying up*] No, is it really?

ŚAKUNTALĀ Yes, see for yourselves.

PRIYAMVADĀ [*examining it delightedly*] Then I'll tell *you* some good news. You'll soon be married.

ŚAKUNTALĀ [*crossly*] Oh, that's just what you want for yourself.

PRIYAMVADĀ No, no, I'm not joking. I heard Father Kaṇva himself say that this would be the omen for your wedding.

ANUSŪYĀ Priyamvadā! So that's why Śakuntalā has been watering the spring creeper so lovingly!

ŚAKUNTALĀ Why shouldn't I water it when it's like a sister to me? [*She pours water from the pot.*]

KING If only she's the sage's daughter by a wife of another caste! * But she *must* be:

21 Without question she is a proper wife for a warrior,
For my heart is noble and yet desires her.
The virtuous, on those matters which admit of doubt,
Are rightly guided by their own inner inclination.

Still, I must find out about her for certain.

ŚAKUNTALĀ [*in alarm*] Oh! There's a bee come out of

*The King, being of the *kshatriya* (warrior) caste, would not be able to marry a girl of pure brahmin descent. His immediate certainty on the question is due not to self-importance but to a lover's optimism.

the jasmine and buzzing round my face. [*She acts being troubled by a bee.*]

KING [*longingly*]

Already, as she moves her lovely eyes 22
To keep the bee in sight, and knits her brow,
She is trying out, though from alarm not love,
The looks a woman uses on her lover.

[*With a show of annoyance*]

You keep touching her trembling eye as she darts a glance at you, 23
You murmur softly in her ear as if to whisper secrets,
Though she waves you away you drink a love draught from her lips.
I stop to speculate, and lose. You, bee, are my victorious rival!

ŚAKUNTALĀ Friends, save me from this wretched bee.

BOTH [*with a grin*] *We* can't help you. You'd better try King Dushyanta – the hermitage is under royal protection.

KING Just the moment to reveal myself! Don't worry –! [*Breaking off discreetly*] No, they'll realize I'm the King. I must play the part of a guest.

ŚAKUNTALĀ The little villain won't leave off. I'll have to move away. [*Taking a step and throwing an agitated glance*] Oh no! He's still following me! Help!

KING [*hastening forward*] Ha!

When a king of Puru's line governs the world, 24
Chastising the unruly,
Who is this who offers an affront
To innocent girls of the hermitage?

[*All the girls show some confusion on seeing the King.*]

ANUSŪYĀ Sir, it wasn't anything disastrous. It was just that our friend here was upset at being pestered by a bee.

KING [*going up to Śakuntalā*] Does your penance prosper?

[*Śakuntalā hangs her head in alarm.*]

ANUSŪYĀ It does, now that we have a distinguished guest.

PRIYAMVADĀ Welcome, sir. Śakuntalā dear, go and fetch fruit and refreshment from the cottage for our guest. We can use this water for his feet.

KING No, dear lady, your words alone are enough refreshment for me.

ANUSŪYĀ Then come and rest yourself, sir, on this cool and shady seat under the saptaparṇa tree.

KING But you're tired yourselves from the duties you've been performing. Sit down for a while with me.

PRIYAMVADĀ [*aside*] Śakuntalā, we must look after our guest. So come, let's sit down.

[*They all do so.*]

ŚAKUNTALĀ [*to herself*] Oh dear, why does the sight of this man fill me with feelings so much at odds with my religious life?

KING [*looking at each of them*] How pleasant it is to see friends so well matched in youth and beauty!

PRIYAMVADĀ [*aside*] Anusūyā, who can this mysterious, dignified stranger be, who speaks so charmingly and shows so much courtesy?

ANUSŪYĀ Just what I was wondering myself. I'm going to ask him! [*Aloud*] You speak so kindly, sir, you encourage me to put a question. Which line of royal sages do you grace – or which country are you causing to repine at your absence? And why has a person of refinement such as yourself taken the trouble to journey to our hermitage?

ŚAKUNTALĀ [*to herself*] Oh, I can relax! Anusūyā is asking exactly what I wanted to know.

KING [*to himself*] Do I reveal myself now, or prevaricate? [*On reflection*] I know what I'll do! [*Aloud*] Lady, I am a scholar charged with the spiritual welfare of cities in this realm, and I have come to this grove in the course of a tour of holy places.

ANUSŪYĀ Holy people have a champion!

[*Śakuntalā displays love shyness.*]

THE TWO FRIENDS [*on observing the demeanour of the other two*] Śakuntalā, think if Father Kaṇva were here!

ŚAKUNTALĀ What then?

BOTH He would insist on giving this distinguished guest what he wanted, even if it were his dearest treasure!

ŚAKUNTALĀ [*pretending annoyance*] Stop it! You've got some silly notion in your head. I'm not going to listen to you.

KING Now *I* have something I should like to ask *you* about your friend.

BOTH It is an honour to be asked, sir.

KING How is it that the revered Kaṇva lives in perpetual chastity and yet your friend here is his daughter?

ANUSŪYĀ I'll tell you, sir. There is a royal sage of great power, whose family name is Kauśika.

KING Yes, we have heard of the revered Kauśika.

ANUSŪYĀ *He* is the procreator of our friend. But Father Kaṇva is her father, because he fostered her when she was abandoned.

KING The word 'abandoned' whets my curiosity. Tell me the whole story from the beginning.

ANUSŪYĀ Well, sir, it seems that once when that royal

sage was practising stringent austerities, the gods became alarmed and sent a nymph called Menakā to disturb his self-restraint.

KING Yes, the gods do have this fear of deep meditation on the part of others. What happened?

ANUSŪYĀ It was a lovely month at the beginning of spring, and when he saw her intoxicating beauty . . . [*She breaks off demurely.*]

KING I understand. At any rate, she is the daughter of the nymph.

ANUSŪYĀ Exactly, sir.

KING I can well believe it.

25 How could such beauty have been born
Of any mortal woman?
The tremulous lightning-flash
Does not spring upwards from the earth.

[*Śakuntalā hangs her head shyly.*]

[*To himself*] Now I can allow scope to my longings!

PRIYAMVADĀ [*after smilingly eyeing Śakuntalā*] You seem to want to say something else, sir.

[*Śakuntalā reproves her friend with a finger.*]

KING You suspect rightly. I am so eager to enquire into good lives that I do have another question.

PRIYAMVADĀ Then do not hesitate, sir. Ascetics have no secrets.

KING Then tell me –

26 Is it till she is given in marriage that she must observe
Her religious vow that hinders thoughts of love?
Or is she destined to live for evermore
With the does she loves because their eyes match hers?

PRIYAMVADĀ She submits to others' guidance on the

matter, sir. But her guardian does plan to bestow her when a worthy suitor appears.

KING [*delightedly to himself*]

Give way to your longings, my heart: 27
All doubts are now at rest.
What you feared might be fire
Is a jewel to be touched.

ŚAKUNTALĀ [*with a show of annoyance*] Anusūyā, I'm going!

ANUSŪYĀ What for?

ŚAKUNTALĀ I'm going to the venerable Gautamī to tell her all about the nonsense that Priyamvadā has been talking. [*She gets up.*]

ANUSŪYĀ But my dear, a member of the community can't leave a distinguished guest unentertained and just go off when she feels like it!

[*Śakuntalā moves off without answering.*]

KING [*to himself*] Is she going? [*Getting up and seeming to want to catch hold of her, then restraining himself*] Ah, a lover's thought is as vivid as the act! For I

Was about to go after the sage's daughter 28
When good manners suddenly halted me,
And without stirring from where I stood
I seemed to go and come back again.

PRIYAMVADĀ [*going up to Śakuntalā*] Listen, you naughty girl, you shouldn't be leaving like this.

ŚAKUNTALĀ [*turning and frowning at her*] And why not?

PRIYAMVADĀ You owe me two lots of tree-watering. Pay me back those, and then you can go. [*She pulls her back.*]

KING But I can see that she is already worn out with watering trees. Look at her –

29 Handling the pot has left her shoulders drooping and her palms reddened,
While her bosom is still heaving with breaths too deep for so slight a frame.
The flower at her ear is sticking to the film of sweat on her face,
And her hairband being loosened, one hand holds her dishevelled locks in place.

I'll discharge her debt myself! [*He hands over his ring.*] [*The two girls, taking it and reading out the name on it, stare at each other.*] Don't misunderstand. It is simply a gift from the King.

PRIYAMVADĀ Then you shouldn't give it up, sir. What you say is enough to free her of the debt.

ANUSŪYĀ Śakuntalā dear, you have been freed by the kind gentleman here, or rather by the King. So you're at liberty to go.

ŚAKUNTALĀ [*to herself*] If I could please myself, I shouldn't leave him.

PRIYAMVADĀ Why aren't you off now?

ŚAKUNTALĀ Do I still have to answer to you? I'll go when I feel like it.

KING [*gazing at Śakuntalā, to himself*] Can she feel towards me as I feel towards her? But yes, I'm sure I have a chance:

30 Although she does not return any words to mine,
She listens closely whenever I speak,
And though she will not face me
She doesn't look very much at anything else.

A VOICE OFF-STAGE Look out, people of the hermitage! Get ready to save the creatures near our grove! King Dushyanta must be nearby on a hunt –

Dust stirred up by his horses' hooves 31
Is falling over the trees of the hermitage,
Settling on the garments of bark spread out to dry
Like a swarm of locusts, red as the setting sun.

KING [*to himself*] Oh heavens, are my soldiers invading the grove in search of me?

AGAIN A VOICE OFF-STAGE Look out, people of the hermitage! Here comes an elephant, throwing old men, women and children into confusion –

With a tree-trunk smashed by a violent blow and caught upon his tusk, 32
And fetters of uprooted vines dragging at his feet,
Scattering the deer, like an incarnate obstacle to our austerities,
He is destroying the grove in his terror at the sight of the chariots.

[*All the girls rise in alarm at the news.*]

KING Oh heavens, have I sinned against these holy people? I must go back.

THE TWO FRIENDS Sir, we're worried by this alarm about the elephant. Give us leave to return to the cottage.

ANUSŪYĀ [*to Śakuntalā*] Śakuntalā dearest, the venerable Gautamī will be very worried. Come, let's get back to her right away.

ŚAKUNTALĀ [*showing difficulty in walking*] Oh dear, I've got a cramp in my leg.

KING Gently, ladies, gently! I will go and see if I can prevent any harm to the hermitage.

THE TWO FRIENDS Sir, we feel we know you. Please forgive this interruption to our hospitality. Since we haven't entertained you properly, may we make amends by asking you to visit us again?

KING Don't trouble yourselves – seeing you has been hospitality enough.

ŚAKUNTALĀ I've cut my foot on a new blade of darbha grass, and I've caught my dress on an amaranth branch! Wait for me while I get myself free. [*Gazing all the while at the King, she follows after her two friends.*]

KING [*with a sigh*] Gone, all of them! Well, I'll be off too. Now that I've met Śakuntalā, I don't feel keen on returning to the city. I'll get my followers to settle well away from the grove. I just can't tear my thoughts from Śakuntalā –

33 My body moves onward,
But my unsteady mind runs back
Like the silk of a banner
Carried into the wind.

[*All withdraw.*]

Act II

[*Enter the Clown.*]

CLOWN [*with a sigh*] Oh Lord, am I fed up with being the friend of this hunting king! We go charging along after deer and boar, in the middle of the day, in the height of summer, down forest tracks with hardly a spot of shade anywhere, and drink nasty, tepid water out of mountain streams – full of leaves and tasting foul. And we burn our tongues on scorching hot meat at any old hour of the day. And the horses and elephants make such a racket you can't get to sleep properly even at night. Then at the crack of dawn those damned birdcatchers and hutsmen wake me up with the deafening row they make going off to the forest. And as if that isn't enough to torment me, there's a pimple on top of the boil. Apparently when he got separated from us chasing after a deer, he came to a hermitage and there, just my luck, met some hermit girl called Śakuntalā. Since when he hasn't said a word about going back to the city. The worry of it's had me tossing and turning all night. Whatever's to be done? Well, I'll go and call on him if he's up and about.

[*Walking about and looking*] Ah, there's my friend coming this way, bow in hand and dreaming of his sweetheart, wearing a garland of wild flowers. Right, I'll stand here, too stiff and sore to move. Perhaps that'll get me a respite. [*He stays leaning on his stick.*]

[*Enter the King as described.*]

KING [*to himself*]

Though my loved one is so hard to win, 1
My heart feels reassured just knowing how she feels.
For even where love remains unsatisfied
To have it returned can be enough to make one happy.

[*With a wry smile*] That's how a lover fools himself, imagining the loved one's thoughts to suit himself!

2 When she looked tenderly even though it was at something else,
When her heavy hips moved languorously as if from thoughts of love,
When she spoke crossly to the friend who kept her from leaving,
I thought it all referred to me – how love sees things in terms of itself!

CLOWN [*staying as he is*] Ho sire, my hand won't move! So I salute you with my voice alone.

KING [*seeing him, with a smile*] Why so paralysed?

CLOWN Why?! That's right – punch me in the eye and then ask why I'm crying.

KING I don't follow – what's this all about?

CLOWN When a reed is bent like a hunchback, is that its own doing or the fault of the river current?

KING It's due to the river current.

CLOWN And in my case it's due to you.

KING What is?

CLOWN It's all very well for *you* to give up affairs of state – not to mention a floor you can walk on without tripping up – and come and live like a savage. I've nothing to say about that. But I'm a brahmin, and this continual chasing after wild animals has shaken up all the ligaments in my joints till now I can't move a muscle. So please – let's take a rest, just for one day.

KING [*to himself*] That's what he wants, and when I think of Kaṇva's daughter I don't feel any enthusiasm myself for going hunting. For after all

3 I can have no heart to string this bow
And aim my arrows at the very deer

Who seem by dwelling with my sweetheart
To have shared the beauty of their eyes with her.

CLOWN [*watching the King*] Your Majesty has been thinking your own thoughts, and I've been crying in the wilderness!

KING [*smiling*] No, I was just stopping to think that I couldn't possibly turn a deaf ear to a friend!

CLOWN [*overjoyed*] Then long may you live, say I! [*Starts to get up.*]

KING Hold on! Hear the rest of what I have to say.

CLOWN Command me, sire.

KING When you've had a rest, I want you to help me in another kind of work, something that won't tire you.

CLOWN Eating sweets?

KING I'll let you know.

CLOWN All right then.

KING Hello, who's there?

[*Enter the Doorkeeper.*]

DOORKEEPER Yes, Your Majesty?

KING Raivataka, ask the General to come here, will you?

DOORKEEPER Yes, sire. [*Withdrawing and re-entering with the General*] This way, General. There is His Majesty over there in conversation. Approach him, sir.

GENERAL [*looking at the King, to himself*] Hunting is a well-known vice,* but it has really done His Majesty nothing but good. Just look at him –

Toughened by the ceaseless friction of the bowstring, 4
Inured to the sun's rays, unaffected by sweat,

*Hunting was classed with pursuits such as gambling as an addiction which could lead to neglect of kingly duties. The Clown is privileged to condemn it openly, but the General in the following scene has to be more circumspect.

Like a wild mountain elephant he has a body that is pure strength –
Thin, but so muscular you don't notice the fact.

[*Approaching him*] Victory to Your Majesty. Sire, we have tracked the game in the forest from the movements of the deer. We await your command.

KING Bhadrasena, Mādhavya here has destroyed my enthusiasm by being so against hunting.

GENERAL [*discreetly to the Clown*] Mādhavya, my friend, you stick to your guns while I humour him. [*Aloud*] Sire, the idiot's talking nonsense. Why, we've only got to look at you! –

5 With the belly lean and free of fat, the body grows nimble and fit for exertion,
And one can observe the minds of living creatures under the strains of fear or anger.
Again, the best possible test of any archer is to score on a moving target.
It's wrong to call hunting a vice – there's no pursuit to equal it!

CLOWN [*angrily*] Get away with you, and leave off tempting him! His Majesty's come to his senses – so why don't *you* just go wandering from one forest to the next yourself, you whoreson, till you fall into the jaws of some old bear hungry for a deer or a jackal.

KING Being near a hermitage, Bhadrasena, I can't approve of what you say. So for the present –

6 Let the buffalo wallow in their drinking-pools, thrashing the water with their horns.
Let the deer cluster in the shade and chew the cud.

Leave the wild boar in peace to tear up the grass by the ponds.
And let this bow of mine take a holiday and stay unstrung.

GENERAL As Your Majesty pleases.

KING So fetch back the beaters who have gone on ahead. And see that the soldiers keep clear of the holy grove and cause no disturbance.

In holy men, who above all things practise calm, 7
There lurks a hidden energy, a power of burning.
They are like sunstones,* pleasant to the touch,
Which yet can burn if kindled by another's fire.

GENERAL Certainly, sire.

CLOWN All right, then, you tempter, off you go!

[*The General withdraws.*]

KING [*looking at his attendants*] Go and take off your hunting clothes, all of you. And Raivataka, be about your business.

DOORKEEPER Yes, Your Majesty. [*He withdraws.*]

CLOWN Well, you've swatted all the flies. So now you sit down on that flat stone under the shade of the tree, so that I can sit comfortably too.

KING Lead the way.

CLOWN Come, sire.

[*Both walk around and sit down.*]

KING Ah, Mādhavya, my friend! You haven't learnt what eyes are for yet, because you haven't seen the one thing that is more worth seeing than anything in the world.

*The sunstone was a jewel supposed to emit fire when exposed to the sun's rays.

CLOWN But here you are, right in front of me!

KING Oh, everyone regards himself as attractive. But I'm talking about that jewel of the hermitage, Śakuntalā.

CLOWN [*to himself*] Right, I'm going to put a stop to this. [*Aloud*] Listen, sire, if she's a hermit girl who can't be wooed, what's the point of seeing or not seeing her?

KING Idiot!

8 Why do you think people bother
To turn their faces upwards
And gaze with unblinking eyes
Upon the crescent of the new moon?

And at any rate Dushyanta's thoughts do not dwell on forbidden objects.

CLOWN Explain to me, then.

KING

9 It seems she was born of an amorous nymph and a sage,
Abandoned by her mother and thus a foundling,
Like a stray jasmine blossom shaken loose
And fluttering by chance onto an arka* plant.

CLOWN [*grinning*] You want her because you're sated with all the gorgeous women of the palace, like someone sickened with sweet dates and yearning for a taste of sour tamarind.

KING My friend, you don't know her or you wouldn't talk like that.

CLOWN Well, anything that can take *your* breath away must be something special.

*A plant of no great beauty, but having religious significance because of its use in sacrificial ceremonies.

KING I tell you, friend –

Whether he drew her in a picture and then breathed life in her, 10
Or mentally fashioned her out of an amalgam of beautiful forms,
When I reflect on her loveliness and the range of the Creator's powers,
I feel that she must be a new way of making a woman.

CLOWN Clearly she puts all other beautiful women in the shade.

KING And what I ask myself is –

That unsmelt blossom, that unsnapped stem, 11
That unpierced gem, that fresh, untasted wine,
That still unharvested fruit of past good deeds, her flawless beauty –
Who in this world, I wonder, will be allowed to enjoy it?

CLOWN Then you'd better get a move on in case she falls into the hands of some oily-haired ascetic.

KING She is a minor, and her guardian is away.

CLOWN Well, but how does she feel towards you?

KING Hermit girls are by nature very modest creatures, my friend. Even so –

When I looked at her she withdrew her gaze, 12
And she smiled while talking about other things.
Being restrained by modesty,
She neither revealed nor exactly hid her love.

CLOWN Were you expecting her to jump on your lap the moment she saw you?

KING But as she was going off with her two friends she

did give me a strong hint of her true feelings. For –

13 Saying she'd cut her foot on a sharp blade of grass,
She suddenly stopped after she'd gone just a step or two,
And with face turned round busied herself with releasing
Her dress from the branches of the trees, although it wasn't caught there.

CLOWN She's given you something to chew on! I should think you've become quite attached to the holy grove.

KING Mādhavya, try to think of some excuse for me to visit the hermitage again.

CLOWN What more excuse do you need – you're the King!

KING And so?

CLOWN Tax the ascetics fifteen per cent on their wild rice.

KING Fool! The tax which ascetics pay is quite a different kind, and far more valuable than piles of jewels:

14 The wealth kings get from society
Is a transitory thing.
But the ascetics of the forest
Yield us an imperishable tithe from their austerities.

VOICES OFF-STAGE Ah, here we are!

KING [*listening*] What strong, calm voices. They must be ascetics.

[*Enter the Doorkeeper.*]

DOORKEEPER Victory, sire. There are two young seers at the door.

KING Show them in at once.

DOORKEEPER Yes, sire. [*Withdrawing and re-entering with the two young seers*] This way!

FIRST SEER [*seeing the King*] How resplendent his form is, and yet how reassuring! But that is to be expected in a king who is virtually a seer.

He too, like a seer, leads a life that is to the good of all, 15
And by protecting his subjects he too accumulates merit every day.
He too knows the virtue of control, and is forever lauded to the skies
Under the holy title of sage – but coupled with the title of king.

SECOND SEER Friend, is that King Dushyanta, comrade of Indra?

FIRST Indeed it is.

SECOND Then

No wonder that he rules the whole earth to the shores of the dark ocean, 16
With his arms as strong as the bolts of a city gate.
For in their wars the gods themselves, battling with the demons,
Look for victory in his ready bow and in the thunderbolt of Indra.

BOTH [*approaching*] Victory, sire!

KING [*rising from his seat*] I salute you both.

SEERS Our good wishes to you. [*They offer him fruit.*]

KING [*accepting it with a bow*] I should be happy to learn the reason for your visit.

SEERS The ascetics have learnt of your presence here, and have a request to make of you.

KING I am their servant: what is their command?

SEERS They say that because the revered head of our community is absent, evil spirits are hindering the practice of austerities, and they ask that you should come with your driver for a few nights and take charge of the hermitage.

KING They do me honour.

CLOWN [*privately to him*] A very agreeable way to have your arm twisted.

KING Raivataka, tell my driver to bring the chariot here, together with my bow and arrows.

DOORKEEPER Yes, Your Majesty. [*He withdraws.*]

SEERS

17 It is fitting that you should act
In imitation of your forebears:
For the descendants of Puru are priests in kingly form
Consecrated to the sacrifice of helping those in need.

KING Off you go. I shall be hard on your heels.

SEERS Victory, sire! [*They both withdraw.*]

KING Well, Mādhavya, do you feel any curiosity to see Śakuntalā?

CLOWN I *was* brimming over with it – but now I've heard about the evil spirits, it's all leaked away.

KING No need to be scared – you can stick close to me.

CLOWN Oh, that makes me your comrade in arms!

[*Enter the Doorkeeper.*]

DOORKEEPER The chariot is ready and awaits your departure to victory, sire. But Karabhaka has arrived here from the city, from the Queen Mother.

KING [*in respectful tones*] Sent by Her Majesty herself?

DOORKEEPER Certainly, sire.

KING Then show him in.

DOORKEEPER [*after withdrawing and returning with Karabhaka*] Karabhaka, there is His Majesty: you may approach him.

KARABHAKA [*approaching and saluting*] Victory, sire, victory! Her Majesty sends the following request.

KING What does she command her servant?

KARABHAKA In four days' time it is the fast day known as the Safeguarding of the Son's Succession. She feels it is essential that Your Majesty should be at her side on that occasion.

KING My duty to the ascetics against the command of my revered parent! What is to be done? I can't ignore either.

CLOWN [*with a grin*] Be like Triśanku * and dangle in the middle!

KING Seriously, I'm worried:

With two duties in different places, 18
My mind is split down the middle –
Like the stream of a river
Dividing against a rock.

[*After reflection*] My friend, the Queen has accepted you as her son. So you go back, explain to Her Majesty that I am busy in helping the ascetics, and take the son's part in the ceremony.

CLOWN Hey, don't think I'm scared of the evil spirits!

KING [*with a grin*] You, born a priest? How could I possibly think such a thing of you?

CLOWN Well, I want to travel in full style, as your younger brother.

*An ancient king whom the powerful sage Viśvāmitra elevated to heaven: the gods hurled him out, but Viśvāmitra arrested his descent and he remained suspended in the sky, forming the Southern Cross.

KING Actually, since I don't want to inconvenience the hermitage anyway, I'll let you have every one of my attendants to accompany you.

CLOWN [*proudly*] Oh my, I'm the Crown Prince!

KING [*to himself*] He's such a chatterbox he might easily let the women of the palace know of my suit. I must do something about it. [*Aloud, taking the Clown by the hand*] Mādhavya, my friend, I'm going to the hermitage out of respect for the seers. Of course I'm not *really* in love with the hermit girl. After all –

19 What have I in common with a girl
Brought up with fawns and a stranger to love?
Those things I said in jest,
Don't take them seriously.

CLOWN Of course not.

[*All withdraw.*]

PRELUDE TO ACT III

[*Enter a pupil of the sacrificial priest, carrying grass for the sacrifice.*]

PUPIL [*in wonder*] What a mighty monarch King Dushyanta is! The moment he appeared, the obstruction to our rituals ceased.

1 No need to fit the arrow:
With no more than the faint sound of the bowstring,
As if it were the twang of the bow being shot,
He puts paid to all obstacles.

I must take this sacrificial grass to the priests to strew on the altar. [*Walking about, seeing someone and speaking into the air*] Oh Priyamvadā, who are you taking that ointment to, and the lotus leaves with fibres? [*Listening*] What's that? Śakuntalā is very unwell with heatstroke, and it's to cool her body? Look after her carefully, Priyamvadā – she is the very breath of life to our revered patriarch. I'll send Gautamī with the soothing water from the sacrifice for her. [*He withdraws.*]

Act III

[*Enter the King, lovesick.*]

KING [*anxiously sighing*]

I know the power of the religious life, 2
I realize that she is dependent on another,
But still, like water in a hollow,
My mind will not leave her.

Oh Love, blessed deity, how can I feel such pain when your arrows are only flowers? [*Recollecting*] Ah, but I know why!

It must be that even now the fire of Śiva's anger 3
Burns within you like the submarine fire in the ocean.
Otherwise how could you be so scorching
To people like me – you, who yourself were burnt to ashes?

In fact you and the moon alike – both of whom we should be able to trust – are perfidious to us lovers:

That you are armed with flowers, that the moon's rays are cool, 4

These are facts not borne out in our experience.
For with its cold rays the moon shoots fire,
While you have turned your flower arrows into adamant.

And yet

5 Though he brings me endless agony of mind
I will still welcome the god of love –
Provided that the passion with which he smites me
Is passion for Śakuntalā and no one else.

Blessed god, do you feel no sympathy at all for me, when thus reproached?

6 In vain, Love, did I make you big and strong,
Feeding you attentively with a thousand thoughts and feelings:
You drew your bow back to your ear
And I was the one you shot your arrow at.

Now that the ascetics have been freed of their troubles and do not require me, where can I find some distraction for my lovesick thoughts? [*With a sigh*] Nowhere where I can't see my loved one. [*Looking up at the heavens*] This is the hot time of day which she usually spends with her friends on the banks of the Mālinī with its bowers of vine: so that's where I'll go. [*Walking about and looking*] I can tell that she must just have passed through this avenue of saplings:

7 The stems from which she has plucked the blossoms
Have not yet closed up.
And there broken twigs can be seen,
Still sticky with sap.

[*Acting a sensation on his body*] How pleasant the breeze is in this part of the wood!

It is a breeze so fragrant with lotus scents, 8
So laden with spray from the rippling river,
That lovers* may safely hug it close to them
To cool their tortured limbs.

[*Looking*] Ha! Śakuntalā must be here in this bower of bamboo and vine. For

In the pale sand at its entrance 9
I can see a fresh line of footprints
Shallow at the toe,
But deep at the heel from the heaviness of her hips.

I'll look through the branches, then. [*Doing so, delightedly*] Oh, what a paradise for my eyes! There is the beloved of my dreams lying on a bed of flowers on top of a slab of stone, being attended by her two friends. I must listen to what they're saying among themselves. [*He stays watching.*]

[*Enter Śakuntalā with her two friends.*]

THE FRIENDS [*fanning her*] Dearest Śakuntalā, is the breeze from these lotus leaves making you feel better?

ŚAKUNTALĀ [*listlessly*] Oh, were you fanning me, my dears?

[*Both look at each other in despair.*]

KING She's very unwell, obviously. [*Musingly*] Now is it the fault of the hot weather, or could it be what I'm thinking? [*After reflection*] But there can be no doubt –

With ointment on her breasts, and loose bracelets solely of lotus fibre, 10

*The breeze from the south was conventionally regarded as inflaming amorous passions.

My loved one's body, tormented though she is, is very beautiful.
Love and the hot season may cause equal agony, it is true,
But summer could never afflict a girl in such a charming way.

PRIYAMVADĀ [*aside*] Anusūyā, Śakuntalā has been restless and anxious ever since she first saw the good King. There can be no other cause for her illness.

ANUSŪYĀ I suspected as much myself. Very well, I'm going to ask her. [*Aloud*] My dear, I must ask you something. You have a very bad fever.

KING That is quite undeniable:

11 See how her bracelets made of lotus fibre,
White as the rays of the moon,
By turning black
Betray her raging temperature.

ŚAKUNTALĀ [*half sitting up*] Dear friend, say what you want to say.

ANUSŪYĀ Śakuntalā my dear, we've no way of knowing what's going on in your mind. But it seems to me that you're experiencing exactly what women in love are said to experience in all the stories. So tell us why you're in such a state. They say there's no cure till you really understand the disease.

KING Anusūyā has the same idea as I do.

ŚAKUNTALĀ My trouble is such a deep one I couldn't tell it to you just like that.

PRIYAMVADĀ She's quite right, my dear: why hide what is bothering you? Every day you're wasting away in body. There's nothing left of you now but a beautiful shadow.

KING It's quite true what Priyamvadā says. Look at her –

Emaciated cheeks, breasts that have lost their firmness, 12
Thin waist, drooping shoulders, complexion drained of
colour:
Languid with love, she seems both piteous and fair –
A spring creeper visited by a breeze that withers its
leaves.

ŚAKUNTALĀ [*with a sigh*] There's no one I'd tell except you. But it will distress you.

BOTH Dear Śakuntalā, that's exactly why we're pressing you. Unhappiness becomes bearable if you share it.

KING

Asked by the friends who share her joys and sorrows, 13
She must surely explain the cause of the trouble in her
heart.
Though she turned so often and looked at me longingly,
My heart's in my mouth to know how she will answer.

ŚAKUNTALĀ Ever since I saw the good King who protects our holy grove – [*She breaks off in embarrassment.*]

BOTH Tell us, my dear.

ŚAKUNTALĀ Ever since then I've become like this from love of him.

BOTH Then thank heavens! Now you're in love with someone worthy of you. But there, where can a great river flow except to the ocean?

KING [*joyfully*] I've heard what I was craving to hear.

Love, the cause of my torment, 14
Has become the author of my joy,
As a sultry, lowering day
Ends by washing away the heat of summer.

ŚAKUNTALĀ So if you approve, try to get the good King to take pity on me. Otherwise, remember me.

KING Her words remove all doubt.

PRIYAMVADĀ [*aside*] Anusūyā, she's so far gone in love we simply can't delay.

ANUSŪYĀ Priyamvadā, what way can there be of quickly and quietly arranging what she wants?

PRIYAMVADĀ Quietly will take a bit of doing. Quickly isn't so difficult.

ANUSŪYĀ How do you mean?

PRIYAMVADĀ Well, the King himself, after showing his feelings for her by the fond way he eyed her, is looking thin with lack of sleep nowadays.

KING It's true, that's exactly how I am! –

15 Night after night, as I lie with my face on my arm,
The hot tears dull the jewels on this golden bracelet:
And again and again I push it back as it slips
Away from my wrist, not even grazing my bow scars.

PRIYAMVADĀ [*after reflecting*] Anusūyā, she must write him a love letter – and I'll hide it in some flowers, pretend they're left over from an offering and see that they get into the King's hands.

ANUSŪYĀ I like it – that's a pretty plan. What do you say, Śakuntalā?

ŚAKUNTALĀ I shan't question your advice.

PRIYAMVADĀ Well, then, think up a nice verse that will give him some idea of your feelings.

ŚAKUNTALĀ All right, but I'm trembling with fear of a snub.

KING

16–17 Here he is and longing to be yours,
That person you're afraid will snub you.

A suitor might or might not succeed with Lakshmī* –
But how could *she* fail to win whoever she wanted?

HER FRIENDS Oh, you do undervalue yourself! Who's going to use an umbrella to keep off the cooling autumn moonlight?

ŚAKUNTALĀ [*with a smile*] Well, since you insist. [*She deliberates.*]

KING No wonder my eyes forget to blink as I gaze on my beloved.

Her face, as she composes, 18
One eyebrow raised in thought,
By the thrilling of the down on her cheek
Declares her love for me.

ŚAKUNTALĀ I've thought of a verse, my dears. But I haven't got anything to write with.

PRIYAMVADĀ Well, just write with your nail on this smooth lotus leaf.

ŚAKUNTALĀ [*doing as directed*] Listen and see if it's properly expressed or not.

BOTH We're listening!

ŚAKUNTALĀ [*reads out*]

I do not know your heart: 19
But day and night in me,
As I yearn for you, cruel one,
The longing sets my limbs on fire.

KING [*approaching suddenly*]

Fair creature, Love sets your limbs on fire, 20
But me he burns to ashes,

*Goddess of beauty and good fortune.

As the day blots the moon completely out
But leaves the waterlily still visible.

THE FRIENDS [*seeing him and arising delightedly*] Welcome to the immediate answer to our prayers!

[*Śakuntalā attempts to get up.*]

KING No, beautiful one, don't exert yourself!

21 Those limbs that have crushed the bed of flowers
And bruised the bracelets of lotus fibre
Must not in their feverish state
Seek to perform acts of courtesy.

ŚAKUNTALĀ [*in confusion to herself*] My heart, have you grown so faint that you can find nothing to say?

ANUSŪYĀ Would Your Majesty condescend to sit down here, on part of the stone slab?

[*Śakuntalā moves over slightly.*]

KING [*sitting down*] Priyamvadā, I hope your friend isn't suffering too much from her fever?

PRIYAMVADĀ [*with a smile*] She should get better now she's having treatment. Your Majesty, the love of the two of you for each other is clear enough. But because I'm fond of her, I want to say something that hardly needs saying.

KING Then don't hang back, my dear – one can regret not saying what one meant.

PRIYAMVADĀ Then hear me, sire.

KING I'm listening.

PRIYAMVADĀ A king has a duty to protect those living in a hermitage.

KING It is his highest duty.

PRIYAMVADĀ Well now, the God of Love has seen fit to reduce our dear friend here to her present condition through her feelings for you. Therefore I ask you to be her saviour and to sustain her life.

KING I am as anxious for this as you are, my dear. And you do me much honour.

ŚAKUNTALĀ [*with a jealous smile*] My dear, don't detain the good King, who must be pining for the women of the palace.

KING

Love of my heart, if you think my heart, 22
This heart which recognizes none but you,
Could ever be unfair to you, fairest one,
Then, pierced by Love's arrows, I am pierced again.

ANUSŪYĀ Sire, it's said that kings have many sweethearts. So please don't let our dear friend here ever become a grief to her family.

KING Need I say more than this, my dear? –

However many wives I have, 23
Two will sustain my line:
The ocean-girdled earth
And this friend of yours.

BOTH We are happy.

[*Śakuntalā shows joy.*]

PRIYAMVADĀ [*aside*] Anusūyā, just see how our friend is reviving more every minute, like a peacock in summer as it feels the wind from the storm clouds.

ŚAKUNTALĀ My dears, ask the King's pardon for anything we said among ourselves that wasn't respectful.

THE FRIENDS [*with a smile*] The one who said it must ask his pardon – no one else has been at fault.

ŚAKUNTALĀ I hope Your Majesty will forgive what you heard. People say all sorts of things when they're alone together.

KING [*smiling*]

24 I will forgive the offence,
Beautiful girl, if you in turn will be so kind
As to soothe my weariness by making room for me
On the bed of flowers that was made to cradle your body.

PRIYAMVADĀ I don't think that will be enough to make her happy!

ŚAKUNTALĀ [*with a show of anger*] Quiet, you ill-mannered girl! Making fun of me in the state I'm in!

ANUSŪYĀ [*looking outside the bower*] Oh, Priyamvadā, there's one of our young fawns looking this way and that – he must have lost his mother. I'll go and take him back to her.

PRIYAMVADĀ He's very frisky, my dear. You can't catch him on your own. I'll come and help you.

[*Both set off.*]

ŚAKUNTALĀ I won't let you go and leave me all alone.

BOTH [*with a smile*] All alone, with the protector of the world at your side? [*They leave.*]

ŚAKUNTALĀ Oh, my friends have left me!

KING Don't be alarmed. Here is a suitor to take the place of your friends. So tell me –

25 Shall I wave the lotus-leaf fan above you
And waft you a breeze moist with refreshing spray –
Or put your lotus-red feet on my lap
And soothingly massage them, loveliest one?

ŚAKUNTALĀ I can't offend the people I should respect. [*She rises feebly and moves off.*]

KING [*checking her*] Beautiful girl, the day is not yet at an end, and you are very weak.

How can you leave your bed of flowers 26
With only a lotus leaf to shield your breast,
And go into the hot sun
When your body is limp with fever?

[*He holds her back.*]

ŚAKUNTALĀ Let go of me! I'm not free to do as I like. But where can I turn, when I have only my friends to help me?

KING Alas, you make me ashamed!

ŚAKUNTALĀ It's not Your Majesty I mean – I blame my fate.

KING Why blame your fate when it's so agreeable?

ŚAKUNTALĀ How can I not blame it for making me love and admire someone when I am not my own mistress?

KING [*to himself*]

Though their own eagerness is great, girls will resist their sweethearts' urging, 27
And though they long for the joys of union, they are nervous of yielding their body.
Far from being plagued by the importunities of Love
It is they who plague Love himself by their hesitations.

[*Śakuntalā actually goes.*]

KING What, am I to lose what I long for? [*He goes after her and catches hold of her dress.*]

ŚAKUNTALĀ Sire, remember who you are, and restrain yourself. There are hermits wandering all about the place.

KING Do not fear your elders, my fair one. The revered Kaṇva is too wise to be annoyed with you.

History tells us of many marriages 28

Entered into as love matches*
By the daughters of royal sages –
And their fathers approved the match.

[*Looking around him*] Oh, I've come out into the open! [*He lets go of Śakuntalā and retraces his steps.*]

ŚAKUNTALĀ [*turning round in mid-step and bending towards him*] Sire, though I haven't fulfilled your desire and you know me only through conversation, don't forget me.

KING My dearest,

29 However far you go
You will not leave my heart,
As the shadow of the tree at evening
Never leaves its root on the eastern side.

ŚAKUNTALĀ [*after going a little further, to herself*] Oh dear, now that I hear that, my feet won't carry me further. Well, then, I'll hide in this clump of amaranth and see where love leads him. [*She does so and stays still.*]

KING What, my love, have you left me when I am lost in love for you, and gone off all uncaring?

30 When your body is so soft
And to be handled so delicately,
Can your heart really be so hard
Like the tough stalk of the acacia flower?

ŚAKUNTALĀ Hearing that robs me of all power to move.

KING What can I do here now, with my sweetheart gone? [*Looking in front of him*] Oh, my path is blocked!

*The Gāndharva form of marriage here referred to was one of mutual consent without consultation of relatives, and was recognized as possible for members of the warrior caste. Given general social attitudes, it is not likely to have been received very often with much enthusiasm, except in romantic stories.

Here, where it has slipped from her wrist, 31
Fragrant with ointment from her body,
Holding me here like a chain around my heart
Is her bracelet of lotus fibre, lying on the ground before me.

[*He takes hold of it reverently.*]

ŚAKUNTALĀ [*looking at her arm*] Oh, the bracelet was so weak and loose it slipped off without my noticing!

KING [*clasping the bracelet to his breast*] Ah, it feels wonderful!

This casual trinket of yours, beloved, 32
By quitting your lovely arm and staying here with me
Has brought more comfort to an unhappy man,
Insentient object though it is, than you have done.

ŚAKUNTALĀ I cannot bear to hold back any more. I'll use this as an excuse to show myself. [*She approaches him.*]

KING [*seeing her, joyfully*] Oh, the mistress of my life is come! I have only to lament and fate is at once kind to me.

Parched with thirst 33
The bird craves water –
And at once a rain-cloud forms
And pours showers into its mouth.

ŚAKUNTALĀ [*standing before the King*] Your Majesty, on my way I remembered that bracelet there which slipped from my arm, and I've come back for it. Something told me you'd picked it up. Let me have it, or it will show both of us up in front of the sages.

KING I'll hand it over on one condition.

ŚAKUNTALĀ What's that?

KING That I can be the one to put it back where it belongs.

ŚAKUNTALĀ [*to herself*] I've no choice. [*She comes closer.*]

KING Let's take the stone seat over here.

[*Both walk about and seat themselves.*]

KING [*taking hold of Śakuntalā's hand*] How wonderful that feels!

34 Though the tree of love was all burnt to ashes
In the fire of Śiva's anger,
Has fate poured down a stream of nectar
And allowed this fresh shoot of it to spring up?

ŚAKUNTALĀ [*showing sensitivity to his touch*] Oh, please hurry, my lord!

KING [*delightedly, to himself*] Now I am reassured: she talks as if I were her husband. [*Aloud*] Fair one, the fastening on this bracelet is not very firm. If you like, I'll refasten it.

ŚAKUNTALĀ [*smiling*] As you please.

KING [*after artful delays fastening it on her*] Look, my fair one –

35 Here is the new moon changed into lotus fibre,
Which has quit the sky in search of greater beauty:
Finding the dark loveliness of your arm
It has joined the tips of its pale crescent around your wrist.

ŚAKUNTALĀ I can't quite see it. The breeze has blown pollen into my eyes from the waterlily at my ear.

KING [*with a smile*] If you like, I'll blow it away for you.

ŚAKUNTALĀ That would be very kind of you. But I don't quite trust you.

KING No, no! A new servant never presumes beyond his instructions.

ŚAKUNTALĀ But all this attentiveness is just what I don't trust.

KING [*to himself*] I'm not going to let slip such a delightful opportunity to do her a service. [*He starts to raise her face.*]

[*Śakuntalā yields while continuing to display resistance.*]

Bewitching creature, stop worrying that I will misbehave!

[*Śakuntalā glances at him and then hangs her head.*]

[*Raising her face with two fingers, to himself*]

My sweetheart's lip, soft and never bruised, 36
Seems, as I thirst for it,
By its sweet trembling
To grant me the permission I crave.

ŚAKUNTALĀ My lord seems slow in doing what he promised.

KING Sweet girl, the dark waterlily at your ear was confusing me by its likeness to your eye. [*He gently blows at her eye.*]

ŚAKUNTALĀ Thank you, my sight is back to normal now. But I'm sorry not to have any way of returning your kindness.

KING No need, my love –

It was enough of a kindness 37
That I could smell your fragrant face.
After all, the bee is satisfied
With the mere scent of the lotus.

ŚAKUNTALĀ But what does he do if he is not satisfied?

KING This! [*He approaches her face resolutely.*]

A FRIEND'S VOICE OFF-STAGE Sheldrake hen, say goodbye* to your mate! Lady night is near at hand.

ŚAKUNTALĀ [*listening, agitatedly*] My lord! Here is the venerable Gautamī, coming to ask after me. You must hide in the branches.

KING Yes. [*He stands aside.*]

[*Enter Gautamī, bowl in hand.*]

GAUTAMĪ Here is the water from the sacrifice, daughter. [*Looking at her and helping her up*] What, unwell and all alone here with the gods?

ŚAKUNTALĀ Priyamvadā and Anusūyā have only just gone down to the river.

GAUTAMĪ [*sprinkling her with the water*] Long life and health to you, my daughter. Is the fever easing? [*She feels her.*]

ŚAKUNTALĀ There is a change for the better, Mother.

GAUTAMĪ The day is drawing to a close. Come, let's get back to the cottage.

ŚAKUNTALĀ [*rising with difficulty, to herself*] My heart, you hesitated at first, when what you wanted was in your grasp. Now you must put up with the consequence. [*Taking a step and turning round, aloud*] Bower of vines that soothed my fever, goodbye until some future time for pleasure!

[*She and Gautamī withdraw.*]

KING [*going back to where he was, with a sigh*] Oh, the obstacles one must surmount to reach one's goal! –

38 The lips she kept covering with her fingers,

*In Indian mythology, sheldrakes of the *chakravāka* species are lovebirds fated always to separate at night.

The sweetly faltering words of prohibition,
The head she turned towards her shoulder,
And then at last the face I lifted up, yet never kissed.

Well, where shall I go now? No, I'll stay where I am for a while, in this bower which has given pleasure to my loved one. [*Looking all round him*]

Here on the stone is her bed of flowers, pressed by her body. 39
Here is the sweet love message which she engraved with her nails on the lotus leaf.
And here, the fibre bracelet that slipped from her arm.
With so much to compel my gaze,
I can't just walk away, empty though the place may be.

[*Reflecting*] Alas, I was wrong to delay once I had won her. So now –

If I am together again with my love in private, 40
I'll lose no time: for happiness is hard enough to come by –
Or so in its frustration my foolish heart calculates:
But when she is there, it seems to be rather more timid.

VOICE OFF-STAGE Sire, sire!

Now that the evening libation is begun, 41
The altar with its fire is thickly thronged
With the fearsome, prowling shadows of the goblins
Ruddy as the tops of the clouds at twilight.

KING [*hearing*, *resolutely*] Hallo there, ascetics! Have no fear, I am coming. [*He goes out.*]

PRELUDE TO ACT IV

[*Enter the two friends, acting the picking of flowers.*]

ANUSŪYĀ Priyamvadā, despite the fact that our dear Śakuntalā has found her happiness in this love match and won a husband worthy of her, I don't feel easy in my mind.

PRIYAMVADĀ Why ever not?

ANUSŪYĀ I'm worried whether, now that the sacrifice has been successfully concluded and the sages have sent the King back to the capital, he will remember her among all those hundreds of court ladies.

PRIYAMVADĀ Oh, rest easy on that score. Men of such distinguished appearance never betray their own nobility. What we have to worry about is what Father Kaṇva will do when he gets back from his pilgrimage and hears about it.

ANUSŪYĀ If you ask me, it's what he wanted.

PRIYAMVADĀ Why's that?

ANUSŪYĀ Well, surely what he hoped for from the start was for his daughter to be given in marriage to someone worthy of her. If fate does the work for him, he's got exactly what he wanted.

PRIYAMVADĀ That's quite true. [*Looking at the flower basket*] My dear, we've picked enough flowers for the offering.

ANUSŪYĀ Don't forget that Śakuntalā has to make an offering for a happy marriage. So let's pick some more.

PRIYAMVADĀ A good idea.

[*Both do so.*]

VOICE OFF-STAGE Hallo there, here I am!

ANUSŪYĀ [*listening*] My dear, I think a visitor is announcing himself.

PRIYAMVADĀ Well, Śakuntalā is by the cottage. [*On reflection*] Oh, but she's far away in her heart today. We'd better make do with the flowers we've got.

[*They set off.*]

THE VOICE What? Do you slight me, a guest?

That one you are thinking of with thoughts for no one else, 1
Because of whom you do not notice that I, a holy sage, am here –
He shall not remember you however much reminded,
Any more than a drunken man remembers what was said.

[*Both despair on hearing this.*]

PRIYAMVADĀ Oh dear, oh dear! It's happened. She's been so absent-minded she's offended some important person.

ANUSŪYĀ [*looking ahead*] And not just any important person, my dear. It's the great sage Durvāsas, who's so short-tempered. There he is striding quickly away again.

PRIYAMVADĀ What has the power to burn except fire? You go and fall at his feet and persuade him to return while I fetch some water to welcome him.

ANUSŪYĀ Right you are. [*She goes out.*]

PRIYAMVADĀ [*on taking another step, acting stumbling*] Oh no! I've tripped in my haste and the flower basket's slipped from my fingers! [*She acts gathering the flowers together.*]

[*Enter Anusūyā.*]

ANUSŪYĀ Oh my dear, he's like anger incarnate. He'd never accept an apology from anyone. But I did get him to relent a little.

PRIYAMVADĀ That's a lot, from him. Tell me.

ANUSŪYĀ He refused to return – so I bowed down at his feet and said, 'Your Reverence, think of your daughter's previous devotion and forgive her the sin she has committed today in failing to acknowledge your holy power.'

PRIYAMVADĀ And?

ANUSŪYĀ And he answered, 'What I have said may not be otherwise. However, the curse on her will be lifted if he sees some ornament given her as a keepsake.' And as he was saying this, he vanished.

PRIYAMVADĀ We can breathe again. Śakuntalā does have a ring marked with the King's own name which he put on her hand himself to remember him by when he was leaving. That will solve the problem automatically.

ANUSŪYĀ Come on then, let's finish what we were doing.

[*They walk about.*]

PRIYAMVADĀ [*looking*] Look, Anusūyā. There she is with her face resting on her left hand, as still as a picture – so full of him she has no attention to spare even for herself, let alone distinguished visitors.

ANUSŪYĀ Let's keep what's happened entirely to ourselves, Priyamvadā. She's such a delicate creature she needs to be shielded.

PRIYAMVADĀ Of course – who would sprinkle a jasmine with hot water?

[*Both withdraw.*]

Act IV

[*Enter, risen from sleep, a pupil of Kaṇva.*]

PUPIL My revered teacher Kaṇva is back from his pilgrimage, and he has asked me to look at the time. So I'll go outside and see how much is left of the night. [*Walking about and looking*] Oh, it's already daybreak:

On one horizon the Lord of Plants* nears the western mountain, 2
On the other the Sun has sent the dawn to herald his arrival.
That one great light should fail as the other grows in splendour
Shows how inexorable is the wheel of this world's fortune.

With the moon vanished, that pond of once blossoming lilies 3
No longer gladdens my sight: its splendour fades into a memory.
But of course the sorrow of those left alone
By a loved one's departure is beyond measure grievous.

Over the jujube trees the early dawn is reddening the dew. 4
The peacock wakes, and quits his grassy perch on the cottage roof.
And from the altar's hoof-marked verge a deer gets up,
Rearing its hind end suddenly, as it stretches itself.

*The moon.

The same moon that towered above the heights of Meru,
greatest of mountains,
And occupied Vishṇu's mid realm, defeating darkness,
Now drops from the sky, its rays grown few and feeble:
No matter how great, too high will mean a fall.

[*Enter Anusūyā.*]

ANUSŪYĀ [*to herself*] Even the most unworldly person can tell that the King has behaved badly towards Śakuntalā.

PUPIL Well, I'll tell my teacher that it's now time for the sacrifice. [*He goes out.*]

ANUSŪYĀ Oh, the day's just dawning! I've woken up bright and early. But what is there for me to do now I *am* awake? My hands won't settle to any of my usual early morning tasks. I only hope the God of Love is satisfied, bringing my pure-hearted friend in contact with such a faithless person. But no, it's not the fault of the good King. This is Durvāsas' curse working itself out. Otherwise how could the King, after saying all he did, not send her so much as a word in all this time? [*On reflecting*] Then we ought to send him the keepsake ring from here. But who to ask among the ascetics, with their serenity and lack of worldly passions? And not wanting to get our friend into trouble, we just can't bring ourselves to tell Father Kaṇva that Śakuntalā is married to Dushyanta and pregnant by him. So what on earth *can* we do?

[*Enter without ceremony* Priyamvadā.*]

*Such an entry was made by pushing through the curtain at the back of the stage, instead of waiting for it to be drawn aside. I have transferred this stage-direction: the manuscripts give it at Anusūyā's entry just above, where it seems inappropriate.

PRIYAMVADĀ Oh hurry, Anusūyā, hurry! There's going to be a farewell ceremony for Śakuntalā.

ANUSŪYĀ [*in amazement*] What on earth do you mean?

PRIYAMVADĀ Listen. Just now I went to ask Śakuntalā if she had slept well.

ANUSŪYĀ And?

PRIYAMVADĀ And there was Father Kaṇva, embracing her while she hung her head in shame, and saying delightedly, 'My dear child, happily the offering has fallen straight into the fire, even though the sacrificer's sight was obscured by the smoke! I know now that I shall not regret you: you are like knowledge received by a good pupil. I'll give you an escort of hermits this very day and send you to your husband.'

ANUSŪYĀ But Priyamvadā, who told Father Kaṇva what had happened?

PRIYAMVADĀ Apparently it was a disembodied voice when he entered the fire sanctuary, speaking a verse to him.

ANUSŪYĀ [*in amazement*] Whatever did it say?

PRIYAMVADĀ Listen. [*Quoting in Sanskrit*]

'Know, brahmin, that your daughter 6
For the well-being of the world
Now bears the vital seed implanted by Dushyanta,
As the pierced firestick holds the seed of fire.'

ANUSŪYĀ [*embracing Priyamvadā*] Oh my dear, how wonderful! But I do feel a sad element mixed in with my pleasure, to know that Śakuntalā is actually leaving today.

PRIYAMVADĀ We'll banish the sadness somehow – the poor girl mustn't have her happiness clouded.

ANUSŪYĀ Well then, in that coconut-shell hanging on the

mango tree branch there are some clusters of long-lasting bakula blossom which I've been keeping there for this very purpose. You wrap them in lotus leaves while I mix up a good luck paste for her out of some yellow orpiment, holy earth and dūrvā grass.

[*Priyamvadā does so.*]

[*Anusūyā withdraws.*]

KAṆVA'S VOICE OFF-STAGE Gautamī, tell Śārngarava and Śāradvata to be ready to escort dear Śakuntalā.

PRIYAMVADĀ [*listening*] Oh hurry, Anusūyā! The hermits who are to go to Hastināpura are already being summoned.

ANUSŪYĀ [*re-entering with the cosmetic paste*] Come on then, my dear.

[*They walk about.*]

PRIYAMVADĀ [*looking*] Look, there's Śakuntalā! She has bathed at sunrise, and she's being showered with rice and blessings by the hermit women. Let's go to her.

[*They do so.*]

[*Enter, attended as described, Śakuntalā together with Gautamī.*]

ŚAKUNTALĀ Reverend ladies, I salute you.

GAUTAMĪ My child, may you win the title of Queen to show your husband's regard.

HERMIT WOMEN May you beget a hero, dear child!

[*Apart from Gautamī, the hermit women withdraw.*]

THE TWO FRIENDS [*approaching*] Dear Śakuntalā, may your bathe have been happy for you!

ŚAKUNTALĀ Welcome, dear friends. Sit down beside me.

THE FRIENDS [*sitting*] Just keep still, darling, while we put the good luck paste on you.

ŚAKUNTALĀ Although that's nothing unusual, it's something to value today. It'll be a long time before my friends put my make-up on for me again. [*She sheds a tear.*]

THE FRIENDS You mustn't cry, my dear, at a happy time like this. [*They wipe away her tears and act adorning her.*]

PRIYAMVADĀ Oh dear, your beauty deserves proper jewellery: the kind of decorations we have in a hermitage don't do justice to it.

[*Enter a young hermit, Hārīta, carrying jewellery.*]

HĀRĪTA Here is a set of ornaments to adorn the young lady.

[*All are astonished to see them.*]

GAUTAMĪ Hārīta, my son, where do these come from?

HĀRĪTA From the spiritual power of Father Kaṇva!

GAUTAMĪ Was it mental concentration?

HĀRĪTA Not at all – listen. Father Kaṇva had ordered us to fetch flowers from the trees for Śakuntalā, whereupon

One tree displayed a linen wedding-dress, pale as the moon, 7
Another exuded red lac to dye the feet.
From yet others the hands of forest deities, like graceful shoots of leaf,
Emerged up to the wrist and offered us jewellery.

PRIYAMVADĀ [*looking at Śakuntalā*] Even if a bee is born in a tree hollow, it's the nectar of the lotus that she longs for!

GAUTAMĪ Such favour foreshadows the regal glory that will be yours in your husband's house.

[*Śakuntalā displays shyness.*]

HĀRĪTA I must go and report this service that the trees have done, to the revered Kaṇva, who has gone down to the Mālinī to bathe. [*He goes out.*]

ANUSŪYĀ My dear, how can we arrange the ornaments when we've had no experience of jewellery? [*Reflecting and regarding her*] Well, we'll follow what we've seen in pictures in putting the ornaments on you.

ŚAKUNTALĀ I know how clever you both are.

[*The friends act fastening the decorations on her.*]

[*Enter Kaṇva, back from his bathe.*]

KAṆVA

8 Śakuntalā leaves today, and my heart is touched with sadness,
Suppressed tears choke my voice, care dulls my vision.
Such weakness due to love, in me a forest-dweller!
How tormented with grief a simple householder must be, when first he loses a daughter.

[*He walks about.*]

THE FRIENDS Śakuntalā dearest, we've finished arranging the ornaments. Now put on these two beautiful linen garments.

[*Śakuntalā gets up and acts putting them on.*]

GAUTAMĪ Daughter, here is your guardian arrived, and almost embracing you with eyes that are brimming with tears of joy. Go and salute him.

[*Śakuntalā shyly pays homage.*]

KAṆVA My child,

9 May you be as esteemed by your husband
As was Śarmiṣṭhā by Yayāti,
And as she begat Puru
May you too beget a son to be emperor of the earth.

GAUTAMĪ Daughter, that is a blessing that has been pronounced on you, not a prayer.

KAṆVA Come, dear child, the offerings have just been made in the sacred fires – walk sunwise round them.

[*All walk about.*]

My child,

Let those three fires of the sacrifice protect you, 10
On their altars ranged around the principal altar,
Heaped with firewood, banked with sacred grass,
Repelling evil with the odours of the sacrifice.

[*Śakuntalā makes a clockwise circumambulation.*]

And now, dear child, go forth. [*Casting his glance about him*] But where are the good Śārngarava and Śāradvata?

[*Enter two pupils.*]

PUPILS Here we are, Your Reverence.

KAṆVA Śārngarava, dear boy, you lead the way for your sister.

PUPIL This way, my sister.

[*All walk about.*]

KAṆVA Oh hear me, trees of the grove that have forest gods within you!

She who would never drink till you yourselves were watered, 11
Who though she loved ornament could never bear to pluck your blossoms,
Who welcomed with joy the time of your first budding,
She, Śakuntalā, is going to her husband's house: all of you, make your farewells.

ŚĀRNGARAVA [*indicating that he hears a cuckoo*] Reverence,

12 The trees that were her companions in her forest life
Have bid Śakuntalā godspeed,
Making an answer to your words
Out of the soft call of the cuckoo.

VOICES OFF-STAGE

13 Fair be her path, with gentle favouring breezes,
In easy stages marked by lakes pink with lotuses,
The sun's hot rays held off by shady trees,
The dust made soft with waterlily pollen.

[*All listen in amazement.*]

GAUTAMĪ Daughter, the forest gods have said farewell with family affection. You must pay them proper homage.

ŚAKUNTALĀ [*after walking round and bowing, aside*] Oh Priyamvadā, although I long to see my husband, as I leave the hermitage I can hardly bear to put one foot before the other.

PRIYAMVADĀ You're not the only one to be upset about your leaving. Just look at the state of the grove itself which is going to lose you:

14 The grass drops from the doe's mouth,
The peahen gives up dancing,
And as their pale leaves fall away
The vines seem to be weeping.

ŚAKUNTALĀ [*recollecting*] Father, I must say goodbye to my sister among the vines, the spring creeper.

KAṆVA Yes, my child, I know how fond you are of it. Look, there it is to the right.

ŚAKUNTALĀ [*going up and embracing the vine*] Sister, embrace me with your tendrils. From now on I'll be far away from you. Father, you must care for this vine as if it were me.

KAṆVA My child,

What I had planned for you, a worthy husband, 15
You have won by your own merits.
Now that my worries for you are at an end,
I will wed this vine to her sweetheart, the mango at her side.

This way, now, to start your journey.

ŚAKUNTALĀ [*going up to her two friends*] My dears, I leave the vine in your hands.

HER FRIENDS And to whose care are *we* entrusted? [*They weep.*]

KAṆVA Anusūyā, Priyamvadā! You mustn't cry – it's you who should be giving support to Śakuntalā.

[*All walk on.*]

ŚAKUNTALĀ Father, this doe who grazes near the cottage because she is heavy with young – when she's given birth happily, you must send someone to tell me the good news. Don't forget.

KAṆVA I shan't forget, dear child.

ŚAKUNTALĀ [*acting an obstruction of her progress*] Oh, who's this at my heels who keeps tugging at my dress? [*She turns to look.*]

KAṆVA

It's the little fawn whose mouth you dabbed with oil of ingudī 16
To heal it when it was cut by the sharp grass,
And whom you gently fed on handfuls of wild millet:
He is your adopted son, and will not leave you alone.

ŚAKUNTALĀ No need to follow me when I am leaving

home, my little one. Just as I looked after you when your mother died while you were still tiny, Father Kaṇva will take care of you now that I am going away. Go back, darling, go back. [*She moves on, weeping.*]

KAṆVA Don't cry, my child – be brave. You must look where you are walking.

17 Be brave, and check the flow of tears
That keep your long-lashed eyes from seeing.
Your feet will come to grief
Unless you watch the hills and hollows on your way.

ŚĀRNGARAVA Your Reverence, it is usual to accompany a loved one as far as the edge of water, remember, and we have come to the bank of the lake. Here is where you should instruct us and go back.

KAṆVA Then let's shelter under the shade of that fig-tree.

[*All do so.*]

Now, what message should I send to His Majesty King Dushyanta? [*He reflects.*]

ANUSŪYĀ Dear Śakuntalā, there isn't a feeling creature around our hermitage that isn't sad to be losing you.

18 Hidden from her by lotus leaves,
The sheldrake fails to answer his anxious mate:
With the lotus fibres hanging forgotten from his bill,
His gaze is fixed on you.

KAṆVA Śārngarava my son, when you present Śakuntalā to the King address him as follows in my name:

19 'Remembering well my holy life and your proud lineage
And the love too that she has shown you, quite unprompted by her family,

Look on this one among your wives with at least an equal regard:
More than that is in the lap of fate, and her kinsfolk do not ask it.'

PUPIL We have the message, Your Reverence.

KAṆVA [*looking at Śakuntalā*] And now I must instruct you, my daughter. Though a forest-dweller I am not ignorant of the world.

PUPIL No, Your Reverence – no subject is outside the scope of the wise.

KAṆVA Daughter, when you have gone from here to your husband's house,

Obey your elders, treat your fellow wives as your friends, 20
Though your husband should ill-treat you, do not cross him in your anger.
Be generally considerate to your servants and not made vain by luxury.
That is how girls become wives: if they are otherwise they are a grief to their family.

But Gautamī, what is your opinion?

GAUTAMĪ It is all a bride need be told. [*To Śakuntalā*] Do not forget these words, my daughter.

KAṆVA Come, dear child, embrace me and your friends.

ŚAKUNTALĀ Oh father, must my friends turn back already?

KAṆVA I shall be giving them in marriage too, my dear. And so it wouldn't be right for them to go there with you. But Gautamī will accompany you.

ŚAKUNTALĀ [*hugging her father*] Torn from my father's breast like a sandalwood vine uprooted from the

Southern Mountain, how can I go on living in foreign soil? [*She weeps.*]

KAṆVA Why so afraid, my dear?

21 When you are honoured as the wife of an illustrious husband,
And continually engrossed in the duties his position brings,
When, not long from now, you bear him an heir as the East brings forth the sun,
You will not think about your grief at leaving me, my dear.

ŚAKUNTALĀ [*falling at his feet*] Father, I salute you.

KAṆVA Daughter, may you have all that I desire for you.

ŚAKUNTALĀ [*going up to her two friends*] Come, my dears, both of you embrace me together.

THE FRIENDS [*doing so*] My dear, if the King should happen to be slow in recognizing you, just show him the ring engraved with his own name.

ŚAKUNTALĀ You make my heart tremble when you raise such a doubt.

FRIENDS No, my dear, don't be scared. Love always fears the worst.

ŚĀRNGARAVA [*looking*] The sun is high in the sky – hurry, my sister.

ŚAKUNTALĀ [*again hugging her father*] Father, when shall I see the holy grove again?

KAṆVA My daughter,

22 When you have long been co-wife with the wide earth,
And when you have borne Dushyanta a son unrivalled in battle,

Your husband will hand the burden to that son, and you and he
Will set foot once more in this hermitage to gain peace of mind.

GAUTAMĪ Daughter, the time for our departure is slipping away. Send your father back. But no, she'll never do it herself – sir, you must go back.

KAṆVA My dear, I am neglecting my duties in the hermitage.

ŚAKUNTALĀ Your religious duties will keep you from missing me, father. But I'm already missing you.

KAṆVA Ah, do you think me so unfeeling? [*With a sigh*]

How can my grief ever leave me, 23
Dearest child, when I can still notice
How the wild rice offering that you once scattered
Has sprouted up at the cottage door?

Go, and God be with you on your journey.

[*Gautamī, Śārngarava and Śāradvata leave with Śakuntalā.*]

THE TWO FRIENDS [*after gazing for a long time, sadly*] Oh dear, Śakuntalā is lost among the trees!

KAṆVA Anusūyā, Priyamvadā, your friend is gone. Check your grief and follow me.

[*All set forth.*]

THE FRIENDS Father, with Śakuntalā gone, the hermitage feels empty as we enter it.

KAṆVA It is love which makes it seem so. [*Walking about in a reflective way*] Now that I have sent Śakuntalā away I feel easier. For –

A daughter is a possession belonging to someone else: 24
And so by sending her now to her husband

I have become at once more tranquil in my mind,
As if I had at last handed over what was given me for safekeeping.

[*All withdraw.*]

Act V

[*Enter the Chamberlain.**]

CHAMBERLAIN [*sighing*] Oh dear, how sadly aged I am!

1 The cane of office which I accepted as a formality
When I was given charge of the women's apartments
I must now, with the passing of the years,
Make use of to support my tottering steps.

I must visit the King in his private quarters and tell him of some business that needs seeing to immediately. [*Going on a little further*] But what was the business? [*After thought*] Oh of course, some ascetics, pupils of Kaṇva, want to see His Majesty. How strange it is!

2 The mind of an old man
Flares brightly for a moment,
Then succumbs to darkness once again,
Like the flame of a dying lamp.

*The Chamberlain, like the Clown, is a stock figure in Sanskrit drama. His advanced years are always emphasized – though the interesting implication of his opening remark here is that real old age was not a prerequisite for appointment.

[*Walking about and looking*] There is His Majesty:

Having seen to his subjects' affairs like a good father, 3
He is enjoying solitude with a quiet mind,
As a lord of elephants who has found grazing for his herd
Seeks out a cool refuge from the heat of the day.

Truth to tell, I feel reluctant to inform His Majesty of the arrival of Kaṇva's pupils when he has only just risen from the seat of judgement. But then, kings never rest:

The sun has never yoked his horses save the once. 4
The wind blows both night and day.
The Great Serpent bears the burden of the earth for all time.
And one who takes the people's tithes accepts a similar duty.

[*He walks about.*]

[*Enter the King, his Clown and his retinue according to rank.*]

KING [*acting exhaustion from work*] Most people feel happy when they get what they want, but for a king every achievement means only more trouble:

Attaining power quiets nothing except ambition: 5
Then come the vexations of safeguarding what one has.
Kingship is less a refreshment than a fresh source of weariness,
Like an umbrella* that needs to be held in one's own hand.

*The reference is to a heavy ceremonial umbrella.

VOICES OF TWO BARDS OFF-STAGE Hail to you, sire!

FIRST BARD

6 Without taking thought for your comfort, you exhaust yourself each day
All for the world's sake – but that is how you were made.
A tree will endure a fierce heat on its crown,
Yet with its shade allay the fever of all who come to it.

SECOND BARD

7 With your royal staff you check those who have taken to evil paths,
You pacify our quarrels, you afford us protection.
In times of prosperity a man may find that he has many kinsmen,
But you act as a kinsman should in all ways and to all your people.

KING [*hearing*] Wonderful – I was tired out with work, but this has quite renewed me!

CLOWN Ah, tell a bull that he's lord of the herd and his tiredness vanishes.

KING [*with a smile*] Well, let's sit down.

[*They both seat themselves while the attendants stand in due order.*]

[*Off-stage the sound of a lute.*]

CLOWN [*listening*] Hey, my friend, listen to the sounds from the music-room. I can hear a lute melody being played in perfect time. It must be Queen Hamsavatī practising her music.

KING Quiet, while I listen.

CHAMBERLAIN [*looking*] Oh, His Majesty is preoccupied. I'll wait for the right moment. [*He stands apart.*]

QUEEN [*sings off-stage*]

Once in your passion for its honey trove 8
The mango blossoms shook to your embraces:
But now, content with dwelling among lotuses,
Have you forgetten, bee, that earlier love?

KING Ah, what a tender song!

CLOWN Tell me, friend, did you get the meaning of the words?

KING [*with a smile*] It means that I used once to be so loving towards Queen Hamsavatī that my neglect of her now is a matter for reproach. Mādhavya, my friend, go and tell the Queen from me that she is right to scold me.

CLOWN Right you are. [*Getting up*] Hey, you're using someone else's hands to grab a bear by the short hairs. I've as much chance of salvation as a randy ascetic.

KING Go on – you're a man of the world: you can cope with her.

CLOWN Oh, I suppose I must. [*He goes out.*]

KING [*to himself*] Now why does hearing a song like that make me feel so full of yearning, even though I am not separated from any loved one? But then

When a man sees beautiful sights or hears sweet sounds 9
And becomes filled with longing although he is perfectly happy,
It must be that in his heart, without knowing it,
He recalls the deep-rooted friendships of another life.

[*He acts restlessness caused by an inability to remember something.*]

CHAMBERLAIN [*coming up*] Victory, sire! Ascetics with womenfolk have arrived here from the foothill forests of the Himālayas, bringing a message from Kaṇva. I await Your Majesty's command.

KING [*in surprise*] Ascetics with womenfolk, bringing a message from Kaṇva?

CHAMBERLAIN Yes, Your Majesty.

KING Then you must ask Somarāta our chaplain to welcome them with due scriptural rite and then himself conduct them to me personally. I shall go and await them in a place that is proper for receiving them.

CHAMBERLAIN Certainly, Your Majesty. [*He withdraws.*]

KING [*getting up*] Vetravatī, lead the way to the Fire Sanctuary.

FEMALE GUARD This way, Your Majesty. [*When they have walked about*] Sire, here is the terrace of the Fire Sanctuary, all freshly cleaned, and with the cow nearby to give milk for the oblation. Ascend, Your Majesty.

KING [*acting ascent, and then pausing to lean on the shoulders of his attendants*] Vetravatī, on what business can the Revered Kaṇva have sent seers to me?

Have the austerities of the devoted sages been spoilt by hindrances?
Or has someone done wrong to the creatures that roam the holy grove?
Can it be that my own misdeeds have stopped the flowering of their plants?
With so many possible conjectures, my mind is sorely puzzled.

FEMALE GUARD How could it be anything like that, Your Majesty, in a contented hermitage defended by your fame? My guess is that the seers have come to honour you in recognition of your great exploits.

[*Enter, in company with Gautamī and bringing Śakun-*

talā, Kaṇva's two pupils; and leading them in the Chaplain and the Chamberlain.]

CHAMBERLAIN This way, good sirs.

ŚĀRNGARAVA Śāradvata, my friend,

For all that he is a mighty king and unfailing in his duty, 11
For all that even the meanest of his subjects never swerve from rightdoing,
Even so my mind is so used to perpetual solitude
That this people-thronged palace seems like a house engulfed in flames.

ŚĀRADVATA You are right to feel so disturbed on entering the city, Śārngarava. I feel the same –

As one who has bathed views one who is still oily, 12
As a clean man a dirty, or one awake a sleeper,
As one who can move freely views someone still in bondage,
That is how I, being liberated, look on anyone tied to this world.

CHAPLAIN That is why we feel in awe of people like you.

ŚAKUNTALĀ [*acting an ill omen*] Oh dear, why is my right eye throbbing?

GAUTAMĪ Daughter, perish the ill omen! Let only happiness be yours.

[*They walk about.*]

CHAPLAIN [*pointing out the King*] Look, ascetics, there is the protector of all castes and conditions of people, already out of his seat and waiting to greet you. Behold him.

ŚĀRNGARAVA His courtesy is much to be praised – and yet I find it unremarkable:

13 Trees bow low because they have fruit to offer,
The rain they bear makes the clouds hang down to us.
Great men are humbled by their wealth.
It is the nature of those that do good to others.

FEMALE GUARD Your Majesty, the sages look quite cheerful and serene.

KING [*eyeing Śakuntalā*] Oh!

14 Who is she who is wearing a veil,
Her beauty showing through obscurely,
Standing among the ascetics
Like a bud among yellow leaves?

FEMALE GUARD She certainly seems very beautiful, sire.

KING Still – one shouldn't look at someone else's wife.

ŚAKUNTALĀ [*putting her hand to her breast, to herself*] Why are you trembling so, my heart? Remember my lord's devotion and take courage.

CHAPLAIN [*coming forward*] Hail to you, sire! Here are the ascetics, whom we have received with due rites. They bring with them a message from their teacher, which Your Majesty may care to hear.

KING [*respectfully*] I am listening.

THE TWO PUPILS [*raising their hands*] Hail, sire, victory to you!

KING [*with a bow*] I salute you all.

PUPILS Blessings upon you, sire.

KING Are your austerities unhindered?

PUPILS

15 Can good people be hindered in their pious work
While you are their protector?
While the sun blazes
How could darkness appear?

KING You give reality to my title of King. And the revered Kaṇva, is he in good health?

ŚĀRNGARAVA Sire, people with religious power such as his control their own health. He sends enquiries as to your own well-being, and the following message.

KING What does he command his servant?

ŚĀRNGARAVA 'I gladly give my approval, sire, to your marriage by mutual consent with this my daughter:

You are known to us as first among worthy men. 16
Śakuntalā is womanly virtue incarnate.
In uniting a bride and groom of equal merit
The Creator at last has acted faultlessly.

Now, therefore, that she is with child, receive her into holy partnership.'

GAUTAMĪ Good sir, I want just to say – that there is nothing for me to say!

KING Speak on, lady.

GAUTAMĪ

She did not consider her guardians, 17
You did not ask permission of her family.
When each has chosen the other
What is there to say to either?

ŚAKUNTALĀ [*to herself*] How is my lord going to answer?

KING [*having listened in doubt and confusion*] What are you getting at?

ŚAKUNTALĀ [*to herself*] Oh, his tone is cold!

ŚĀRNGARAVA What are we getting at? Why, you surely know the ways of the world better than we do!

Though she is blameless, people will suspect otherwise 18

If a girl has a husband yet lives all the time with her family.
And that is why relatives ask a wife to stay
With the man who married her, whether he loves her or not.

KING Did I once marry this lady?

ŚAKUNTALĀ [*to herself, despairingly*] Oh my heart, your fears have come true!

ŚĀRNGARAVA Sire!

19 Is it usual in a king,
This turning from duty because you now dislike what you did?

KING Why do you make these false assumptions?

ŚĀRNGARAVA [*angrily*]

19 cont. Such aberrations generally take hold
In men who are drunk with power.

KING You are gravely insulting me.

GAUTAMĪ [*to Śakuntalā*] Daughter, don't be shy – let me take your veil off, and then the King will recognize you. [*She does so.*]

KING [*looking at Śakuntalā, to himself*]

20 Seeing such flawless beauty offered like this to me
And wondering if I could somehow once have made it mine,
Like a bee at daybreak finding a jasmine with cold dew inside it
I can neither reach for it nor leave it alone.

FEMALE GUARD [*to herself*] What a scrupulous man the King is! Who else would hesitate on finding such a fine woman so easily available?

ŚĀRNGARAVA Sire, why so silent?

KING Good ascetic, however hard I think about it I can't remember marrying this lady. So how can I accept her when she is clearly pregnant, and condemn myself in my own eyes as an adulterer?

ŚAKUNTALĀ [*to herself*] Alas, he doubts our very marriage! All my fond hopes are dashed to the ground.

ŚĀRNGARAVA Not so!

Is it for you to spurn the sage 21
When he approves your seduction of his daughter,
And by presenting you with the stolen property
Turns you from a thief to an honest man?

ŚĀRADVATA That is enough, Śārngarava. Śakuntalā, we have said what we had to say, and you have heard how the King has spoken. Reply to him.

ŚAKUNTALĀ [*to herself*] When such a love has become so changed, what is the use of reminding him of it? But no, I have to clear myself, and so I must bring myself to do it. [*Aloud*] My lord – [*breaking off*] But no, my right to call you that is being questioned. Descendant of Puru, then – is it right, do you think, to reject me with such words after the way I opened my heart to you at the hermitage and you made promises to me and cherished me?

KING [*stopping his ears*] Perish the evil!

Why are you trying to sully your name 22
And at the same time drag me down,
Like a river tearing at the bank
That both muddies its clear current and destroys the tree on the shore?

ŚAKUNTALĀ Very well, if you are really doing this

because you suspect me of being someone else's wife, I have a token that will put your doubts at rest.

KING That's the first essential.

ŚAKUNTALĀ [*feeling where the ring should be*] Oh no, oh no! My finger's bare! [*She looks despairingly at Gautamī.*]

GAUTAMĪ Child, the ring must have slipped off when you were worshipping the water at Indra's Ford.

KING A typical piece of female quick-wittedness.

ŚAKUNTALĀ Well, fate has intervened there – but I can mention something else.

KING So now we're reduced to verbal evidence?

ŚAKUNTALĀ There was that day in the bower of bamboo and vine when you had some water in your hand in a lotus-leaf cup.

KING I'm listening.

ŚAKUNTALĀ At that moment the fawn who was my adopted son came up to us. You took pity on him and coaxed him to drink first. But he wouldn't come and drink out of your hand because you were a stranger. Then, when I held out the same water, he was happy with it. Whereupon you laughed and said, 'True enough, we all trust those who smell the same, for you and he are both creatures of the forest.'

KING These are the sweet, lying words of designing women that lure the susceptible.

GAUTAMĪ Your Majesty! You have no right to say that. She has been brought up in a hermitage and knows noth ing of deceit.

KING Venerable lady,

23 You will find that the female has an untaught cunning

Even among animals, let alone when she has a human brain.
Until her brood takes to the air
The cuckoo, it's said, gets other birds to feed them.

ŚAKUNTALĀ [*angrily*] Vulgar man, it seems you judge everything by the standard of your own heart. Others don't all behave like you, putting on a false cloak of virtue, like a well covered over with grass.

KING [*to himself*] Her anger really seems like the artless anger of a country girl!

Her eyes are red and stare straight at me, 24
Her voice is harsh, without any drawling inflections,
Her whole lip is trembling as if with cold,
And her curving eyebrows have knitted together in a disfiguring frown.

The anger looks so genuine it throws me into uncertainty –

Is it *my* heartlessness in failing to remember, 25
My refusal to acknowledge a secret love,
That has made her break the graceful curve of that brow
As if in her anger she were snapping the bow of Love?

[*Aloud*] Young lady, my conduct as king is an open book to my subjects, and anything of this kind is unheard of.

ŚAKUNTALĀ So be it – I'm now no better than a whore because, trusting a member of the family of Puru, I fell into the clutches of a man with a mouth of honey and a heart of stone. [*She weeps, wiping her eyes with the edge of her dress.*]

ŚĀRNGARAVA This shows the damage that can be done by unbridled impulse –

26 This is why one should show caution in entering
Most especially into any secret liaison.
Unless one knows a man's heart
Love may turn, as here, to hatred.

KING Oh, what's this? Do you heap accusations on me just because you rely on what this young woman says?

ŚĀRNGARAVA [*scornfully*] Your ideas are upside down –

27 If someone has never been taught duplicity in her whole life,
What she says can carry no weight;
While those who make a science out of doing others down
Are, it would seem, the people one must trust.

KING Well, well, Mr Honest Broker – let's just suppose for a moment that I am as you say I am. What exactly will I gain from wronging her?

ŚĀRNGARAVA Your own downfall!

KING It is beyond belief that kings of Puru's line should court their own downfall.

ŚĀRNGARAVA Sire, what is the point of bandying words? We have done as our teacher commanded us, and now we shall go home.

28 Here, then, is your bride
Whether you reject or accept her.
A husband's power over his wife
May be used in any way he chooses.

Gautamī, lead the way.

[*They set off.*]

ŚAKUNTALĀ I've been played false by this deceiver – are you abandoning me as well? [*She starts to follow them.*]

GAUTAMĪ [*turning round and seeing her*] Śārngarava, my son, Śakuntalā is following us, crying pitifully. What is the poor girl to do now that her husband has been treacherous enough to reject her?

ŚĀRNGARAVA [*turning angrily*] You forward girl! Why are you being so self-willed?

[*Śakuntalā trembles in terror.*]

ŚĀRNGARAVA Listen to me:

If you are as the King says you are 29
What will your father have to do with you, when you have disgraced your family?
But if you know your own conduct to be pure,
You will bear even servitude in your husband's house.

Stay here. We must be on our way.

KING Oh ascetic! Why do you deceive her?

The moon makes only the night lilies bloom. 30
The sun awakens only the day lotuses.
Those who discipline their conduct
Can never embrace another man's wife.

ŚĀRNGARAVA But Your Majesty, just suppose some distraction has made you forget what you have done: how could anyone who fears to do wrong reject his own wife?

KING [*to his Chaplain*]* Sir, I ask *you* to tell me which is more important:

When there is this doubt whether I am deluded 31
Or she is speaking falsely,
Do I reject my own wife
Or defile myself by touching the wife of another?

*Stage direction introduced in translation.

CHAPLAIN [*after pondering*] Suppose one were to act as follows –

KING Instruct me, I am your pupil.

CHAPLAIN Let the young lady remain in my house until her confinement.

KING Why so?

CHAPLAIN Seers have already prophesied that the first son you beget will be emperor of both worlds. If the sage's daughter gives birth to a son bearing the necessary marks, you may welcome her into your household. If not, she can still return to her father.

KING I defer to my teacher.

CHAPLAIN [*rising*] This way, my child – come with me.

ŚAKUNTALĀ Oh holy mother Earth, swallow me up!

[*She moves off weeping, together with the Chaplain, the ascetics and Gautamī.*]

[*The King still muses about Śakuntalā, his memory clouded by the curse.*]

[*Voices off-stage exclaim in wonder.*]

KING [*listening*] What on earth can that be?

[*Enter the Chaplain.*]

CHAPLAIN [*in amazement*] Your Majesty, something quite extraordinary has happened!

KING Whatever is it?

CHAPLAIN When Kaṇva's pupils had turned to go,

32 Śakuntalā, bewailing her wretched fate,
Had just flung up her arms and begun to weep –

KING Yes?

CHAPLAIN

32 cont. When all at once, from near the Nymphs' Pool, a flash of light shaped like a woman

Seized hold of the girl and immediately vanished with her.

[*All show amazement.*]

KING Sir, we have already dismissed the matter. There is no point in pursuing it with vain speculations. You may retire.

CHAPLAIN Victory, sire! [*He withdraws.*]

KING Vetravatī, I feel thoroughly worn out. Conduct me to the bedchamber.

FEMALE GUARD This way, Your Majesty.

KING [*walking about, to himself*]

The sage's daughter whom I repudiated, 33
I have no memory of having married her.
But such is the pain in my heart
I yet could almost believe that I had done so.

[*All withdraw.*]

PRELUDE TO ACT VI

[*Enter a police superintendent, with two guards leading a man with his hands tied behind him.*]

THE GUARDS [*beating the man*] Come on, you thieving scum! Tell us where you got that ring with the King's name inset in jewels.

MAN [*showing terror*] Oh please, sirs! I wouldn't do a wicked thing like that.

FIRST GUARD I suppose the King gave it to you as a mark of respect because you're such a fine brahmin.

MAN Oh listen, please! I'm a fisherman from Indra's Ford.

SECOND GUARD Did we ask you for your address and occupation, you cheating scum?

SUPERINTENDENT Lẹt him tell it as it comes, Sūchaka. Don't interrupt, either of you.

BOTH GUARDS Just as you say, Chief. Come on then, you, talk.

FISHERMAN Well, I support my family by the use of nets, hooks and other fishing tackle.

SUPERINTENDENT [*with a laugh*] That's a clean trade you've got!

FISHERMAN Don't say that, master –

1 They say that if a man's born to a trade
He shouldn't give it up however low it may be.
Even the softest-hearted butcher
Is in the cruel job of slaughtering animals.

SUPERINTENDENT Well, go on.

FISHERMAN Well, one day I was cutting up a carp, and inside its belly I came on this ring, all bright with gems. And while I was showing it round looking for a buyer, I got arrested by your officers. Kill me or let me go – that's all there is to tell about how I got the thing.

SUPERINTENDENT [*sniffing the ring*] It's been in the belly of a fish, Jānuka, there's no doubt about that – that's how it's got this fishy smell. We'll have to look into how it was found. Come on, we must go to the palace.

GUARDS [*to the fisherman*] Move, pickpocket, move!

[*They walk about.*]

SUPERINTENDENT Sūchaka, you two stand guard at the main gate here while I go into the palace, and wait here until I return.

BOTH In you go, Chief, and good luck with the King.

SUPERINTENDENT Right you are. [*He goes out.*]

SŪCHAKA (FIRST GUARD) The Chief's taking a long time, Jānuka.

JĀNUKA (SECOND GUARD) Well, you have to pick the right moment to approach a king.

SŪCHAKA You know, Jānuka, my fingers are itching – [*indicating the fisherman*] to finish off this pickpocket here.

FISHERMAN You wouldn't want to kill someone without a reason, sir!

JĀNUKA [*looking*] Here comes the Chief, bringing the royal decree. [*To the fisherman*] So you'll either be seeing your family again, or feeding the vultures and the jackals.

[*Enter the Superintendent.*]

SUPERINTENDENT Quick, grab hold of that fisherman –

FISHERMAN [*interrupting*] Oh, I'm done for! [*He acts despair.*]

SUPERINTENDENT – and untie his bonds at once. Apparently his story about the ring is all right. The King told me so personally.

SŪCHAKA Just as you say, Chief. Well, here's someone who's certainly come back from the other world. [*He releases the fisherman from his bonds.*]

FISHERMAN [*bowing to the Superintendent*] Master, I owe you my life. [*He falls at his feet.*]

SUPERINTENDENT Get up, get up! The King has been kind enough to give you this reward, which is equal in value to the ring. Here, take it. [*He hands the fisherman a bracelet.*]

FISHERMAN [*joyfully taking it*] How I'm favoured!

JĀNUKA Yes, the King favours him so much he's rescued him from the stake and set him on an elephant!

SŪCHAKA Chief, you can tell from the reward that the King must have thought a lot of the precious gems in that ring.

SUPERINTENDENT Oh, it wasn't because of the value of the gems that he was so pleased. It was just that . . .

BOTH What?

SUPERINTENDENT I think that seeing it reminded the King of someone in his heart, because for a moment when he saw it, though he is calm and dignified by nature, he was very moved.

SŪCHAKA The King's very pleased with you, then, Chief.

JĀNUKA Pleased with this murderer of poor little fishes here, you mean. [*He glares at the fisherman.*]

FISHERMAN Gentlemen! Half of it's for you, to buy a few drinks.

JĀNUKA Fisherman, suddenly you're my best friend. And what we need to seal the friendship is some wine. So come on, let's get off to the tavern.

[*They all go out.*]

Act VI

[*Enter, flying through the air, Miśrakeśī.*]

MIŚRAKEŚĪ I have finished my spell of duty at the Nymphs' Pool, and so I'll just see for myself what's been happening to the good King. Because of my connection with her mother Menakā, Śakuntalā is one flesh with me now, and she has asked me to do this for her. [*Looking around her*] Now why does there seem to be no sign of celebration of the Festival in the palace, even though it's now the proper time of day? If I wanted to, I could learn everything through mental concentration. But I must respect my friend's feelings. Well then, I'll station myself beside those two garden girls there, and stay invisible while I find out more. [*She acts descent and stays still.*]

[*Enter a servant girl, examining a mango shoot, and another behind her.*] 2

FIRST

With its flower stalks turning from green to red
Like the first stirrings of spring,
Now that the mango has put forth shoots
I know that the time of festival is here.

SECOND Little Cuckoo, what's that you're saying to yourself?

FIRST Hello, Little Bee. Didn't you know that cuckoos are always excited when they see the fresh mango shoots?

SECOND [*delightedly*] What, you mean that spring is here?

FIRST Yes, Little Bee – it's time for you too to buzz and be intoxicated.

SECOND Hold me, my dear, while I stand on tiptoe so that I can get at the mango bud and worship the God of Love.

FIRST All right, provided I can have half the merit of the worship.

SECOND That goes without saying, dearest, since you and I are one flesh together. [*Leaning on her friend and acting the plucking of a mango bud*] Ah there, although it hasn't opened, the mango bud smells sweet when I snap the stem. [*Cupping her hands together*] Salutations to the holy God of Love.

3 When I give you, mango bud,
To Love with his bow in his hand,
Be an arrow better than all his five,
Aimed at young wives whose husbands are away.

[*She casts the mango bud forth.*]

[*Enter without ceremony in anger the Chamberlain.*]

CHAMBERLAIN Stop it, you silly girl! What do you mean plucking mango buds when His Majesty has expressly forbidden the Spring Festival?

BOTH [*frightened*] Oh please, sir, please! We had no idea.

CHAMBERLAIN Hm! You mean you two girls hadn't heard of His Majesty's command, which even the spring trees and those that dwell in them have deferred to? Why,

4 The mango buds have long been out, and yet they produce no pollen.
Though the amaranth blossom has formed, it still stays tightly folded.
The cuckoo's call dies in his throat, though winter is long past.
And Love himself, I think, has timidly replaced the arrow half drawn from his quiver.

MIŚRAKEŚĪ No doubt of it, he is a king of mighty power!

FIRST Oh sir, it's only a few days since we were sent here to the Queen by her brother Mitrāvasu, and given this pleasure garden to look after. That's why we hadn't heard anything until now about all this, being newcomers.

CHAMBERLAIN In that case don't do it again.

BOTH Sir, we do feel curious. If it's for people like us to

hear, please tell us why His Majesty has forbidden the Spring Festival.

MIŚRAKEŚĪ Kings are usually fond of festivals – so the reason must be a strong one.

CHAMBERLAIN The matter's common knowledge – no reason why I shouldn't tell you. The gossip must have reached you about the rejection of Śakuntalā.

BOTH Yes sir, we heard about it from the King's brother-in-law, up to the point where the King saw the ring.

CHAMBERLAIN Then there is little left to tell. The moment he saw the ring and remembered that he really had secretly married Śakuntalā and then in his delusion repudiated her, His Majesty became seized with remorse:

Pleasures disgust him, he is not available each day to his ministers as before,
He passes the nights without any sleep at all, tossing about on his bed.
And when from politeness he offers some remark to the women of the palace,
He muddles their names and is plunged into long embarrassment.

MIŚRAKEŚĪ Good, good!

CHAMBERLAIN So it is because of the monarch's depression that the Festival has been cancelled.

BOTH Yes, we see.

FEMALE GUARD'S VOICE OFF-STAGE This way, sire.

CHAMBERLAIN [*listening*] Oh, His Majesty's coming this way. Off with you, then – be about your work.

[*The two girls withdraw.*]

[*Enter, dressed as appropriate in his remorseful state, the King, together with the Clown and the female guard.*]

CHAMBERLAIN [*looking at the King*] How attractive those of truly distinguished appearance are, no matter what state they are in! For sunk in gloom though he is, His Majesty is pleasant to behold:

6 Rejecting all special insignia and wearing on his left arm
Just one gold bracelet, now loose, his lips inflamed with sighing,
Eyes red with anxious wakefulness, he has such qualities of brilliance
That like a great gem ground down with polishing, one does not notice how he is worn away.

MIŚRAKEŚĪ [*looking at the King*] I do not wonder that Śakuntalā pines for him, for all that he disgraced her by turning her away.

KING [*pacing about slowly, deep in thought*]

7 My cursed heart that once slept
Though my sweetheart sought to waken it
Is now all too awake again
And tortured with remorse.

MIŚRAKEŚĪ Such is the poor girl's fate!

CLOWN [*to himself*] Another bout of Śakuntalā-sickness! I don't know what we can do to cure him.

CHAMBERLAIN [*approaching*] Victory, sire! I have inspected the grounds of the pleasure garden. Your Majesty may care to visit its delights at your leisure.

KING Vetravatī, tell Minister Piśuna in my name that today I'm suffering too much from sleeplessness to think of sitting in judgement. Any business concerning the citizens that he looks into, he can commit to writing and send on to me.

FEMALE GUARD Certainly, Your Majesty. [*She goes out.*]

KING Pārvatāyana, you are free to go too.

CHAMBERLAIN Yes, sire. [*He goes out.*]

CLOWN That's got rid of the flies. Now you can relax in this garden, which is very pleasant now that the cold weather's gone.

KING [*sighing*] Oh my friend, it's very true what they say, that misfortunes always find out your weak spots. See –

No sooner has my mind been freed of the darkness
That stopped me remembering my love for the sage's
daughter
Than Love himself, wanting to finish me,
Has fitted the mango arrow to his bow.*

With memory restored by the signet ring
Of my loved one spurned for no good reason,
I weep for her with remorse and longing –
And at once the joys of the scented month assail me.

CLOWN Well, friend, hold on and I'll destroy Love's arrow with this stick. [*He lifts his stick and tries to bring down the mango blossom.*]

KING [*with a smile*] All right, I've seen your brahmin power. But friend, where can I sit and rest my eyes among the vines that remind me of her beauty?

CLOWN Well, you told your maidservant Chaturikā that you were going to pass the time in the arbour of spring creepers, and you asked her to bring you there the portrait of Śakuntalā that you yourself painted in a picture.

KING It's the only way I have of comforting myself. Lead the way to that arbour, then.

*i.e. spring, the most erotic season of the year, has arrived.

CLOWN This way, sire.

[*They walk about.*]

[*Miśrakeśī follows after them.*]

CLOWN See, the arbour of spring creepers with its marble bench is so quiet and private it seems to be offering you a silent welcome. Let's go in and sit down.

[*Both do so.*]

MIŚRAKEŚĪ I'll hide among the creepers and just take a look at my friend's portrait. Then I can tell her of the strength of her husband's love.

KING [*sighing*] Oh my friend, I can remember it all now! I told you how I first met Śakuntalā. But you weren't with me when I turned her away, and even before that you had never so much as mentioned her. I suppose that like me you had forgotten her?

CLOWN Oh no, I hadn't forgotten. But after you'd told me everything, you finished up by saying that it was all a joke and not really true. And I was so thick-witted I accepted that. But really it's a case of fate being all-powerful.

MIŚRAKEŚĪ That's true.

KING [*after brooding*] Oh my friend, help me!

CLOWN Hey, what's this? That isn't like you. Heroes shouldn't give way to grief. Mountains aren't shaken even by storms.

KING Oh but Mādhavya, when I remember how she was after the shock of being rejected, I just don't know what to do.

10 Spurned by me and deciding to follow after her family,
But halted by the brusque command of her father's pupil, for he was a father to her,
She again turned her eyes, clouded with flooding tears,
On me, cruel me – oh, it burns like a poisoned dart.

MIŚRAKEŚĪ Such care for right conduct! I am glad that he is so distressed.

CLOWN If you ask me, she must have been spirited away by some creature of the air.

KING No one else would dare lay hands on that faithful wife. Her friends told me that her real mother is supposed to be the nymph Menakā. So I suspect that it was either she herself or her companions that took her.

MIŚRAKEŚĪ The wonder is that he was ever deluded, rather than that he has come to his senses.

CLOWN Oh well, if that's the case, you can breathe easy. You and she will be united.

KING How so?

CLOWN Why, no mother or father can bear to see their daughter separated for long from her husband.

KING Friend,

Whether it was a dream, an illusion, a mental aberration, 11
Or whether it simply exhausted all that was due me for past good deeds,
I am quite certain all hope is gone –
Over the precipice and beyond recall.

CLOWN Oh no, don't say that. Why, the ring itself proves how the most unthought-of reunions are destined to take place.

KING [*looking at the ring*] Unhappy ring, to have fallen from a place so difficult to gain!

To judge from the result, poor ring, 12
Your good deeds must have been as scant as mine.
Among her fingers with their bright red nails
You won a place, but then you slipped from favour.

MIŚRAKEŚĪ If it were on anyone else's hand, then it

really would be worth pitying. Oh Śakuntalā, my dear, you're far off, and I'm the only one who hears these delicious words.

CLOWN What about this signet ring, how did you broach the question of getting her to wear it?

MIŚRAKEŚĪ He's voicing the same curiosity as I have myself.

KING Listen, friend. When I was leaving for the city, she tearfully asked me how long I would remember her for –

CLOWN And you?

KING I put this ring on her finger, saying

13 'Count off one letter of my name
Each day on this ring, and as you reach the end
Someone will arrive, my dearest, to escort you
To join the women of my palace.'

But in my cruel distraction I never did it.

MIŚRAKEŚĪ A sweet appointment ruined by fate!

CLOWN Then how did it get like a fish hook into the carp's mouth?

KING It slipped from my wife's hand when she was worshipping the water at Indra's Ford.

CLOWN Oh, I see.

MIŚRAKEŚĪ That must be why the King, who would fear to behave immorally, was uncertain if he had married poor Śakuntalā. But on the other hand a love such as his doesn't need proofs of identity – so what is it all about?

KING Well then, I'm going to scold this ring.

CLOWN [*grinning*] And I think I'll scold this stick: what do you mean by being crooked when I'm straight?

KING [*not listening*]

How could you possibly have left 14
Her soft curving fingers and sunk into the water?

But no –

A mindless thing wouldn't notice merit:
How could *I* have spurned my sweetheart?

MIŚRAKEŚĪ He's admitting the very charge I wanted to put.

CLOWN Listen, I'm really going to die of hunger.

KING [*ignoring him*] Beloved, when my heart is on fire with remorse at having rejected you for no reason, please take pity on me and show yourself again.

[*Enter, carrying a picture, a maidservant.*]

MAIDSERVANT Sire, here is your Queen in a picture. [*She shows the picture.*]

KING [*looking*] What a beautiful subject for a picture!

Eyes that stretch back, brows that arch gracefully, 15
Lips red as berries, bathed in the radiance of her smile:
Yes, this is her face, and even in a picture
It seems to speak, alive with feminine charm.

CLOWN [*looking*] Ah, a delightful picture, full of feeling! My eyes almost trip up on those curves and hollows. In fact, I'm so expecting the picture to be filled with life it makes me want to start a conversation with it.

MIŚRAKEŚĪ What a skilful artist the King is! I feel as if my friend is there in front of me.

KING Friend,

Anything not perfect in this picture 16
Is simply painted wrongly.
But still the portrait does show
A little of her beauty.

MIŚRAKEŚĪ A natural sentiment for love sharpened by remorse.

KING [*sighing*]

17 By first rejecting my love, when she was there before me,
And worshipping her now, when she is in a picture,
I have ignored the brimming river in my path,
Then ended, friend, by thirsting for a mirage.

CLOWN I can see three figures, and they're all beautiful. So which of them is the lady Śakuntalā?

MIŚRAKEŚĪ The poor fellow knows nothing of my friend's beauty. The gift of sight has done him no good if he has never seen her.

KING Well, which one do *you* think she is?

CLOWN [*after examination*] I think she's the one you've painted against the vine round the mango tree, with the vine leaves glossy because they've just been watered – the one who's got flowers falling from her loosened hair-braid, drops of sweat on her face, slender drooping arms and a loosely tied dress, and who's looking a little tired: and the other two are her friends.

KING That's very clever of you. There are signs of my feelings on the picture itself:

18 Around the edges, where my sweating fingers have been pressing,
You can see a dirty streak.
And here a tear that fell from my cheek
Is made visible by the swelling of the paint.

Chaturikā, I've still only half painted the landscape in. So would you go and fetch me some brushes?

MAIDSERVANT Mādhavya, sir, could you please hold the picture while I'm gone.

KING I'll hold it myself. [*He does so.*]

[*The maidservant goes out.*]

CLOWN Well, what else do you have to paint in here?

MIŚRAKEŚĪ I think he'll want to paint in the places that she was fond of.

KING I'll tell you, friend:

I must put in the river Mālinī with pairs of geese on its sandy banks, 19
And on either side the holy foothills of Himālaya, where yaks are resting.
And under a tree whose branches are hung with garments of bark,
I want to show a doe rubbing her eye on the horn of the buck.

CLOWN [*privately*] It sounds to me as if he ought to fill the thing with crowds of long-bearded ascetics.

KING Oh, and I've forgotten to paint in a favourite ornament of Śakuntalā's.

CLOWN What could that be?

MIŚRAKEŚĪ It must be something that an unmarried country girl would naturally wear.

KING

I haven't put in the acacia flower, my friend, 20
With its stalk at her ear and its stamens brushing her cheek –
Nor the necklace of lotus fibre lying between her breasts
As soothingly soft as the rays of the autumn moon.

CLOWN But why is the lady covering her face with her lotus-pink fingers and looking so frightened? [*Inspecting the picture*] Ah! There's a wretched bee that plunders flower nectar and wants to get at the lotus of her face.

KING Well, stop the villain!

CLOWN You're the one who can punish misconduct.

KING True. Hey there, bee, why bother hovering over here when you would be welcomed by the flowering vines?

21 There in the flower the female bee,
Although she's feeling thirsty,
Is waiting out of love for you,
And won't drink the nectar till you join her.

MIŚRAKEŚĪ A very polite way of discouraging him.

CLOWN Creatures of that kind can be very stubborn.

KING [*in anger*] What, you won't do as I tell you? Then just listen to me:

22 If you dare bite my sweetheart's red lip
As enticing as the virgin blossom on a young tree,
Which in our lovemaking I drank so tenderly,
Then, bee, I'll have you shut up in a lotus.

CLOWN Well, you'll certainly terrify him if you're as savage as that! [*With a laugh, to himself*] He's so crazy I'm getting just as bad from associating with him!

KING What, is he still there despite the warnings?

MIŚRAKEŚĪ Love can affect the strongest minds!

CLOWN [*aloud*] It's just a picture, you know.

KING Just a picture?

MIŚRAKEŚĪ I already knew it, but he was living in his own world!

KING What piece of officiousness was this!

23 When I was feeling the joy of seeing her
In full reality because my mind was identified with her,
You awoke my memory and once again
Turned my beloved into a picture.

[*He sheds a tear.*]

MIŚRAKEŚĪ The way he yearns for her now is in such strange contradiction with his past behaviour.

KING Oh my friend, why is there nothing to give me a rest from my unhappiness?

My sleeplessness puts paid 24
To any thought of meeting her in a dream.
And my tears will not allow me
To gaze at her even in a picture.

MIŚRAKEŚĪ I have watched you atone fully, friend, for the unhappiness you caused my dear friend Śakuntalā when you spurned her.

[*Enter Chaturikā.*]

CHATURIKĀ Your Majesty, I was coming here with the paintbox –

KING And?

CHATURIKĀ – and Queen Vasumatī appeared with Pingalikā, and snatched it away from me saying she would bring it to you herself.

CLOWN How did you get away?

CHATURIKĀ Her Majesty's dress got caught on a branch, and while her maid was freeing her I disappeared.

VOICE OFF-STAGE This way, mistress!

CLOWN [*listening*] Oh, it's the tigress of the women's apartments coming to pounce on Chaturikā and gobble her up like a doe.

KING Friend, the Queen is coming and she is proud of my esteem for her. You had better keep this portrait safe.

CLOWN And keep you safe, don't you mean? [*Taking the picture board and getting up*] If you manage to escape from the toils of the women, you can come and call me in the Cloud Palace. And I'll hide this up there where no one but the pigeons will see it. [*He runs off.*]

MIŚRAKEŚĪ Ah, even when his heart is elsewhere, the King continues to be considerate towards an earlier love. So his affection is a lasting thing.

[*Enter, holding a document, the female guard.*]

FEMALE GUARD Victory, Your Majesty.

KING Vetravatī! Surely you must have passed Queen Vasumatī on your way?

FEMALE GUARD Yes, I did, sire. She turned back when she saw I had a document in my hand.

KING Her Majesty is discreet enough to avoid interrupting my business.

FEMALE GUARD Sire, the Minister begs to say that there was so much revenue business that he has looked into only one citizen's case, which he has committed to writing for Your Majesty to deal with personally.

KING Here, show me the document.

[*The female guard does so.*]

KING [*reads out*] 'Be it known to Your Majesty as follows: An overseas trader called Dhanavriddhi has been drowned in a shipwreck. He is childless, and has wealth amounting to many millions, which now becomes the property of the Crown. We await Your Majesty's instructions.'

KING [*despondently*] It is a grievous thing to be childless. Vetravatī, since he was so rich he must have had many wives. Find out whether by any chance one of them is pregnant.

FEMALE GUARD It is said that one of his wives, the daughter of a leading merchant in Ayodhyā, has just performed the ceremony to ensure a male child.*

*This ceremony was performed in the third month of pregnancy.

KING Well, the unborn child deserves to inherit his father's estate. Go and tell the Minister so.

FEMALE GUARD Yes, Your Majesty. [*She starts to go.*]

KING One moment.

FEMALE GUARD [*turning back*] Here, sire.

KING On second thoughts, what does it matter whether he has offspring or not?

Whenever my subjects suffer 25
The loss of a loving relative,
Let it be proclaimed that I, Dushyanta,
Will be in all lawful respects that relative to them.

FEMALE GUARD It shall be so proclaimed. [*Going out and re-entering*] Your Majesty, your command has been welcomed by the people like rain in due season.

KING [*after long sighing*] This is how lack of offspring robs a fortune of its basis, so that it passes to strangers when the head of the family dies. And the same will happen to the dynasty of Puru when I myself am gone.

FEMALE GUARD God forbid, sire!

KING Shame on me for spurning the good that came my way!

MIŚRAKEŚĪ He's certainly thinking of my friend when he blames himself so.

KING

My lawful wife, the support of my race, 26
Deserted by me, her own husband, though I had implanted myself in her –
Like earth sown with seed in due season,
Then abandoned before it could yield the riches of its harvest!

MIŚRAKEŚĪ Your desertion of her is at an end now.

CHATURIKĀ [*aside*] Lady, the Minister has made things twice as bad for His Majesty by sending him that document. You should go and fetch Master Mādhavya from the Cloud Palace to make him feel better.

FEMALE GUARD You are right. [*She goes out.*]

KING Alas, the ancestors that receive my offerings are now in danger:

27 Wondering if there will be anyone in our family after me
To prepare and present their oblations with due ritual,
My forefathers are probably drinking as a water offering
The pure tears which I shed at my lack of offspring.

MIŚRAKEŚĪ Though there is light, it is so veiled from the good King that he feels himself in darkness.

CHATURIKĀ Sire, do not torture yourself. You are in the prime of your life, and you will have fine sons by other queens to pay your debt to your ancestors. [*To herself*] His Majesty pays no attention to what I say. But then it's only the right medicine that cures the disease.

KING [*showing grief*]

28 This race of Puru, pure in descent from earliest times,
Has come to grief in my barrenness,
As the stream of the Sarasvatī
Peters out in the common sand of the desert.

[*He loses consciousness.*]

CHATURIKĀ [*in alarm*] Wake up, sire, wake up!

MIŚRAKEŚĪ Should I make him happy now? No, I heard from the Mother of the Gods * herself, when she was comforting Śakuntalā, that it would be the gods themselves, in their concern to secure their share of the

* Aditi, wife of Kaśyapa.

sacrifice, who would see to it that her husband would soon welcome her as his lawful wife. And so I shouldn't linger here. I must encourage my dear friend Śakuntalā with news of these events. [*She flies up and away.*]

CLOWN'S VOICE OFF-STAGE Help, sacrilege!

KING [*recovering consciousness and listening*] Oh, that sounds like Mādhavya calling for help.

CHATURIKĀ Your Majesty, I hope poor Mādhavya hasn't been caught red-handed with the picture by Miss Pingalikā!

KING Go, Chaturikā, and tell the Queen that I am displeased that she doesn't restrain her servants.

CHATURIKĀ Yes, Your Majesty. [*She goes out.*]

CLOWN'S VOICE Help, sacrlege!

KING My brahmin friend's voice sounds genuinely altered by terror. Hallo, who's there!

[*Enter the Chamberlain.*]

CHAMBERLAIN Yes, Your Majesty?

KING Find out why poor Mādhavya is yelling so.

CHAMBERLAIN I'll go and see. [*He goes out and returns in an agitated state.*]

KING Pārvatāyana, nothing terrible has happened?

CHAMBERLAIN Yes, it has.

KING Why are you shaking so?

The tremor of old age 29
Has given way to a real trembling
That is shaking all your limbs
Like the wind blowing through a pipal tree.

CHAMBERLAIN Save your friend, sire!

KING From what?

CHAMBERLAIN Great danger.

KING Speak plainly, man.

CHAMBERLAIN The palace for distant views, Cloud Palace –

KING What about it?

CHAMBERLAIN

30 From its topmost point, which even the palace peacocks
Cannot reach without frequent pauses in their ascent,
Some being of invisible form
Has seized your friend and taken him away.

KING [*rising suddenly*] No! Are there beings who invade my very home? But kings run many such risks –

31 No one can recognize from day to day
Even the errors committed through his own oversights.
Could a king therefore ever know in full
Who is behaving in what way among his subjects? *

CLOWN'S VOICE Oh quickly!

KING [*hearing and acting a change of pace*] Don't be afraid, my friend, don't be afraid!

CLOWN'S VOICE What do you mean, don't be afraid? There's someone here forcing my head back and trying to snap my neck like a piece of sugarcane.

KING [*casting his eye around*] My bow, my bow!

[*Enter a Greek girl.*]

GREEK GIRL Here, Your Majesty – your bow and arrows and your handguard.

[*The King takes them.*]

ANOTHER VOICE OFF-STAGE

32 Seeking the fresh blood that will gush from your throat,

* In the strict Indian theory, a king was responsible for (and therefore liable to divine punishment for) all the misdeeds in his realm which he did not recognize and redress.

I'll kill you as you struggle like a tiger killing cattle.
Now let Dushyanta try to save you,
Who seizes his bow to rescue the needy.

KING [*angrily*] Is that me he's talking about? Oh, wait there, you corpse-eating whoreson! This is the end of you. [*Stringing his bow*] Pārvatāyana, to the staircase!

CHAMBERLAIN This way, sire.

[*All approach hastily.*]

KING [*looking round him*] There's no one here!

CLOWN'S VOICE Help! I can see you, but you can't see me. I've as much hope of surviving as a mouse caught by a cat.

KING You there, arrogant in your power of invisibility! Do you think my weapon can't see you either? Stay still, and don't imagine you can use my friend as a shield. I am aiming an arrow

That will kill its proper victim, you, 33
And save the one that should be saved, the brahmin,
As a goose will take up milk
And leave the water that was mixed with it.

[*He aims his weapon.*]

[*Enter Mātali and the Clown.*]

MĀTALI Sire,

God has given you the demons for a target: 34
They are the ones on whom you should bend that bow.
Noble people direct upon a friend
Kind, gentle eyes rather than cruel arrows.

KING [*urgently withdrawing his weapon*] What! Is it Mātali? Welcome, charioteer of the King of the Gods!

CLOWN Hey, he nearly succeeded in slaughtering me, and you give him a joyful welcome.

MĀTALI [*with a smile*] Sire, hear why Indra has sent me to you.

KING I am listening.

MĀTALI There is a brood of demons, born of Kālanemi, that go by the name of Durjaya.

KING Yes, I have already heard of them from the seer Nārada.

MĀTALI

35 Them, it would appear, your comrade Indra may not slay,
For you are the one destined to kill them in the forefront of the battle.
The darkness of night which the sun cannot destroy
It is the part of the moon to drive away.

And so mount the chariot of the gods, just as you are, with your bow strung, and set out to victory.

KING I am much honoured by such a mark of favour from Indra. But why did you treat Mādhavya in the way you did?

MĀTALI Let me explain that too. I could see that for some reason you were in the grip of emotional distress, and accordingly I acted as I did to arouse you to anger. For

36 Fires blaze when stirred,
Snakes spread their hoods when injured.
In fact whatever has the spark of energy within it
Will show that spark if roused.

***Stage direction introduced in translation.**

KING [*to the Clown*]* Friend, one cannot disobey an order from the Lord of the Heavens. So go and tell Minister Piśuna what has happened, and give him this message from me:

'For the time being your counsel alone 37
Shall safeguard our subjects:
This bow that I have strung
Is employed on other business.'

CLOWN As you command. [*He goes out.*]
MĀTALI Mount the chariot, sire.
[*The King does so.*]
[*All go out.*]

Act VII

[*Enter, flying through the air and in a chariot, the King and Mātali.*]

KING Mātali, I've done the work Indra entrusted me with, but I still feel thoroughly unworthy of the honours heaped on me.

MĀTALI What you should realize is that *neither* of you feels satisfied!

You have done Indra the service you have, 1
Yet think it little compared with the honour he has shown you:
He himself reckons that even such honour
Cannot measure the size of your exploit.

KING Oh never! The distinction he paid me when I took my leave went far beyond anything I could have dreamed of. Before the assembled gods, as I shared his throne with him,

2 Glancing with a smile at his son Jayanta,
Who stood nearby and was inwardly longing for the same,
Indra fastened round me his garland of coral-tree flowers,
Smudged with the yellow sandal paste from his own chest.

MĀTALI And isn't that what you deserve from the King of the Gods? Think, sire –

3 For Indra, seeking to live in peace from the demons,
Two things have freed heaven of the thorn of their presence:
One is your smooth-jointed arrows, just now deployed,
The other, in earlier times, the claws of the Man-lion.*

KING But that is only an indication of Indra's own greatness:

4 However momentous the work in which an agent is successful,
It merely reflects the esteem in which his master holds him.
Would dawn have power to destroy the darkness
If the thousand-rayed sun had not yoked it to the task?

MĀTALI Such a thought is worthy of you. [*After proceeding a little further*] Look, sire, how the glory of your fame is spread across the vault of the heavens!

5 With paint that the nymphs have used in their own adornment,

*The god Vishṇu.

See how the gods of the sky
Are inscribing your exploits on silk from the wishing-trees' branches,
Turning them into a theme for their poetry.

KING Mātali, I was too eager to do battle with the demons to notice my surroundings on the ascent yesterday. So tell me, in which path of the winds are we?

MĀTALI

This is the path, sanctified by Vishṇu's second stride, 6
Of the wind called Pravaha, free of all worldly dust,
Which sustains the divine third of the Ganges' course,*
And causes the lights of heaven to revolve, distributing their rays.

KING No wonder that my senses without and my soul within are all at peace. [*Looking down at the wheel of the chariot*] I think we have descended to the path of the clouds.

MĀTALI How can you tell, sire?

KING

With cloud cuckoos flying out from among its spokes, 7
And its steeds that glisten in the flickers of lightning,
And the rims of its wheels all damp with spray,
Your chariot shows that we move over rain-swollen clouds.

MĀTALI Quite so – and in a moment, sire, you will be over the land you rule.

KING [*looking below*] Mātali, we're descending so fast the human world looks very strange:

As the mountains rear, the earth seems to drop away from their peaks. 8

*The Ganges is said to flow through heaven, earth and hell.

Trees cease to be hidden by their leaves as their trunks
  thrust upwards.
Rivers, so thin that their waters were lost, emerge and
  grow broad.
Do you see? I feel someone is throwing the ground up
  at me.

MĀTALI Truly observed, sire. [*Gazing appreciatively*] How intensely beautiful the earth is!

KING Mātali, what is that mountain I can see plunging down to the eastern and western oceans, fiery with liquid gold like a cloud at sunset?

MĀTALI Sire, it is Golden Peak, the mountain of the Kimpurusha sprites and place of final fulfilment for ascetics.

9 It is here that Kaśyapa, Lord of Creatures,
Who was born of Marīchi, son of the self-born Brahmā,
He whom the gods and demons revere as their father,
Together with his wife follows the ascetic life.

KING [*reverently*] Then let us not neglect our spiritual well-being. I should like to walk sunwise round the holy one before we go on.

MĀTALI An undeniable proposal, sire. [*Acting descent of the chariot*] There, we have landed.

KING [*in astonishment*] Mātali!

10 The rims of the chariot-wheels make no sound.
There is no stir of dust to be seen.
Because there has been no jolting contact with the
  ground,*
One could never tell that you have landed the chariot.

*It is a sign of divinity to walk the earth without touching it.

MĀTALI Yes, it is the one difference between Indra's chariot and your own, sire.

KING In which direction is Kaśyapa's hermitage?

MĀTALI [*pointing with his hand*] Look,

It is where that sage stands as still as a post, facing the sun's disc, 11
Half buried in an ant-hill, with the slough of a snake for a second sacred thread,
Tightly squeezed round the throat by the coiling tendril from an ancient vine,
His unkempt hair falling round his shoulders and filled with the nests of birds.

KING [*looking*] My homage to him in his harsh austerities.

MĀTALI [*tightening the reins*] There, we have entered Kaśyapa's hermitage, with its coral-trees tended by his wife Aditi.

KING Oh, here is a place of greater bliss than heaven! I feel as if I had plunged into a lake of nectar.

MĀTALI [*halting the chariot*] Dismount, sire.

KING [*dismounting*] What about yourself?

MĀTALI The chariot will stay as it is, now that I have halted it. So I shall dismount as well. [*Doing so*] Just look, sire, at the grounds of the holy grove of these reverend seers!

KING I am looking, and the contrast astonishes me:

Air is their chosen means of maintaining the vital powers, in a grove where wishing-trees abound, 12
Their ritual bath is in water tawny with golden lotus pollen.
They meditate in marble halls, control their senses amid heavenly nymphs.

They practise austerities among the very things which other seers by their austerities are seeking.

MĀTALI The ambitions of the great soar high. [*Walking about, and then speaking into the air*] Venerable Śākalya, how is the holy Kaśyapa occupied? [*Listening*] What do you say? Being questioned by Aditi concerning the proper conduct of a faithful wife, he is expounding the matter to her.

KING [*hearing*] Oh, then our business must wait its turn.

MĀTALI [*looking at the King*] Why not stay in the shade of this aśoka tree, sire, until I inform Indra's father of your presence?

KING Just as you suggest.

[*Mātali goes out.*]

KING [*indicating an omen*]

13 I have no hope of what I want:
Why do you vainly throb, my arm?
I have already spurned my salvation
And turned it into a source of misery.

HERMIT WOMAN'S VOICE OFF-STAGE Stop it! Don't be so headstrong – you want your own way the whole time!

KING [*listening*] This is a strange place for bad behaviour. Who can it possibly be who needs such checking? [*Looking in the direction of the sound, in surprise*] Why, there is a child, with two hermit women trying to restrain him – but a child with more than a child's strength:

14 He is dragging along by main force
A lion cub that he wants to play with,
Which has only half-sucked its mother's milk
And whose mane is all tousled in the struggle.

[*Enter a child as described and two hermit women.*]

CHILD Come on, lion cub, open your mouth. I want to count your teeth.

FIRST WOMAN You bad boy! What do you mean by ill-treating our animals that are like children to us? Really, your wildness is getting worse. No wonder the hermits have called you Sarvadamana, the all-conquering.

KING Why should my heart feel as drawn to this child as if he were a son of my own loins? [*Musing*] No doubt because being childless makes me tender.

SECOND The lioness there will spring on you if you don't let go of her baby.

BOY [*with a grin*] Ooh, now you've really frightened me! [*He bites his lip aggressively.*]

KING [*in astonishment*]

This young boy seems to me 15
To be the seed of some great future brilliance,
Like the fire that smoulders in an ember,
Waiting for fuel to feed on.

FIRST WOMAN Darling, let go of the baby lion and I'll give you something else to play with.

BOY Where is it? Show me. [*He holds out his hand.*]

KING [*looking at the hand*] Why, he has the birthmark of a universal emperor!

As he stretches his hand out in eagerness for the bribe, 16
He reveals that its fingers are linked as in a web,
Like the solitary lotus, showing no space between its
petals,
That is prised open by the first pink glow of dawn.

SECOND WOMAN It's no good, Suvratā. It'll take more than words to stop him. Go – in my hut there's a painted clay peacock that belonged to young Mankaṇaka. Give him that.

FIRST WOMAN Right. [*She goes out.*]

BOY Meanwhile I'm going to play with this.

WOMAN [*looking and laughing*] Let him be!

KING I really feel fond of this naughty child. [*Sighing*]

17 When children reveal their budding teeth in causeless laughter,
And stumble charmingly in their attempts to speak,
When they clamour to be lifted onto a lap, blessed are the fathers,
As they pick them up, to be stained by the dust from their limbs.

WOMAN [*shaking her finger*] Oh, you take absolutely no notice of me! [*Turning her head*] Which of the hermit boys is there? [*Seeing the King*] Oh sir, please come and make this little boy let go of the lion cub he's tormenting. He's got a grip of iron.

KING Of course. [*Approaching, with a smile*] Hey there, little son of some mighty sage –

18 Why behave in a way so foreign to a hermitage:
Why violate, so early in life,
The hermit's forbearance that takes pleasure in the company of living things,
Like some young cobra violating the sandal-tree that shelters it?

WOMAN Oh no, sir, he isn't a hermit boy.

KING I should have known from his behaviour, which is of a piece with his appearance. But I assumed otherwise because of where I found him. [*Doing as he is requested and so touching the child, to himself*]

Such is my pleasure when my limbs are touched 19
By this offspring of some stranger's family,
What bliss the child must bring to the heart
Of the lucky man from whose loins he is sprung!

WOMAN [*looking at both of them*] How extraordinary!

KING What is, lady?

WOMAN I was marvelling at how alike you are to the boy, even though you're not related. And although he's so wild and you're a stranger, he isn't at all wary of you.

KING [*stroking the child*] If he isn't one of the hermits' children, lady, what is his family name?

WOMAN Paurava.*

KING [*to himself*] The same clan as myself? So that's why she sees a resemblance. [*Aloud*] The Pauravas do, it is true, have just such a religious dedication:

They choose as guardians of the world to spend 20
Their earlier life in white-stuccoed palaces.
But later the roots of trees become their home,
Where only the vows of an ascetic are observed.

But how could any mortal decide for himself to live in such a place as this?

WOMAN What you say is true, sir. But this boy's mother, being related to one of the heavenly nymphs, was able to give birth to her child in Kaśyapa's hermitage.

KING [*to himself*] Ha, here is another reason to be hopeful! [*Aloud*] What, then, is the name of the royal sage to whom that good lady is married?

WOMAN Who would speak the name of such a man, who rejected his own lawful wife?

KING [*to himself*] Such words must surely refer to me.

*i.e., descendant of Puru.

Perhaps I might ask after the name of the child's mother? [*On reflection*] But no, it is not honourable to show curiosity about another man's wife.

[*Enter the first hermit woman, holding a clay peacock.*]

FIRST WOMAN Look, Sarvadamana, see how beautiful the śakunta bird is!

BOY [*looking about him*] Mummy? Where is she?

[*Both women laugh.*]

FIRST He's so fond of his mummy the similarity of names* has misled him.

SECOND She was only telling you to see how nice the peacock is.

KING [*to himself*] Is his mother's name Śakuntalā? But coincidences of name are possible. I pray god this is not some mirage that will end in heartbreak.

BOY Oh, I like that nice peacock! [*He takes the toy.*]

FIRST [*looking, in alarm*] Oh dear, his amulet's not on his wrist!

KING Don't worry, ma'am. Here it is – it must have slipped off in his scuffle with the lion cub. [*He starts to pick it up.*]

BOTH No, no! [*Looking*] Why, he's got it! [*They gaze at each other, their hands to their breasts in amazement.*]

KING Why did you two ladies try to stop me?

FIRST Listen, sir. It is a divine charm of great potency called The Invincible, which the holy Kaśyapa gave to the child at his birth ceremony. No one except himself or his parents can pick it up off the ground if it falls.

KING And if someone does?

FIRST It turns into a snake and bites him.

* The ambiguity of the original Prakrit was more complete: the child misunderstood *saünta-lāvaṇṇaṃ* 'beauty of the bird' as *Saüntalā-vaṇṇaṃ* 'colour of Śakuntalā'.

KING Have you ever seen this happen?

BOTH Several times.

KING [*joyfully*] Then I may surely give thanks that all that I have longed for has now come true! [*He embraces the child.*]

SECOND Come, Suvratā, let's go to Śakuntalā where she is busy with her religious duties, and tell her what has happened.

[*They go out.*]

BOY Let me go. I want to go to my mummy.

KING My son, you and I will go to your mother together and make her happy.

BOY Dushyanta's my daddy, not you.

KING [*with a smile*] That objection makes me more confident than ever.

[*Enter Śakuntalā, her hair done in a single braid.*]

ŚAKUNTALĀ [*doubtfully*] When I heard that Sarvadamana's amulet stayed as it was when it should have changed, it seemed as if I could not trust my good fortune. But when I remember what Miśrakeśī told me, I know that it may be true. [*She walks about.*]

KING [*looking at Śakuntalā, with both joy and distress*] Ah, there is my wife Śakuntalā –

Dressed in grey garments, 21
Face gaunt with fasting, hair worn in a single braid,
Steadfastly true though I have been so cruel,
She still observes the long vow of separation from me.

ŚAKUNTALĀ [*seeing the King pale with remorse*] That is not my husband! Who can it be defiling my son with his embrace, when the amulet should have protected him?

BOY [*going to his mother*] Mummy, here's a strange man who calls me son!

KING My dearest, the cruelty with which I treated you has come full circle: now it is I who ask to be recognized by you.

ŚAKUNTALĀ [*to herself*] Take courage, my heart. Fate has ceased to be unkind and taken pity on me. It really is my husband.

KING

22 Memory has pierced, thank god, the darkness of my delusion,
And you my fairest one stand before my eyes.
The eclipse is at an end, and Rohiṇī
Is once more united with her consort the Moon.

ŚAKUNTALĀ Victory, victory to – [*She breaks off, her throat choked with tears.*]

KING Beloved,

23 Though tears may prevent that word of victory,
My victory has already been won,
When I can see that face before me
With its lips so pale and unadorned.

BOY Mummy, who is this man?

ŚAKUNTALĀ Ask fate, my child.* [*She weeps.*]

KING

24 Oh my fairest, banish the pain of that rejection from your heart:
Somehow my mind was in the grip of a delusion.
Victims of darkness treat even the best of good fortune in that way –

*i.e., she still dare not say that it is his father.

Put a garland on a blind man, and he'll tear at it for fear
it is a snake.

[*He falls at her feet.*]

ŚAKUNTALĀ Rise, my lord, rise! I must have done something in a former life to prevent my own happiness, and it was working itself out at that time, or someone so compassionate as you would not have acted as you did.

[*The King rises.*]

How, then, did you come to recall this unhappy person, my lord?

KING I will tell you, once I have plucked out the barb of my grief:

The teardrop which once troubled your lip, my fairest,
And which in my infatuation I then ignored,
Today, beloved, while it still clings to your curling
lashes,
I must wipe off, if I am to be free of my remorse.

[*He does as he says.*]

ŚAKUNTALĀ [*her tears wiped away, seeing the ring*] My lord, that is the ring!

KING Yes, certainly. It was the strange recovery of it that restored my memory.

ŚAKUNTALĀ And so that succeeded in the task of convincing you which I found so difficult!

KING Well then, let the vine now receive the blossom which will proclaim its union with the season of spring.

ŚAKUNTALĀ No, I don't trust it. Wear it yourself, my lord.

[*Enter Mātali.*]

MĀTALI Congratulations, sire, on your reunion with your lawful wife, and on beholding the face of your son!

KING My desires are all the better rewarded because a friend has been instrumental in bringing them about. But Mātali, can Indra have realized that this would happen?

MĀTALI [*with a smile*] What is hidden from the gods? Come, the revered Kaśyapa has granted you an audience.

KING Dearest, take hold of our son. I should like to take you with me when I see His Holiness.

ŚAKUNTALĀ Oh, but I am shy of appearing before my elders in the company of my husband!

KING It is the proper thing to do on a happy occasion. Come, my dear.

[*They walk about.*]

[*Enter, enthroned, Kaśyapa, together with his wife Aditi.*]

KAŚYAPA [*looking at the King*] Daughter of Daksha,

26 There is the one who leads the field in your son Indra's
battles,
He who is called Dushyanta, lord and husband of the
world:
Because of his bow, the sharp thunderbolt of Indra
Has abandoned its task and become a mere ornament.

ADITI One could tell from his looks the majesty that is within him.

MĀTALI Look, sire, the parents of the gods are gazing at you with eyes that reveal affection for a son. Approach them.

KING Mātali,

27 Is this the couple declared by sages to be the origin of
the twelvefold energy,*

*The Sun during the twelve months of the year; the next line refers to Indra, and the following to Vishṇu.

They who begat the lord of the three worlds and ruler of the gods of the sacrifice,
They in whom the Man that is higher than Brahmā placed himself to be born,
The couple born of Daksha and Marīchi, one generation removed from the Creator?

MĀTALI It is.

KING [*falling down before them*] Dushyanta, servant of Indra, salutes you both.

KAŚYAPA My child, long may you guard the earth.

ADITI May you be without rival in battle, my son.

[*Śakuntalā falls with her son at their feet.*]

KAŚYAPA My daughter,

Your husband is Indra's counterpart, 28
And your son is the image of Jayanta:
There is no wish for you that need be uttered but this –
May you be as blessed as is Paulomī.*

ADITI Daughter, may you live honoured by your husband, and may your noble son here do credit to both his parents' families. Come, be seated.

[*All sit down.*]

KAŚYAPA [*indicating each in turn*]

Here is Śakuntalā the virtuous wife, 29
Here the fine son, and here Your Majesty:
Faith, Wealth and Performance –
The three are most happily met together.

KING Holy sir, to be granted our wishes first and afterwards to see you – that is a favour quite unique. Why,

Flowers come first, and fruit thereafter, 30

*Wife of Indra, as Jayanta is his son.

First clouds and then the rain.
That is the law of cause and effect –
And yet our good fortune has preceded your benevolence.

MĀTALI Sire, that is what marks the benevolence of the parents of the universe.

KING Your Holiness, in first wedding your handmaid here in a love match and then repudiating her through a loss of memory when her relatives brought her to me some time later, I have sinned against one who is of your own lineage, the revered Kaṇva. It was not until subsequently when I saw the ring that I remembered having married her – a fact which I find very extraordinary:

31 As if an elephant had wandered by
Before my very eyes, and I had felt doubt,
But then on seeing his footprints had become convinced:
That is the way in which my mind has worked.

KAŚYAPA My son, you need not feel guilty. Your delusion was entirely natural. Let me explain.

KING I am listening.

KAŚYAPA The moment Menakā came to my wife from the Nymphs' Pool bringing her daughter Śakuntalā in a state of collapse because of her rejection, I discovered through meditation what had happened – that the poor girl had been disowned by her lawful husband as a result of a curse laid upon her by Durvāsas. And the curse would be ended by the sight of the ring.

KING [*with a sigh of relief, to himself*] At last I am freed from blame.

ŚAKUNTALĀ [*to herself*] Thank heavens! My husband had no wish to spurn me, but genuinely did not remember me. In fact I must have been so absent-minded that I failed to hear the curse, for my friends were very careful to tell me to let him see the ring.

KAŚYAPA Daughter, now you have learnt the facts you must feel no resentment towards your husband. Consider –

You were harshly spurned by your husband when the curse clouded his memory, 32
But now that the darkness has left him he is yours to command.
A reflection cannot form while a mirror is grimed with dirt,
But shows up easily the moment the surface is clear.

KING It is as you say, Holiness.

KAŚYAPA My son, you have I hope welcomed to you this son born to Śakuntalā, for whom I myself have duly performed the ceremonies of birth and all subsequent rituals?

KING Holiness, he is the one in whom rests the security of my line.

KAŚYAPA Know that such is his heroic temperament that he will be a universal emperor:

Crossing the oceans in a chariot smooth and silent, 33
He is destined to govern without rival the seven continents of earth.
Known here as Sarvadamana because he subdues the animals,
He will be newly named as Bharata, supporter* of the world.

*The root *bhar* 'support' is cognate with English *bear*.

KING My hopes for him are boundless, when it was Your Holiness who performed his rites of initiation.

ADITI Now that his daughter's wishes have come true, Kaṇva must be given the news. Her mother Menakā of course is here, attending on me.

ŚAKUNTALĀ [*to herself*] Her Holiness has voiced the wish in my own heart.

KAŚYAPA The power of his austerities is such that the revered Kaṇva can perceive for himself all that has happened.

KING So that is why the sage did not unleash his anger upon me.

KAŚYAPA [*on reflection*] Even so it is right that we should send him the good news. Hallo, who's there!

[*Enter a pupil.*]

PUPIL Yes, Your Holiness?

KAŚYAPA Gālava, fly at once to the revered Kaṇva and report to him from me the joyful tidings that Śakuntalā, blessed with a son, has been accepted back by Dushyanta, who has regained his memory now that Durvāsas' curse is at an end.

PUPIL Certainly, Your Holiness. [*He goes out.*]

KAŚYAPA [*to the King*] And you, my son, take your wife and your heir and set off in your friend Indra's chariot for your capital.

KING Most certainly, Your Holiness.

KAŚYAPA And now

34 Let Indra send abundant rain upon your people,
And do you in turn please the gods by offering sacrifice.
And let that be the pattern of his acts and yours through the cycle of a hundred ages,

Reciprocating good with good for the sake of both god and man.

KING Holiness, I shall strive for such welfare to my utmost.

KAŚYAPA My son, what further service may I do you?

KING Holiness, could any further service be possible? Yet let this be:

Let the monarch work for the good of his people. 35
Let the utterance of those mighty in their learning be esteemed.
And let Śiva the self-existent, in his infinite power,
Extinguish forever the cycle of my rebirths.

[*All go out.*]

Rākshasa's Ring
by Viśākhadatta

Viśākhadatta

Although Viśākhadatta furnishes the names of his father and grandfather, we know little else about him. Estimates of the date of *Rākshasa's Ring* have varied widely. Professor A. L. Basham suggests the sixth century A.D., which would put the work neatly half way between the other two plays in this volume. However, if the reference to Chandra Gupta in the final, benedictory stanza of the play is authentic, there are good arguments for identifying this monarch as Chandra Gupta II, already mentioned in connection with Kālidāsa, who reigned about A.D. 376–415. The intention can hardly be to refer to the emperor Chandra Gupta Maurya, of 700 years before, who appears in the play, since these final stanzas are not attached to the dramatic situation but are addressed directly to the audience. But variant readings which appear to centre around the name Avantivarman also occur, and the question cannot be taken as settled. *Rākshasa's Ring* is Viśākhadatta's only surviving play, although there exist fragments of another work probably to be ascribed to him.

The titles of Viśākhadatta's father and grandfather do indicate one point of interest: that he came of a princely family, certain to have been involved in political administration at least at a local level It seems very possible in fact that Viśākhadatta came to literature from the world of affairs. Stylistically he stands a little apart from other dramatists. A proper literary education is clearly in no way lacking, and in formal terms he operates within the normal conventions of Sanskrit literature, but one does not feel that he cultivates these conventions very enthusiastically for their own sake. It would be as much a travesty to suggest that one can detect in his writing a clipped, quasi-military diction as it would be to think of Kālidāsa as an untutored child of nature simply because he shows himself less steeped than Bhavabhūti in philosophical erudition. But it is fair to say that Viśākhadatta's prose passages in particular often have a certain stiffness compared with the supple idiom of both Kālidāsa and Bhavabhūti. And in relative rather than absolute terms his style inclines towards the principle of 'more matter and less art'.

There have been other cases of contributions to Sanskrit literature by men of action – for instance the three plays ascribed to the celebrated monarch Harsha Vardhana. The ascription is plausible, and the plays are talented and worthy pieces. But unlike *Rākshasa's Ring* they adhere closely to conventional literary ideals. Harsha no doubt wished to show that he could write as well as he could rule: yet in the last resort one suspects that he would have been more interesting to know as a man than as a dramatist. We do not know whether Viśākhadatta, on the other hand, if he *was* some kind of politician, was as such either original or successful: but as a playwright he is both.

The historical setting of the play is, as mentioned above, at least 700 years earlier than Viśākhadatta's own time, and belongs to the period immediately following Alexander the Great's Indian expedition of 327–325 B.C. Alexander effectively penetrated no further than the area of modern Pakistan. To the east lay the empire of the Nandas, with its capital of Pāṭaliputra, the modern Patna. Greek sources tell us that a young Indian called Sandracottus tried unsuccessfully to persuade Alexander to attack this empire. Sandracottus is the Chandra Gupta of our play, and after

Alexander's withdrawal he managed the task for himself and seized the throne, thereby founding the great empire of the Mauryas – his grandson Aśoka is the best known and most remarkable of all the kings of ancient India. It is very likely that Chandra Gupta Maurya was indeed aided by a minister called Kauṭilya or Chāṇakya, but we need not suppose that he was as dependent on his guidance as the present play makes out.

Rākshasa's Ring is unique in Sanskrit literature. If, as suggested earlier, a Sanskrit play may be looked on as a fairy tale subjected to a process of literary sophistication, then this play is such a fairy tale subjected to a further process of political sophistication. It cannot be seen, that is to say, as a realistic political drama – even in the ancient Indian context, where cloak-and-dagger enterprise and Machiavellian intrigue probably made a more significant contribution than they would today to the course of important political events. The work is unashamedly a piece of colourful story-telling, but deeply imbued at the same time with a sense of man as a political animal – a celebration, in fact, of the human goal of *artha* or worldly advancement. Indian tradition distinguished three Ends of Man: *dharma*, duty to God and one's fellow creatures, *artha*, worldly (and more particularly political) advancement, and *kāma*, sensual (especially sexual) pleasure. (A fourth goal, transcending these three, was often added: that of *moksha* or release from worldly bondage.) The theme of *dharma* is never absent from Sanskrit literature. But the theme of *artha* is more prominent in this play than is that of *kāma* in *Śakuntalā* or even in *Mālatī and Mādhava*. And just as Bhavabhūti shows himself conversant with the Indian *ars amatoria*, and indeed at one point actually quotes directly from the *Kāma Sūtra*, so Viśākhadatta shows himself equally conversant with the theory of statecraft (*artha-śāstra* or *nīti-śāstra*) and in Act III makes a direct reference to its teachings.

Nothing shows the political sophistication of the play more plainly than the nature of the conflict between the two main characters. The hero is Rākshasa, the exiled Chief Minister of the deposed dynasty of the Nandas, a man in equal measure intelligent, experienced, courageous and loyal. But his political opponent, far from being the villain of the piece, is a sort of super-hero – the inhumanly competent ascetic Kauiṭlya, the man who originally engineered the Nandas' destruction. And the theme of the play is Kauṭilya's struggle not to destroy Rākshasa but to win him over to his own side to be his successor as Chandra Gupta's Chief Minister, so that he himself can retire from all involvement in practical politics. Rākshasa is outmanoeuvred because of the poor quality and treachery of his associates, the undisciplined warmth of his human feelings, and ultimately his unswerving loyalty – the very quality above all which Kauṭilya values him for.

The fact that Rākshasa is outsmarted by Kauṭilya at every turn would make him a poor sort of hero if the two characters were on the same dramatic level. But Kauṭilya is presented as no ordinary human being, in fact scarcely as a real person at all. He has no human weaknesses – for the anger which inspired his implacable enmity towards the Nanda Emperor is no more seen as a weakness than is that of the sage Durvāsas in *Śakuntalā*. Rather, he is the idealized embodiment of *artha-śāstra* itself. Indeed the textbook on statecraft which has come down to us under that name is traditionally attributed to his authorship (though the attribution is certainly false), and the audience would have been keenly aware of this fact, which underlines his mythical and semi-divine character. His differing status from Rākshasa is emphasized also by the difference in their relationship to the young Emperor. Kauṭilya is Chandra Gupta's guru, the man who chose to put him on the throne: the question of his being a loyal or disloyal servant of the Emperor cannot arise, since the obligation is all on the other side. Rākshasa, on the other hand, once he has been manoeuvred into accepting Chandra Gupta as the true heir of the Nandas' power (and it is hinted that the young man is in fact an illegitimate son of the late Emperor), transfers to the new monarch the absolute commitment which he had given to the old. It becomes a central part of his own particular *dharma* to put his political talents unreservedly at the disposal of his new master. Kauṭilya, the austere and self-disciplined sage, lacks all worldly ties, and his motivations are not those of ordinary men. But in Rākshasa, utterly loyal servant and devoted friend and husband as well as experienced statesman, the conflicting claims of *dharma*, *artha* and *kāma* meet and take their proper place within a single human being.

One of the delights of *Rākshasa's Ring* is its intricate and perfectly interlocking plot. To help the reader a little in keeping the characters distinct I have taken one or two minor liberties with nomenclature. As against the usual practice in transcription, I have divided most compound names – thus Śakaṭa Dāsa rather than Śakaṭadāsa. And while the playwright alternates the names Kauṭilya and Chāṇakya, I have eliminated the latter completely, since two other major characters have names beginning with *chan*. No reader should let himself be put off by Kauṭilya's long explanatory monologue at the beginning of Act I (which to my mind is something of a flaw in the dramatic construction, since few members of any audience could be expected to keep all of it clear in their heads): those who plunge straight on into the lively ensuing dialogue will find that the main lines of the plot unfold quite naturally as the play progresses.

Rākshasa's Ring

CHARACTERS IN THE PLAY

**Sanskrit speakers are marked with an asterisk. Characters not appearing on stage are mentioned in brackets.*

THE RULING FACTION

*THE EMPEROR of India, Chandra Gupta Maurya, familiarly called 'Vrishala'
*KAUṬILYA, his preceptor and acting Chief Minister
*A PUPIL, Śārngarava, living in Kauṭilya's household
A FEMALE GUARD of the Emperor, Śoṇottarā
*CHAMBERLAIN to the Emperor, Vaihīnari

KAUṬILYA'S AGENTS

A SPY, Nipuṇaka, disguised as a votary of the God of Death
SIDDHĀRTHAKA, pretending friendship to Śakaṭa Dāsa and to Rākshasa
A JAIN MONK, Jīva Siddhi, in reality a brahmin called Indu Śarman
*BHĀGURĀYAṆA, pretending friendship to Malaya Ketu
MAN WITH A ROPE, supposed friend of a friend of Chandanadāsa
SAMIDDHĀRTHAKA, Siddhārthaka's friend
(Three brahmin brothers, the eldest called Viśvāvasu, disguised as traders)
(Bhadra Bhaṭa, Purusha Datta, Hingu Rāta, Bala Gupta, Rājasena, Rohitāksha, Vijaya Varman, allies of Chandra Gupta now supposedly disloyal)

THE OPPOSING FACTION

*PRINCE MALAYA KETU, son of Chandra Gupta's murdered ally King Parvataka

*RĀKSHASA,† Chief Minister of the deposed Nanda dynasty, now adviser to Malaya Ketu

CHANDANADĀSA, a rich jeweller, Rākshasa's friend

*ŚAKAṬA DĀSA, a letter-writer, Rākshasa's friend

*VIRĀDHA GUPTA, Rākshasa's friend, now his agent and disguised as a SNAKE-CHARMER

*SECOND BARD at Chandra Gupta's court, Stanakalaśa, Rākshasa's agent

KARABHAKA, Rākshasa's agent

MANSERVANT of Rākshasa, Priyamvadaka

*CHAMBERLAIN to Malaya Ketu, Jājali

FEMALE GUARD of Malaya Ketu, Vijayā

MANSERVANT of Bhāgurāyaṇa Bhāsvaraka

(Five princes, Chitra Varman, Siṃha Nāda, Pushkarāksha, Sindhusheṇa, Megha Nāda, allies of Malaya Ketu)

Also *FIRST BARD, Rākshasa's DOORKEEPER, a MANSERVANT of Malaya Ketu, a MANSERVANT of Chandra Gupta, WIFE and SON of Chandanadāsa

†This name has the inauspicious literal meaning of 'demon'.

The action of the play takes place in the imperial capital Pāṭaliputra (or 'the Flower City') and elsewhere in Northern India towards the end of the fourth century B.C.

*Benediction**

'Who is that lucky one on your head?' 'Moon crescent.' 1
'Is *that* her name?'
'Of course, but you knew it well – how could you have forgotten?'
'My question concerns a woman, not your moon.' 'Ask Vijayā then, if the moon's no help.'
Śiva's skill, thus guarding Gangā from his wife, be your protection.

As with cautious steps he avoids the earth's certain collapse 2
And mimes with arms always bent that could outreach the universe,
Letting his blazing eye rest nowhere for fear of fire,
May the dance protect you, cramped by its stage, of the Triple City's Victor.

*Śiva's consort Pārvatī is conventionally depicted as jealous of the Ganges, which flows from Heaven to Earth through his hair: he fends off her questions by deliberately misinterpreting them. Vijayā is Pārvatī's handmaiden. Śiva's dancing is capable of being highly destructive, but in the second stanza he is described as performing with a self-denying restraint which causes him some discomfort, in order to avoid bringing any harm to the world.

The stanzas mirror in divine terms the theme of the play, which is *nīti*, 'politics, worldly success', as practised with supreme skill by Kauṭilya: he like Śiva has to use subterfuge and double-talk, and he too has to cramp his own style in order to control Rākshasa without destroying him.

PROLOGUE

[*After the Benediction, enter the Director.*]

DIRECTOR Enough, enough! The audience directs me to present the play called 'Rākshasa's Ring', a work of the writer Viśākhadatta, son of Mahārāja Bhāskaradatta, and grandson of Lord Vaṭeśvaradatta. And indeed it gives me the greatest pleasure to perform before so discriminating a public. For

3 Even a fool can farm
When he lights on fertile ground.
Rich crops have no need
Of merit in the sower.

So first I'll go home and rehearse my company. [*Walking about and looking*] Here is our house. I'll enter. [*Entering and looking*] Hallo, what's going on? Is it some celebration, with all the maidservants so busy? Look –

4 Here's one fetching water, here's one grinding perfume,
Here's one weaving colourful garlands.
And here's one at the pestle
Humming softly as she works.

I must call my wife and ask her. [*Looking off-stage*]

5 Talented wife, treasure-house of contrivance,
Source of security, my path to Pleasure, Virtue and Success,
Science of Polity incarnate in my household,
Teacher and counsellor – come here at once.

PROLOGUE

[*Enter an actress.*]

ACTRESS Here I am, sir. Favour me with your commands.

DIRECTOR Never mind my commands for the moment, dear wife. Tell me, have *you* favoured our house by inviting holy brahmins here, or have honoured guests perhaps turned up, to justify all this cooking?

ACTRESS I have invited holy brahmins, sir.

DIRECTOR For what purpose?

ACTRESS Because there's going to be an eclipse of the moon.

DIRECTOR Who says so?

ACTRESS That's what people have been saying in the city.

DIRECTOR My dear wife, I have laboured much upon the sixty-four branches of the science of astronomy. By all means go on with your cooking for the brahmins. But as for an eclipse of the moon, someone has been misleading you. Let me explain –

Now the fierce Demon joins with Ketu, 6
Seeking by force to overpower
Chandra the full-orbed moon –

A VOICE OFF-STAGE [*interrupting him*] Who! Who dares, while I am here!

DIRECTOR

– But the wise planet Mercury safeguards him. 6 cont.

ACTRESS Sir, who was that human being wanting to save the moon from an eclipse?

DIRECTOR *I* couldn't tell either. This time I'll listen carefully for his voice –

Now the fierce Demon joins with Ketu, 6 rptd
Seeking by force to overpower

Chandra the full-orbed moon –

A VOICE OFF-STAGE Who! Who is it, who is it? Who while I am here dares try to overthrow Chandra Gupta?

DIRECTOR [*listening*] Now I know! It is Kauṭilya –

[*The actress shows fear.*]

7 It is Kauṭilya of wily counsel,
Who consumed the House of Nanda in the fire of his anger.
Hearing mention of the moon's eclipse, he imagines
Some threat to the Maurya emperor who has the same name as the moon.

Let us be off.

[*They withdraw.*]

Act I

[*Enter, angrily fingering his loosened braid of hair,* Kauṭilya.*]

KAUṬILYA Who is it, who is it? Who while I am here dares try to overthrow Chandra Gupta?

Who is that doomed fool who even now 8
Wants to see this lock of hair unbound,
This dark serpent that bit the House of Nanda,
This thick black plume of smoke from the fire of my wrath?

Who blunders like a moth into my blazing anger 9
Which burnt the Nanda forest,
So little able to measure his strength and mine
That he invites his own destruction?

Śārngarava, Śārngarava!

[*Enter his pupil.*]

PUPIL Command me, preceptor.

KAUṬILYA A seat, boy.

PUPIL Why, sir, there is a bamboo seat already here in the entrance-hall. Please be seated, sir.

KAUṬILYA I have many affairs on my mind, dear boy – don't think I'm just a teacher picking fault with his

*He had once unbound his hair and vowed not to bind it up again until the Nandas were destroyed. That vow is over and done with; but here, as at the end of Act III, he unbinds his hair again and threatens to begin a new vow.

pupil. [*To himself, sitting down*] So the news is out, is it, that Rākshasa has made a pact with Parvataka's son Malaya Ketu, and with the large forces of the barbarian princes whom Malaya Ketu has won to his side, is getting ready to attack the Emperor – Rākshasa in revenge for the destruction of the House of Nanda, Malaya Ketu indignant at his father Parvataka's murder and inflamed by the prospect of winning the whole Nanda empire. [*Reflecting*] But what of it? No matter how strong the public alarm is, I can quiet it – I am Kauṭilya, who vowed before the whole world to slay the Nanda race, and then fulfilled that impossible vow:

10 Clouding the moon-lovely faces of my enemy's wives with the smoke of grief,
Spattering his counsellors with ashes of confusion borne on the wind of strategy,
Burning the tender shoots of his House, while his subjects scattered like startled birds,
My forest-fire of wrath has paused for lack of fuel, not from exhaustion.

11 Those who once in helpless grief saw me dragged from my high place,
Their gaze averted, protests dying on their lips for fear of the King,
Let them now see how Nanda with all his brood
Lies felled from the throne, like an elephant felled from the mountain-top by a lion.

Now with the burden of my vow discharged, it is only regard for Vrishala that keeps me in office. For I

12 Have uprooted the Nine Nandas like a canker from the soil,

And planted sovereignty in the Maurya as surely as a lotus in a pool.
On friend and foe with full deliberation
I have justly apportioned the fruits of my displeasure or regard.

But no. Until I have Rākshasa, the House of Nanda is undisturbed and Chandra Gupta's sovereignty has no firm roots. [*Reflectively*] Oh how unswerving is Rākshasa's loyalty to the Nandas! While even a single member of the Nanda family remained alive, it would have been impossible to get him to serve under Vrishala. But once blocked on that front, he'll be manageable. That was why I had the wretched Sarvārtha Siddhi killed, though he retired to a hermitage. Meanwhile Rākshasa has won Malaya Ketu to his side, and shows himself more determined than ever to destroy me. [*Addressing himself to the air*] Bravo, Minister Rākshasa! Bravo, divine pattern of a counsellor!

While he has power, people serve their lord for gain, 13
And those who follow him into adversity are hoping for his restoration.
Hard it is to find men with loyalty such as yours,
Selflessly shouldering the burden of duty even when their master is dead.

That is why I strive to win you to our side, to persuade you to favour us by accepting office under Vrishala.

What merit has a timid, stupid man, however loyal? 14
What use is a brave and clever man if he lacks loyalty?
Those who unite brains, courage and devotion, are the servants

That profit a king. In good times or in bad the rest are
concubines.

And so I am unresting in my struggle to win him over. This is what I have done:

First, I have used the mystery of King Parvataka's murder. I have made sure that among the people a rumour unfavourable to Rākshasa circulates, that it was he who employed the poison-girl to kill our great ally, in the belief that the murder of Parvataka would harm me as much as the murder of Vrishala himself. To convince everyone that this was obviously true, my agent Bhāgurāyaṇa spoke privately to the murdered man's son, Prince Malaya Ketu, and first alarmed him with the opposite tale – that it was I, Kauṭilya, who had had his father killed – then helped him to escape. For if Malaya Ketu leads a rebellion against me, even one backed by Rākshasa, I can deal with him; but for me to have arrested him here would have wiped out all the mounting unpopularity which King Parvataka's murder has been earning Rākshasa.

Secondly, I have used spies disguised in various ways and commanding a variety of manners, costumes and dialects, to help me learn who is loyal and who is mutinous both among ourselves and among the enemy. They are using their talents to investigate people living here in Pāṭaliputra who were friends of Rākshasa.

Then there are Bhadra Bhaṭa and certain others who fought on Chandra Gupta's side: various pretexts have been manufactured to give the enemy the impression that they can be easily seduced from their allegiance to us.

Fourthly, I have ensured that the King is constantly attended by men of proven reliability, alert against any poisoners the enemy may employ.

And last, there is my friend and colleague of student days, the brahmin Indu Śarman. He is a man learned both in political science and in all branches of astrology. When I first swore to destroy the race of Nanda, I introduced him into this city disguised as a Jain monk and had him cultivate the friendship of all the Nanda ministers. In particular he enjoys Rākshasa's full confidence. He plays an important part in my plans.

So I have left nothing to chance. Vrishala himself sits at ease, entrusting all cares of state to me his Chief Minister. But then kingship cannot bring pleasure unless it is free of the special vexations that accompany it:

If they must forage for themselves, 15
Then, however strong they are,
Lords of men and lords of the herd alike
Grow vexed and weary.

[*Enter a spy with a canvas depicting the God of Death.*]

SPY

Bow at the feet of Death – 16
What use of other gods?
O you who worship other gods,
It is he who will snatch your throbbing life.

From this harsh god, appeased by prayer, 17
Man's life is won.
From him who slaughters all,
From the God of Death we have our being.

I'll enter this house, show my death-canvas and sing my songs. [*He walks about.*]

PUPIL [*seeing him*] Good fellow, you can't come in here.

SPY Hallo my fine brahmin, whose house is this?

PUPIL It is the house of my teacher, the revered preceptor Kauṭilya.

SPY [*with a laugh*] Why, then it is the house of my very own religious brother. So let me in, and I'll instruct your preceptor in the true faith.

PUPIL [*angrily*] Dolt! Do you know more of such things than he does?

SPY Don't be annoyed, young brahmin. After all no one can know everything. Your preceptor has his knowledge, and people like me have our own.

PUPIL Blockhead! You question my preceptor's omniscience?

SPY If your preceptor is omniscient, sir, he should know whom the Moon displeases.

PUPIL What use could there be in knowing that?

SPY Your preceptor, sir, will know the point of knowing it. As for you, you need only know this much – the Moon displeases the lotuses:

18 The lotuses, fair though they be,
Belie their looks by their behaviour,
For they are the enemy
Of the full-orbed splendour of the Moon.

KAUṬILYA [*listening, to himself*] Ha! He means that he knows of men disloyal to Chandra Gupta.

PUPIL What nonsense is this, you idiot?

SPY Why, sir, it would all make sense enough –

PUPIL If what?

SPY If I could find someone who understood to listen to me.

KAUṬILYA Come in, good fellow. You'll find someone to listen, and to understand.

SPY I enter! [*Entering*] Victory to you, sir.

KAUṬILYA [*to himself, looking at him*] Ah, this is Nipuṇaka, whom I employed to sound out feeling among the citizens. [*Aloud*] You are welcome, my good fellow. Be seated.

SPY As you command, sir. [*He seats himself on the floor.*]

KAUṬILYA Now, what progress? Are the citizens loyal to Vrishala?

SPY More loyal than ever, sir, as you remove various possible reasons for discontent. But there are at present in this city three men who, out of the love and esteem they have always borne Rākshasa, cannot endure the glorious reign of His Majesty the Emperor.

KAUṬILYA [*in anger*] Cannot endure to live, you mean! Do you know their names?

SPY Would I approach you, sir, if I did not?

KAUṬILYA Then I am waiting to hear them.

SPY Yes, sir. First there is a Jain monk working for the enemy.

KAUṬILYA [*to himself, in pleased tones*] A Jain monk working for the enemy?* [*Aloud*] What is his name?

SPY He is called Jīva Siddhi, and he ensured that King Parvataka was killed by the poison-girl engaged by Rākshasa.

KAUṬILYA [*to himself*] That one at any rate is my own agent. [*Aloud*] Who else, my good fellow?

SPY There is another good friend of Minister Rākshasa, a letter-writer called Śakaṭa Dāsa.

KAUṬILYA [*to himself, smiling*] A letter-writer is a person of small consequence. But it would be wrong to disregard even the meanest opponent, and I have already

*Jain monks were regarded as inauspicious: cf. Act IV, p. 248, and Act V, p. 250.

ordered my agent Siddhārthaka to cultivate his acquaintance. [*Aloud*] And the third?

SPY The third too is an intimate friend, one very dear to Minister Rākshasa's heart, the master-jeweller and banker Chandanadāsa. It was in his house that Minister Rākshasa placed his wife when he left the city.

KAUṬILYA [*to himself*] A close friend indeed! Rākshasa would never entrust the safety of his wife to a mere acquaintance. [*Aloud*] Tell me, my dear fellow, how do you know that Rākshasa has left his wife in Chandanadāsa's house?

SPY This signet-ring should enlighten you, sir. [*He hands him a ring.*]

KAUṬILYA [*taking it and reading out the name* 'Rākshasa', *to himself in delight*] Why, I have Rākshasa himself, entwined around my finger! [*Aloud*] Tell me in detail how you came by this ring.

SPY Listen, sir. Being employed by you to enquire into the activities of the citizens, I was wandering the city with this death-canvas by means of which I may enter strange houses without exciting suspicion, and I went into the house of the master-jeweller Chandanadāsa, where I spread my canvas and began to chant my songs.

KAUṬILYA What happened?

SPY From an inner apartment an attractive child about four or five years old, his two eyes widening in the easy curiosity of childhood, began to show himself. In the apartment I could hear sounds of confusion, alarmed women urgently whispering 'Oh, he's got out, he's got out!'; then a woman, just showing her face round the door, scolded the child and caught hold of him with a slender arm, while he was still emerging. As she moved her hand hastily to check him, that signet-ring, which is made to fit a man's finger, slipped off and fell onto the threshold. It bounced off and rolled towards me, quite unnoticed by her, and lay motionless at my feet, like a well-bred woman silently saluting me. Seeing that it was engraved with Minister Rākshasa's name, I brought it to Your Honour. And that is the story of how I came by it.

KAUṬILYA I have noted it, my dear man. Go, and you will soon be well rewarded for your efforts.

SPY As you command, sir. [*He goes out.*]

KAUṬILYA Śārngarava! Śārngarava!

PUPIL [*entering*] Command me, sir.

KAUṬILYA Bring me an ink-pot and paper.

PUPIL Yes, sir. [*Withdrawing and re-entering*] Here you are, sir.

KAUṬILYA [*accepting them, to himself*] How shall I phrase this letter? It must bring victory over Rākshasa.

[*Enter the female guard.*]

FEMALE GUARD Victory be yours, Your Honour.

KAUṬILYA [*delightedly, to himself*] I accept the omen of victory! [*Aloud*] Śoṇottarā, what brings you here?

FEMALE GUARD Sir, His Glorious Majesty the Emperor Chandra Gupta salutes you with his hands folded to his forehead, and begs to say: 'I wish with Your Honour's permission to perform the obsequies of His Majesty King Parvataka, and would therefore bestow the decorations he wore upon revered brahmins.'

KAUṬILYA [*delightedly, to himself*] Well done, Vrishala! You have consulted with my own heart in expressing such a wish. [*Aloud*] Śoṇottarā, answer Vrishala in my name as follows: 'Bravo, dear child, bravo! You show that you know what is proper. Do what you propose.

And as to the decorations worn by Parvataka, they are of the finest quality and should be bestowed upon brahmins worthy of them. I will send you therefore brahmins whose worth I can vouch for.'

FEMALE GUARD As you command, sir. [*She goes out.*]

KAUṬILYA Śārngarava, Śārngarava!

PUPIL [*entering*] Sir?

KAUṬILYA I have a message for Viśvāvasu and his two brothers: they are to go to Vrishala to accept a gift, and then to come to me.

PUPIL Yes, sir. [*He goes out.*]

KAUṬILYA I have the second half of the letter, but how shall it begin? [*After reflection*] Ah yes! My agents inform me that prominent among the barbarian forces are five princes especially friendly with Rākshasa –

19 Chitra Varman of Kulūta, stout Siṃha Nāda of Málaya,
Pushkarāksha of Kashmir, mighty Sindhusheṇa of Sindh,
And fifth Megha Nāda, commander of horsemen, ruler of the Persians.
I'll write their names now, and leave them to be cancelled by the Clerk of Death.

No, on second thoughts, I won't spell things out. Śārngarava, Śārngarava!

PUPIL [*entering*] Yes, sir?

KAUṬILYA My boy, a scholar's handwriting is always illegible however hard he tries. So give Siddhārthaka this message: 'Have the letter-writer Śakaṭa Dāsa copy out this letter. Explain that it has no address on it, because it is intended to be read aloud. When you have done this, bring it to me here. And do not mention to him that it is Kauṭilya who wants it copied.'

PUPIL Yes, sir. [*He goes out.*]

KAUṬILYA [*to himself*] This means victory over Malaya Ketu!

[*Enter Siddhārthaka with the letter.*]

SIDDHĀRTHAKA Victory be yours, sir. Here is the letter, copied by Śakaṭa Dāsa.

KAUṬILYA [*taking it*] Ah, a most attractive hand! [*After reading it through*] Siddhārthaka, seal it with this signet-ring.

SIDDHĀRTHAKA Yes, sir.

KAUṬILYA Śārngarava, Śārngarava!

PUPIL [*entering*] Yes, sir?

KAUṬILYA Boy, tell the Chief of Police in my name that the following is the Emperor's command: 'The Jain monk Jīva Siddhi, who, being in the employ of Rākshasa, made use of a poison-girl to murder King Parvataka, shall after proclamation of the aforesaid offence be banished in disgrace from the city.'

PUPIL Yes, sir. [*He walks off.*]

KAUṬILYA Wait, there is more. 'And the letter-writer Śakaṭa Dāsa, who, being likewise in the employ of Rākshasa, is forever seeking to do violence to my person, shall after proclamation of the aforesaid offence be impaled, and his household imprisoned.'

PUPIL Yes, sir. [*He goes out.*]

SIDDHĀRTHAKA I have sealed the letter: what now, sir?

KAUṬILYA My dear man, I have an extremely confidential task that I want to employ you on.

SIDDHĀRTHAKA [*delightedly*] You do me too much honour, sir. What may this humble servant do for you?

KAUṬILYA First, go to the Execution Ground and angrily wink your right eye as a signal to the executioners. When they get the signal they will pretend to panic and run about, and you must rescue Śakaṭa Dāsa and convey him to Rākshasa. Rākshasa will be delighted with you for saving his friend's life: accept whatever gift of gratitude he makes you, and serve him devotedly thereafter. But when the enemy is close to this city, I want you to do as follows – [*He whispers in his ear*] Like that! [*To himself, in preoccupied tones*] Have I the obstinate Rākshasa within my grasp?

SIDDHĀRTHAKA Yes, fully grasped, sir!

KAUṬILYA [*to himself in delight*] Ha! Rākshasa is fully grasped! [*Aloud*] Fully grasped? How do you mean?

SIDDHĀRTHAKA My instructions, sir. I know what to do. And so I'll be off to accomplish my mission.

KAUṬILYA [*handing him the sealed letter*] Go, my dear Siddhārthaka. And all success be yours in your task.

SIDDHĀRTHAKA Yes, sir. [*He salutes and goes out.*]

[*Enter a pupil.*]

PUPIL Sir, the Chiefs of Police and Prison beg to inform Your Honour that His Majesty's commands are being fulfilled.

KAUṬILYA Excellent, my boy. Now I should like to see the master-jeweller Chandanadāsa.

PUPIL Yes, sir.

[*He goes out and returns with Chandanadāsa.*]

PUPIL This way, Master Chandanadāsa.

CHANDANADĀSA [*to himself*]

When the ruthless Kauṭilya
Sends an urgent summons,
Even the innocent are worried,
Let alone the guilty.

That is why I have told them at home that the accursed Kauṭilya may be going to have our house searched, and that they must smuggle my lord Rākshasa's family away – though for myself what must be, must be.

PUPIL This way, Master Chandanadāsa.

CHANDANADĀSA I am coming, good sir.

[*They both walk about.*]

PUPIL [*approaching Kauṭilya*] Here is the master-jeweller Chandanadāsa, sir.

CHANDANADĀSA Victory, sir, victory!

KAUṬILYA [*seeing him*] My dear Master Chandanadāsa! Welcome! Here is a seat for you – do sit down.

CHANDANADĀSA As Your Honour surely knows, inappropriate courtesies cause an inferior more discomfort than do insults. So let me just sit here on the ground as is fitting.

KAUṬILYA Oh my dear Master Chandanadāsa, not a bit of it, not a bit of it! It is perfectly fitting for you to sit together with one such as my poor self. Sit, therefore, on the seat.

CHANDANADĀSA [*to himself*] He's found out something. [*Aloud*] As you say, sir. [*He sits down.*]

KAUṬILYA Tell me, Master Chandanadāsa, is business flourishing?

CHANDANADĀSA Most certainly, sir. By Your Honour's favour, business is as good as ever.

KAUṬILYA Perhaps Chandra Gupta's shortcomings make people remember the merits of bygone rulers?

CHANDANADĀSA [*stopping his ears*] Perish the thought!

Like a full moon risen 21
On a clear autumn evening
His Serene Majesty Chandra Gupta
Gladdens the hearts of his people.

KAUṬILYA If so, Master Chandanadāsa, a king likes some return from his satisfied subjects.

CHANDANADĀSA Command me, sir: what and how much do you want?

KAUṬILYA Master Chandanadāsa! This is the reign of Chandra Gupta, not the reign of the Nandas! What pleased Nanda, with his itch for money, was the piling up of wealth; what pleases Chandra Gupta is your peace of mind.

CHANDANADĀSA [*happily*] I am favoured, sir.

KAUṬILYA Master Chandanadāsa, I was waiting to hear you say, 'And how may one show one's peace of mind?'

CHANDANADĀSA Command me, sir.

KAUṬILYA In a word, by not acting against the Emperor.

CHANDANADĀSA Your Honour, what unlucky man do you suppose to be acting against the Emperor?

KAUṬILYA You, for a start.

CHANDANADĀSA [*stopping his ears*] Perish the thought! How can straws act against fire?

KAUṬILYA They can, as you have, harbour in their house the family of Rākshasa, a man who is acting treasonably.

CHANDANADĀSA Your Honour, this is some calumny that some villain or other has reported to you.

KAUṬILYA Do not be alarmed, my dear Master Chandanadāsa. When frightened officials of a former king leave their families in the houses of citizens (all unwilling though those citizens may be) before making off somewhere else, there is no crime except in subsequent concealment of the family.

CHANDANADĀSA Yes, you are right. Minister Rākshasa's family *was* left in my house at that time.

KAUṬILYA First a calumny, now 'it *was* left there!' Your words have a certain lack of internal consistency.

CHANDANADĀSA I did speak misleadingly, sir.

KAUṬILYA While Chandra Gupta is on the throne, Master Chandanadāsa, no 'misleading' will be tolerated.

So hand over Minister Rākshasa's family, and let all misleading cease.

CHANDANADĀSA Please sir, what I mean to say is that Minister Rākshasa's family *was* in my house, then.

KAUṬILYA And is now where?

CHANDANADĀSA I don't know.

KAUṬILYA [*smiling grimly*] Oh, you don't know? Master-jeweller, the danger, as we say, is about you, and the healing herbs far away on the mountain-top. And let me tell you this: you need be under no illusion that just as Nanda was overthrown by Vishṇugupta* – [*breaking off and showing modesty*] I mean of course by *Chandra* Gupta, so Chandra Gupta in turn might be overthrown by Rākshasa. Consider –

All those brave and brilliant counsellors, like Vakranāsa, 22
Could not make the light of sovereignty rest tranquilly
 on Nanda.
Now that it gladdens the world with an unflickering
 glow
Who will wrest it from Chandra Gupta, any more than
 the moonlight from the moon?

When the lion's mouth stretches in a yawn, 23
Who will extract the glittering fang
Ruddy as the crescent moon at twilight
That gleams with elephant's blood?

CHANDANADĀSA [*to himself*] Your boasting is justified by the facts.

[*Off-stage a commotion.*]

KAUṬILYA Śārngarava, Śārngarava, find out what that is.

*Vishṇugupta is Kauṭilya's own name.

PUPIL Yes, sir. [*Going out and returning*] Sir, it is a traitor, the Jain monk Jīva Siddhi: on His Majesty Chandra Gupta's orders he is being banished in disgrace from the city.

KAUṬILYA A Jain monk? Oh! But he must reap the reward of his treachery. Good Master-jeweller, you can see how severely His Majesty deals with traitors. Take a friend's good advice. Hand over Rākshasa's family. Enjoy for many years to come all the benefits that royal favour can bestow.

CHANDANADĀSA I cannot hand over what I have not got.

[*Off-stage further commotion.*]

KAUṬILYA Śārngarava, Śārngarava, find out what *that* is.

PUPIL Yes, sir. [*Going out and returning*] Sir, it is another traitor, the letter-writer Śakaṭa Dāsa: on His Majesty's orders he is being taken to be impaled.

KAUṬILYA Let him reap the reward of his actions. Good Master-jeweller. A king who is so severe towards traitors is not going to overlook your concealment of Rākshasa's wife. At the cost of the wife of another, save your own wife – and your own life.

CHANDANADĀSA Why do you threaten me, Your Honour? Even if Rākshasa's family were in my house I should not surrender them, and at any rate they are not.

KAUṬILYA Chandanadāsa, are you resolved?

CHANDANADĀSA Yes, completely.

KAUṬILYA [*to himself*] Then bravo, Chandanadāsa –

24 When all the profit lies
In turning informer,
Who but another Śibi*

*A legendary king, renowned for generosity, who once offered his life to protect a dove.

Would choose the difficult course?

[*Aloud*] Chandanadāsa, are you resolved?

CHANDANADĀSA Yes, completely.

KAUṬILYA [*angrily*] Villainous shopkeeper! Then suffer the Emperor's wrath.

CHANDANADĀSA I am ready, sir. Live up to your office.

KAUṬILYA [*angrily*] Śārngarava, tell the Chief of Police to have this villain arrested at once – no, wait! Tell the Governor of the Prison to seize this man and his goods, and hold him in gaol with his wife and children until I have reported to Vrishala. Vrishala himself shall pass the sentence of death.

PUPIL Yes, sir. This way, Master-jeweller.

CHANDANADĀSA [*getting up*] I am coming. [*To himself*] Thank God I am dying for a friend, and not for any crime.

[*He walks about and goes out with the pupil.*]

KAUṬILYA [*in delight*] Now I have Rākshasa. For

Just as one, when the other is in trouble, 25
Gives up his life as something worthless,
So assuredly when *he* is in trouble
The other will not think of his own skin.

[*Off-stage a commotion.*]

PUPIL [*entering*] Sir, it's Siddhārthaka! He has rescued Śakaṭa Dāsa from execution and escaped with him!

KAUṬILYA [*to himself*] Bravo Siddhārthaka, the work is begun. [*Aloud*] Escaped? [*Angrily*] Tell Bhāgurāyaṇa to capture him at once.

PUPIL [*going out and returning*] Oh sir, oh sir! Bhāgurāyaṇa has run away as well!

KAUṬILYA [*to himself*] Success go with him. [*Aloud, angrily*] Boy, take a message to Bhadra Bhaṭa, Purusha

Datta, Hingu Rāta, Bala Gupta, Rājasena, Rohitāksha and Vijaya Varman: they are to go after the villain Bhāgurāyaṇa at once and catch him.

PUPIL Yes, sir. [*Going out and returning, in despair*] Oh sir, oh sir! Everything is upside down. All of them have run away already – they left before dawn.

KAUṬILYA [*to himself*] And let success attend every one of them. [*Aloud*] Do not despair, my boy. Look,

26 Those who have schemed and gone, had left us long ago in their hearts.
And those who stay may plot to go if they will.
Let just one thing not desert me, for it can do more than a thousand armies –
My mind, to whose power a dynasty destroyed bears witness.

[*Rising*] I will go and catch your wicked fugitives. [*To himself*] Wretched Rākshasa, where will you go? See, I will get you before long:

27 You are my wild elephant, self-willed and solitary,
Plunging through the jungle in rutting pride,
Whom I with guile will trap and then break in,
Making you apt for service under Vrishala.

[*All go out.*]

Act II

[*Enter a snake-charmer.*]

SNAKE-CHARMER

If you see a man who knows about administering, 1
Who cultivates the right circles*
And likes to get in a good spell,
He must be a snake-charmer, if he's not a politician.

[*Addressing the air*] What's that you say, sir? Who am I? Sir, I am a snake-charmer: Jīrṇavisha † is my name. What's that? You too would like to amuse yourself with snakes? Well, sir, what do you do for a living? You have a post in the palace? Then, my dear sir, you do play with snakes. Listen,

A snakeman that doesn't know his spells and herbs, 2
A rider that mounts an elephant in rut,
A palace official flushed with success –
All three of them are doomed.

Oh, the man's gone! [*Addressing the air once more*] What's that, sir? What's in these boxes and hampers? Poisonous snakes! You want to see them, you say? Not here, sir, if you don't mind. If you're interested, come with me and I'll put on a show inside this house. This is Minister Rākshasa's house, you tell me, and no admission for the likes of us? Then *you* can be off, but I have a profession that will allow me in. Oh, *he's* gone too!

*Alludes also to mystical diagrams.
†'Digester of Venom'.

[*Glancing about and then speaking in educated tones*] Ah, it is extraordinary: I see Chandra Gupta with Kauṭilya to advise him, and despair of Rākshasa's chances – then I see Malaya Ketu with Rākshasa to advise him, and Chandra Gupta seems as good as toppled from his throne.

3 Kauṭilya's wits had, I thought, roped and bound
Fortune to the Mauryan dynasty:
But Rākshasa's plotting seizes on the ropes
And seems to be loosening the knots again.

And as these two great statesmen dispute, Fortune seems perplexed –

4 The two ministers are violently disputing,
Like two wild elephants rampaging through the world.
And in her uncertainty, like a fearful she-elephant,
Fortune is exhausted with running from one to the other.

Now I will call on Minister Rākshasa.

[*Enter, on a couch in his house and attended by a man-servant, Rākshasa in anxious thought.*]

RĀKSHASA [*weeping*] Alas, alas!

5 Once the Nandas had courage and skill to conquer all their foes,
But now Destiny has cruelly doomed them like Krishṇa's clan,*
And worn with care, sleepless by day or night,
I go on painting a picture on a non-existent canvas.

But

*The Vrishṇi (or Yādava) clan, whose capital Dvārakā is said to have been submerged by the sea within seven days of Krishṇa's death.

It is not that I have forgotten my loyalty, or steeped my mind in worldly things, 6
Not that I fear for my life or seek my own security,
If I now enslave myself to another and plunge into politics –
It is only so that my master in heaven may be avenged.

[*Gazing up, with tears*] Blessed Goddess of Fortune, truly you ignore merit.

Why did you forsake your joy the Nanda monarch 7
For that cursed son of the Mauryas, oh why?
Why, fickle one, did you not vanish on the spot,
Like the streak of ichor when the musk-elephant dies?

Base creature!

Are kings of noble line all dead and burnt 8
That you have chosen the Mauryan upstart for your consort?
But fickle by nature as the petal of a full-blown flower
Is the mind of woman, and loath to judge men aright.

Very well, my wench. I shall frustrate you by robbing you of him you lean on.

[*Reflectively*] I did well to leave my family in my dear friend Chandanadāsa's house before I left Pāṭaliputra. My lord's dependants who are working there in our cause will know that I am committed to taking the city, and will not slacken in their efforts. I have put large resources at Śakaṭa Dāsa's disposal to encourage the poisoners we are employing against Chandra Gupta, and also for use in propaganda. And I have set Jīva Siddhi and other friends to the hourly collecting of information about the enemy and the undermining of their unity. In fact

9 That tiger-cub which my dear lord cherished as the son he longed for
Only to be struck down with all his kin,
I will in turn strike down with the arrow of my thought,
Unless he has an invisible shield of fate about him.

[*Enter a chamberlain.*]

CHAMBERLAIN

10 Old age has killed desire in me, and strengthened virtue,
As it might be Kauṭilya establishing the Mauryan where Nanda ruled.
Now virtue flourishes like the Mauryan, and greed like Rākshasa
Seizes its chance to strike but cannot win.

Here is Minister Rākshasa's house. I will go in. [*Walking about and approaching*] Greetings to you, sir.

RĀKSHASA Sir, I salute you. Priyamvadaka, a seat!

MANSERVANT Here you are, sir. Please sit down.

CHAMBERLAIN [*sitting down*] Minister, His Highness Prince Malaya Ketu begs to say that he has long grieved in his heart to see Your Honour without proper adornment of your person. Though your former master's virtues can never be forgotten, he begs you to honour his request. [*Producing decorations*] His Highness, sir, has taken these decorations from his own person and sent them for you to wear.

RĀKSHASA Noble Jājali, please take this answer to His Highness: 'In my admiration of Your Highness's virtues I have forgotten the virtues of my former Lord. But

11 This feeble and humiliated body
Shall bear no trace of adornment

Until the circle of your foes is laid low
And your gold throne, great hero, set in the River Palace.'

CHAMBERLAIN Now that you, sir, are guiding him, that is easy for His Highness to achieve. Therefore I ask you to honour the first request His Highness has ever made of you.

RĀKSHASA Noble sir, I can offend you no more than I can His Highness: I will do as the Prince commands.

CHAMBERLAIN [*after arranging the decorations on him*] Thank you, sir, I will take my leave.

RĀKSHASA Sir, I salute you.

[*The Chamberlain withdraws.*]

RĀKSHASA Priyamvadaka, find out who is waiting at the door to see me.

MANSERVANT Yes sir. [*Going out and seeing the snake-charmer*] Who are you, sir?

SNAKE-CHARMER I am Jirṇavisha, a snake-charmer, my dear man. I should like to perform with my snakes before the Minister.

MANSERVANT Wait here while I tell the Minister. [*Approaching Rākshasa*] A snake-charmer, sir, who wants to perform before you.

RĀKSHASA [*indicating an inauspicious throbbing of the left eye, to himself*] What! See snakes now?* [*Aloud*] I don't feel interested in snakes, Priyamvadaka. Give him something and send him away.

MANSERVANT Yes, sir. [*Going out and approaching the snake-charmer*] My master thanks you without seeing the snakes, sir, and would prefer not to see them.

SNAKE-CHARMER Tell your master from me that I'm

*i.e., immediately after the ill omen of the twitching of the eye.

not just a snake-charmer. I'm also a poet in the common tongue. If he won't favour me with an audience, perhaps he will be so good as to read this. [*He hands over a sheet of paper.*]

MANSERVANT [*taking it and going up to Rākshasa*] Sir, he says he is a poet as well as a snake-charmer, and would you be so good as to read this.

RĀKSHASA [*takes the paper and reads it out*]

12 'The probing bee has used his power
To drink the nectar of the flower.
The honey that he makes of it
Is work for others' benefit.'

[*After reflection, to himself*] This verse must mean that the writer has news of the Flower City, Pāṭaliputra, and is an agent of mine. I have so much on my mind, and so many agents, that I was forgetting. But I remember now. It must be Virādha Gupta disguised as a snake-charmer. [*Aloud*] Priyamvadaka, show him in. He is a good poet, and I want to hear more from him.

MANSERVANT Yes, sir. [*Approaching the snake-charmer*] Come in, sir.

SNAKE-CHARMER [*approaching and looking at Rākshasa, to himself*] Here is Minister Rākshasa,

13 Whom Fortune turns anxiously to watch, as she lies in the Mauryan's embraces,
With one arm loosely placed around her lover.
Though he draws her other arm about him, it always falls away
And even now she will not let him crush her other breast against him.

[*Aloud*] Victory, sir, victory!

RĀKSHASA [*seeing him*] Why, good Vi— [*breaking off*] good vigorous growth of beard you've got there, my man! Priyamvadaka, there's no snake-show for the moment. The servants can take a rest. And you too go about your work.

MANSERVANT Yes, sir.

[*He withdraws with the attendants.*]

RĀKSHASA My dear Virādha Gupta. Here, sit down.

VIRĀDHA GUPTA* Thank you, Minister. [*He seats himself.*]

RĀKSHASA [*taking in his appearance*] What a state we loyal subjects of His Majesty are reduced to! [*He weeps.*]

VIRĀDHA GUPTA Do not grieve, Minister. You will soon restore our former glory.

RĀKSHASA Virādha Gupta, my dear friend. Tell me what has been happening in Pāṭaliputra.

VIRĀDHA GUPTA Much has been happening, Minister. Where shall I begin?

RĀKSHASA I want to know how the poisoners and others I employed have been faring since Chandra Gupta first entered the city.

VIRĀDHA GUPTA Well, then: with Pāṭaliputra now beseiged on all sides by the great horde of Scythians, Greeks, Hill Tribesmen, Cambodians, Persians, Bactrians and all the others, numberless as the ocean waters at Doomsday, that make up the forces of Chandra Gupta and Parvataka under Kauṭilya's guidance –

RĀKSHASA [*in agitation, drawing his sword*] What, who threatens the city while I am alive? Quick, Pravīraka, quick now!

*Now that he is Virādha Gupta and not Jīrṇavisha the snake-charmer, he speaks again in educated tones – i.e. in Sanskrit (see Introduction).

14 Man the ramparts at once with archers!
Put elephants at the gates to break the enemy elephants' attack!
Lay fear of death aside, resolve to strike our nerveless foe,
March out with me all you who look for glory!

VIRĀDHA GUPTA Minister, calm yourself. We are talking of the past.

RĀKSHASA The past? To me it all seemed to be happening again. [*Relinquishing his sword and weeping*] Oh Nanda, my beloved Emperor! Well do I remember how you favoured me at such times.

15 'There are elephants massing like a storm-cloud,' you would say – 'send Rākshasa there!'
'Rākshasa must stem the tidal wave of cavalry!'
'Rākshasa shall destroy their infantry!' Such were your orders,
For you loved me so well you thought the city had a thousand Rākshasas.

Well go on.

VIRĀDHA GUPTA With Pāṭaliputra now besieged on all sides and the privations of the siege continuing day after day, His Majesty the Emperor Sarvārtha Siddhi could not bear to let the people go on suffering and for their sake made his escape through the secret passage and retired to a hermitage. The loss of their lord dampened the enthusiasm of your own forces, and when the boldness of the resistance to Chandra Gupta's victory proclamation revealed your presence in the city, you yourself left by the secret passage to work for the later restoration of Nanda rule. It was then that the poison-girl you engaged to kill Chandra Gupta brought about the death of poor Parvataka –

RĀKSHASA How strange that was, friend!

She was like the once-for-all weapon* that Karṇa kept to kill Arjuna, 16
Which instead helped Krishṇa by killing Hiḍimbā's son.
I had been keeping her for Chandra Gupta, but alas,
She did Kauṭilya's work by killing Parvataka.

VIRĀDHA GUPTA It was the sport of fate, Minister. What can one do?

RĀKSHASA Go on.

VIRĀDHA GUPTA His father's death frightened Prince Malaya Ketu into escaping, but his uncle, Parvataka's brother Vairodhaka, was given assurances of safety. It was proclaimed that Chandra Gupta would enter the Nanda Palace, and Kauṭilya called all the carpenters in the city together and told them that because of a favourable astrological juncture the Entry into the Palace would take place at midnight on that same day, and that they were to decorate the whole royal palace beginning with the Eastern Gate. The carpenters informed him that one of their number, Dāru Varman, had contrived sumptuous decorations for the royal gateway, including a golden triumphal arch, as soon as he

*In the *Mahābhārata* it is recounted how Karṇa, the half-brother but bitter enemy of the five Pāṇḍavas and especially of Arjuna, had been given by the god Indra a special weapon which would be fatal but could be used only once: he attempted to kill Arjuna with it, but instead it struck Ghaṭotkacha, the son of Arjuna's powerful brother Bhīma and the demoness Hiḍimbā. The god Krishṇa was Arjuna's protector, acting as his charioteer in the battle.

had heard that Chandra Gupta would enter the palace, and it only remained for them to decorate the interior. That fellow Kauṭilya seemed delighted to hear that Dāru Varman had decorated the palace gateway without waiting to be asked, praised his talents at considerable length, and said that it wouldn't be long before he earned a reward in keeping with his enterprise.

RĀKSHASA [*disturbed*] Why should the fellow be so pleased, friend? I can guess that Dāru Varman's efforts were not rewarded, at least not in the way he intended: he was mad to act before being commissioned, and make Kauṭilya suspicious – or rather he was too zealous in the service of his rightful king. What happened?

VIRĀDHA GUPTA Kauṭilya made sure that the craftsmen and the citizens at large knew that because of a favourable astrological juncture Chandra Gupta was due to enter the palace at midnight. Then on the stroke of the hour he set Parvataka's brother Vairodhaka on the throne with Chandra Gupta and divided the empire between them.

RĀKSHASA He gave away to Vairodhaka the half-share in the empire which had been promised to Vairodhaka's brother?

VIRĀDHA GUPTA Exactly.

RĀKSHASA [*to himself*] Then the cunning villain can only have been plotting to have the poor wretch quietly killed, and contrived this act of public good faith to wipe out the unpopularity which Parvataka's murder was earning him. [*Aloud*] Go on.

VIRĀDHA GUPTA It had already been proclaimed that Chandra Gupta would enter the palace that night. The ceremony of consecration was performed and the Emperor was robed in silk corselet encrusted with strings of snow-white pearls. A jewelled crown fitted closely round his gleaming head. His chest glowed with a fragrant mantle of flower garlands. His closest friends would not have recognized him. On the accursed Kauṭilya's orders, he was mounted on Chandra Gupta's own mount, the she-elephant Chandra Lekhā, and attended by Chandra Gupta's own vassal princes; but the Emperor who entered the Nanda Palace was not Chandra Gupta but Vairodhaka. Supposing him to be Chandra Gupta, your agent the carpenter Dāru Varman set the mechanism of the arch in motion to fall on him. The vassal princes reined in their mounts outside the gateway, but Chandra Lekhā's driver Varvaraka, who was also your agent, reached for his gold staff, hanging on a gold chain, intending to take out the dagger he had concealed within.

RĀKSHASA Alas! It was not the moment for either attempt! Yes?

VIRĀDHA GUPTA The elephant expected a blow on the rump, and quickened her pace. The release of the mechanical arch had been calculated on her previous speed and when it fell it missed its target and instead killed poor Varvaraka while his hands were occupied with the dagger he had drawn, and before he could reach Vairodhaka – whom he supposed to be Chandra Gupta. Dāru Varman knew that the release of the arch had signed his own death warrant, and since he was already perched on top of it he seized the iron bolt that had triggered the mechanism and killed Vairodhaka where he was on the elephant.

RĀKSHASA Alas, two equal disasters – Chandra Gupta still alive, Vairodhaka and Varvaraka killed! The carpenter Dāru Varman, what happened to him?

VIRĀDHA GUPTA Stoned to death by Vairodhaka's infantry.

RĀKSHASA [*weeping*] We have lost a loving friend! And the doctor, Abhayadatta, what of his work?

VIRĀDHA GUPTA It is done.

RĀKSHASA [*in delight*] He has killed Chandra Gupta?

VIRĀDHA GUPTA As fate would have it, he has not.

RĀKSHASA Then why tell me his work is done?

VIRĀDHA GUPTA He prepared medicine for Chandra Gupta containing a fatal powder. When the accursed Kauṭilya inspected it, he saw that the gold cup it was in had changed colour, and he said, 'Vrishala, don't drink it, it's poisoned.'

RĀKSHASA He's a cunning villain. What happened to the doctor?

VIRĀDHA GUPTA The doctor was made to drink his own medicine, and died.

RĀKSHASA [*despondently*] The world has lost a very learned man. What has happened to Pramodaka, the steward of the bed-chamber?

VIRĀDHA GUPTA The same as to the others, sir.

RĀKSHASA [*alarmed*] How do you mean?

VIRĀDHA GUPTA When he got the huge sum of money you allowed him, the fool began spending extravagantly. On being asked to account for his wealth he told a confused variety of stories – and on Kauṭilya's orders he was put to death by torture.

RĀKSHASA [*in despair*] Does fate strike us down yet again? And those we employed to kill the Emperor in bed, who were already living in a secret passage inside the bedchamber – Bībhatsaka and the others, what news of them?

VIRĀDHA GUPTA Grim news, I fear.

RĀKSHASA Grim? Did Kauṭilya discover they were there?

VIRĀDHA GUPTA He did. Before Chandra Gupta occupied the bedchamber, Kauṭilya entered it and made a sudden inspection. He saw a column of ants emerging with bits of food from a crack in the wall, and realizing there were men in the room had the place fired. As it was burning Bībhatsaka and his companions were blinded by the thick smoke and could not find the way out, which they had closed behind them, and they perished in the flames.

RĀKSHASA [*weeping*] See, friend, that accursed Chandra Gupta's luck:

The poison-girl I secretly engaged to kill him 17
By chance killed Parvataka, who would have taken half his empire.
My agents die themselves by the knives and poisons that they use.
It is the Mauryan reaps the benefit of every plan I make.

VIRĀDHA GUPTA Even so, Minister you must not give up. Think, sir.

Obstacles deter the worst from starting 18
And turn the mediocre from what they have begun.
But the best and noblest like yourself will persevere
Though obstacles beset them time and time again.

Does the Serpent feel no ache, that he does not throw off the earth? 19
Has the sun no weariness that it does not pause to rest?
A great man is ashamed to give up like a commoner.
The noble have one family-law, to do what they have promised.

RĀKSHASA My friend, you see for yourself that I cannot give up. Continue.

VIRĀDHA GUPTA Thereafter Kauṭilya became a thousand times more vigilant for Chandra Gupta's safety, and by tracking everything that happened to its source he uncovered your most trusted agents in the city.

RĀKSHASA [*in alarm*] Whom did he discover?

VIRĀDHA GUPTA First the Jain monk Jīva Siddhi, whom he banished in disgrace from the city.

RĀKSHASA [*to himself*] That at least is endurable: loss of home will not bear hard on a man without ties. [*Aloud*] Friend, for what offence was he banished?

VIRĀDHA GUPTA For being employed by you to have Parvataka killed by a poison-girl.

RĀKSHASA [*to himself*] Bravo, Kauṭilya!

You avoid unpopularity, transfer it to me,
And dispose of a claimant to half the empire.
You sow one seed of policy
And harvest many fruits.

[*Aloud*] What then?

VIRĀDHA GUPTA Then Śakaṭa Dāsa was publicly proclaimed to have employed Dāru Varman and others in plots against Chandra Gupta, and was impaled.

RĀKSHASA [*weeping*] Oh Śakaṭa Dāsa, dearest friend, you did not deserve such a death. But you died in your master's cause: it is not you who should be mourned, but I, who think of living when the House of Nanda has perished.

VIRĀDHA GUPTA No, Minister, no! You must live to serve our master's cause.

RĀKSHASA Friend,

It is because of that cause 21
That I still love life,
And am so disloyal
As not to follow my lord into the next world.

VIRĀDHA GUPTA You put it wrongly, Minister –

It is because of that cause, 22
Not because you love life,
That you are loyal to your Lord
And keep from following him into the next world.

RĀKSHASA Speak on, my friend. I am waiting to hear of other disasters to those I love.

VIRĀDHA GUPTA Hearing the news, Chandanadāsa, out of the love he bears you, got your wife safely away.

RĀKSHASA He did ill to oppose one so merciless as Kauṭilya.

VIRĀDHA GUPTA Would he have done better to betray a friend?

RĀKSHASA What happened?

VIRĀDHA GUPTA When he was pressed to hand her over and refused, Kauṭilya grew angry –

RĀKSHASA [*in alarm*] And had him killed?

VIRĀDHA GUPTA No sir, not that. His goods were confiscated and he was thrown into gaol with his wife and son.

RĀKSHASA Then why tell me in pleased tones that he got my wife safely away? Tell me rather that *I* am in gaol with *my* wife and son.

[*Enter the manservant.*]

MANSERVANT Victory, sir. Sir, Śakaṭa Dāsa is waiting in the entrance-hall.

RĀKSHASA Is this true?

MANSERVANT Can Your Honour's own household lie to you?

RĀKSHASA What can this mean, Virādha Gupta?*

VIRĀDHA GUPTA It may be true, sir. Destiny looks to what must be.

RĀKSHASA If it is true, then hurry, Priyamvadaka! Show him in at once and put new heart in me.

MANSERVANT Yes, sir. [*He goes out.*]

[*Enter, with Siddhārthaka in attendance, Śakaṭa Dāsa.*]

ŚAKAṬA DĀSA [*to himself*]

23 When I saw the stake set firm as the Mauryan in the earth,
When I felt the garland as heavy on my heart as his royal glory,
When I heard the trumpet of execution as harsh as my lord's defeat,
My mind only held firm because it was hardened by earlier blows.

[*Looking joyfully*] There stands Minister Rākshasa:

24 He goes on serving his master's cause,
His devotion alive though Nanda is dead.
He stands as the supreme example
Of all on earth who are loyal to a master.

[*Approaching*] Victory to you, Minister.

RĀKSHASA [*seeing him, joyfully*] Dearest Śakaṭa Dāsa, thank God I see you! Embrace me! [*After embracing him*] Here, sit down.

ŚAKAṬA DĀSA Yes, sir. [*He sits down.*]

*This is despite Rākshasa's elaborate efforts earlier to conceal Virādha Gupta's identity. In contrast to Kauṭilya, his emotions are stronger than his calculating mind.

RĀKSHASA Śakaṭa Dāsa, dear friend, what have I to thank for this happiness?

ŚAKAṬA DĀSA [*indicating Siddhārthaka*] My dear friend Siddhārthaka here frightened off the executioners and rescued me from the Execution Ground.

RĀKSHASA [*joyfully*] Good Siddhārthaka, this is nothing, I know, for such a service, but take it. [*He removes Malaya Ketu's decorations from his body and offers them.*]

SIDDHĀRTHAKA [*taking them and going down on his knees, to himself*] My master Kauṭilya has given me my instructions: I will carry them out. [*Aloud*] Minister, I am a newcomer here, and I don't know anyone I would be happy to entrust with your generous gift. May I seal it with this signet-ring and deposit it in your Honour's own strong-room? Then I can take it when I have need of it.

RĀKSHASA My dear man, why not? See to it, Śakaṭa Dāsa.

ŚAKAṬA DĀSA Yes, sir. [*Looking at the signet-ring, aside*] This signet-ring has Your Honour's name engraved on it.

RĀKSHASA [*looking at it, to himself*] So it has. My wife took this ring from my finger as a keepsake when I was leaving the city. How has it fallen into his hands? [*Aloud*] Siddhārthaka, my dear fellow, where did you get this from?

SIDDHĀRTHAKA Minister, there is a master-jeweller called Chandanadāsa in Pāṭaliputra, and I found it lying at the gate of his house.

RĀKSHASA That certainly fits.

SIDDHĀRTHAKA What fits, Minister?

RĀKSHASA Finding such a thing lying at the gate of such a rich man's house.

ŚAKAṬA DĀSA Siddhārthaka, my friend, the ring has the Minister's name engraved on it, and he will give you much more than it is worth. So let him have it.

SIDDHĀRTHAKA I shall be well rewarded, Minister, if you will do me the honour of accepting it. [*He hands over the ring.*]

RĀKSHASA Use this ring, Śakaṭa Dāsa, in your administrative duties.

ŚAKAṬA DĀSA Yes, sir.

SIDDHĀRTHAKA May I say something, sir?

RĀKSHASA Speak freely.

SIDDHĀRTHAKA Your Honour knows that as one who has given offence to Kauṭilya I cannot return to Pāṭaliputra. I should like to enter your Honour's service if your Honour would be so kind.

RĀKSHASA My dear man, I should be delighted. I did not know how you would feel about it, or I should have had the politeness to ask you myself. Let it be so.

SIDDHĀRTHAKA [*delighted*] I am honoured.

RĀKSHASA Śakaṭa Dāsa, my friend, see that Siddhārthaka is made comfortable.

ŚAKAṬA DĀSA Yes, sir.

[*He goes out with Siddhārthaka.*]

RĀKSHASA And now dear Virādha Gupta, the rest of the news from the city. Are Chandra Gupta's subjects responding to our overtures?

VIRĀDHA GUPTA Indeed they are, sir. In fact they are increasingly coming over to our side.

RĀKSHASA Why is that, my friend?

VIRĀDHA GUPTA Ever since Malaya Ketu's escape, Chandra Gupta has been putting pressure on Kauṭilya, and Kauṭilya, flushed with success, has increased

Chandra Gupta's irritation by defying him on a number of occasions. This is something I myself can confirm.

RĀKSHASA [*delighted*] Virādha Gupta, my friend, keep your disguise as a snake-charmer and go back to Pāṭaliputra. I have a good friend called Stanakalaśa living there disguised as a bard. Tell him in my name that when Kauṭilya defies Chandra Gupta's commands, he should address the Emperor in stanzas calculated to inflame him further. And he should report progress very discreetly via Karabhaka.

VIRĀDHA GUPTA As you command, Minister. [*He goes out.*]

[*Enter the manservant.*]

MANSERVANT Victory to you, sir. Śakaṭa Dāsa begs to say that these three ornaments are being offered for sale, and would you examine them.

RĀKSHASA [*looking at them, to himself*] Why, what valuable jewels! [*Aloud*] Tell Śakaṭa Dāsa to give the trader a good price for them and accept them.

MANSERVANT Yes, sir. [*He goes out.*]

RĀKSHASA [*to himself*] I must send Karabhaka to Pāṭaliputra. [*Getting up*] Ah, if Chandra Gupta can just be split from the cursed Kauṭilya! But I see that the thing has been done for me –

The Mauryan is supreme ruler of all the monarchs of the earth,
And Kauṭilya swells with pride at having made him so.
One has achieved his kingly ambitions, the other has fulfilled his vow:
Success in itself will be enough to break their friendship.

[*All withdraw.*]

Act III

[*Enter a chamberlain.*]

CHAMBERLAIN

1 It was the use of my senses that gave you birth,
But now my senses are dull and tell me little,
While my limbs that were your servants have lost their cunning:
Desire, old age has beaten you and you repine in vain.

[*Walking about, and addressing the air*] Ho there, officials of the River Palace! His Majesty the Emperor Chandra Gupta of auspicious name has declared his intention of enjoying the spectacle of the city celebrating the Full Moon Festival, and desires that the upper terrace of the Palace be made ready for him to watch from. [*Listening*] What's that you say? Does His Majesty not know that the Full Moon Festival has been cancelled? Doomed fools! Such talk will cost you your lives. Quick now,

2 Let yaktail plumes lustrous as moonbeams be massed
About pillars fragrant with incense and wreathed in garlands.
Too long the earth has languished beneath a heavy throne:
Revive it with flower-strewn water of sandalwood.

[*Addressing the air*] What do you say? 'At once, sir!' Well, be quick, be quick. Here comes His Majesty the Emperor:

3 The heavy yoke his elder bore so long and confidently,

Trained in the task, surefooted in the roughest ground,
He is resolved to bear aloft now in his time of youth,
And though new to the yoke and headstrong, he does not stumble or feel distress.

VOICE OF FEMALE GUARD OFF-STAGE This way, sire, this way.

[*Enter the Emperor and a female guard.*]

FMPEROR [*to himself*] A kingdom brings little pleasure if the king is intent on doing his duty.

In seeing to others' interests a king loses sight of his own. 4
And a sovereign whose interests are unregarded is surely no sovereign.
For if he puts another's good before his, why, he is in bondage.
And how is a man in bondage to know what pleasure means?

And even where a king is his own master, success is a hard mistress:

If he is stern, she recoils; if he is mild, she fears contempt and shuns him. 5
Fools she can't stand, yet never loves the over-learned.
A hero she is afraid of, a coward she despises –
Success is as hard to please as a capricious whore.

And now my revered preceptor tells me I must pretend to quarrel with him and rule for a time on my own account. I have agreed reluctantly, as to something sinful. And yet I *have* always ruled by myself, while his guidance has illuminated all my decisions.

While he acts well, a pupil is never checked: 6
It is when his wits go wandering that he feels the goad.

And therefore, self-disciplined, the good are never curbed,
For they never wish to stray beyond the limits of their independence.

[*Aloud*] Noble Vaihīnari, lead me to the River Palace.

CHAMBERLAIN This way, sire.

[*They walk about.*]

CHAMBERLAIN Here is the River Palace, Your Majesty. Have a care as you ascend.

EMPEROR [*acting the ascent and gazing at the heavens*] How lovely the skies are in the rich splendour of autumn:

7 Now they are calm, with sandbanks of scattered cloud,
And strewn with flocks of softly calling cranes.
At night they fill with stars like blossoming waterlilies:
The skies are like rivers flowing away into the distance.

8 The rains are gone, and autumn corrects the world,
Teaching the swollen waters their proper limits,
Making the rice bow down in its time of richness,
Drawing from peacocks like venom their fierce passion.

9 Though Gangā was swollen with rage at her faithless spouse,
Autumn has brought her back to her true self,
And like a go-between skilled in love's adventures
Has led her sweet and calm to her lord the Ocean.

[*Looking all around*] What is this? Is the city not celebrating the Full Moon Festival? Vaihīnari, was my proclamation of a holiday made known in the city?

CHAMBERLAIN Assuredly, sire. On your Majesty's orders a Full Moon Festival was proclaimed in Pāṭaliputra.

EMPEROR Then have the citizens rejected my orders, sir?

CHAMBERLAIN [*stopping his ears*] Perish the thought, sire! Till now Your Majesty's command has prevailed throughout the earth: could it fail among your own citizens?

EMPEROR In that case, sir, why do I see even now no sign of holiday-making in the city?

The streets are not thronged with harlots, broad-hipped and walking slow,
Pursued by rakes that flirt and joke with them.
Nor have the solider citizens, vying with each other in the splendour of their houses,
Put aside cares to enjoy with their wives the longed-for holiday.

CHAMBERLAIN The fact is, sire . . .

EMPEROR Is what?

CHAMBERLAIN It's this.

EMPEROR Speak out, sir.

CHAMBERLAIN The Full Moon Festival has been cancelled, Your Majesty.

EMPEROR [*angrily*] What! By whom?

CHAMBERLAIN I can tell Your Majesty no more than that.

EMPEROR Can the revered Kauṭilya have robbed us of this beautiful spectacle?

CHAMBERLAIN Sire, who else who valued his life would dare transgress Your Majesty's orders?

EMPEROR Śoṇottarā, a seat.

FEMALE GUARD Here is the throne, sire: be seated.

KING [*sitting*] Vaihīnari, I wish to see the revered Kauṭilya.

CHAMBERLAIN Yes, Your Majesty. [*He goes out.*]

[*Enter in angry thought, seated and in his house, Kauṭilya.*]

KAUṬILYA [*to himself*] Does the wretched Rākshasa dare fight me?

11 He thinks that, as Kauṭilya left the city like a wounded snake
Then slew the Nandas and made the Mauryan king,
He in his turn can dim the light of this Mauryan moon –
He is determined to be cleverer than I!

[*Gazing into the air as if he could see him*] Rākshasa, Rākshasa, give up this obstinate attempt.

12 Chandra Gupta is no Nanda,
Ruling arrogantly with the aid of incompetent ministers,
And you are no Kauṭilya – the comparison holds
In one point alone, in our hatred of the ruler.

[*On reflection*] But I need not be too concerned.

13 My agents are all about Parvataka's son, and waiting for their chance;
Siddhārthaka and other spies are working keenly at their tasks.
Now I shall feign a quarrel with the King, and use my talents
To split off his opponent from mine.

[*Enter the Chamberlain.*]

CHAMBERLAIN It is hard to be in service!

14 One has the King to fear, his ministers, his favourites,
And all the court parasites that have chanced to catch his ear.

The obsequious fawning, the struggling for scraps –
'A dog's life' is just the name for such degrading service.

[*Walking about and looking*] Here is the revered Kauṭilya's house. I'll go in. [*Entering and looking*] Why, this man, minister of the King of Kings, lives in extraordinary luxury! –

Here is a piece of stone for breaking cow-dung, 15
Here is a heap of grass collected by his pupils for the sacrifice.
And the house itself, I can see, is broken-walled,
For the drying firewood makes the gables sag.

No wonder that His Majesty Chandra Gupta is simply 'Vrishala' to him.

When even honest, clever men, ignobly eloquent, 16
Praise a king for non-existent virtues till their jaws break,
It shows what power greed has – for otherwise
In their indifference they would treat him as a wisp of straw.

[*Looking, in awe*] Oh, here he is, Kauṭilya –

Who vanquished the world, and ordained with no pause between 17
The setting of Nanda and the rise of the Mauryan king.
His splendour outshines the splendour of the shining sun,
Which must shift its realm and vary heat with cold.

[*Falling on his knees to the ground*] Victory to Your Honour!

KAUṬILYA [*seeing him*] Vaihīnari, what brings you here?

CHAMBERLAIN Sir, His Majesty the Emperor Chandra

Gupta, whose feet are dappled by the light of jewels in the crowns of princes that bow down in homage to him, worships at Your Honour's feet and begs to say that he would like to see you at the earliest moment convenient to yourself.

KAUṬILYA Vrishala wants to see me? Can it be, Vaihīnari, that my cancellation of the Full Moon Festival has come to his ears?

CHAMBERLAIN It has, my lord.

KAUṬILYA [*angrily*] Ha! Who told him?

CHAMBERLAIN [*terrified*] May it please Your Honour, His Majesty observed for himself from the River Palace that Pāṭaliputra was not celebrating the Festival.

KAUṬILYA I see! Whereupon in my absence you inflamed Vrishala against me. Of course!

[*The Chamberlain stands in terrified silence with face bent down.*]

How the Court loves to see Kauṭilya in disgrace! Where is Vrishala?

CHAMBERLAIN His Majesty was in the River Palace when he sent me to Your Honour.

KAUṬILYA [*rising*] Conduct me there.

CHAMBERLAIN This way, my lord.

[*Both walk about.*]

CHAMBERLAIN Here is the River Palace. Have a care, my lord, as you ascend.

KAUṬILYA [*ascending and looking, with pleasure to himself*] Ah, Vrishala is seated on the throne! That is well.

18 The throne is rid of Nandas, who took no thought of
their duty,
And occupied by Vrishala, Bull* of Kings.

*Play upon *Vrishala* and *vrisha*, 'bull'.

At last it is graced by a monarch worthy of it.
This threefold good thrice multiplies my joy.

[*Approaching*] Victory to you, Vrishala.

EMPEROR [*rising from his throne and clasping Kauṭilya's feet*] Chandra Gupta salutes you, sir.

KAUṬILYA [*taking him by the hand*] Rise, dear child, rise.

From Himālaya, cooled by the Sacred River's spray, 19
To the shore of the southern ocean, lit by its jewels of many flashing hues,
May awestruck princes come to do you homage in their hundreds,
Forever bathing your feet in the jewelled radiance of their crowns.

EMPEROR By Your Honour's favour the wish is already granted. Let Your Honour be seated.

[*Both sit in their respective seats.*]

KAUṬILYA Why did you summon me, Vrishala?

EMPEROR To favour myself with your sight.

KAUṬILYA [*smiling grimly*] Enough of these courtesies. Masters do not summon their stewards without a reason. Let me know the reason.

EMPEROR What good does Your Honour see in cancelling the Full Moon Festival?

KAUṬILYA [*again smiling grimly*] So Vrishala, I have been summoned to be reprimanded!

EMPEROR Not to be reprimanded, no.

KAUṬILYA What, then?

EMPEROR To be questioned politely.

KAUṬILYA In that case, Vrishala, the whims of those he must 'question politely' are surely bound to be respected by a pupil?

EMPEROR Of course they are, sir. But the fact that Your Honour's whim could never operate without a motive gives me some excuse for my question.

KAUṬILYA You understand well, Vrishala – even in dreams my actions are always motivated.

EMPEROR And it is my wish to know your motive which makes me so persistent.

KAUṬILYA Listen, Vrishala. Textbooks on statecraft distinguish three types of government – monarchical, or ministerial, or monarchical and ministerial. You have a ministerial government – no need to tire your tongue and brain with searching after reasons: that is *my* job.

[*The Emperor turns away his face in a show of anger.*]

[*Off-stage two bards recite.*]

FIRST BARD

20 As the sky is lit with an ash whiter than kāśa down,
And moonbeams banish the elephant grey of rainclouds,
Dressed in bright moonlight like a garlanding of skulls,
With a smile of geese in flight may autumn like Śiva
ease your cares.

21 When in the first moment he screws his face against the
brightness of the jewel-lamps,
While body-racking yawns bring tears to his languorous
eyes,
And he makes to rise from his broad serpent's couch,
where his pillow is the serpent's hood,
May Vishnu's glance still dazed and red with sleep be
your salvation.

SECOND BARD

22 Some men for some reason the Creator has filled with
his glory,

To outshine in power the rutting lords of the herd.
As is the breaking of his fang to the fierce pride of the king of beasts,
So is the breaking of his command to a monarch of the earth, great king, like you.

It is not luxury and pomp 23
That make a king a king.
It is when his orders are never disobeyed
That he has earned a title such as yours.

KAUṬILYA [*listening, to himself*] The earlier recitation was a blessing, and described the present season of autumn in terms of a particular god – but what is the point of the other? [*On reflection*] Ah, I see! This is Rākshasa's doing. Villain, you are detected! Kauṭilya is awake.

EMPEROR Vaihīnari, give these bards a hundred thousand gold pieces.

CHAMBERLAIN Yes, Your Majesty. [*He gets up and moves away.*]

KAUṬILYA [*angrily*] One moment, Vaihīnari, one moment – don't go. Vrishala, what is this ludicrous piece of extravagance?

EMPEROR If you are going to thwart my every action like this, sir, it will make me feel more like a prisoner than a king.

KAUṬILYA A natural affliction for a king that does not see to his own affairs. If you don't like it, do the job yourself.

EMPEROR That is exactly what I am doing now.

KAUṬILYA Excellent! And I shall do my job.

EMPEROR Then tell me why you should want to cancel the Full Moon Festival.

KAUṬILYA You just tell me why you should want to celebrate it?

EMPEROR To see my command obeyed, for a start.

KAUṬILYA And for a start I want it cancelled to see your command *dis*obeyed –

24 As far as the ocean's edge where the jungle is dark with flowering blackwood
And the waters teem with darting whale,
Your command is worn like an ever-blooming garland by countless princes:
That it cannot encompass *me* gives a becoming modesty to your kingship.

EMPEROR And what other reason have you?

KAUṬILYA I will tell you.

EMPEROR Do so.

KAUṬILYA Śoṇottarā, tell Achala the letter-writer that I should like to have that list of Bhadra Bhaṭa and the others.

FEMALE GUARD Yes, Your Honour. [*Going out and returning*] Here is the list, Your Honour.

KAUṬILYA [*taking it*] Hear this, Vrishala.

EMPEROR I am listening.

KAUṬILYA [*reads out*] 'A list of eminent associates of His Majesty the Emperor Chandra Gupta who have defected to Malaya Ketu:

(1) Bhadra Bhaṭa, superintendent of elephants
(2) Purusha Datta, superintendent of horse
(3) Hingu Rāta, nephew of Chandra Bhānu, the Chief Equerry
(4) Prince Bala Gupta, His Majesty's connection by marriage
(5) Rājasena, His Majesty's own former tutor

(6) Bhāgurāyaṇa, younger brother of General Siṃhala
(7) Rohitāksha, son of the King of Malwa
(8) Vijaya Varman, head of a warrior family.'

EMPEROR I should like to know their reasons for defection.

KAUṬILYA Then listen: Bhadra Bhaṭa and Purusha Datta, the superintendent of elephant and horse, were given over to women, drinking and hunting, neglected their duties and accordingly were removed from their posts by me and put on subsistence pay. In their indignation they have now defected to Malaya Ketu, each to serve in his own capacity.

As for Hingu Rāta and Bala Gupta, being excessively greedy they were dissatisfied with the pay they got from you and defected to Malaya Ketu in the expectation of greater rewards.

Your old tutor Rājasena by your favour found himself in sudden possession of vast resources of money, elephants and horses. He defected for fear of being deprived of this wealth with equal abruptness.

General Siṃhala's younger brother Bhāgurāyaṇa was very close to King Parvataka, and on the strength of this he told Malaya Ketu some tale of my being responsible for his father's death, and got him away from the city. Later when other malefactors such as Chandanadāsa were being arrested for treason against you, the guilty knowledge of his own offence led him to defect to Malaya Ketu, who in gratitude to him for saving his life and in memory of his friendship with his father, has admitted him to his closest personal counsels.

Finally Rohitāksha and Vijaya Varman defected because in their vanity they could not bear your awarding equal shares to their kinsmen. Those were the motives for the various defections.

EMPEROR Why, sir, did you not take action against them at once, knowing those motives?

KAUṬILYA I could not, Vrishala.

EMPEROR You mean you lacked the skill, or you had some reason?

KAUṬILYA How could I lack the skill? I had a reason, of course.

EMPEROR Then I should like to hear what this reason can have been for your failing to take action.

KAUṬILYA Hear what I have to say, my child, and mark it well.

EMPEROR I am doing both. Continue.

KAUṬILYA There are two kinds of action, Vrishala, that one can take against subjects with a grievance – reward them, or punish them. We will take reward first. In the case of Bhadra Bhaṭa and Purusha Datta, dismissed from their posts, this would have meant reinstating them. And to reinstate men whom their vices have made so incompetent would be to strike at the very foundations of government, our forces of elephant and horse. Rewarding Hingu Rāta or Bala Gupta was an impossibility – they were so greedy that giving them the whole empire would not have satisfied them. Rewarding Rājasena or Bhāgurāyaṇa would have been an irrelevance: they were afraid, one of losing his wealth, the other of losing his life. And if Rohitāksha and Vijaya Varman were so vain that having the same share as their kinsmen vexed them, what reward would have been big enough to give them positive pleasure? So the former alternative was ruled out.

But so was the latter. If we who have just taken over

power from the Nandas start severely punishing our own most prominent supporters, how could we avoid losing the confidence of citizens who previously supported the House of Nanda? Thus Malaya Ketu has acquired these former servants of ours. He lends an ear to Rākshasa's schemes. He has the large forces of the barbarian chieftains to support him. He is incensed at his father Parvataka's murder. And he is poised to attack us. This is a time for work, not play. What place has a Full Moon Festival, when we should be looking to our defences? There you have the reason why I cancelled it.

EMPEROR There is much, sir, to question in this.

KAUṬILYA Question away, Vrishala. I have much to reply.

EMPEROR Then I will ask.

KAUṬILYA And I will answer.

EMPEROR Malaya Ketu, the cause of all the trouble – why did you let him get away?

KAUṬILYA If I had not let him get away, Vrishala, I could have done one of two things: suppress him, or give him half the empire as promised. By suppressing him we would have put our signatures to a confession that we treacherously murdered Parvataka. By giving him half the empire, we should have avoided the charge of treachery but gained nothing else. And that is why I let Malaya Ketu get away.

EMPEROR Granted that is so, sir; but you also let Rākshasa himself go on living here right in the heart of the city. What answer have you to that?

KAUṬILYA Rākshasa had the full confidence of the citizens that supported Nanda: they knew his character through his steadfast devotion to his master and through his staying with them for so long. He had brains and courage, a wealth of allies, plenty of money. If he had gone on living here he would have stirred up a lot of internal disorder. But if removed to a distance, though he might stir up external disorders he would not be difficult to deal with. These were my reasons for letting him escape.

EMPEROR Why did you not find means to defeat him while he was still here?

KAUṬILYA Isn't that what I did? I found the means to pluck him out like a rankling dart and remove him to a distance – and I've already told you why he had to be removed.

EMPEROR But why not have seized him by force?

KAUṬILYA Vrishala, you are speaking of Rākshasa. If he had been seized by force, either he would have died himself or he would have destroyed your forces. Either way it would have been a misfortune.

25 If such a competent minister had perished,
You, Vrishala, would have lost a great man.
If he had killed the flower of your forces, an equal blow.
He had, then, to be managed like a wild elephant, with cunning.

EMPEROR I cannot defeat you in argument, sir, but at all events it is Minister Rākshasa whom one must admire.

KAUṬILYA [*angrily*] Rather than me, you mean? Never! Vrishala, what has he done?

EMPEROR I'll tell you, if you don't know. That great man

26 When the city was taken, stayed as long as he liked, putting his foot on our neck;
He created resistance to our army – for instance in the victory-proclamation;

And by a wealth of strategems he has so bemused our wits
That we don't trust even our loyalest supporters.

KAUṬILYA [*with a laugh*] So, Vrishala, that is what Rākshasa has done?

EMPEROR Yes.

KAUṬILYA I really thought he must have overthrown you and crowned Malaya Ketu Emperor of the World, as I overthrew Nanda and crowned you.

EMPEROR That was another's doing – what did it have to do with you?

KAUṬILYA Oh envious one!

Who was it loosed his top-knot with fingers that shook with rage 27
And swore before the world the long and dreadful oath to kill the whole race of his foes?
Who took the proud Nandas, owners of wealth untold,
And slew them one by one like sacrificial beasts, under the very eyes of Rākshasa?

With a ring of vultures slowly wheeling in the sky above, 28
And smoke that kills the sunlight and clouds the heavens,
Look, the funeral fires still burn with a reek of melting fat,
Delighting the beasts that prowl in the Nandas' cemetery.

EMPEROR That was the doing of Destiny that hated the Nandas.

KAUṬILYA The stupid always appeal to Destiny.

EMPEROR While the wise are duly modest.

KAUṬILYA [*showing anger*] Vrishala, you want to degrade me to a servant!

29 This hand flies to loose my bound hair yet again.
[*Stamping the ground with his foot.*]
This foot runs to embrace my vow again.
My wrath was extinguished when the Nandas were destroyed,
But you, doomed fool, are kindling it again.

EMPEROR [*in alarm, to himself*] What, can His Honour be genuinely angry?

30 Though tears of emotion from his quivering eyelids seek to quench it,
The tawny blaze of his eyes bursts into flame beneath his smoking brow.
And as if remembering Śiva in his Terror Dance,
The earth trembles violently and scarcely bears the stamping of his foot.

KAUṬILYA [*checking his show of anger*] Vrishala, enough of recriminations. If you respect Rākshasa more than me, here, let him have my sword of office. [*Relinquishing his sword and rising; then to himself, gazing into the air as if he could see him*] Rākshasa, Rākshasa, so much for your superior wisdom, which you hope will defeat me!

31 'When the Mauryan loses the loyalty of Kauṭilya,'
You tell yourself, 'I can beat him easily.'
Well, here is the split between us that you planned,
But it will only redound to your own undoing.

[*He goes out.*]

EMPEROR Vaihīnari, let the people be told that from now on the Emperor will administer the affairs of state in person, without reference to Kauṭilya.

CHAMBERLAIN [*to himself*] Plain 'Kauṭilya', with no

title of honour? Alas, he really has been dismissed. But in truth I cannot blame His Majesty for this.

It is the minister's fault 32
If the king acts ill,
As it is the driver's incompetence
That makes a rogue elephant.

EMPEROR What is keeping you, sir?

CHAMBERLAIN Nothing, Your Majesty. I was only thinking how glad I am that Your Majesty has now become a true king.

EMPEROR [*to himself*] While they view me in this light, let His Honour achieve the success he wants. [*Aloud*] This arid dispute has given me a headache, Śoṇottarā. Conduct me to my bedchamber.

PORTERESS This way, sire.

EMPEROR [*rising from his throne, to himself*]

At his own bidding I have slighted my teacher, 33
And I feel that I want to sink into the ground.
When others commit such impiety in earnest
Why do their hearts not split in two with shame?

[*All go out.*]

Act IV

[*Enter someone dressed as a traveller.*]

TRAVELLER Oh heavens above!

A thousand miles or more there and back! 1
Who would ever make such journeys? –
Except when his master's orders
Mean more than the discomfort of travel.

So now I have to call on Minister Rākshasa. [*Walking about wearily*] Here is my master the Minister Rākshasa's house. Ho there, doormen! Tell your master that Karabhaka has come like a camel* from Pāṭaliputra!

[*Enter a doorkeeper.*]

DOORKEEPER Hey, good sir, not so loud! Our master Minister Rākshasa has a headache brought on by overwork and insomnia, and he hasn't yet left his bed. Wait a minute while I pick the right moment to let him know you've come.

TRAVELLER Right you are, then.

[*Enter, in his bed with Śakaṭa Dāsa seated beside him, Rākshasa, careworn.*]

RĀKSHASA [*to himself*]

2 When I think how little Fate has been my ally in the struggle
And how devious has been the plotting of Kauṭilya,
For all my successful winning of his subordinates,
My nights pass in sleepless bewilderment.

3 Contriving the first faint outlines of a plot, and then elaborating,
Causing the hidden seeds to germinate unsuspected,
Cleverly managing the crisis, drawing together all the sprawling threads –
In these painful anxieties of creation I am working like a playwright.

I pray then that Kauṭilya may know –

DOORKEEPER [*approaching*] Victory –

RĀKSHASA – the bitterness of defeat!

*His name Karabhaka itself means 'camel'.

DOORKEEPER – be yours, Minister!

RĀKSHASA [*indicating an inauspicious throbbing of his left eye, to himself*] Must Kauṭilya, then, know victory, and the bitterness of defeat be mine? [*Aloud*] What do you want to tell me?

DOORKEEPER Minister, Karabhaka has arrived from Pāṭaliputra and is asking to see you.

RĀKSHASA Show him in at once.

DOORKEEPER Yes, sir. [*Withdrawing and approaching the traveller*] There is the Minister, friend. You may approach him. [*He goes out.*]

KARABHAKA [*going up to Rākshasa*] Victory, sir, victory!

RĀKSHASA [*seeing him*] Good Karabhaka, welcome! Sit down.

KARABHAKA Yes, sir. [*He seats himself on the floor.*]

RĀKSHASA [*to himself*] I have so many affairs on hand I can't remember what it was I sent this agent to do. [*He acts anxious thought.*]

[*Enter a man bearing an official staff.*]

MAN Make way, sirs, make way! Be off, you people, be off! Do you not realize –

Like the fair lords of the heavens, 4
The fair lords of this world
Are hard for those less fortunate
Even to see, let alone come near to.

[*Addressing the air*] What's that you say, sirs? Why are we clearing the road? Sirs, His Highness Prince Malaya Ketu is coming this way, to see Minister Rākshasa, having heard that he has a headache. That's why we're clearing the road. [*He goes out.*]

[*Enter with Bhāgurāyaṇa and attended by his Chamberlain, Malaya Ketu.*]

MALAYA KETU [*with a sigh, to himself*] It's ten months now since father died, and in a vain act of manly pride I have not offered even a handful of water in his memory. I have sworn an oath that first

5 My enemies' wives shall beat their breasts till their bangles break and their garments fall apart,
Piteous in their cries of woe, dust roughening their hair,
And they shall know all the grief my mother knows
Before I make the offering of water to my sire.

In short

6 I must bear the hero's yoke,
And either tread my father's fatal path in battle
Or snatch the tears from my mother's eyes
And put them in the eyes of the enemy's womenfolk.

[*Aloud*] Noble Jājali, tell the princes in my name that I want to go on alone and give Minister Rākshasa the pleasure of a surprise visit. So they need not trouble to attend me.

CHAMBERLAIN Yes, Your Highness. [*Walking about and addressing the air*] Princes! His Highness states that he does not wish you to attend him! [*Looking, with pleasure*] See, Your Highness: they have all turned back as soon as they learnt of Your Highness's command –

7 Some, pulling hard on the reins, have checked their steeds,
Which rear with necks arched back, breaking thin air with their hoofs.
Others turn their stately elephants about, bells faltering into silence.

These princes respect your command as the sea respects the shore.

MALAYA KETU Noble Jājali, you too go back with my servants. No one but Bhāgurāyaṇa need attend me.

CHAMBERLAIN Certainly, Your Highness.

[*He goes out with the servants.*]

MALAYA KETU Bhāgurāyaṇa, my friend, when Bhadra Bhaṭa and his companions arrived here, they said to me, 'We are not seeking asylum with Your Highness through Minister Rākshasa: it was Your Highness's general Śikharasena who, when we sickened of seeing Chandra Gupta in the clutches of an evil minister, enabled us to take refuge with Your Highness, as your amiable qualities had made us long to do.' I have been turning their words over in my mind for a long time, but I can't decide what they were getting at.

BHĀGURĀYAṆA It is simple enough, Your Highness. It is natural surely to wish to turn to a master who is both determined and talented, and to do so through a dear and good friend of that master.

MALAYA KETU But Bhāgurāyaṇa, Minister Rākshasa himself is the dearest and best of friends.

BHĀGURĀYAṆA No doubt, Your Highness. But their reasoning is as follows. Minister Rākshasa is fighting Kauṭilya, not Chandra Gupta. Suppose by some chance Chandra Gupta were to find Kauṭilya's arrogance impossible to bear, and were to dismiss him from his post. Out of his loyalty to the House of Nanda, since Chandra Gupta is after all of Nanda stock, or else for the sake of his friends in prison, Minister Rākshasa might come to terms with Chandra Gupta – who for his part might accept him, as being his minister by family tradition.

Now in such circumstances Your Highness might suspect their own loyalty as well.

MALAYA KETU Yes, I see what you mean. Lead the way to Minister Rākshasa's house.

BHĀGURĀYAṆA This way, Your Highness.

[*They both walk about.*]

BHĀGURĀYAṆA Here is the house. Enter, Your Highness.

MALAYA KETU I do so.

[*They act entering.*]

RĀKSHASA Ah, I remember! [*Aloud*] Did you see Stanakalaśa the bard in Pāṭaliputra, my dear man?

KARABHAKA Certainly, sir.

*

MALAYA KETU Bhāgurāyaṇa, my friend, they are discussing events in Pāṭaliputra. Let's not interrupt, but simply listen.

8 For fear of destroying his resolve
Ministers say one thing to a prince's face,
And quite another when they are speaking freely
And saying what they mean.

BHĀGURĀYAṆA By all means, Your Highness.

*

RĀKSHASA Was your mission successful, my dear man?

KARABHAKA Quite successful, if it pleases Your Honour.

*

MALAYA KETU What mission, Bhāgurāyaṇa?

BHĀGURĀYAṆA A minister's affairs are complicated, Your Highness. This is hardly enough to go on. Just listen attentively.

*

RĀKSHASA Tell me in detail what happened.

KARABHAKA You had instructed me, sir, to go to Pāṭaliputra and tell Stanakalaśa the bard in your name that when the accursed Kauṭilya infringed some command or other of the Emperor he should address inflammatory stanzas to the Emperor.

RĀKSHASA Yes?

KARABHAKA So I went to Pāṭaliputra and gave Stanakalaśa your message, sir.

RĀKSHASA Go on.

KARABHAKA At this point, to dispel the gloom which the destruction of the House of Nanda has cast over the city, Chandra Gupta proclaimed that Pāṭaliputra should celebrate the Full Moon Festival. The return of this Festival after so long an absence delighted the people and they greeted it as affectionately as a long-lost relative.

RĀKSHASA [*weeping*] Alas, Nanda my emperor!

What Full Moon Festival can there be today 9
Though the moon shine never so full?
For it was you, great king,
Who were the full moon of this world.

Go on, my dear fellow, go on.

KARABHAKA Then this glorious spectacle was cancelled by the accursed Kauṭilya against the Emperor's wishes. Upon which Stanakalaśa addressed two inflammatory stanzas to Chandra Gupta. [*He repeats the two stanzas of the Second Bard* (*Act III*, *verses 22 and 23*).]

RĀKSHASA [*delightedly*] Bravo, Stanakalaśa, my friend! This seed of dissension so opportunely sown is sure to bear fruit:

When his pleasure is rudely shattered, 10
Even a common man will not endure it –

What then of emperors, lords of the earth,
Men of no common splendour?

*

MALAYA KETU He is right there.

*

RĀKSHASA And what then?

KARABHAKA Then Chandra Gupta, furious at being disobeyed, praised Your Honour's ability at some length and stripped Kauṭilya of his powers.

*

MALAYA KETU Friend Bhāgurāyaṇa, if he praised his ability, it shows that Chandra Gupta is sympathetic towards Rākshasa.

BHĀGURĀYAṆA Yes, but not so much because he praised him, Your Highness, as because he dismissed Kauṭilya.

*

RĀKSHASA Tell me, was this cancellation of the Festival the sole reason for Chandra Gupta's displeasure at Kauṭilya, or was there something else as well?

*

MALAYA KETU Bhāgurāyaṇa, what point does he see in looking into the reasons for Chandra Gupta's displeasure?

BHĀGURĀYAṆA I will explain, Your Highness. Since Kauṭilya is a sensible man, why should he anger Chandra Gupta over such a trivial matter? And since Chandra Gupta knows what he owes him, why should he offer Kauṭilya disrespect just over this? At all events if there is rich cause for their estrangement, it will then be lasting.

*

KARABHAKA Yes, Minister, Chandra Gupta does have other grievances against Kauṭilya. He allowed Prince Malaya Ketu and yourself to escape.

RĀKSHASA [*delightedly*] Dear Śakaṭa Dāsa, now I know I have Chandra Gupta in the palm of my hand! This means Chandanadāsa's release from prison, and your own reunion with your wife and children.

*

MALAYA KETU What does he mean, Bhāgurāyaṇa – he has Chandra Gupta in the palm of his hand?

BHĀGURĀYAṆA He must think it will be easier to defeat Chandra Gupta now that he is without Kauṭilya, Your Highness – I'm sure it can't be anything else.

*

RĀKSHASA Now the fellow's lost his post, where is he?

KARABHAKA He is still living in Pāṭaliputra, sir.

RĀKSHASA [*in disquiet*] Still living there? Hasn't he retired to a hermitage, or sworn a second oath?

KARABHAKA It's said, sir, that he is going to retire to a hermitage.

RĀKSHASA [*still disquieted*] Śakaṭa Dāsa, this doesn't make sense:

How can he, who could not endure the insult of dismissal 11
By His Majesty the Emperor Nanda, god on earth,
Possibly in his arrogance endure this slight
From the Mauryan, the king that he himself has made?

*

MALAYA KETU Bhāgurāyaṇa, how will it help him if Kauṭilya retires to a hermitage or enters on a second vow?

BHĀGURĀYAṆA Simple enough, Your Highness. Anything will help him that keeps Kauṭilya away from Chandra Gupta.

*

ŚAKAṬA DĀSA Do not trouble yourself, Minister: it does make sense. Consider –

12 Now that the Mauryan has set his foot upon the gleaming crowns of princes,
He will never let one of his own people flout his rule,
And Kauṭilya, even in his anger recalling the painful discipline of a vow,
Having been lucky once will not risk a future failure.

RĀKSHASA Yes you are right, Śakaṭa Dāsa. Go, then, and see that Karabhaka is made comfortable.

ŚAKAṬA DĀSA Certainly, Minister.

[*He goes out with Karabhaka.*]

RĀKSHASA And I must go to see His Highness.

MALAYA KETU Here I am, sir, come to see you.

RĀKSHASA [*seeing him*] Oh, Your Highness! [*Rising from his seat*] Here, please be seated, Your Highness.

MALAYA KETU Thank you. Be seated yourself, sir.

[*They sit in their respective seats.*]

Is your headache better, my lord?

RĀKSHASA How could it be so until Your Highness's title of Prince is eclipsed by the title of Emperor?

MALAYA KETU Since you have engaged on the task, sir, that will not be difficult of fulfilment. How long must we sit passively with our forces massed in this way, watching for a deficiency in the enemy?

RĀKSHASA Why delay a moment longer, Your Highness? Set out to victory.

MALAYA KETU Have we found a deficiency in the enemy, sir?

RĀKSHASA Most certainly we have, Your Highness.

MALAYA KETU What?

RĀKSHASA No less than a deficiency in ministers! Chandra Gupta has fallen out with Kauṭilya.

MALAYA KETU A deficiency in ministers, sir, is no deficiency.

RĀKSHASA In the case of other kings, Your Highness, that may be true, but not in Chandra Gupta's case.

MALAYA KETU Surely particularly in Chandra Gupta's case?

RĀKSHASA Why so?

MALAYA KETU It is Kauṭilya's faults which have made Chandra Gupta's subjects disloyal. With Kauṭilya out of the way, his subjects, already loyal to him, will now display more loyalty than ever.

RĀKSHASA That is not so, Your Highness. His subjects are of two kinds: those who helped him to power and those who are loyal to the Nandas. Kauṭilya's faults have been estranging his own supporters, not those who are loyal to the Nandas. The latter are bitterly hostile and resentful at Chandra Gupta's treachery in destroying the House of Nanda, his own father's family, and they have accepted him only because they have no one else to turn to. But with a champion like yourself that they can rely on to defeat the enemy, they are rapidly leaving him and coming over to you – as Your Highness may judge from my own case.

MALAYA KETU Is this deficiency in ministers the one and only reason for attack, or is there something else?

RĀKSHASA It doesn't matter how many others there might be, Your Highness. This is the one that counts.

MALAYA KETU Why is it the one that counts, sir? Is Chandra Gupta incapable of entrusting the administration of his empire to another minister or of taking it on his own shoulders and meeting our challenge on his own?

RĀKSHASA Quite incapable.

MALAYA KETU Why?

RĀKSHASA Such a course is open to kings whose government is either monarchical or monarchical and ministerial. But the wretched Chandra Gupta has always depended on a totally ministerial government, and sees no further than a blind man into the workings of the administration: what resistance can he possibly offer us on his own?

13 An inexperienced king torn from his minister
Is like a babe in arms snatched from the breast.
Confused and knowing nothing of the world around him,
He cannot manage by himself for a single moment.

MALAYA KETU [*to himself*] How lucky that mine is not a ministerial government! [*Aloud*] Even so, sir, the success of an attacker who is concentrating on the enemy's ministerial deficiency will obviously be more complete when there are a good many reasons for attacking.

RĀKSHASA Your Highness may count on a truly complete success:

14 With yourself at the head of a mighty force and the city loyal to Nanda,
With Kauṭilya dismissed and estranged, and the Mauryan a fledgling king,
With myself free to act at last –
[*Breaking off modestly*]
as your counsellor, pointing out your path,

Our success waits now, sire, only on your word of command.

MALAYA KETU If you think it is the moment to attack, sir, let's not delay:

Lofty as its lofty sides, rut flowing down into its flowing stream, 15
Dark as its bordering woods, with bees to match the murmuring of its ripples,
Their tusks attacking from above the banks that the current strikes at from below,
My elephants, vermilion-red, shall churn the Red River's waters.*

With a deep roaring and a spewing forth 16
Of showers of water mixed with their own ichor,
Like thunder-clouds beating upon the Vindhyas
My troops of elephants shall storm Pāṭaliputra.

[*He goes out with Bhāgurāyaṇa.*]

RĀKSHASA Hallo, hallo, there!

SERVANT [*entering*] Command me, sir.

RĀKSHASA Priyamvadaka, find out what astrologers are available.

PRIYAMVADAKA Yes, sir. [*Going out and returning*] I've found an astrologer, sir, the Jain monk –

RĀKSHASA [*to himself, indicating an ill omen*] Oh, and the first thing is a Jain monk!

PRIYAMVADAKA – called Jīva Siddhi, sir.

*The Red River is a tributary which joins the Ganges from the south west just above Pāṭaliputra. The bees as usual are depicted clustering round the elephants for the rut-fluid.

RĀKSHASA [*aloud*] Make him look respectable,* Priyamvadaka, and bring him in.

PRIYAMVADAKA Yes, sir. [*He goes out.*]

[*Enter the Jain monk Jīva Siddhi.*]

JĪVA SIDDHI

17 Follow the teachings of the Sages,
Physicians that treat the sickness of illusion,
Whose medicine at first is bitter
But afterwards will cure.

[*Going up to Rākshasa*] The true faith be yours, brother.

RĀKSHASA Reverend sir, would you please determine for me the auspicious day for setting forth?

JĪVA SIDDHI [*after reflection*] It is determined, brother. The day of the full moon is auspicious and will be wholly favourable to you in the afternoon. And the Lunar Mansion in the south will favour your march from the north.

18 As the Sun sinks to its setting
And the full-orbed Moon rises,
Seize the moment of union with all-powerful Mercury,
When Ketu's brief hour is at an end.

RĀKSHASA The very day is evil, sir!

JĪVA SIDDHI Brother,

19 The day counts as one,
The mansion counts as four,
The juncture counts as sixty-four –
Such is the teaching of astrology.

*Jain monks went about naked, and were regarded as inauspicious (cf. Act I, p. 187).

The juncture with wise Mercury is auspicious. 20
Avoid the ill-omened Ketu.
Long life will be yours
If you go by the Moon.

RĀKSHASA Sir, will you confirm this with other astrologers?

JĪVA SIDDHI Confirm it yourself, brother. I am leaving.

RĀKSHASA You are not angry with me, sir?

JĪVA SIDDHI *I* am not, no.

RĀKSHASA Who, then?

JĪVA SIDDHI Destiny, because you shun what is meant for you, and look for good in the wrong place. [*He goes out.*]

RĀKSHASA Priyamvadaka, find out what hour it is.

PRIYAMVADAKA Yes, sir. [*Going out and returning*] The sun will soon be setting, sir.

RĀKSHASA [*rising from his place and looking*] True, the sun will soon be setting:

Struck by his radiance as he rose at dawn, the trees of the wood 21
Ran eagerly before him to offer him their shade.
But see how they all turn back as his orb sinks westwards:
For a master is ever shunned in his decline by those who served him only with their shadow.

[*All go out.*]

PRELUDE TO ACT V

[*Enter, carrying a letter and a jewel-case, both sealed, Siddhārthaka.*]

SIDDHĀRTHAKA Oh amazing!

1 Nourished by the waters of his wisdom
Streaming from watering-cans of place and time,
Kauṭilya's strategy is a fertile vine
Yielding rich crops of successes.

I have with me the letter originally commissioned by His Honour Kauṭilya but stamped with Minister Rākshasa's own seal – *and* this jewel-case, also stamped with his own seal. And now I must look as if I'm making for Pāṭaliputra. Off I go then. [*Walking about and looking*] Oh, here comes a Jain monk! I must ward off the ill omen by looking at something pure.

[*Enter the Jain monk Jīva Siddhi.*]

JĪVA SIDDHI

2 My salutation to the Sages,
Who by their profound wisdom
Can find satisfaction in this life
By transcendental paths.

SIDDHĀRTHAKA Greetings, reverend sir!

JĪVA SIDDHI The true faith be yours, my brother. [*Scrutinizing him*] I notice, brother, that you seem to be planning some untimely journey.

SIDDHĀRTHAKA How can you tell that, reverend sir?

JĪVA SIDDHI It doesn't need much fathoming, my brother. That bird to give you omens on the road and the letter in your hand, they give the game away.

SIDDHĀRTHAKA Yes, you've guessed the truth, reverend

sir. I'm off to foreign parts. So tell me: what kind of day have I got for it?

JĪVA SIDDHI [*laughing*] What, brother, ask the omens when you've already shaved?

SIDDHĀRTHAKA No harm in it even now, reverend sir. Come, tell me. If it's all right, I'll go. Otherwise I'll turn back.

JĪVA SIDDHI You can't leave Malaya Ketu's camp nowadays, brother, whether the omens are all right or not.

SIDDHĀRTHAKA Why not?

JĪVA SIDDHI I'll tell you. At one time people could come and go at will in this camp. But now we're so near Pāṭaliputra, no one is allowed to go out or come in without a pass. So if you've got a pass stamped by Bhāgurāyaṇa, go with an easy mind. Otherwise turn back and keep quiet – or the guards will tie you hand and foot and march you to the Prince's headquarters.

SIDDHĀRTHAKA Don't you know then, reverend sir, that I'm Siddhārthaka, one of Minister Rākshasa's men? No one has the power to stop me leaving even if I don't have a pass.

JĪVA SIDDHI Rākshasa, goblin or ghost,* it makes no difference. If you haven't got a stamped pass you can't leave.

SIDDHĀRTHAKA Don't be angry with me, reverend sir. Give me good luck on my errand.

JĪVA SIDDHI Go, my brother, and good luck be with you. But speaking for myself, I'm going to ask Bhāgurāyaṇa for a pass.

[*They withdraw.*]

**Rākshasa* means 'demon'.

Act V

[*Enter Bhāgurāyaṇa, attended by a manservant.*]

BHĀGURĀYAṆA [*to himself*] The revered Kauṭilya's strategy is wonderfully various!

3 Sometimes revealed, sometimes buried deep out of sight,
Now complex, now simple, as the task requires,
Now withering in the seed, now bearing rich fruit –
His statecraft is as manifold as destiny.

[*Aloud*] Bhāsvaraka, His Highness wants me to keep near at hand. So put a seat right here in the audience-hall.

MANSERVANT Here is the seat, sir. Be seated.

BHĀGURĀYAṆA [*sitting down*] Show in anyone who wants to see me about a pass.

MANSERVANT Yes, sir. [*He goes out.*]

BHĀGURĀYAṆA [*to himself*] Alas, this Prince Malaya Ketu is so fond of me – it's hard that I have to deceive him! But then

4 When someone has renounced family, shame, honour and reputation,
To sell himself to a rich man, being greedy for a moment's wealth,
When he does that other's bidding, what has he, a mere hireling,
Who has passed beyond problems of right and wrong, to do with such reflections?

[*Enter Malaya Ketu, attended by a female guard.*]

MALAYA KETU [*to himself*] Oh my mind is in such a storm of conflicting thoughts about Rākshasa, I can decide nothing for certain –

His loyalty to the House of Nanda is strong, and the Mauryan is of Nanda's line:
Now that in victory he has rid himself of Kauṭilya, will Rākshasa treat with him?
Or put constancy first and keep his word to me?
My mind is on a potter's wheel, whirling and whirling round.

[*Aloud*] Vijayā, where is Bhāgurāyaṇa?

FEMALE GUARD There he is, Your Highness, seeing to passes for people who want to leave the camp.

MALAYA KETU Tread softly for a moment, Vijayā, and I'll put my hands over his eyes while he's not looking!

FEMALE GUARD Yes, Your Highness.

[*The manservant enters.*]

MANSERVANT Sir, there is a Jain monk who wants to see you about a pass.

BHĀGURĀYAṆA Show him in.

MANSERVANT Yes, sir. [*He goes out.*]

[*Enter Jīva Siddhi.*]

JĪVA SIDDHI The true faith be yours, my brother.

BHĀGURĀYAṆA [*seeing him, to himself*] Why, it's Rākshasa's friend Jīva Siddhi. [*Aloud*] Reverend sir, are you going on some business of Rākshasa's, then?

JĪVA SIDDHI [*stopping his ears*] Perish the thought! I'm going, brother, where I shan't even have to hear his name.

BHĀGURĀYAṆA A quarrel with a friend is particularly bitter. What has Rākshasa done to injure you, reverend sir?

JĪVA SIDDHI Rākshasa's done nothing to injure me, brother. Wretch that I am, I am injuring myself.

BHĀGURĀYAṆA You rouse my curiosity, sir.

MALAYA KETU [*to himself*] And mine.

BHĀGURĀYAṆA I should like to hear more.

MALAYA KETU [*to himself*] So should I!

JĪVA SIDDHI Why want to hear something so unspeakable?

BHĀGURĀYAṆA If it's a secret, sir, let it be.

JĪVA SIDDHI No secret, brother, just very dreadful.

BHĀGURĀYAṆA If it's not a secret, tell me.

JĪVA SIDDHI But no, I'll not tell you, brother.

BHĀGURĀYAṆA And I won't let you have a pass.

JĪVA SIDDHI [*to himself*] It's all right to tell him now that he presses me. [*Aloud*] You leave me no alternative, brother. Listen. Wretch that I am, when I was formerly living in Pāṭaliputra I became a friend of Rākshasa. And at that time he secretly arranged to employ a poison-girl to kill King Parvataka.

MALAYA KETU [*to himself, weeping*] What! Rākshasa, not Kauṭilya, killed my father?

BHĀGURĀYAṆA Go on, sir.

JĪVA SIDDHI Then the accursed Kauṭilya had me banished in disgrace from the city as a friend of Rākshasa. And now with his political schemes, he's plotting something that will get me banished from the world of the living.

BHĀGURĀYAṆA We had heard, reverend sir, that it was Kauṭilya, not wanting to divide the empire as promised, who committed that crime, not Rākshasa.

JĪVA SIDDHI Brother, Kauṭilya hadn't so much as heard of the poison-girl.

BHĀGURĀYAṆA Here, you can have your pass, reverend sir. Come and let His Highness hear this.

MALAYA KETU

He has heard it, friend – a tale to split the ears, 6
A tale of an enemy straight from the mouth of his friend,
Which makes the evil of my father's murder,
Though done long since, seem suddenly twice as great.

JĪVA SIDDHI [*to himself*] Ah, the accursed Malaya Ketu has heard! My job is done. [*He goes out.*]

MALAYA KETU [*gazing into the air as if he could see him*] Rākshasa, was this well?

When my father was happy in his mind because you were his friend 7
And being confident entrusted everything to you,
You killed him, bringing sorrow to his kin –
Aptly named Rākshasa! you are in truth a devil.

BHĀGURĀYAṆA [*to himself*] His Honour Kauṭilya's instructions are to safeguard Rākshasa's life. So be it. [*Aloud*] Do not overexcite yourself, Your Highness. If you will sit down, there is something I should like to say to you.

MALAYA KETU [*sitting down*] What is it, friend?

BHĀGURĀYAṆA In this life, Your Highness, those who practise politics choose enemies, allies and neutrals on political grounds, not on grounds of personal preference like ordinary people. At that particular time, when Rākshasa wanted Sarvārtha Siddhi to be Emperor, it was His Majesty King Parvataka of glorious memory who, being even more powerful than Chandra Gupta, was the most awkward obstacle in Rākshasa's path and his greatest enemy, and that is why he did this to him: in a sense I do not blame him. Consider, Your Highness –

8 Turning friend into foe, foe into friend,
On grounds of practical advantage,
Politics takes a man while he still lives
Into another birth where earlier memories are lost.

So don't take Rākshasa to task over this, but treat him well until you win the empire. Afterwards Your Highness can please himself whether to keep him or drop him.

MALAYA KETU What you say, friend, is very sensible. And if he were executed, it could cause popular unrest and jeopardize our chances of victory.

[*Enter the manservant.*]

MANSERVANT Victory to Your Highness. The Captain of the Guard begs to state that they have caught a man without a pass trying to leave the camp with a letter, and have brought him to be interviewed by His Honour.

BHĀGURĀYAṆA Bring him in, my good fellow.

MANSERVANT Yes, sir. [*He goes out.*]

[*Enter, in the company of the manservant, Siddhārthaka, bound.*]

SIDDHĀRTHAKA [*to himself*]

9 All homage to Loyalty,
Mother of such as me,
Who puts me in the path of right
And averts my gaze from wrong.

MANSERVANT [*approaching*] Here is the man, Your Honour.

BHĀGURĀYAṆA [*looking at him*] Is he a stranger here, or in someone's service?

SIDDHĀRTHAKA Sir, I am in Minister Rākshasa's service.

BHĀGURĀYAṆA Then why, my good man, were you leaving the camp without a pass?

SIDDHĀRTHAKA It was an emergency, sir, and I was in a hurry.

BHĀGURĀYAṆA What kind of emergency, to override a royal edict?

MALAYA KETU Bhāgurāyaṇa, take his letter.

BHĀGURĀYAṆA [*taking the letter from Siddhārthaka's hand*] Here it is, Your Highness. [*Looking at the seal*] This seal bears Rākshasa's name.

MALAYA KETU Open it with the seal intact and show me.

[*Bhāgurāyaṇa does so.*]

[*Takes it and reads out*] 'Greetings. Someone somewhere sends the following message to a most distinguished person. In dismissing our rival, the Truthful One has shown himself to be as good as his word. He should now give pleasure by granting to our allies who have already entered into an agreement with him the price of the agreement as previously promised. They will thus be encouraged to reward their benefactor by making an end of their present protector. We bring this to the Truthful One's attention, though he will not have forgotten it. Of the allies in question some are seeking the enemy's treasury and armed forces, others his territory. The three ornaments sent by the Truthful One have been received. We in turn are sending something to support the present letter. This should be accepted and a verbal message received from our most trusted messenger Siddhārthaka.'

MALAYA KETU Bhāgurāyaṇa, my friend, what does the letter mean?

BHĀGURĀYAṆA Who is this letter for, Siddhārthaka?

SIDDHĀRTHAKA I don't know, sir.

BHĀGURĀYAṆA You're taking a letter, you scoundrel, and you don't know who to? All right, all right. Who is to hear your message?

SIDDHĀRTHAKA You are.

BHĀGURĀYAṆA We are?

SIDDHĀRTHAKA Now you've arrested me, I don't know what to say.

BHĀGURĀYAṆA [*angrily*] Then you soon shall. Bhāsvaraka, take him outside and beat him till he talks.

MANSERVANT Yes, sir. [*Going out with Siddhārthaka and coming in again*] Sir, as he was being beaten, this little box fell out of his pocket.

BHĀGURĀYAṆA [*examining it*] Your Highness, this too is stamped with Rākshasa's seal.

MALAYA KETU It must be the thing that was to support the letter. Keep the seal intact again and open it and show me.

[*Bhāgurāyaṇa does so.*]

[*Looking*] Oh, it is the jewellery I took from myself and sent to Rākshasa. This must be a letter to Chandra Gupta.

BHĀGURĀYAṆA We'll soon clear up any doubts. Beat him again, Bhāsvaraka.

MANSERVANT Yes, sir. [*Going out and coming in again*] Sir, now he is beaten he says he wants to tell His Highness in person.

MALAYA KETU Bring him in.

MANSERVANT Yes, Your Highness.

[*He goes out and comes back with Siddhārthaka.*]

SIDDHĀRTHAKA [*falling at the Prince's feet*] Grant me a pardon, Your Highness, I beg you.

MALAYA KETU My good fellow, a servant who was merely obeying his master has nothing to fear. Speak out.

SIDDHĀRTHAKA Hear me, Your Highness. Minister Rākshasa told me to take this letter to Chandra Gupta.

MALAYA KETU And now let me hear the message.

SIDDHĀRTHAKA Your Highness, Minister Rākshasa told me to say: 'The following five princes, close friends of myself, have allied themselves with you: Chitra Varman, Prince of Kulūta; Siṃha Nāda, Prince of Malaya; Pushkarāksha, Lord of Kashmīr; Sindhusheṇa, Prince of Sindh; Megha Nāda, Ruler of the Persians. Of them the first three seek Malaya Ketu's territory, the other two his troops of elephant. And so just as, noble sir, you have pleased me by dismissing Kauṭilya, so you should allow them too the above-mentioned requests.' Such was my message.

MALAYA KETU [*to himself*] What, Chitra Varman and the others betraying me too? But of course, that is why they have been so extremely friendly with Rākshasa. [*Aloud*] Vijayā, I should like to speak to Rākshasa.

FEMALE GUARD Yes, Your Highness. [*She goes out.*]

[*Enter, seated at home, attended by his manservant, Rākshasa in anxious thought.*]

RĀKSHASA [*to himself*] Our army is full of Chandra Gupta's men, and truly I am not easy in my mind:

If its aim is clear, its parts well-knit, the whole securely based,
An army like an argument wins every conflict.
But when it is suspect, at war with itself, full of equivocation,
The man that marshals it ensures his own defeat.

And yet these people all had clear reasons for their defection to us, and they had already accepted our overtures: there's no need for me to feel uneasy. [*Aloud*]

Priyamvadaka, take this message in my name to the princes who attend His Highness: 'We are now drawing nearer to Pāṭaliputra every day. Henceforth during our advance you should keep to your planned positions – namely,

11 In the van with me shall march the men of Khasa and
Magadha;
The Greek kings of Gāndhāra shall form the core of the
advance;
In the rear will be the valiant Scythian princes, sup-
ported by the Chedis and the Hūṇas;
The lord of Kulūta and the other princes shall guard
His Highness on the march.'

MANSERVANT Yes, Your Honour. [*He goes out.*]

[*Enter the female guard.*]

FEMALE GUARD Victory to you, Minister. His Highness asks to speak with you.

RĀKSHASA Then wait a moment. Hallo, hallo there!

[*Enter another manservant.*]

MANSERVANT Yes, Your Honour?

RĀKSHASA Tell Śakaṭa Dāsa that since His Highness has presented me with decorations, I must not go into His Highness's presence undecorated, and that I should therefore like to have one of the three sets of ornaments we bought.

MANSERVANT Yes, Your Honour. [*Going out and coming in again*] Here are the ornaments, Your Honour.

RĀKSHASA [*inspecting the jewellery, decorating himself and getting up*] Conduct me to headquarters.

FEMALE GUARD This way, Minister.

RĀKSHASA [*to himself*] A post of authority causes even the most blameless man much anxiety.

Fear of his master may possess a servant, 12
Or fear of the people about him may grip his heart;
An exalted post earns the envy of the wicked,
And in his thoughts one who has climbed high can foresee a fall as great.

FEMALE GUARD [*walking about*] There is His Highness, Minister: approach him.

RĀKSHASA [*looking*] So, there is His Highness,

Gazing fixedly at his feet, 13
But with thoughts elsewhere, not seeing them,
His face supported by his hand,
As if bowed down by the weight of all his problems.

[*Approaching*] Victory to Your Highness.

MALAYA KETU Greetings, sir. Here, be seated.

RĀKSHASA [*sitting*] Why did you summon me, Your Highness?

MALAYA KETU I was worried, sir, at not seeing you for so long.

RĀKSHASA Your Highness, it is my preoccupation with arrangements for the march that has earned me this rebuke.

MALAYA KETU I should be glad to hear what your arrangements for the march are.

RĀKSHASA I will repeat to Your Highness the orders which I gave Your Highness's vassal princes –

'In the van with me shall march the men of Khasa and Magadha; 11 rptd
The Greek kings of Gāndhāra shall form the core of the advance;
In the rear will be the valiant Scythian princes, supported by the Chedis and the Hūṇas;

The Lord of Kulūta and the other princes shall guard His Highness on the march.'

MALAYA KETU [*to himself*] Am I to be surrounded then, by the very men who want to endear themselves to Chandra Gupta by killing me? [*Aloud*] Sir, have you anyone visiting Pāṭaliputra or coming here from there?

RĀKSHASA Any need for such comings and goings is past, Your Highness. After all we shall be there ourselves in five days' time.

MALAYA KETU [*to himself*] That settles it. [*Aloud*] In that case, sir, why did you send this man with a letter to Pāṭaliputra?

RĀKSHASA [*seeing him*] Why, Siddhārthaka! What is all this?

SIDDHĀRTHAKA [*weeping and looking ashamed*] I'm sorry, sir, I'm sorry. I couldn't keep it secret when they beat me.

RĀKSHASA Keep what secret? What do you mean?

SIDDHĀRTHAKA I mean I just couldn't keep it secret when they beat me.

MALAYA KETU Bhāgurāyaṇa, he is too afraid and embarrassed in front of his master to speak out. Tell His Honour yourself.

BHĀGURĀYAṆA As you wish, Your Highness. He tells us, Minister, that you gave him a letter and a verbal message and sent him to Chandra Gupta.

RĀKSHASA Siddhārthaka, my good man, is this true?

SIDDHĀRTHAKA [*looking ashamed*] I let it out when they beat me.

RĀKSHASA It is false, Your Highness. A man who is beaten will say anything.

MALAYA KETU Show him the letter, Bhāgurāyaṇa. His own servant can tell him the verbal message.

BHĀGURĀYAṆA Here is the letter, Minister. [*He hands it over.*]

RĀKSHASA [*reading it*] This is a trick by the enemy, Your Highness.

MALAYA KETU You sent that jewellery to support the letter, sir. How might that be a trick by the enemy?

RĀKSHASA [*examining the jewellery*] I didn't send this, Your Highness. This was given me by Your Highness, and I gave it to Siddhārthaka to reward him for a service he had rendered me.

BHĀGURĀYAṆA Is this a suitable person, Minister, to be given jewels of such value, particularly when they had been presented to you by His Highness from his own person?

MALAYA KETU It says in the letter: 'And a verbal message should be received from our most trusted messenger Siddhārthaka.'

RĀKSHASA Verbal message, Your Highness? The letter itself is none of mine.

MALAYA KETU Then whose is this seal on it?

RĀKSHASA Wicked men are quite capable of appending a false seal.

BHĀGURĀYAṆA Minister Rākshasa is right, Your Highness. Siddhārthaka, my man, who wrote this letter?

[*Siddhārthaka glances at Rākshasa's face, then stays silent, staring down.*]

Don't get yourself beaten again. Speak up.

SIDDHĀRTHAKA It was Śakaṭa Dāsa, sir.

RĀKSHASA Your Highness, if Śakaṭa Dāsa wrote it, then I wrote it myself.

MALAYA KETU Vijayā, I want to see Śakaṭa Dāsa.

FEMALE GUARD Yes, Your Highness. [*She moves off.*]

BHĀGURĀYAṆA [*to himself*] No agent of the revered Kauṭilya would take an unnecessary risk. [*Aloud*] Your Highness, Sakaṭa Dāsa will never admit in front of Minister Rākshasa that he wrote the letter. So let us get something else written by him, and a comparison of the handwriting will settle the matter.

MALAYA KETU Yes, see to that, Vijayā.

FEMALE GUARD Shall I ask for the seal as well, Your Highness?

MALAYA KETU Yes, both.

FEMALE GUARD Yes, Your Highness. [*Going out and coming in again*] Your Highness, here is a letter just written by Śakaṭa Dāsa in his own hand, together with the seal.

MALAYA KETU [*comparing them both*] Minister, the characters agree.

RĀKSHASA [*to himself*] The characters agree! But Śakaṭa Dāsa is my friend, and there's one character at odds. Is it conceivable that Śakaṭa Dāsa

14 Remembered his wife and children
And forgot his loyalty to our Lord,
Eager for transient advantage
Instead of imperishable glory?

But it must be so:

15 The signet-ring does not leave his finger, Siddhārthaka is his friend;
The treacherous letter is his, as the other letter shows:
Clearly he has been plotting with enemies who know how to sow dissension,
Forgetting affection, saving his skin by treachery.

MALAYA KETU Is that, sir, one of the three ornaments whose receipt was acknowledged in the letter? [*Examining them, to himself*] Why, it is jewellery my father used to wear! [*Aloud*] Where did you get these jewels?

RĀKSHASA They were bought from traders.

MALAYA KETU Vijayā, do you recognize them?

FEMALE GUARD [*examining them and weeping*] How could I fail to, Your Highness? They are what His Majesty King Parvataka of blessed memory used to wear.

MALAYA KETU [*weeping*] Oh father!

These were the jewels you loved, beloved hero; 16
Ornament of our house, these were the jewels that adorned you,
That shone on you, beneath the moon-radiance of your face,
Like autumn stars against the evening sky.

RĀKSHASA [*to himself*] Once worn by King Parvataka, she says? Then the traders who sold them to me must have been agents of Kauṭilya.

MALAYA KETU It is hardly likely, sir, that you could have bought valuable jewels once worn by my father, especially when they had fallen into Chandra Gupta's hands. Or rather it's all too likely:

The seller was Chandra Gupta 17
Looking for a handsome profit,
And the price that you fixed on for them,
Monster, was me.

RĀKSHASA [*to himself*] Alas, the enemy's trap is carefully sprung!

No use to say it is not my letter, when the seal on it is mine. 18

That Śakaṭa Dāsa has broken faith would never be credited.
And who would believe that the Mauryan Emperor could sell his jewels? –
Better admit the charge than vulgarly dispute.

MALAYA KETU Let me ask Your Honour this –

RĀKSHASA Ask one that *has* honour, Your Highness. I have no honour left.

MALAYA KETU

19 The Mauryan is your master's son, I am your friend's son eager in your service.
He would be your benefactor: here you are mine, and always listened to.
There minister means politely treated slave, here it means master.
What gain can you long for, to make you so dishonoured?

RĀKSHASA Your Highness, you have answered yourself –

19 rptd The Mauryan is my master's son, you my friend's son, eager in my service.
He would be my benefactor: here I am yours, and always listened to.
There minister means politely treated slave, here it means master.
What gain *can* I long for, to make me so dishonoured?

MALAYA KETU [*indicating the letter and the jewellery*] And what of these?

RĀKSHASA [*weeping*] It is the hand of Destiny:

20 It is the hand of Destiny blighting man's efforts,

The same that has killed off the kings who could judge a man right;
Though servitude means contempt, yet those kings in their love
Being grateful and wise looked on me as their son.

MALAYA KETU [*angrily*] Do you still deny it? This is the hand of Destiny, is it, not your own greed? Dishonoured one –

You have already treacherously primed a girl with deadly poison 21
And turned my too trusting father into a memory.
Now you are obsessed with becoming the enemy's minister
And try to sell me in turn like so much raw meat.

RĀKSHASA [*to himself*] Here is a still unkinder thrust! [*Aloud, stopping his ears*] Perish that thought! I am guiltless towards Parvataka.

MALAYA KETU Then who did kill my father?

RĀKSHASA You must ask fate.

MALAYA KETU Ask fate? Not Jīva Siddhi the Jain?

RĀKSHASA [*to himself*] What, is Jīva Siddhi too working for Kauṭilya? Alas, my enemies have made my very heart their own.

MALAYA KETU [*angrily*] Bhāsvaraka, take the following order to General Śikharasena: 'The five princes who have made a pact with Rākshasa and wish to do violence to my person to please Chandra Gupta – namely, Chitra Varman of Kulūta, Siṃha Nāda of Malaya, Pushkarāksha of Kashmīr, Sindhusheṇa of Sindh, Megha Nāda of the Persians – shall be executed: the three first, who want my land, shall be put in a pit and covered with earth; the two last, who want my troops of elephant, shall be trampled to death by an elephant.'

MANSERVANT Yes, Your Highness. [*He goes out.*]

MALAYA KETU Rākshasa, I am not Rākshasa the traitor: I am Malaya Ketu. Go, seek out Chandra Gupta with all your heart –

22 Kauṭilya, yes, and the Mauryan
Though they unite with you
I can destroy as surely
As evil drives out good.

We shall delay no longer. Let our troops march forth this very minute to take Pāṭaliputra.

23 Greying the Eastern women's cheeks that were fragrant with lodhra pollen
And spoiling the bee-dark blackness of their curling locks,
Columns of dust from our troops, born of the horses' galloping, then cut down
By the stream of our elephants' ichor, shall fall on the heads of our enemies.

[*Malaya Ketu and his retinue go out.*]

RĀKSHASA [*in distress*] Alas, poor Chitra Varman and the rest all killed! Does Rākshasa work to kill his friends and not his enemies? Miserable wretch that I am, what shall I do?

24 Shall I go to a hermitage? Austerities will not calm my embittered heart.
Follow my lord? While the enemy lives, that is a woman's way.
Fall with my sword on the foe? That would not be ill

Did gratitude not prevent it, and tell me that Chandanadāsa must be freed.

[*He goes out.*]

PRELUDE TO ACT VI

[*Enter Siddhārthaka, decorated and in high spirits.*]

SIDDHĀRTHAKA

Glory to Krishṇa, dark as a cloud, slayer of the demon,* 1
Glory to Chandra Gupta, a full moon to the eyes of all good people,
Glory to that which has prepared our forces for victory,
The revered Kauṭilya's strategy that vanquishes our foes.

Now at long last I may seek out my good friend Samiddhārthaka. [*Walking about and looking*] But there is good Samiddhārthaka coming this way. I'll go and meet him. [*Enter Samiddhārthaka.*]

SAMIDDHĀRTHAKA

The friends we embrace in our drinking-bouts 2
Who bring joy to our festivities,
When they are gone, though they stay in our hearts,
They grieve us by their absence.

Now I have heard that my dear good friend Siddhārthaka is back from Malaya Ketu's camp. So I'm off to find him. [*Walking about and seeing him*] There he is! [*Going up to him*] How are you, my dear friend?

SIDDHĀRTHAKA [*seeing him*] Hallo – it's my good friend

*Keśin, who took the form of a horse and was slain by Krishṇa with his bare hands.

Samiddhārthaka! [*Coming up to him*] Samiddhārthaka! Are you well, my dear friend?

[*They embrace each other.*]

SAMIDDHĀRTHAKA How can I be well, when you come back after such a long time and still haven't been to my house?

SIDDHĀRTHAKA I'm sorry, my friend, I'm sorry. The moment he saw me, His Honour Kauṭilya told me to go and tell my news to His Glorious Majesty the Emperor. I told His Majesty and received marks of his royal favour, and I was just on my way to your house to see you, dear friend.

SAMIDDHĀRTHAKA If I'm allowed to hear it, tell me what was the good news you told His Majesty?

SIDDHĀRTHAKA There's nothing I'd keep from you, friend. Listen. The accursed Malaya Ketu's mind was so deluded by the strategy of His Honour Kauṭilya that he dismissed Rākshasa and executed Chitra Varman and four other leading princes. At which the remaining princes, thinking him reckless and wicked, left Malaya Ketu's camp for their own good, and attended by the rest of the soldiery in a state of fear and trembling set off for their respective domains. Then Malaya Ketu was arrested by Bhadra Bhaṭa, Purusha Datta, Hingu Rāta, Bala Gupta, Rājasena, Bhāgurāyaṇa, Rohitāksha, Vijaya Varman and others.

SAMIDDHĀRTHAKA Friend, everyone said Bhadra Bhaṭa and the others had defected from his Majesty the Emperor and gone over to Malaya Ketu. So why do they start one way and end another like a bad play?

SIDDHĀRTHAKA Do homage, friend, to the noble Kauṭilya's strategy, that flows as silently as the heavenly Ganges.

SAMIDDHĀRTHAKA Go on, friend.

SIDDHĀRTHAKA Thereupon Kauṭilya marched out with large picked forces and overcame the princes and their soldiers.

SAMIDDHĀRTHAKA Where, friend?

SIDDHĀRTHAKA Over there, friend, where

Elephants rear up and trumpet, 3
Dark as swollen clouds in their high rutting frenzy,
And horses, trembling in fear of the whip,
Surge forward in a flood as they hear the victory cry.

SAMIDDHĀRTHAKA But never mind that – why has the noble Kauṭilya resumed his post of minister after publicly renouncing it and standing aside for so long?

SIDDHĀRTHAKA You're a fool, my friend, if you think you can fathom Kauṭilya's mind when even Minister Rākshasa couldn't, up till now.

SAMIDDHĀRTHAKA And where is Minister Rākshasa at the present moment?

SIDDHĀRTHAKA His Honour Kauṭilya has had a report that he escaped from Malaya Ketu's camp in the confusion, and has arrived here in Pāṭaliputra, shadowed by a spy they call The Rat.

SAMIDDHĀRTHAKA You mean that, after leaving here resolved to restore the Nanda Empire, Minister Rākshasa has come back again without achieving his aim?

SIDDHĀRTHAKA I thinks it's out of his love for Chandanadāsa, friend.

SAMIDDHĀRTHAKA Do you think Chandanadāsa will be freed, then?

SIDDHĀRTHAKA Freed, that unlucky man? On Kauṭilya's orders you and I, my friend, have got to take him right away to the Execution Ground and kill him.

SAMIDDHĀRTHAKA [*angrily*] Has His Honour Kauṭilya no executioners, employing us on such a loathsome errand?

SIDDHĀRTHAKA My friend, no one questions Kauṭilya's orders if they want to stay in this world. So come on. Let's dress ourselves as outcasts and take Chandanadāsa to the Execution Ground.

[*Both go out.*]

Act VI

[*Enter a man carrying a rope.*]

MAN

4 Firmly twisted from the Six Strands
And with a noose fashioned from the Chain of Tactics,
Victory to the rope of Kauṭilya's strategy
Waiting to bind the enemy.

Here is the place His Honour Kauṭilya heard about from The Rat, where His Honour has instructed me to meet with Rākshasa. [*Looking*] Ah, there is Minister Rākshasa, coming this way with his face covered. I'll hide among the trees of this overgrown park and watch where he seats himself. [*He walks about and then stays still.*]

[*Enter Rākshasa as described, carrying a sword.*]

RĀKSHASA [*weeping*] Alas, alas!

5 Like a whore frightened by losing her man, Fortune has gone to another's house,
And the people have followed after her like sheep, their loyalty forgotten.

And even the best, finding courage unrewarded, have given up the task.
But what could they do? Limbs do not last when the head is lopped.

Leaving her husband, a great emperor of noble birth, 6
Fortune has eloped to the Mauryan, low-born harlot to low-born man,
And sticks to him. What can I do, I whose hardest struggles
Are frustrated by Fate, which seems to side against me?

For

When my king went to heaven, never deserving such a death, 7
I centred all my efforts on Parvataka.
When he was killed, I turned to his son – but all without success.
Truly Fate is the Nanda's enemy, not the brahmin.

How poor an understanding the barbarian has!

A man who still serves his masters though they are dead and gone, 8
How could that same man while he has strength conspire with their bitterest enemies?
The barbarian in his blind folly could not see that –
But the mind that fate has smitten turns everything upside down.

Why, even now if Rākshasa falls into his enemy's hands, he shall die rather than bargain with Chandra Gupta. To be wilfully false to one's word is a greater disgrace than to be worsted by the enemy's tricks. [*Looking all about him and weeping*] Is this then the parkland about

Pāṭaliputra whose ground was once hallowed by my Emperor's tread?

9 In these parts, with slackened reins as he drew the bow,
His Majesty at full gallop would shoot at moving targets.
In this avenue he stayed, here gave audience – lacking such kings
The lands of the city are a most melancholy sight.

Where shall I go in my wretchedness? [*Looking*] Ah, I see an overgrown park. I will go in and try to get news of Chandanadāsa from someone. [*Walking about*] Alas, the good and evil turns of man's condition creep on him all unnoticed!

10 Once, with the townsfolk pointing at me, as at the rising moon,
I went forth from the city like a prince, attended by a thousand princes.
Now here I am again, returning to the same city in despair,
And darting, fearful as a thief, into an overgrown garden.

But then the very ones whose favour made it possible are themselves no more. [*Entering and looking*] How dreary the park is!

11 The pavilion is in ruins, like a family that once did mighty things.
The lake is dried up, like a good man's heart when his friends all die.
The trees are barren of fruit, like schemes that are blighted by fate.
The ground is smothered with weeds, as the mind of a fool with error.

And

Grievously wounded by the sharp axe 12
And moaning their pain through the pigeons' ceaseless cries,
The branches of trees are bandaged by sighing snakes
With strips of their slough, in pity for their friends.

Poor trees!

All withered up within, 13
Weeping their tears of woodworm dust,
Sunk in despair and mourning vanished shades,
They seem to be preparing for their funeral.

Here is a broken slab of stone that suits my degradation. I will sit down for a moment. [*Sitting down and listening*] Oh, what is the sudden sound of cheering I can hear, mixed with the noise of conch and drum?

Bruising the fragile ear with its heavy din 14
So loud the houses spew it back again,
This cheering, swelled by the sounds of conch and drum,
Leaps up to take the measurement of heaven.

[*On reflection*] Oh of course! It means that Malaya Ketu's capture is being celebrated by the Emperor's – [*breaking off*] Alas, I mean the Mauryan's court. [*Weeping*] Oh wretchedness!

I have been made to hear the enemy's triumph, 15
I have been made to come and see it:
Now it would seem that Fate is striving
To make me live* it too.

***By thinking of the Mauryan as the Emperor.**

MAN He is sitting down. Now to put His Honour Kauṭilya's plan into operation. [*Pretending not to notice Rākshasa, he stands in front of him fastening the noose on himself.*]

RĀKSHASA [*seeing him*] What's this, he's using a rope on himself! Why, the poor fellow must be as unhappy as I am. I must ask him. [*Going up to him*] My dear man, what are you doing?

MAN [*weeping*] I'm doing what any unlucky man like me would do, when he grieves the loss of a dear friend.

RĀKSHASA [*to himself*] I could tell right away that he was in the same plight as myself. I'll certainly ask him. [*Aloud*] Fellow student in misery, if it is not a secret or too painful to tell, I should be glad to hear why you are ending your life.

MAN It's not a secret, sir, nor too painful to tell. But my heart is so heavy with grief at the loss of my friend that I cannot bear to delay my own death for even a single moment.

RĀKSHASA [*to himself with a sigh*] Alas, this man is a lesson to me, when I sit here as indifferent as a stranger to the plight of my friend. [*Aloud*] Since it's not a secret or painful, my dear man, I should be glad to hear.

MAN Oh how persistent you are, sir! Well, if you insist, I'll tell you. There is a master-jeweller in this city called Jishṇudāsa.

RĀKSHASA [*to himself*] So there is, and he is a great friend of Chandanadāsa.

MAN And Jishṇudāsa is the dear friend I mentioned.

RĀKSHASA [*to himself in delight*] A dear friend, he says! The connection is very close: he is bound to have news of Chandanadāsa.

MAN [*weeping*] He has now given away his wealth to

brahmins and other deserving people, and left the city to enter fire. And I have come to this old park to kill myself before I could hear what I dreaded to hear about him.

RĀKSHASA My dear man, why did your friend want to kill himself? –

Was he afflicted with a fearful disease beyond the aid of 16
medicine?

MAN No, no, sir!

RĀKSHASA

Was he ruined by the King's wrath, deadly as fire or 16 cont.
poison?

MAN Assuredly not, sir. In Chandra Gupta's realm, we are not treated so harshly.

RĀKSHASA

Did he fall in love with some lovely woman forbidden 16 cont.
to him?

MAN [*stopping his ears*] Perish the thought, sir! He is incapable of such indecency.

RĀKSHASA

Then did he, like you, have a friend who was doomed 16 cont.
to die?

MAN Exactly, sir.

RĀKSHASA [*to himself, in alarm*] Chandanadāsa is his friend, and the loss of a friend is his reason for suicide? I am shaken with fear for Chandanadāsa. [*Aloud*] Your friend too, in his devotion to a friend, has done a deed worth telling. I should like to hear of it in detail.

MAN No sir, I can delay my death no longer, unhappy wretch that I am!

RĀKSHASA It is a noble story: you must tell it, my dear man.

MAN Well, if you insist, sir. Listen.

RĀKSHASA I am listening.

MAN There is living in this city, in the Square of Flowers, a master-jeweller called Chandanadāsa.

RĀKSHASA [*to himself in despair*] Now Fate opens the door that consecrates me to death. Be firm, my heart. You have worse to hear. [*Aloud*] Yes, he is reputed to be a good man, devoted to his friends. What of him?

MAN He too is a close friend of Jishṇudāsa.

RĀKSHASA [*to himself*] The thunderbolt is near.

MAN And today Jishṇudāsa, out of the love he bears his friend, petitioned Chandra Gupta.

RĀKSHASA What was the petition?

MAN That he had adequate resources for the support of his family, which he was offering in exchange for the release of his dear friend Chandanadāsa.

RĀKSHASA [*to himself*] Bravo, Jishṇudāsa! What love you have shown for your friend!

17 The wealth sons coldly kill their fathers for, and fathers their sons,
For which friends withdraw their friendship from a friend,
You wanted to give up for a loved one in distress.
You are a merchant, but you use your money well.

[*Aloud*] How did the Mauryan receive this petition?

MAN Chandra Gupta replied that he hadn't imprisoned Chandanadāsa to get money, but because he had sheltered Minister Rākshasa's family and wouldn't hand them over despite repeated demands. And so he would be released if he handed them over, and if he didn't he would be condemned to death. After which the Emperor ordered Chandanadāsa to be taken to the Execution Ground. Then Jishṇudāsa decided to enter the fire before he could hear such dreadful news of his friend, and left the city. And I have decided to kill myself before I can hear such dreadful news of Jishṇudāsa, and that is why I came to this old park.

RĀKSHASA Has Chandanadāsa been executed, my good man?

MAN They aren't actually executing him yet. At the moment they are asking him over and over again for Rākshasa's family, but he goes on refusing them out of love for his friend. And all that is delaying the execution.

RĀKSHASA [*to himself joyfully*] Bravo, my dearest Chandanadāsa!

The fame that Śibi won 18
By protecting the helpless
You now win for yourself
Though the friend you protect has deserted you.

[*Aloud*] Go, my dear man. Hurry to stop Jishṇudāsa from entering the fire. I shall go and rescue Chandanadāsa.

MAN How can you rescue Chandanadāsa, sir?

RĀKSHASA [*drawing his sword*] Why with this sword, my comrade in misfortune! Look!

This sword, the colour of the cloudless sky, 19
That seems to sparkle with lust to fight as it feels the grasp of my hand,
Whose fine-tempered strength my enemies have tried on the touchstone of war,

Calls me to adventure for love of my friend, all powerless though I now am.

MAN You want to save Master Chandanadāsa, and you have known better times? I cannot clearly tell, sir, but are you His Honour Minister Rākshasa of glorious name?

RĀKSHASA I am that one who has seen his master's house destroyed and brought ruin on his friends, a man dishonoured and of most inglorious name, and truly called Rākshasa.

MAN [*falling joyfully at his feet*] Oh wonder! Thank god I have found you.

RĀKSHASA Get up, get up, my dear man. There's not a moment to lose. Tell Jishṇudāsa that Rākshasa is going to save Chandanadāsa. [*He draws his sword and strides forth, again reciting*]

19 rptd This sword, the colour of the cloudless sky,
That seems to sparkle with lust to fight as it feels the grasp of my hand,
Whose fine-tempered strength my enemies have tried on the touchstone of war,
Calls me to adventure for love of my friend, all powerless though I now am.

MAN [*falling at his feet*] Listen to me, Your Honour, please! The accursed Chandra Gupta once ordered the Honourable Śakaṭa Dāsa to be taken to the Execution Ground and someone came and rescued him. Chandra Gupta was enraged by the negligence which had cheated him of Śakaṭa Dāsa's death, and quenched his anger by having the executioners put to death. And ever since then if the executioners see anyone they don't know anywhere near them, then to protect their own lives they kill their prisoner without waiting to get to the proper spot. So if Your Honour goes there carrying a sword, it will only hasten Chandanadāsa's death. [*He goes out.*]

RĀKSHASA [*to himself*] I can't see what that fellow Kauṭilya is up to.

If I was deliberately sent Śakaṭa Dāsa by the enemy, 20
Why should he grow angry and kill the executioners?
But if it wasn't a trick, how explain the letter?
My mind fills with doubts, I can see nothing for certain.

[*After reflection.*]

This is no time for the sword – the executioners have learnt their lesson. 21
Plots take their time to mature – no use for them here.
I cannot sit idle, when a friend is going to a hideous death for me.
Ah, but I have the answer – to trade my life for his.

[*He goes out.*]

Act VII

[*Enter an executioner.**]

EXECUTIONER Away, sirs, away! Be off!

If you want to keep safe 1
Your wealth and your life, your wife and your family,
Be sure you shun like the plague
All acts of treason to the Emperor.

*In reality Siddhārthaka.

2 A man can grow sick or die
If he does things that don't agree with him.
But if he does what doesn't agree with the king,
The disease is fatal to the whole of his family.

If you have any doubt, just look at the traitor Master Chandanadāsa here, being led to execution with his wife and son. [*Listening, and then addressing the air*] What's that you say? Has he no way out? Yes, if he surrenders Minister Rākshasa's family. What? He tenderly protects the helpless, he would never consider such wickedness just to save his own skin? Well in that case, he's quite happy, isn't he? Why bother with trying to save him?

[*Enter, attended by another executioner,* Chandanadāsa dressed as a condemned man and carrying the stake on his shoulder. His wife and son accompany him.*]

CHANDANADĀSA Alas!

3 If even men like me
That dread the thought of sin
Can die the death of thieves,
Then I bow to the God of Death.

But a cruel man can never distinguish between those who don't wish him harm and those who do.

4 When the innocent deer, renouncing flesh,
Live only on grass for fear of taking life,
Why is it that the huntsman
Is so stubbornly bent on their destruction?

[*Looking about him*] Oh my dear friend Jishṇudāsa, do you make me no reply? But few are the men who will so much as show themselves at such a time. [*Weeping*]

* Samiddhārthaka.

There I see my friends, with nothing but their tears to help me, retreating with sad faces still turned towards me, following me only with their weeping eyes.

THE TWO EXECUTIONERS Master Chandanadāsa, you have come to the Execution Ground. Say goodbye to your family.

CHANDANADĀSA Dear wife, you must go back now with our son. This is as far as you can come.

WIFE [*weeping*] You are off to another world, sir, not a foreign country. It would not be right for a true wife to leave you now.

CHANDANADĀSA Ah! What are you planning?

WIFE To bless myself by following in my husband's footsteps.

CHANDANADĀSA An ill resolve, my wife. Keep your blessings for our son here, who knows nothing yet of the world.

WIFE Let the blessings of our family gods fall kindly upon him. My son, kneel to your father for the last time.

SON [*falling at his feet*] Father, what should I do without you?

CHANDANADĀSA My son, you must live somewhere beyond Kauṭilya's reach.

EXECUTIONERS Master Chandanadāsa, the stake is now fixed. Prepare yourself.

WIFE Save him, sirs, save him!

CHANDANADĀSA What love of life is this? Why are you calling? The Nanda kings who pitied the distressed are all gone to heaven.

FIRST EXECUTIONER Hey, Bilvapattraka, take hold of Chandanadāsa!

SECOND EXECUTIONER Right you are, Vajralomaka!

CHANDANADĀSA One moment, sir, while I embrace my

son. [*Putting his lips to his son's head*] My son, even though death should be certain, you must die still doing your duty to your friends.

SON Need you say it, father? That is the tradition in our family. [*He falls again at his feet.*]

EXECUTIONERS Take hold of him. His family will leave by themselves.

WIFE Help, sirs, help!

[*Enter without ceremony Rākshasa.*]

RĀKSHASA Have no fear, lady, have no fear! Ho there, officer, you need not kill this good man:

5 The man who once watched his lord's family being killed like the family of an enemy,
And in the plight of his friends stayed at his ease as if it were a holiday,
Who loved his own life though it held nothing but trickery and humiliation,
That is the man, and I am he, who must wear this garland leading to the world of death.

CHANDANADĀSA [*looking at him and weeping*] What is this, Minister?

RĀKSHASA An imitation, as you see, of a part of your goodness.

CHANDANADĀSA You have done me no service, sir, to make all my efforts useless.

RĀKSHASA Well, dear Chandanadāsa, everyone thinks of himself first in this world. Don't blame me. Tell the accursed Kauṭilya, my good man.

EXECUTIONERS What?

RĀKSHASA

6 'Here I am, for whose sake this worthy man made himself your enemy,

Sacrificing himself for another, in this evil Kali age which loves the wicked:
By his side the glory of Śibi pales to nothing,
And his saintly heroism eclipses the deeds of the Buddhas.'

FIRST EXECUTIONER Well, Bilvapattraka, you'd better take Master Chandanadāsa and wait over there in the shade of the tree in the Burning Ground while I go and tell His Honour Kauṭilya that we've caught Minister Rākshasa.

SECOND EXECUTIONER Right you are, Vajralomaka.

[*He goes out with Chandanadāsa and the wife and son.*]

FIRST EXECUTIONER [*walking about with Rākshasa*] Hey, there at the gate! Report to His Honour Kauṭilya, the thunderbolt that pulverized the Nanda Mountain, establisher of the House of Maurya and light of truth to the citizens –

RĀKSHASA [*to himself*] Must Rākshasa hear even this?

EXECUTIONER – that here, with his cleverness and bravery trapped in the noose of His Honour Kauṭilya's skill, stands Minister Rākshasa, a prisoner.

[*Enter, but with the curtain concealing his body and only his face visible, Kauṭilya.*]

KAUṬILYA Tell me, good fellow, tell me –

Who caught the fire with its leaping flames and put it in his pocket? 7
Who roped the restless wind and kept it still?
Who trapped the lion that reeked of elephant rut and caged him?
Who swam the ocean, with its sharks and crocodiles?

EXECUTIONER Why, you, Your Honour, with your strategic brilliance.

KAUṬILYA No, my man, no! It was Destiny, hating the race of Nanda. [*Seeing Rākshasa, to himself in joy*] Ah, here is Minister Rākshasa, that great and noble man, who

8 Long exercised my mind
And Vrishala's army
With that wearying need for alertness
Which caused many sleepless hours.

[*Putting off the curtain and approaching him*] Minister Rākshasa, I Vishṇugupta salute you.

RĀKSHASA [*seeing him, to himself*] 'Minister'? That is a title which shames me now. So here is the accursed – no, here is the great Kauṭilya!

9 Mine of all learning
As the ocean is of gems,
Whose worth we take no pleasure in
Because of our own envy.

[*Aloud*] Vishṇugupta, don't touch me – I am defiled by the touch of an outcast.

KAUṬILYA He is no outcast, Minister Rākshasa. He is someone you know already – Siddhārthaka, a servant of the Emperor, who pretended to be friends with Śakaṭa Dāsa and got the poor fellow at my instigation to write that false letter all unwittingly. And the other executioner was another of the Emperor's servants, called Samiddhārthaka.

RĀKSHASA [*to himself*] Thank god my doubts about Śakaṭa Dāsa are set at rest!

KAUṬILYA In fact, to tell you briefly –

10 Bhadra Bhaṭa and his friends, the letter, Siddhārthaka,

Those jewels you bought, your friend the supposed monk,
The poor wretch in the park and the plight of his friend the merchant
Were all schemes of mine –
[*He breaks off modestly.*]
– of Vrishala's, to gain, noble sir, your allegiance.

And here comes Vrishala to see you. Look.

RĀKSHASA [*to himself*] What can I do? I must see him.

[*Enter the Emperor with his retinue in order of rank.*]

EMPEROR [*to himself*] I feel almost ashamed to think that my preceptor has beaten the enemy's formidable forces without even a fight.

Though their aim is achieved, my arrows lie 11
Ashamed that they have not been called upon,
Hanging their heads as if in grief
Observing a vow of lying in their quiver.

But no –

Though his bow stays unstrung 12
That man has won all that on earth may be won,
In whose realm even while he sleeps
There are guardians like mine to watch over his affairs.

[*Approaching Kauṭilya*] Chandra Gupta bows to you, sir.

KAUṬILYA Vrishala, all your hopes are fulfilled. Salute Minister Rākshasa here – your hereditary Chief Minister.

RĀKSHASA [*to himself*] He has made the connection.

EMPEROR [*approaching Rākshasa*] Sir, Chandra Gupta salutes you.

RĀKSHASA [*looking at him, to himself*] Here is Chandra Gupta, who

13 Even as a child was known to the world
As one of extraordinary promise,
And by degrees has grown to Emperor
As an elephant grows to be lord of the herd.

[*Aloud*] Victory, sire!

EMPEROR Sir,

14 What victory is left me
To win, pray, in this world
When I have Your Honour as my guardian
Vigilant instructor in the Six Strands of government.

RĀKSHASA [*to himself*] This pupil of Kauṭilya is making me his servant. But no, this is courtesy on Chandra Gupta's part: my jealousy makes me misinterpret it. No wonder Kauṭilya has won such glory:

15 If he finds a worthy and ambitious man,
The dullest-witted counsellor is sure of renown,
While the cleverest minister, relying on a fool,
Is undermined, like a tree on the bank of a river.

KAUṬILYA Minister Rākshasa, do you want Chandanadāsa to live?

RĀKSHASA How can you ask, Vishṇugupta?

KAUṬILYA I ask because you have not granted Vrishala the favour of accepting the sword of office. If you really want Chandanadāsa to live, accept it.

RĀKSHASA Impossible, Vishṇugupta! I am not worthy to accept it, particularly when it has been yours.

KAUṬILYA Do not talk of worthy and unworthy, sir.

Look at our elephants, backs swollen with the rubbing of their accoutrements, 16
Robbed of the joys of bathing, feeding, roaming, drinking, sleeping when they would,
And the horses too, exhausted with endless bridling, their saddles never empty –
All due, wise counsellor, to that brave resolution which has humbled your enemy's pride.

But that is all beside the point: if you won't accept office, Chandanadāsa's life is forfeit.

RĀKSHASA [*to himself*]

Love for the Nandas fills my heart, yet I must serve their enemies. 17
The trees I watered and made tall are all cut down.
To protect a friend I must bear the sword of office.
The things that happen make us all Fate's servants in the end.

[*Aloud*] Then Vishṇugupta, I bow to that love of friends which may lead one anywhere. I have no choice, I am ready.

KAUṬILYA [*joyfully handing over the sword of office*] Vrishala, Vrishala, Minister Rākshasa has now graciously consented to accept office under you. My congratulations to you.

EMPEROR Chandra Gupta acknowledges this great blessing from Your Honour.*

[*Enter a manservant.*]

MANSERVANT Victory to Your Honour. Bhadra Bhaṭa, Bhāgurāyaṇa and their companions have brought

*This is addressed to Kauṭilya and is a normal response to the formula of congratulation.

Malaya Ketu to the gate, bound hand and foot. What is Your Honour's desire in the matter?

KAUṬILYA Tell Minister Rākshasa, my dear man. He is the judge now.

RĀKSHASA [*to himself*] Does Kauṭilya first enslave me then make me the Emperor's adviser? Well, what choice have I! [*Aloud*] Your Majesty, as you well know, I was in Malaya Ketu's service for some time. For that reason I ask you to spare his life.

[*The Emperor looks at Kauṭilya.*]

KAUṬILYA Vrishala, you must honour the first request which Minister Rākshasa makes of you. [*To the manservant*] Tell Bhadra Bhaṭa and the others in my name that, in response to a request by Minister Rākshasa, His Majesty the Emperor grants Malaya Ketu those territories which are his by ancestral right. They are therefore to go back with him and return when they have seen him established.

MANSERVANT Yes, sir. [*He moves off.*]

KAUṬILYA Wait a moment. Here is another message – for the Governor of the Prison: 'Out of the affection he bears Minister Rākshasa, His Majesty the Emperor commands that the master-jeweller Chandanadāsa be granted the title of Chief Merchant in all cities throughout the world. And furthermore, let all be freed from bondage save the horses and elephants. But no! With Minister Rākshasa to guide us, what need of horses and elephants? Now therefore

18 Save only for draught animals
Let every bond be loosed.
With the vow I swore fulfilled,
I will keep nothing bound except my hair.

MANSERVANT As Your Honour commands. [*He goes out.*]

KAUṬILYA Chandra Gupta, what further service may I do you?

EMPEROR

I have Rākshasa's friendship, 19
I am established on the throne,
The Nandas are all rooted out:
What further service could there be?

RĀKSHASA Yet let this be –

Vishṇu, who once, incarnate in the sturdy body of a boar, 20
Held the Earth safe amid chaos on the tip of his tusk,
And now, incarnate as a king shelters her in his strong arms from the barbarians' threats,
Long let him save the world, prospering his people and his house, our monarch Chandra Gupta.

[*All go out.*]

Mālatī and Madhava
by Bhavabhūti

Bhavabhūti

It is possible to say a little more about the biography of Bhavabhūti than about that of either Kālidāsa or Viśākhadatta, though the evidence is still by almost any standard extremely tenuous and uncertain. There seems good reason to accept the statement in a twelfth-century source that both he and the poet Vākpatirāja were protégés of King Yaśovarman. This fixes Bhavabhūti to the early part of the eighth century A.D. He was born into a learned brahmin family of southern India. His birthplace, Padmapura, has not been identified for certain, but it was probably in the Vidarbha country (modern Berar) and not far from the river Godāvarī (cf. the affectionate reference to the Godāvarī in Act IX of the present play). However, he came north, perhaps like his hero Mādhava (who himself comes from Vidarbha) to further his philosophical studies. The scene of *Mālatī and Mādhava*, the only one of his plays whose setting is not determined by legend, is laid in the city of Padmāvatī – now no more than an archaeological site, 100 miles south of Agra. 150 miles to the east, and 75 miles south of Yaśovarman's capital Kanauj, lay the city or town of Kālapriya, on the south bank of the Yamunā river. All three of Bhavabhūti's plays were written for performance at the festival of a god Kālapriyanātha, and the evidence would suggest that this is a title ('Lord of Kālapriya') of the Sun-god, a shrine dedicated to whom is stated in various sources to have been established at Kālapriya.

The three plays of Bhavabhūti which survive (it is quite

possible that he wrote others) are, in what seems their most likely order of composition: *The Story of the Great Hero*, a re-telling in dramatic form of the major adventures of the great epic hero Rāma; *Mālatī and Mādhava*; and finally *The Later Story of Rāma*, which tells how after his triumph Rāma is forced to renounce his beloved wife Sītā and is reunited with her only after long years of sorrow.

It is not irrelevant that Bhavabhūti came from a scholarly family and was himself, as his work makes abundantly clear, an extremely highly educated person (although, as the prologue of the present play makes equally clear, he took no pedantic pride in such achievements). He is a very deliberate and, by the standards of Sanskrit literature, an unusually self-aware artist. His plays are full of echoes of one another, and although the matter awaits further study, it seems certain that sometimes at least these are intended to awaken echoes in his audience's mind. In *Mālatī and Mādhava* he sets out to run the gamut of dramatic art, and this basically cheerful and spring-like piece is famous for its evocation in Act V of that rarest of *rasas*, the Repulsive. In particular, one suspects, both the type of play and the theme were chosen as an opportunity to display those aspects of his craft for which there had been least scope in the earlier epic play, such as amorous intrigue and the refinements of feminine passion; and I doubt whether the charge (levelled with monotonous regularity) that Bhavabhūti lacks a sense of humour would survive a stage performance of Act VII.

Although it is an 'invented drama', *Mālatī and Mādhava* (unlike that other famous *prakaraṇa*, the *Toy Cart* of Śūdraka) is as remote in its own way as any *nāṭaka* from the atmosphere of ordinary life. The plot is colourful, improbable and highly romantic. Supernatural elements feature prominently, as do frequent swoonings and other literary manifestations of heightened sensibility. In some ways Bhavabhūti has taken advantage of an existing dramatic genre to provide a theatrical equivalent of the prose romance, which had reached its sophisticated culmination in the work of the seventh-century writer Bāṇa. The relationship of the teenage hero and heroine embodies the perfection of a cultural ideal, and we may feel a more immediate sympathy with the comparatively down-to-earth love affair between Madayantikā and Makaranda. Madayantikā accepts with cheerful relish, rather than with heart-wringing conviction, the convention that the pangs of love have brought her to death's door. Her description of her feelings in Act VII underlines the fact that in India women have traditionally been seen as having if anything even stronger sexual appetites than men – a fact complemented, however, by the expectation of absolute commitment to one man throughout their life, and by the requirement that sexual behaviour should be a strictly private matter. We are not intended to suppose that Mālatī's feelings are less physical and more ethereal than Madayantikā's, merely that the expression of them is held in check by a more sensitive refinement and womanly reserve. Another point of difference from the traditional sexual patterns of Western culture, abundantly illustrated in the relationship of Mādhava and Makaranda, is that overt physical attraction and warmth between two men (or two women) is not regarded as having any sexual overtones.

In many respects, and in particular in the direct expression of intense feeling, Bhavabhūti often seems to be testing the language and conventions of Sanskrit poetry to their limits. The weight of Kālidāsa's genius must sometimes have rested heavily upon him. In his case the quality of 'Limpidity' is not one which one would single out for special praise, even though his language is often both clear and graceful. For he can be at his most interesting when he seems to be struggling to make Sanskrit say things which it has never said before. In the first act of the *Later Story of Rāma*, Rāma, with Sītā asleep on his arm, reflects on their mutual love:

This state where there is no twoness in responses of joy or sorrow,
Where the heart finds rest, where feeling does not dry with age,
Where concealments fall away in time and the essential love is ripened –
Blessed is this state of human fulfilment, which we find once if ever.

The use here of the word *āvaraṇa*, 'covering, concealment', to refer to psychological defences is probably unique to Bhavabhūti. And in the last line the word *sumānuṣa*, evidently his own coinage, which I have translated by 'state of human fulfilment' and which literally means 'good human being-ness', seems to have baffled all Western and many Indian commentators. It might at first sight mean 'good human being', and so they have taken it, unfortunately wrecking both grammar and sense.* Two other explanations have come down to us: one, that it means 'being a good person', also a linguistic misinterpre-

*A note to Sanskritists: Bhavabhūti's use of an apparently ambiguous word is not a piece of artistic incompetence, but does reveal how educated he expected his audience to be: those properly alive to the use of *bhadram* with a genitive (Pāṇini 2.3.73), once alerted by the neuters in the preceding relative clauses, would have recognized *tasya sumānuṣasya* as a neuter, and would therefore have been in no danger of misinterpreting it.

tation, though a more subtle one; the other, that it means 'married partnership', an accurate statement of the word's reference rather than of its meaning, though obviously deriving in the first place from someone who had understood the stanza correctly

Clearly, then, even in his own country a proper understanding of Bhavabhūti's intentions was a fragile thing. It is his ideas, not just his language, which cause the difficulty, and one of the basic reasons seems to be that he pursued psychological introspection to a point unusual in his cultural environment. In itself the ideal of human partnership expressed in the stanza just quoted is not original to Bhavabhūti. It is implicit in the whole Indian tradition. Kālidāsa also gives moving expression to it, but by portraying it in action rather than by analysing it. The notion that feeling is conveyed in literature by finding an adequate 'objective correlative' for it was very familiar to Indian critics, as the mention of 'determinants' in connection with the theory of *rasa* will have indicated. Naturally, as a dramatist, Bhavabhūti himself does not fail to realize the ideal in human terms – in one sense his whole *Later Story of Rāma* is an objective correlative for this theme. But where his poetical contribution is, if not at its most important, then certainly at its most distinctive is in his ability to make such a powerfully direct analytical statement of the theme, and see it within the wider context of the human quest for self-fulfilment.

Another stanza, spoken by a minor character in the same play, illustrates both Bhavabhūti's search for underlying conceptual unities and his artistic readiness to play upon his audience's awareness that they are participating in a work of fiction. On the surface the words refer to the sufferings of his heroine Sītā. Secondarily they refer, with their mention of the theatrical doctrine of *rasa*, to the drama which he has made out of her sufferings and to the great epic poem, the *Rāmāyaṇa*, on which his drama is based. But in this reference to an underlying singleness of *rasa*, at a time when the philosophical implications of the *rasa* theory had been little studied, it does not seem too fanciful to glimpse something of Bhavabhūti's own vision of life. The Sanskrit name of the Sorrowful *rasa*, *karuṇa*, most literally means 'pitiable', and there are therefore overtones of a human community of suffering which are difficult to bring out in translation:

TAMASĀ: What a course this story has run!
One *rasa*, the Sorrowful, made various by its varied causes,
Assumes one manifestation or another,
As water the form of whirlpools, bubbles, waves,
And yet the whole is water.

Malatī and Mādhava

CHARACTERS IN THE PLAY

**Sanskrit speakers are marked with an asterisk. Characters not appearing on stage are mentioned in brackets.*

[The KING, ruler of Padmāvatī]
[BHŪRIVASU, a minister of the King]
MĀLATĪ, Bhūrivasu's daughter
LAVANGIKĀ, Mālatī's foster-sister

[DEVARĀTA, minister to the King of the southern state of Vidarbha]
*MĀDHAVA, Devarāta's son
*MAKARANDA, Mādhava's friend
KALAHAMSAKA, Mādhava's servant, in love with Mandārikā

[NANDANA, minister and intimate friend of the King]
MADAYANTIKĀ, Nandana's sister and friend of Mālatī

*KĀMANDAKĪ, Buddhist mendicant nun, friend of both Bhūrivasu and Devarāta
AVALOKITĀ, chief pupil of Kāmandakī
BUDDHARAKSHITĀ, pupil of Kāmandakī and friend of Madayantikā
MANDĀRIKĀ, servant girl of the convent, sweetheart of Kalahamsaka

*AGHORAGHAṆṬA, a Śaivite adept and worshipper of Karālā (a form of the Fierce Goddess)

*KAPĀLAKUṆḌALĀ, Aghoraghaṇṭa's pupil
*SAUDĀMANĪ, former pupil of Kāmandakī, now a Śaivite adept

Also PORTERESS and two MAIDSERVANTS of Bhūrivasu's household, *MAN (official in Nandana's household)

The action of the play takes place in or near the city of Padmāvatī.

*Benediction**

1 When Śiva dances, and Kumāra's peacock, drawn by the exultant thunder of Nandin's drum,
Has sent the frightened Snake King spiralling into his trunk,
May Gaṇeśa's frantic head-shakings, which make the heavens buzz
With bees that swarm from his temples, long protect you.

And

2 Opposing the skulls of their garland to the Ganges' stream,
Blending their radiance with his forehead-eye lightning,

*The first benedictory stanza invokes the elephant-headed Gaṇeśa, god of obstacles and their elimination. Peacocks dance in the thunder of the rainy season, and are the natural enemies of snakes. Bees gather on an elephant's cheeks and forehead in search of his ichor or rut-fluid. Thus when Śiva's attendant Nandin beats the drum for Śiva's cosmic dance, this thunder-like sound attracts the peacock belonging to Śiva's son Kumāra. Frightened by the appearance of a peacock, the Snake King Vāsuki, or Śesha, whom Śiva often wears twined about his person, dives for shelter into Gaṇeśa's trunk, and Gaṇeśa's attempts to shake him off dislodge all the bees that have clustered around his head.

The second stanza invokes Śiva the skull-bearing ascetic: he carries the crescent moon on his head, and the river Ganges flows from heaven to earth through his matted red hair. On his forehead Śiva has a third eye, capable of flashing forth a deadly flame.

BENEDICTION

Harbouring like a tender spike of ketaka the crescent moon,
Bound with their tendrils of snakes, may the matted locks of the Lord of Ghosts protect you.

PROLOGUE

[*After the Benediction, enter the Director.*]

DIRECTOR [*looking eastwards* *] Behold, the holy lamp of all the continents of Earth is almost risen, and I do homage –

Of glory you are the abode, O God of infinite forms; 3
Then in your mercy a pre-eminent splendour upon me bestow.
Whatever is ill, avert it, Lord of the World, from this your suppliant;
Whatever is good, turn it, O holy one, to my greater blessedness.

[*Looking off-stage*] My assistant, the auspicious preliminaries have been attended to, and people have come from many parts for the festival of the blessed Kālapriyanātha. What then are the actors waiting for?

[*Enter his assistant.*]

ASSISTANT Sir, the assembly of the wise and learned is asking to be entertained with a new comedy,† and we

*By a zonal convention, this was always to the front of the stage.

†In fact a *prakaraṇa* (see Introduction, p. 18).

are at a loss for a work which meets their requirements.

DIRECTOR What do our noble and learned patrons demand?

ASSISTANT

4 'A work which plumbs the depths of every emotion,
Action that is informed with human feeling,
Fiery spirits tempered by the tender laws of love,
A marvellous tale and eloquence in its telling.'

DIRECTOR [*miming inspiration*] I have it!

ASSISTANT What, sir?

DIRECTOR There is in the south a city called Padmapura where lives a certain family of brahmins, followers of the Taittirīya recension and descended from the great seer Kaśyapa, expounders of the Veda, men whose presence will purify the row in which they sit, guardians of the five sacred fires, strict in their vows, drinkers of soma, by name Udumbara.

5 They are scholars who, in the cause of truth alone,
Apply themselves ceaselessly to the study of Holy Writ.
For charity alone do they study worldly advancement.
Only for offspring they marry, and only with a view to
penance do they seek to prolong their lives.

Now a descendant of that same family, grandson of Bhaṭṭa Gopāla of auspicious memory and son of Nīlakaṇṭha of pure renown, son also of Jātūkarṇī, a descendant I say bearing the title Śrīkaṇṭha and named Bhavabhūti, being a poet with a natural affection for actors, has handed us one of his own compositions, one full of the qualities you have listed. And about it this is his declaration:

Whoever they are who declare their contempt for my work 6
Must think as they please: I have not laboured for them.
But there will be born some kindred spirit to mine –
For time is endless, and the world is wide.

Again –

Study of the Vedas, knowledge of the Upanishads, of sānkhya and of yoga – 7
Why talk of all that? It confers no merit on a play.
Mature and sensitive language, profundity of thought,
From *these* are inferred the learning and craftsmanship.

ASSISTANT So that is why you have been rehearsing us all in that same work! But sir, the aged Buddhist mendicant Kāmandakī – it is you yourself who have been reading her first scene, while I have taken the part of her disciple Avalokitā.

DIRECTOR What of it?

ASSISTANT Well, how are you going to get into the costume of the hero of this play, Mālatī's sweetheart Mādhava?

DIRECTOR I shall manage it while Kalahamsaka and Makaranda are making their entrances.

ASSISTANT In that case let us do honour to our respected audience by performing the work.

DIRECTOR By all means. See, I am now Kāmandakī.

ASSISTANT And I Avalokitā.

[*They withdraw.*]

PRELUDE TO ACT I

[They now enter seated and wearing robes of red cloth.]

KĀMANDAKĪ Avalokitā, my dear.

AVALOKITĀ Command me, Reverence.

KĀMANDAKĪ How much I long for this marriage between Bhūrivasu's daughter Mālatī and Devarāta's son Mādhava! [*Delightedly, indicating an auspicious throbbing of the left eye*]

8 So even my left eye
Can see into the heart of things,
And by its throbbing promises
That all will turn out well.

AVALOKITĀ You are very exercised in your mind over all this, Reverence. It seems so strange that Minister Bhūrivasu should put you to such work – you who wear a mendicant's robes and live by the begging bowl. And you for your part, to commit yourself to it now that you have rid your mind of worldly attachments!

KĀMANDAKĪ No, no, dear child!

9 That the Minister employs me as his servant
Is due to his affection – the strongest proof of his regard.
And if by sacrificing my life or my vows
I can achieve my friend's desires, then achieved they shall be.

Do you not know how we all met as students and formed

a lasting bond of friendship? It was then, in front of Saudāmanī and myself, that Bhūrivasu and Devarāta solemnly swore that they would make a marriage between their children. And that is why Devarāta, now that he is minister to the King of Vidarbha, has done well to send his son Mādhava from Kuṇḍinapura to study logic here in Padmāvatī.

He has both reminded his beloved friend 10
Of the oath they swore of uniting their offspring
And at the same time revealed for our delight
A son of such merit as is seldom seen in this world.

AVALOKITĀ In that case, Reverence, why does Minister Bhūrivasu himself not bestow Mālatī upon the young man, instead of setting you to arrange a clandestine match?

KĀMANDAKĪ

Nandana, the King's close friend, is asking for her hand, 11
And doing so through the mouth of the King himself.
A direct rebuff might therefore anger both,
While all may be well by the use of this stratagem.

AVALOKITĀ It is extraordinary: from his lack of concern you would think that Minister Bhūrivasu had never even heard of Mādhava.

KĀMANDAKĪ Deliberate secrecy!

From Mālatī and Mādhava above all, 12
In their youthful openheartedness,
He must be careful to conceal
The real truth of his intentions.

13 But if the fact that they have fallen in love
Becomes a matter of common gossip,
It will suit us well: for that is the way
That Nandana and the King can be misled.

Consider –

14 In outward behaviour thoroughly charming and compliant,
Concealing from others the slenderest clue to his intentions,
The wise man all by himself can fool the world,
As he quietly furthers his own ends and keeps his own counsel.

AVALOKITĀ I have done as you asked and found various excuses to make Mādhava walk along the highway near Minister Bhūrivasu's mansion.

KĀMANDAKĪ Yes, Mālatī's foster-sister Lavangikā has been telling me

15 That, as he strolls again and again on the city road nearby,
Mālatī, gazing and gazing again from a window high up in the house,
As if she were Rati confronted with Kāma reborn,
With limbs which her love has made charmingly weak, is pining.

AVALOKITĀ It is so. And to distract her longing she has painted a portrait of Mādhava, which this morning Lavangikā put into Mandārikā's hands.

KĀMANDAKĪ [*thoughtfully*] Lavangikā has acted well, for Mādhava's attendant Kalahamsaka is in love with this selfsame Mandārikā, the servant-girl of our convent.

And so if it passes through their hands, this portrait could well provide the preface to our tale.

AVALOKITĀ I have also persuaded Mādhava to go at dawn this morning to the park where they are celebrating the Festival of Love. I heard that Mālatī was going there, and thought they might meet.

KĀMANDAKĪ Well done, dearest child, well done! In your eagerness to help me you remind me of my very first pupil Saudāmanī.

AVALOKITĀ Reverence, Saudāmanī herself has now achieved magical power and is on the Holy Mountain, observing the vows of a Śaivite adept.

KĀMANDAKĪ How did you hear that?

AVALOKITĀ Here in this city at the Great Burning-ground is an image of the Fierce Goddess,* named Karālā.

KĀMANDAKĪ Yes, one who demands the sacrifice of living creatures of every kind, or so adventurous people have reported.

AVALOKITĀ From the Holy Mountain has come a skull-bearing magician named Aghoraghaṇṭa, a prowler by night, who is living in the nearby woods. He has a powerful disciple Kapālakuṇḍalā who visits the goddess at each twilight, and it is from her that I have the news.

KĀMANDAKĪ Where Saudāmanī is concerned, nothing is impossible.

AVALOKITĀ So much for that. But Reverence, if Mādhava's companion and boyhood friend Makaranda

*Śiva's consort Devī ('The Goddess') has a benign form in which she is known by such names as Umā or Pārvatī, and complements Śiva in his benign aspect. In her fierce form, known as Durgā, Kālī, Chāmuṇḍā, etc., she parallels rather than complements the terrible aspect of Śiva – and was the object of a special and rather sinister cult.

could marry Nandana's sister Madayantikā, that would be a further blessing upon Mādhava.

KĀMANDAKĪ I have engaged her friend Buddharakshitā upon the task.

AVALOKITĀ That was well done, Reverence.

KĀMANDAKĪ Come then, let us find out how Mādhava has been faring, and then let us go and see Mālatī.

[*Both rise.*]

[*Thoughtfully*] Mālatī is a girl of delicate sensibility, and in modelling myself uponthe 'entrusted go-between'* I must use all my skill.

16 May she in her beauty delight the noble youth
As the autumn moon delights the waterlily, and may he in turn win her:
After such skilful fashioning of complementary virtues
Let the Creator's work be fruitful and gladden the world.

[*They withdraw.*]

*The kind that has total discretion to manage matters according to her own judgement – one of the categories of go-between recognized by the *Kāma Sūtra*.

Act I

[*Enter Kalahamsaka, carrying a picture and drawing materials.*]

KALAHAMSAKA Where now can I find my master Mādhava, the one who has overthrown Mālatī's heart by a grace of form that matches the Love God's own? [*Walking about*] I'm tired. I'll rest for a moment in this garden before I look for my master, Makaranda's friend. [*Enters the garden and sits down.*]

[*Enter Makaranda.*]

MAKARANDA Avalokitā says that Mādhava has gone to the park of the Love Temple, and so I'll go and look for him. [*Walking about and seeing him*] Ah! here comes my friend. [*Looking closely*] But his

Walk is slow, his eye is vacant, his body ill at ease, 17
His breathing quickened. What can it be? But what else,
Except that love's writ runs everywhere and youth is in disarray
As one sweet emotion chases another, bringing all resistance to nought.

[*Enter Mādhava as described.*]

MĀDHAVA [*to himself*]

If I think for a moment of that countenance lovely as the moon, 18
Hardly thereafter can I tear my mind from it,

All my shame defeated, my self-control lost, my strength of mind
Shattered, and my wits quite suddenly bemused.

Strange!

19 Arrested by wonder, lost to all other sensation,
Becalmed with joy as in a lake of nectar –
All this when she was there, and yet now
My suffering heart seems kissed by coals of fire.

MAKARANDA Over here, Mādhava my friend!

MĀDHAVA Why, there is my dear friend Makaranda!

MAKARANDA [*coming up to him*] Dear Mādhava, the sun is scorching to the face: why not sit in this garden for a moment?

MĀDHAVA Just as you say, friend.

KALAHAMSAKA [*seeing them*] Ah, Mādhava and his friend Makaranda are gracing this very same garden. I'll show him the painting of himself which brought relief to the love-tormented eyes of Mālatī. But no, let him enjoy a rest.

MAKARANDA Let us sit down where this mountain ebony is perfuming the garden with the coolly astringent scent of its blossoms.

[*They do so.*]

MAKARANDA Dearest Mādhava, you are back from the park of the Love Temple, where all the women of the city have been celebrating the Festival of Love, and you look quite unlike yourself. I am wondering whether you too may not have come a little under the influence of the god?

[*Mādhava stares at the ground in embarrassment.*]

[*Smiling*] Why are you keeping your lotus face bent downwards? After all

The god who between the sluggish mass of mankind 20
And the great Lord of the Universe makes no distinction
Is one whose power is everywhere recognized:
Do not hang back in shame from telling me.

MĀDHAVA Friend, am I refusing to tell you? Listen. My interest aroused by Avalokitā, I went to the temple of the Love God. And after I had strolled around, I felt tired, and stopped beneath a young bakula tree which stood in the temple courtyard, ornamented with clusters of buds on which the bees were thickly swarming, drawn there by its wine-sweet perfume. Scattered beneath it was a great quantity of fallen blossoms, and I began to amuse myself by weaving them into an intricate garland. Then suddenly, as if I were seeing the very banner of world victory which accompanies the Love God himself, there emerged from the temple sanctum someone whose girlish dress, arranged with elaborate skill, proclaimed her maiden state – a girl of noble appearance, attended by a magnificent retinue of servants.

Of loveliness she was the guardian deity, 21
Or if you will, the abode of essential beauty.
Moonlight and lotus fibre, nectar and autumn nights,
Of such, friend, was she made, and Love himself the maker.

Then in answer to the fond entreaties of her maidservants, who had taken it into their heads to pick the thickly clustering flowers, she came towards the very spot where the young bakula tree stood. And I realized that she must have been many days pining for love of some lucky man. For

22 Her body was wasted as a trampled lotus stalk,
She could scarcely respond to the urgings of her attendants,
And the pale beauty of a spotless moon
Was there in the fresh-cut ivory of her cheek.

But from the moment that I caught sight of her my eyes felt bathed in nectar, and my heart was drawn to her as is iron ore to the lodestone. And in short

23 To the end that I am racked with unceasing torment,
My thoughts without seeking the reason are fixed on her.
Man's lot is a mixture of good and ill
Apportioned him by an irresistible fate.

MAKARANDA You cannot, dear Mādhava, talk in the same breath of love and of seeking reasons:

24 It is some inner cause that is the binding force –
Affections do not dwell upon the surface of things.
For the searing sun makes the lotus bloom,
And the moon's cold rays can melt the moonstone.

What happened then?

MĀDHAVA Thereupon

25 With eyebrows quivering, saying to each other 'There he is!',
Having seen and seemingly having recognized me,
Her companions, skilled in reading each other's thoughts,
Stole nectarous glances at me, sweet with smiles.

MAKARANDA [*to himself*] How's this – they recognized him?

MĀDHAVA Then they playfully clapped their hands together, shaking the rows of bracelets on their wrists, and with a graceful flurry of foot-movements which set their anklets sweetly jingling and which mingled with the tinkling of the tiny bells about their waists, they turned and said, 'Mistress, we are in luck, for here is someone's sweetheart' – slyly pointing me out as they spoke.

MAKARANDA Oh, signs of a love already strong!

KALAHAMSAKA What's this, what do I hear? – seductive talk of women?

MAKARANDA And what then?

MĀDHAVA

At this, in a way too heavenly to describe, 26
She showed that Love's teaching had disciplined her wholly,
Flashing a trembling loveliness into her lotus eyes,
Demanding the surrender of her limbs, confounding all resistance.

And then

With eyes which blossomed into stillness while her slender eyebrows danced, 27
Which again turned softly to buds yet lengthened at the corners,
Which, falling upon my encountering eye, withdrew,
She made me the varied object of her gaze.

Shyly and fondly turning or scarcely seeming to move, 28
The pupils glinting with a wonder that blossomed in her still,
Those covert glances of her long-lashed eyes found my heart
Defenceless – stole it and pierced it, swallowed it, tore it from me.

Yet helpless though I was made by the passion-thrilling nearness of one who had so devastated my heart, I did my best to hide my confusion and managed somehow or other to finish the rest of the garland of bakula which I had started. She joined the large retinue of eunuchs armed with swords and canes of office that surrounded her elephant, and mounting upon it set out along the road to the city. And then

29 As she receded, she kept turning her face towards me,
Bending round like a lotus upon the stalk of her neck,
Her long-lashed eyes implanting in the depths of my heart
A glance that was barbed at once with nectar and with poison.

And ever since,

30 Indefinable in any words,
Beyond anything I have ever known in this birth
Plunging my senses into a great forest of delusion,
An inner turmoil has both numbed me and set me on fire.

31 I cannot discriminate even what is before my eyes,
And even over what I know well, my memory plays me false.
Nothing will allay my fever, neither cool lakes nor moonlight,
And my mind is untethered and pictures things as it will.

KALAHAMSAKA Some girl has certainly won his heart – could it be Mālatī?

MAKARANDA [*to himself*] He is totally infatuated. Ought I then to discourage him? But no –

'Do not be deluded by the self-born God of Love,' 32
'Do not cloud your mind with these turbulent passions,'
– Useless indeed would such exhortation be now,
Where love and fresh youth have shown themselves in strength.

[*Aloud*] Tell me, friend, did you find out her name and family?

MĀDHAVA Listen. While she was mounting her elephant, there was one girl among her great crowd of companions who lingered behind, and as she picked the flowers of the young bakula tree drew gradually closer to where I was. She saluted me, and pretending that she was talking about the garland I had made, 'Sir,' she said, 'the delightfulness of your fashioning has filled my mistress with longing. She is quite unused to anything of the sort. I hope therefore that all this cleverness will not be in vain. So lovely a product of the Creator's skill ought not to go to waste, but rather to be enhanced by lying at last against her bosom.'

MAKARANDA Oh, cleverly put!*

MĀDHAVA When I questioned her she told me that her mistress was Bhūrivasu's daughter, Mālatī, and that she herself was her mistress's foster-sister and favourite companion Lavangikā.

KALAHAMSAKA [*delightedly*] Mālatī? Then the God of Love has smiled on us – victory is ours!

MAKARANDA Minister Bhūrivasu's daughter? That is very impressive. Indeed, Her Reverence Kāmandakī is always talking about Mālatī. There is even a rumour that

*The preceding word-play in the Sanskrit original is more elaborate.

the King himself has requested her on behalf of Nandana.

MĀDHAVA At her earnest request I took the bakula garland from my neck and handed it to her. Glancing meaningfully at the part where looking at Mālatī had made my work clumsy and uneven, she accepted it with many protestations of gratitude. And then in the great press of townsfolk leaving the festival I lost sight of her, and so came here.

MAKARANDA Friend, it all fits in with your seeing that Mālatī was in love. Quite obviously the paleness of cheek and all the other signs which you detected were due to you – all we need to know is where she can have seen you before. For it is certainly impossible that such a high-born girl, once her affections have been fixed in one quarter, should fall in love at first sight with someone else. Besides which

33 When her friends exchanged glances
And spoke of 'someone's sweetheart',
It was a sign that she already loved you –
And so was the veiled speech of her foster-sister.

KALAHAMSAKA [*coming up to them*] And so is this. [*He shows them the portrait.*]

[*Both look at it.*]

MAKARANDA Kalahamsaka, who painted this portrait of Mādhava?

KALAHAMSAKA The same who stole his heart.

MAKARANDA Mālatī?

KALAHAMSAKA Exactly.

MĀDHAVA Dear Makaranda, it looks as if your guess was right.

MAKARANDA Where did you get it from, Kalahamsaka?

KALAHAMSAKA From Mandārikā – and she in turn got it from Lavangikā.

MAKARANDA What reason did Mandārikā give why Mālatī should have drawn Mādhava's portrait?

KALAHAMSAKA To calm her longing.

MAKARANDA Dear Mādhava, breathe easy:

She who is moonlight to your eyes 34
Has in turn made you the noble object of her love.
And that you will be united is not in doubt,
When Love and Fate have worked so hard to achieve it.

I must know what she looks like to cause you such turmoil: draw Mālatī's portrait here too.

MĀDHAVA As you wish, friend. [*While drawing*] Oh Makaranda!

Time and again the flooding tears cloud my vision, 35
And the thought of her paralyses my limbs.
With sweat starting forth and fingers endlessly trembling,
How can I set my hand to drawing?

But still I am determined. [*He spends a long time drawing and then displays the result.*]

MAKARANDA [*examining it*] Well, your infatuation is not surprising. [*With interest*] A stanza, so quickly composed? [*He reads it out*]

'The world knows many experiences naturally sweet, 36
The new moon's crescent and much beside, sights to gladden the heart.
But that my eyes should have seen on this earth such moonlight
I count as the one true happiness of my life.'

[*Enter in haste Mandārikā.*]

MANDĀRIKĀ Kalahamsaka, Kalahamsaka, I've tracked you down! [*Seeing the others, in embarrassment*] Oh, these gentlemen are here too! [*Approaching them*] Greetings, sirs.

BOTH Mandārikā! Here, sit down.

MANDĀRIKĀ [*seating herself*] Kalahamsaka, give me the picture.

KALAHAMSAKA [*obtaining it*] Here you are.

MANDĀRIKĀ [*looking at it*] Kalahamsaka! Who drew Mālatī's picture here and why?

KALAHAMSAKA The person she herself drew, and for the same reason.

MANDĀRIKĀ [*in delight*] Then the Creator's skill is rewarded!

MAKARANDA Mandārikā, is it true what your sweetheart here has been telling us?

MANDĀRIKĀ Entirely, sir.

MAKARANDA But where had Mālatī seen Mādhava?

MANDĀRIKĀ Lavangikā says it was from her window.

MAKARANDA Friend, we do often walk along the road by the Minister's house, and so this is quite possible.

MANDĀRIKĀ Will you give me leave, sirs? I must tell my friend Lavangikā how the God of Love has shown himself.

MAKARANDA An excellent idea.

[*Mandārikā goes out with the picture-box.*]

MAKARANDA Friend, the midday sun is burning harshly – come, let us go back.

[*They get up and walk about.*]

MĀDHAVA Thus I imagine –

37 The sweat which now cascades
Across the innocent beauty of her face

Is setting at nought the skill of her attendants,
The morning elaboration of saffron-painted lines.*

Now when the opening buds have unsheathed the jasmine 38
And poured its perfumed nectar out on you,
Stroke softly, wind, her gentle eyes and curving body,
Then touch me too upon my every limb.

MAKARANDA

Alas, the implacable Love God 39
Bears hard on Mādhava's tender limbs,
Working a cruel change from mind to body
Like horn-fever wasting the young elephant.

Then we must look to Her Reverence Kāmandakī to help us.

MĀDHAVA Oh strange!

Here first, then here, before me and behind, 40
Within, without, all around, the vision of her appears,
Her face an unfolding golden lotus
With eyes which she cannot keep from turning towards me.

Oh Makaranda,

My body has broken out in fever 41
And delusion veils my senses.
My longing mounts, my limbs whirl.
My mind burns within me, and loses itself in her.

[*All withdraw.*]

* Ornamental painting of musk over saffron was applied cosmetically to the cheeks and breasts of women.

PRELUDE TO ACT II

[*Enter the maidservants.*]

FIRST My dear, what was that you were talking to Avalokitā about, over by the music room?

SECOND Well, it seems, my dear, that Her Reverence has now heard all about what happened in the park of the Love Temple from Mādhava's friend Makaranda. So she now wants to see Mālatī, and she has sent Avalokitā to find out where she is. I was telling Avalokitā that our mistress is alone with Lavangikā.

FIRST But Lavangikā stayed behind in the park to pick flowers – do you mean that she is back?

SECOND Exactly. The moment she arrived, our mistress seized hold of her, sent all the servants away and took her up to the upper terrace.

FIRST To talk about the young man, of course.

SECOND [*with a sigh*] Much good it will do her. Seeing him face to face today will only have made her more infatuated than ever. And this very morning the Minister gave his answer when the King asked for her hand on Nandana's behalf.

FIRST What did he say?

SECOND He said, 'It is for Your Majesty to dispose of your daughters as you will.' So I am afraid that this love for Mādhava is going to be nothing but a dart that will rankle for the rest of her life.

FIRST Perhaps Her Reverence will show what she is capable of.

SECOND Foolish optimist – come on, away.

[*They withdraw.*]

Act II

[*Enter, seated, Mālatī pining with love, attended by Lavangikā.*]

MĀLATĪ Oh, and what then, dearest Lavangikā?

LAVANGIKĀ Then the young man presented me with this bakula garland.

MĀLATĪ [*taking it and delightedly examining it*] Lavangikā, one side of the work is unevenly woven!

LAVANGIKĀ Well, you're the one to blame for that particular imperfection.

MĀLATĪ What do you mean?

LAVANGIKĀ I mean that it was you who made the dark-limbed youth so clumsy.

MĀLATĪ Dear Lavangikā, you are always ready to encourage me.

LAVANGIKĀ My dear, encourage you? Nothing of the sort. Good heavens, you saw him yourself, looking at you with those eyes like blossomed lotuses stirring in the soft breeze, held in check by his pretended interest in the garland, but growing wider and wider in spite of himself, while above the long corners which were frozen with astonishment his eyebrows danced and quivered like the bow of the God of Love himself!

MĀLATĪ [*hugging her*] Oh but dear Lavangikā, was the way he looked just a natural expression, and likely to deceive someone who has only seen him for a moment, or was it really as you imagine?

LAVANGIKĀ [*with a smile, ironically*] And I suppose the ballet without music which you danced at the same moment was no more than natural to *you*?

MĀLATĪ [*smiling in confusion*] Well, what happened then?

LAVANGIKĀ I lost him in the crush of the returning procession, and went on to see Mandārikā. I had given her that portrait at first light this morning.

MĀLATĪ Why?

LAVANGIKĀ Mādhava's servant Kalahamsaka is in love with her and I wanted her to show it to him. And Mandārikā had good news for me.

MĀLATĪ [*to herself*] Kalahamsaka will certainly have shown the picture to his master. [*Aloud*] What good news was that, my dear?

LAVANGIKĀ This! Something with which your tormentor, being himself tormented, momentarily eased the dreadful pangs of his hopeless love – a portrait of yourself. [*She shows it to Mālatī.*]

MĀLATĪ [*sighing with happiness and examining it at length*] What a pessimist I'd need to be, to think of doubting encouragement like this! Why, there is writing as well. [*She reads it out*]

'The world knows many experiences naturally sweet,
The new moon's crescent and much besides, sights to gladden the heart.
But that my eyes should have seen on the earth such moonlight
I count as the one true happiness of my life.'

[*Happily*] Sir, your words match your creation in sweetness. But though seeing you is delightful at the time, it brings endless torment after it, and I envy those girls who have never seen you – or who manage to keep control over their own hearts.
[*She weeps.*]

LAVANGIKĀ My dear, do you still refuse to hope?

MĀLATĪ Why should I hope?

LAVANGIKĀ Because the very one for whom you have been pining like a fading jasmine blossom has been made by the god to feel a similar torment.

MĀLATĪ Then I wish him well of it, but for me there is no hope. [*Weeping*] And now especially, dearest Lavangikā –

This passion spreads and spreads like a sharp poison. 1
It burns like a blaze fanned into smokelessness.
Like a heavy fever it racks me in every limb.
There is none who can save me, neither father, nor mother, nor you.

LAVANGIKĀ The meetings of good people are always so – immediate delight and then the pangs of separation. And besides, if seeing him for a moment from a window reduced you to a state where the moon's cool rays could scorch like fire until in the end the cruel workings of passion had put your very life in danger – well then, now that you have come face to face with him at last, is it surprising if you are tormented? I know only this, my dear: in this world union with a noble lover truly worthy of one's love is something to be praised, and something which comes about only after much heartache.

MĀLATĪ You prize my life too dearly – I will not listen to your reckless talk. [*Weeping*] But no, I am the guilty one, looking out for him time after time as I did, giving way to my misery and losing all sense of shame and right behaviour. But Lavangikā, even so

Let the moon blaze full in the sky night after night, 2
And let Love scorch – for what, more than death, can they threaten?

I shall hold dear my noble father, my mother of unblemished line,
A spotless family – but never myself nor my life.

LAVANGIKĀ [*to herself*] What help is there now?

[*A porteress half shows herself on stage.*]

PORTERESS There is Her Reverence Kāmandakī –

BOTH Her Reverence?

PORTERESS – come to see you, mistress.

BOTH Then show her in at once.

[*The porteress withdraws.*]

[*Mālatī hides the picture.*]

LAVANGIKĀ [*to herself*] This has certainly happened at the right moment.

[*Enter Kāmandakī and Avalokitā.*]

KĀMANDAKĪ Excellently done, Bhūrivasu my dear friend: 'It is for Your Majesty to dispose of your daughters as you will' – that is an answer to keep both parties happy. And to judge by events in the park of the Love Temple today, it seems that fate itself is on our side. What has happened over the bakula garland and the exchange of portraits gives me an extraordinary thrill of joy. For the highest of all blessings in marriage is mutual love. As the sage Angiras has declared, 'Where his mind and eye are drawn, there is the woman in whom a man may find his wealth.'

AVALOKITĀ Here is Mālatī.

KĀMANDAKĪ [*gazing on her*]

3 Thin beyond measure, delicate as the pith of the fresh plantain,
Lovely to the eye as the waning crescent of the moon,
Wasted by the torturing fires of passion,
This fair one at once gladdens and alarms my heart.

With her cheek that is dusty pale, 4
She has become yet lovelier.
On those born fair
Love scores his victory gracefully.

Without a doubt she is imagining union with her loved one. For I see

A heaving of the fastening of her skirt, a quivering lip and drooping arms, 5
A beading of sweat, eyes with moist, soft, unfocused pupils,
Her limbs unstrung, her bud-shaped breasts rising and falling,
The down on her cheek erect, a state between swooning and consciousness.

[*She approaches them.*]

[*Lavangikā nudges Mālatī. Both stand up.*]

MĀLATĪ Greetings, Reverence.

KĀMANDAKĪ Noble daughter, may you meet with all that you desire.

LAVANGIKĀ Here is a seat for you, Reverence.

[*All seat themselves.*]

MĀLATĪ Is all well with you, Reverence?

KĀMANDAKĪ [*with a sigh*] Well enough!

LAVANGIKĀ [*to herself*] Here is the prologue to some drama of intrigue! [*Aloud*] The heavy tears which choke your throat, Reverence, have quite altered your voice. What can be causing you such distress?

KĀMANDAKĪ Why, this very friendship so at variance with my mendicant's garb.

LAVANGIKĀ What do you mean?

KĀMANDAKĪ Then you have not heard that

6 This triumphant earthly weapon of the God of Love,
This girlish body so abounding in amorous graces,
Is destined for a disastrous match
And a sour end to all its promise?

[*Mālatī shows distress.*]

LAVANGIKĀ It is true. To please the King, the Minister is giving Mālatī to Nandana, and everyone hates him for it.

MĀLATĪ [*to herself*] What, Father sacrificing me to the King?

KĀMANDAKĪ Extraordinary!

7 How could he so disregard merit? But no –
What is love of one's child to a mind obsessed with politics? –
His only thought, that giving his daughter away
Would win him the friendship of that crony of the King's.

MĀLATĪ [*to herself*] Father thinks less of his own daughter than of pleasing the King!

LAVANGIKĀ You must be right, Reverence – or surely the Minister would have hesitated over such an old and ugly suitor.

MĀLATĪ [*to herself*] Oh, I am finished, destroyed by a thunderbolt.

LAVANGIKĀ Please therefore, Reverence, save our dearest Mālatī from this living death – to you too she is a daughter.

KĀMANDAKĪ Why, you simpleton, what do you think 'Her Reverence' can do in the matter? Two things determine a girl's future, generally speaking – fathers and fate. And as for Śakuntalā, Kauśika's offspring, in love with Dushyanta, or the nymph Urvaśī who loved Purūravas, as history informs us (and then of course there *was* Vāsavadattā, who gave herself to Udayana, when her father had bestowed her on King Sanjaya, and so on) – those were very reckless escapades and by no means to be recommended. In fact

In deliberately bestowing on the King's great friend and counsellor 8
His very own daughter, let the Minister find satisfaction –
And let her too be united with the ill-favoured one,
As is the moon's fair digit with the smoky Demon of Eclipse.

MĀLATĪ [*weeping*] Oh Father, if you treat me so, then greed has triumphed everywhere.

AVALOKITĀ You have stayed long, Reverence. Remember that the noble Mādhava is not well.

KĀMANDAKĪ Yes, I am going now. Give me leave, dear child.

LAVANGIKĀ [*aside*] Mālatī dear, now we can find out from Her Reverence where that young man comes from.

MĀLATĪ My dear, I *am* curious.

LAVANGIKĀ [*aloud*] Who *is* this Mādhava for whom you feel so much affection, Reverence?

KĀMANDAKĪ It is a long and not very relevant story.

LAVANGIKĀ Even so, Reverence, tell us, if you please.

KĀMANDAKĪ Listen, then. The King of Vidarbha has a minister, the brightest jewel of all his eminent statesmen, one Devarāta by name – your father indeed knows him as a former fellow-student and as a man whose great abilities are universally recognized.

9 Their brilliant fame spreading to the far corners of the earth,
Embodying in themselves nature's mightiest manifestations,
Of unrivalled distinction, blessed beyond measure,
Men such as he are few enough in this world.

MĀLATĪ [*aside*] Lavangikā, this man she mentions is someone whom Father is always calling to mind.

LAVANGIKĀ I believe they studied together – so people say who remember those days.

KĀMANDAKĪ

10 From him as from the Eastern Mountain,
Full and shining in the splendour of merit,
A joy to all in this world who are blessed with sight,
Sprang like the moon an only child.

LAVANGIKĀ [*aside*] Can it be Mādhava, my dear?

KĀMANDAKĪ

11 He while yet a boy has left his home to study,
And is come here, sweet as the rounded autumn moon,
And when he is near, excited female glances
Seem to fill the city's windows with waterlilies.

With his childhood friend Makaranda he is here studying philosophy. And *he* is Mādhava.

MĀLATĪ [*joyfully*, *aside*] Lavangikā, did you hear?

LAVANGIKĀ My dear, where could the coral tree spring from but the great ocean?

KĀMANDAKĪ Oh, the time has flown – now

12 Shattering the sleep that marked the reconcilement
Of mating birds* who now wake to loneliness,

*These are the *chakravākas* or sheldrakes, lovebirds fated always to separate at night.

And growing thereafter more resonant in the echoing
houses,
The sound of the evening conch-shell spreads loudly
through the air.

Stay where you are, dear child.
[*They rise.*]

MĀLATĪ [*to herself*] What, Father sacrificing me to the King? He thinks less of his own daughter than of pleasing his sovereign. [*Tearfully*] Oh Father, if you treat me so, then greed has triumphed everywhere. [*Delightedly*] What, is that youth born of a noble family? Rightly Lavangikā says that the coral tree can spring only from the ocean. Oh, shall I ever see him again?

LAVANGIKĀ Here, Avalokitā, let us go down this way.

KĀMANDAKĪ [*to herself*] Excellent! Without betraying my interest, I have carried out the duties of the entrusted go-between –

She now dislikes the other suitor, and doubts her 13
father,
And old tales have shown her the path that she must
take.
I have praised in passing the nobility, in birth and
character,
Of my dearest Mādhava – and all that remains is to
bring them together.

[*They all withdraw.*]

PRELUDE TO ACT III

[*Enter Buddharakshitā.*]

BUDDHARAKSHITĀ Avalokitā, Avalokitā, do you know where Her Reverence is?

AVALOKITĀ What are you thinking of, Buddharakshitā? Does she ever leave Mālatī's side nowadays except during the alms round?

BUDDHARAKSHITĀ Oh! But where did *you* get to?

AVALOKITĀ Her Reverence sent me to Mādhava to tell him to go to the Flower Garden by the temple of Śankara, and wait in the grove of red aśoka trees which borders on the kubjaka arbour. And that is where he has now gone.

BUDDHARAKSHITĀ But why there?

AVALOKITĀ This is the last day of the dark fortnight, and Mālatī will be going to the Śankara Temple with her mother and Her Reverence. Then Her Reverence will advise the picking of flowers for a good luck offering to the god, and she will take Mālatī with Lavangikā into the Flower Garden itself. But where are you off to?

BUDDHARAKSHITĀ My friend Madayantikā is also on her way to the Śankara Temple, and she has asked me to go with her. And so I am going as soon as I have taken leave of Her Reverence.

AVALOKITĀ What of the business that Her Reverence asked you to see to, how is it going?

BUDDHARAKSHITĀ As Her Reverence asked, I have had all sorts of intimate talks with Madayantikā about Makaranda and his qualities, until she is half in love with him already, and longing to get a glimpse of him.

AVALOKITĀ Well done, Buddharakshitā.

BUDDHARAKSHITĀ Let us be on our ways then.

[*They withdraw.*]

Act III

[*Enter Kāmandakī.*]

KĀMANDAKĪ

So within a few short days, 1
Despite her natural modesty,
I have worked successfully upon Mālatī
Until she treats me as her confidante.

And so now

She grows weary at my absence, is comforted by my presence, 2
Is pleased if we are alone, and talks to me warmly.
When I must go, she follows and clings desperately to my neck,
Then with an abrupt appeal makes me swear to return.

And my greatest reason for hope is that

When casually I have brought into the conversation 3
Stories from the past, like the tale of Śakuntalā,
She will listen, cradled in my arms,
And for a long time stay lost in thought.

And now with Mādhava nearby, I will move things on a little. [*Looking off-stage*] This way, dear children.

[*Enter Mālatī and Lavangikā.*]

MĀLATĪ What, Father sacrificing me to the King? He thinks less of his own daughter than of pleasing his sovereign. [*Delightedly*] Is that young man born of a noble family? Rightly Lavangikā says that the coral tree can spring only from the ocean.

LAVANGIKĀ Dear Mālatī, see how delightfully you are caressed by the breeze from the Flower Garden. For now that the fluttering of the cuckoos, as they playfully cram their beaks with the nectar-soaked blossom, has shaken the swarming bees from the boughs of the mango tree and sent them off to open the magnolia flowers, the wind has become most wonderfully perfumed and blows as cool as sandalwood about your fair face that is bedewed with the effort of directing your feet under the wide burden of your hips – so let us go on into the garden itself.

[*They walk about and enter the garden.*]

[*Enter Mādhava.*]

MĀDHAVA Ah, Her Reverence is come, who

4 Seen before my loved one appears,
Causes me to catch my breath,
As the young peacock, burnt by the summer's heat,
Trembles at the lightning flash that heralds rain.

And oh, here with Lavangikā is Mālatī!

5 Strange, when the spotless moon of her face appears
My mind is for a moment frozen,
Then, like a true moonstone of the mountain,
Knows a fluid transformation.

Mālatī is lovelier now than ever!

6 The fires of my love blaze up,
My heart is gladdened, my eye satisfied,
As I gaze on limbs which, tired and tremulous,

Have the grace of a garland of drooping magnolia flowers.

MĀLATĪ Shall we pick our flowers in this arbour of kubjakas?

MĀDHAVA

The first words of my beloved 7
Make the hairs on my body thrill,
As raindrops from the massing clouds
Instantly awaken the buds on the kadamba.

LAVANGIKĀ Yes my dear, let's do so.

[*They act the picking of flowers.*]

MĀDHAVA Her Reverence is a wonderfully skilful teacher!

MĀLATĪ Dear Lavangikā, need we pick any further?

KĀMANDAKĪ [*hugging Mālatī*] No, stop! You're exhausted. Why,

Your voice falters and every limb grows slack, 8
Sweat beads upon your face,
Your eyes are closing – tiredness, fair child, has given you
The look of a woman gazing upon her lover.

[*Mālatī looks confused.*]

LAVANGIKĀ Quite right, your Reverence.

MĀDHAVA This teasing pierces me to the heart.

KĀMANDAKĪ Sit down, then – I have something to tell you.

[*All seat themselves.*]

[*Lifting up Mālatī's chin*] Listen to this extraordinary story, dear child.

MĀLATĪ I am listening.

KĀMANDAKĪ I did once mention in passing a young man

called Mādhava, who like yourself is a tie which binds me to this world.

LAVANGIKĀ We remember.

KĀMANDAKĪ Well, ever since the day of the Festival in the park of the Love Temple, he has been sick at heart and apparently at the mercy of some bodily fever.

9 That he finds no pleasure in the moon or in the company of friends
Betrays, for all his courage, the cruel agony of his mind.
His limbs, by nature dark as the black vine,
In their sweet pallor grow ever more wasted and more beautiful.

LAVANGIKĀ That was what Avalokitā said at the time, when she asked you to hurry, Reverence – that Mādhava did not feel well.

KĀMANDAKĪ Now I have heard that it is Mālatī who is the cause of his passion. And I am sure it is so –

10 This lovely face without a doubt
Has come like the moon within his ken,
For the still waters of his heart
Are shaken and turbulent now with longing.

MĀDHAVA How well she uses words to exalt me! But then

11 Education together with innate understanding,
Boldness allied to practised eloquence,
Tact combined with quick-wittedness
Are what brings men success in their affairs.

KĀMANDAKĪ And so in his horror of life he courts danger at every turn. He

Lets himself look on the young mango-tree, in bud and alive with cuckoos, 12
And exposes his limbs to the bakula-scented breezes.
In a longing to be burnt, with no more to protect him than a fresh lotus leaf,
He surrenders his wasted body to the killing rays of the moon.

MĀDHAVA She tells her story in a strikingly fresh way!

MĀLATĪ [*to herself*] Oh, he is too reckless.

KĀMANDAKĪ And so it happens that this youth, who is naturally very delicate (and, I suspect, quite unacquainted until now with torments of this kind), is greatly to be pitied, for it is now only too likely that he may die.

MĀLATĪ [*aside*] Lavangikā, Her Reverence is frightening me with her fears that something may happen on my account to this noble ornament of the world. Whatever is to be done?

MĀDHAVA Thank heaven, I am pitied!

LAVANGIKĀ Since you have told us this, Reverence, I will speak out. My mistress too, from catching many brief glimpses of him on the road in front of the house, has grown even lovelier for the tormented beauty of her limbs, like a lotus beneath the strong caress of the sun, and she too is causing her companions pain. She takes no pleasure in any pastime, but spends her days with her cheek cupped in the open lotus of her hand. And the breeze which blows about the garden of our house, fragrantly charged with the nectar of the full-blown lotuses and the budding jasmine and mango, is causing her to wilt.

And ever since that day of the Festival, when he

graced the park like the God of Love himself taking bodily form to observe the success of the celebrations in his honour, when she attained the happiness of meeting him face to face, the happiness of finding in true love the meaning and value of her youth, her curiosity sharpened by the annoying need of avoiding his glance, while her body weak with fright was sweating and thrilling and trembling – ever since that day which so rejoiced her friends, her condition has grown steadily and cruelly worse, and like a night-lotus when the momentary bliss of the full moon's presence is past, she is fading away.

And yet if she can even for a moment fill her mind with the thought of union with her lover, then she revives like the earth sprinkled with a fruitful shower – of that much I am certain. For when her pearl-like teeth flash out from her quivering lips, and tears of pleasure course unendingly across downy cheeks that are thrilling with excitement, when the dark lotuses of her eyes, with pupils unfocused and hardly seeming to move, stare upwards and fold softly into buds, when the crescent of her forehead is thickly dewed with sweat, then we her friends find ourselves wondering if it is really a virgin that we are gazing on.

Later when the moon's rays set the cool moonstones of her necklace flowing, and her friends prepare her a bed of cool lotuses and hasten to her with young plantain leaves saturated with fresh sandalwood and camphor, still she passes the night without sleep. Or if she somehow attains a moment's oblivion, then with sweat washing the red lac from the soles of her feet, with the girdle slipping down sideways from her restless thighs, with her slim arms folded across breasts that heave with the sighing of her agitated heart, she wakes with a start, and seeing at once that the bed beside her is empty, swoons away in a faint. And if our panic-stricken efforts do succeed in reviving her, the only signs of life which reward us are the endless sighs which she lets escape, until we pray for an end to our own lives and have nothing left to do but rail at the unrelenting harshness of fate.

Think, Reverence. These limbs are delicate: they were created out of almost nothing but beauty. How much longer can they survive the cruel onslaught of love? Will these spring nights, when the darkness is split by the rising moon, its orb as soft as a southern woman's cheek veined with an angry glow at her lover's teasing, or when later the whole courtyard of heaven is awash with moonlight in a milky flood and the horizons are misted with the southern breeze, langorously thick with the scent of trumpet flower and bakula blossom – will these spring nights not prove disastrous for her?

KĀMANDAKĪ Truly, Lavangikā,

If he is the one her love has fixed upon, 13
Clearly this comes of recognizing merit –
But my joy at this thought is checked,
And my heart breaks to hear of her sad condition.

MĀDHAVA Her Reverence has every reason to be alarmed. Oh heavens!

A naturally graceful body, the essence of fragility; 14
And the Five-arrowed God proving in truth merciless;
And then, what is more, the season of the lovely moon,
When the mango blossom stirs in the southern breeze!

LAVANGIKĀ And another thing, Reverence. This picture of Mādhava, and [*moving aside the bosom of Mālatī's dress*] this bakula garland which hangs at her neck because he wove it with his own hands, these are the two things which keep her alive.

MĀDHAVA [*passionately*]

You have won the whole world, dear bakula garland,
If you are beloved of her.
On her breasts pale as a fresh-cut lotus stalk,
You are the banner of victorious love.

[*Off-stage uproar. All listen.*]

AGAIN OFF-STAGE Look out, everyone in the Śankara temple! This fierce tiger in a fury of youthful pride has smashed his iron cage and broken the chain which fastened him to it, and now in lusty pursuit of his natural sport, waving his thick tail like a terrifying banner to signal the fearful magnificence of his beauty, he has sprung out of his cell and stalks through the temple playing a deadly game. Already he has greedily gulped down the bodies of countless people, and their bones are being crunched in his huge jaws. He has pounced like a thunderbolt on men and horses alike, and the gurgling of their flesh in his throat is re-echoing in the wide cavern of his mouth, putting to flight those whom it does not frighten to death. Here he comes, muddying his path with the blood of the victims he has mercilessly clawed! Save your lives, everyone, save your lives!

[*Enter Buddharakshitā.*]

BUDDHARAKSHITĀ Help, help! Minister Nandana's sister, dear Madayantikā, is being attacked by the dreadful tiger, and all her servants are killed or run away!

MĀLATĪ Lavangikā, oh no!

MĀDHAVA *[springing forward]* Where is she, Buddharakshitā, where is she?

MĀLATĪ *[to herself, in joyful agitation]* Oh, has *he* been here too?

MĀDHAVA *[to himself]* Oh, I am blessed! She, with eyes shining at this unexpected encounter,

Seems to bind me with a lotus garland hand and foot, 16
Seems to bathe me with a flowering stream of milk,
Swallows me with her widening eyes,
Drenches me in nectar whether I will it or not.

BUDDHARAKSHITĀ Sir, at the end of the road outside the park.

[Mādhava strides purposefully forward.]

KĀMANDAKĪ Oh dear child, be careful as well as brave!

MĀLATĪ Lavangikā, Lavangikā, there is dreadful danger!

[All move about in great haste.]

MĀDHAVA *[with revulsion]* Ah!

With bits of carcase scattered about 17
Latticed with adhering pieces of broken gut,
And mud made wading-deep by the flowing blood,
Hideous is the clawing monster's track.

Oh horror! We are too far away, and the beast is on the girl.

ALL Madayantikā!

KĀMANDAKĪ *and* MĀDHAVA *[in delighted excitement]*

Why, snatching a weapon from a man killed by the beast, 18
Suddenly from somewhere Makaranda is between them!

THE REST Oh bravely done, sir.

KĀMANDAKĪ *and* MĀDHAVA [*in fear*]

18 cont. Is savagely struck by the beast and knocked unconscious.

THE REST Oh dreadful!

KĀMANDAKĪ *and* MĀDHAVA

18 cont. But at once revives and kills the sharp-fanged monster.

THE REST Thank god the horror is averted!

KĀMANDAKĪ [*alarmed*] Oh, Makaranda has blood pouring from the wounds of the tiger's claws. He has stuck his sword in the ground to keep himself steady, and a terrified Madayantikā is holding him up, for he is on the verge of fainting.

THE REST Oh heavens, the young nobleman is dreadfully wounded.

MĀDHAVA What, fainted? Oh help, Reverence, help!

KĀMANDAKĪ Not so nervous, dear child. Come, we will see about it.

[*They all withdraw.*]

Act IV

[*Enter in a fainting condition, supported by Madayantikā and Lavangikā respectively, Mādhava and Makaranda; with them Kāmandakī, Mālatī and Buddharakshitā, all agitated.*]

MADAYANTIKĀ Oh, Reverence, save this young man who pities the distressed and put his life in danger for my sake.

THE REST Oh heavens! What must we witness now?

KĀMANDAKĪ [*sprinkling them both with water from her*

*jar**] All of you, fan them with the border of your dresses.

[*Mālatī and the others do so.*]

MAKARANDA [*regaining consciousness and seeing Mādhava*] Dear worried friend, what is this? See, I am perfectly all right.

MADAYANTIKĀ [*joyfully*] Oh, Makaranda has revived!

MĀLATĪ [*putting her hand on Mādhava's forehead*] Good news, sir! All is well. Your friend has recovered.

MĀDHAVA [*reviving*] Oh reckless friend, come to me! [*He embraces him.*]

KĀMANDAKĪ [*kissing each of them on the head*] Thank heaven, my children are alive.

THE REST All is well!

[*All show delight.*]

BUDDHARAKSHITĀ [*aside*] Madayantikā, my dear, this is the one!

MADAYANTIKĀ Yes, I knew that this was Mādhava, and that the other was the one you mentioned.

BUDDHARAKSHITĀ Was I speaking the truth about him?

MADAYANTIKĀ *You* could not have favoured anyone unworthy. [*Looking at Mādhava*] And my dear, how delightful to think of Mālatī's being in love with this noble youth. [*She once more confines her gaze to Makaranda.*]

KĀMANDAKĪ [*to herself*] This meeting between Madayantikā and Makaranda has been marvellously opportune. [*Aloud*] But Makaranda, dear child, how did Fate come to direct you here and cause you to save Madayantikā's life?

MAKARANDA I heard some news in the town today

*A simple water-pot was one of the few worldly possessions of the mendicant.

which I was afraid would upset Mādhava very much, and so when Avalokitā told me that you were all at the Flower Garden, I rushed straight here – and came upon this young lady being threatened by the tiger.

[*Mālatī and Mādhava grow thoughtful.*]

KĀMANDAKĪ [*to herself*] The news he heard must be Mālatī's betrothal. [*Aloud*] Mādhava, my dear child, a moment ago you received congratulations on your friend Makaranda's recovery. You ought to make Mālatī some gift of friendship in return.

MĀDHAVA Reverence,

1 When I fainted because a friend had fainted from his wound,
She in the goodness of her heart dispelled my anguish –
As a present to the bearer of such good news,
I offer my heart and life to dispose of as she will.

LAVANGIKĀ My friend accepts the kind offer.

MADAYANTIKĀ [*to herself*] This young man certainly knows how to speak well.

MĀLATĪ [*to herself*] What can Makaranda have heard that was so upsetting?

MĀDHAVA But friend, what was this news that might upset me?

[*Enter a man.*]

MAN Madayantikā, dear child, here is a message from your elder brother, the Minister Nandana. He says: 'Today His Majesty came to our house, and as a mark of confidence in Minister Bhūrivasu and of favour towards myself, he has personally bestowed Mālatī upon me. So come home and share our joy.'

MAKARANDA That, friend, was the news.

[*Mālatī and Mādhava change colour.*]

MADAYANTIKĀ [*embracing Mālatī delightedly*] Dearest Mālatī, we have lived in the same city, and played in the dust together as children, and you have always been my own dear friend and my sister. Now you will grace the very house I live in!

KĀMANDAKĪ Good Madayantikā, let me congratulate you on your brother's winning of Mālatī.

MADAYANTIKĀ It was through the favour of your prayers, Reverence. Dear Lavangikā, our wishes are fulfilled in gaining you!

LAVANGIKĀ No, ours in gaining you, my dear.

MADAYANTIKĀ Buddharakshitā, let us go to the celebration.

BUDDHARAKSHITĀ Come then, my dear.

[*They both rise.*]

LAVANGIKĀ [*aside*] Reverence, from the looks of wonder and delight now linking Madayantikā and Makaranda like a garland of dark waterlilies, I think that in their thoughts they are already wed.

KĀMANDAKĪ [*smiling*] They must indeed be exploring the delights of their imagined consummation. For

Their faces, awkwardly angled and drawn at the sides, 2
Made by Love motionless yet quivering, the eyebrows
quirking slightly,
The eyelashes drooping and stilled with the knowledge
of ecstasy,
Clearly those faces, their unfocused eyes, announce
it.

MAN This way, Madayantikā.

MADAYANTIKĀ Oh, Buddharakshitā, shall I see him again, this handsome man who saved my life?

BUDDHARAKSHITĀ Yes, if Fate is kind.

[*She and Madayantikā withdraw, together with the man.*]

MĀDHAVA [*apart*]

3 Snap at last, fragile lotus-thread of hope.
Spread unchecked, my fearful agony of spirit.
Yoke of madness, rest openly upon me.
Be easy, Destiny – and Love, have your way.

But in truth –

4 I aspired to one beyond me, and one whose love matched mine:
If Destiny has worked against me, what is odd in that?
Oh, but her face torments me, when she heard she was betrothed,
Its colour drained like the light of the moon at morning.

KĀMANDAKĪ [*aside*] The dear child's misery is torture to me, and Mālatī too is in such despair she hardly draws breath. [*Aloud*] Let me put a question to you, sir: had you been thinking that Bhūrivasu would give Mālatī to you?

MĀDHAVA [*in confusion*] No, no!

KĀMANDAKĪ Then you are no worse off than you were before!

MAKARANDA Reverence, what worries us is that she is now promised elsewhere.

KĀMANDAKĪ Yes, I heard the news. There is certainly no doubt that when the King asked for Mālatī to be given to Nandana, Bhūrivasu said to him, 'It is for Your Majesty to dispose of your daughters as you will.'

MAKARANDA Precisely.

KĀMANDAKĪ But what we were told a moment ago was that it's the King himself who has given Mālatī in marriage. Now, my dear child, the whole conduct of human affairs is based on words: on words depend the distinctions from which pleasant and unpleasant effects derive. And Bhūrivasu's words were essentially false. Mālatī is *not* the King's daughter, and to defer to a king in giving one's daughter in marriage has no sanction in either morality or custom. So you must examine the statement carefully. And anyway, dear child, do you really think I will do nothing? Consider –

I could not wish even on your enemies 5
The disaster threatening both her and you.
Though it should cost me my life,
My every effort must be to unite you with her.

MAKARANDA You are right in everything you have said, Reverence. Indeed

Your heart, though turned from worldly things, has been melted 6
By pity or by love for these your children.
That is why, against all a mendicant's principles,
You make such efforts – and yet an evil fate prevails.

A VOICE OFF-STAGE Reverend Kāmandakī, our Mistress* asks you to bring Mālatī and come quickly.

KĀMANDAKĪ Rise, my child.

[*All rise and begin to move.*]

[*Mālatī and Mādhava gaze at each other with tender affection.*]

MĀDHAVA Alas, must the worldly contact of Mālatī and Mādhava be no more than this? Oh cruel!

At first showing nothing but kindness 7

*Mālatī's mother.

Like a comforting friend,
Fate, turned suddenly tormentor,
Brings only agony in the end.

MĀLATĪ [*to herself*] Noble sir, gladdener of my sight, shall I see no more of you?

LAVANGIKĀ Alas, the Minister has brought his daughter to the very verge of death.

MĀLATĪ This is what has come of my thirst for life. And by his hardness Father has shown himself an ogre. My dreadful fate is ending as cruelly as it promised to do. Whom can I blame, alas – whom can I turn to for help, when I am helpless?

LAVANGIKĀ This way, my dearest.

[*She and Mālatī withdraw, together with Kāmandakī.*]

MĀDHAVA [*to himself*] Her Reverence's words cannot be more than an attempt to console me, the result of her anxious affection. [*In great agitation*] My life is losing its meaning. What can I do? [*After thought*] I know no way out but the selling of human flesh.* [*Aloud*] Makaranda, my friend, are you in love with Madayantikā?

MAKARANDA Of course –

8 I am ravished to think of how, when she saw me wounded,
She bent with no thought of the garment that slipped from her shoulder,
And with a gaze as tremulous as that of a year-old doe
Clasped me in arms which seemed to be made of nectar.

MĀDHAVA You will easily win Buddharakshitā's friend. In fact

*Apparently in order to obtain supernatural help: the attempt is described in the following act.

How can she love another? She accepted your embrace 9
When you were her rescuer from the murderous tiger.
And the functioning of her lotus eyes
Was charmingly prevented by her obvious love of you.

MAKARANDA Come, let's bathe at the confluence of the Pārā and the Sindhu, and then return to the city.

[*They rise and walk about.*]

MĀDHAVA There is the place where the two great rivers meet –

Its banks are thronged with women risen from bathing 10
Their shapes betrayed by water-compacted garments,
Who place the *svastika** of their arms
Against the bright gold pitchers of their breasts.

[*They withdraw.*]

PRELUDE TO ACT V

[*Enter, flying through the air, in terrifying radiance, Kapālakuṇḍalā.*]

KAPĀLAKUṆḌALĀ

To the God whose self abides within the Circle of the Sixteen Veins, 1
Granting power to them that know him when they have realized him in their hearts,
Whom devotees with unwavering minds search after,
To Śiva, Lord of Energy, is victory.

The self enveloped in the Six Limbs mystically touched, and manifested in the lotus of the heart, 2
I now by absorption behold as God, and am come here.

*A very ancient good luck symbol. The word means 'well-being'.

In the order of swelling of veins I have drawn from my body the five essences:
Therefore my flying cannot tire me as I split the clouds in my path.

3 As the skulls of the garland at my breast roll and slip
And set the gaping bells ringing,
The rush of my passage through the firmament
Enhances the awful splendour of my form.

For

4 Though tightly confined, my hair flies all about.
On my whirling club the bell reverberates shrilly.
Its streamers fly in the wind which loudly howls
In the hollows of skulls and engenders a ceaseless carillon.

[*Looking before her and sniffing the air*] Below, the smoke of pyres, smelling of garlic fried in old neem oil, reveals the great Burning-ground. There next to it is the temple of Karālā, where my teacher Aghoraghaṇṭa, of miraculous power, has ordered me to assemble the materials of sacrifice. For today he must fulfil his vow of sacrificing to Karālā a jewel among women – a jewel such as is known to reside in this very city. I will search her out. [*Looking in curiosity*] But who is this young man looking so earnest and charming, who comes to the Burning-ground with his mass of curly hair bound up and a sword in his hand? –

5 Dark as the blue waterlily, yet his body dusty pale,
Graceful and dignified, with a face as lovely as the moon,
Yet whose left hand proclaims him a desperate adventurer,

Smeared thickly with blood, with dead men's flesh
dangling from it.

[*Looking more closely*] It is Mādhava, that son of Kāmandakī's friend, here to sell human flesh. What of him? I'll go on with what I have to do. For the hour of twilight is almost past. Now

The horizon is overgrown with clustering creepers of darkness, 6
And earth seems to drown in a turbid accession of water.
And like a thick smoke that is twisted and spread by the wind,
Already the night is maturing its blackness in the forests.

[*She withdraws.*]

Act V

[*Enter Mādhava as described.*]
MĀDHAVA [*wistfully*]

Let me know again those sweet betraying signs of love, 7
Melting in tenderness, born of her passion.
If my longing no more than pictures them for a moment,
My mind's dissolving in joy confounds my senses.

And

Oh, as she delicately withholds her breast 8
For fear of crushing the garland I once wove,

Burying my face below her ear
Let me embrace her.

But no, I ask no more than this –

9 Let me again see her face, the temple of love,
Made out of all crescent moons' collected essence,
Which, when it falls to anyone to behold,
Happiness swells into an ecstasy of bliss.

Yet in truth I hardly know the difference between seeing her and not. For such was the overwhelming earlier impression on my senses, that there remains alive in me as a perpetual memory a perception of my beloved which no conflicting perception can obscure, so that my consciousness takes on the very shape and substance of her –

10 Absorbed, or mirrored she seems, or painted, or sculptured,
Inset, cemented or engraved,
Nailed to my mind by the Mind-god's five arrows,
Tightly sewn there by a close embroidery of thought.

[*Off-stage uproar.*]

MĀDHAVA Ha, now the great Burning-ground is wild with strutting ghosts!

11 Pressing in, thick and viscid, the blackness of night
Illuminates the flaring brilliance of the pyres,
And shrieking with joy in their merrymaking
Goblins of every sort make common uproar.

I'll call to them, then. [*Calling out*] Ho there, ghosts that live in this burning-ground –

12 Flesh not hallowed by the knife,

Taken from human limbs,
Without fraud I offer you:
Come and buy, come and buy.

[*Off-stage a commotion.*]

MĀDHAVA At my cry the prowling ghosts raise a great hubbub, and the whole ground seethes as they press forward. Oh heavens!

Fire flashing in the grins that stretch from ear to ear, 13
Pointed fangs hideous, the fire-faced ghouls are scurrying.
Hair, eyes, brows, matted beards like flickering lightning,
Their faces throng the air, their withered bodies hardly visible.

And

Here is a circle of goblins, feeding the wolves that howl around 14
With titbits of corpse-flesh, half fallen from untidily munching jaws.
Their shanks are long as date-palms, and their aging bony frames
Are knotted with sinew and hung with blackened skin.

[*Looking about, with a laugh*] Ha, how odd these goblins look. Here are some

With straggling bodies and cavernous mouths that open 15
Repulsively on huge, thick tongues,
Looking like old and blasted trees
Where slithering snakes lurk in the hollows.

Oh, what ghastliness is here?

This starveling ghost, having ripped at the skin and feasted 16

On bloated, stinking cuts of shoulder, rump and rib,
Has removed eyes, tendons and guts, and with bared teeth
Sits quietly picking at the bones of the carcase on his lap.

And

17 From many a pyre where heat-sweating bones have cooked the marrow,
Goblins drag off the still smouldering corpses
And detaching from its joints a shank-bone with the meat slipping from it
Are gulping down the emerging streams of liquid.

[*With a laugh*] The goblins have evening diversions!

18 With guts for bracelets, and elegant flower-chains of hearts,
And women's lac-painted hands for red lotuses at their ears,
With thick blood for make-up, the demon women join their lovers
And drink in skull goblets the marrow wine.

[*Moving about and again calling out*]

12 rptd Flesh not hallowed by the knife,
Taken from human limbs,
Without fraud I offer you –
Come and buy, come and buy.

Oh, suddenly the ghosts have dropped their terrifying ways and vanished! You cowards! [*Despondently*] And the Burning-ground is here completely cut off. For in front of me

I see the river which skirts the ground, its waters loudly sucking at the bank, 19
Deterring the passenger by its flotsam of skulls and bones.
On its fearful shores the jackals howl and jump
At the shrieking troops of owls in their noisy coverts.

A VOICE OFF-STAGE Oh, my hard-hearted father, the daughter who was to find you favour with the King is near to death!

MĀDHAVA [*listening with great emotion*]

A sound as sweet and shrill as the frightened osprey's call 20
Compels my mind. It has a familiar note.
My heart shatters in confusion, my limbs are unstrung,
My frozen body stumbles. What can it be, what is it?

From the Karālā temple 21
That fearful sound
Must clearly have come – well assuredly
It would be the place for such horrors.

I will look. [*He walks about.*]

[*Enter in the act of worship Kapālakuṇḍalā and Aghoraghaṇṭa, with Mālatī as sacrificial victim.*]

MĀLATĪ Oh my hard-hearted father, the daughter who was to find you favour with the King is near to death. Oh my loving mother, harsh fate destroys you. Reverence, you who have made me your life, and my welfare your only happiness, affection has finally acquainted you with sorrow. And oh dearest Lavangikā, never again will you see me except in your dreams.

MĀDHAVA It is my beloved, no doubt of it. Can I yet save her? [*He hurries forward.*]

KAPĀLAKUṆḌALĀ *and* AGHORAGHAṆṬA Fierce Goddess, homage to you:

22 Hail to your dance, whose firm steps shake and bend the globe of earth,
Till the shell of the Turtle* sags and his trembling puts the universe out of joint,
And the seven seas surge up into your cheeks as cavernous as hell –
Hail to that prospering dance which wins the applause of Śiva's court.

23 As your whirling skirts of elephant hide scratch with their flying claws at the moon,
Starting a trickle of nectar to revive your garland of skulls
At whose wild laughter frightened multitudes turn to your worship;
As pressure upon the hissing black snakes which tightly bracelet your upper arms
Brings a blossoming of their hoods and a hideous flaring of poison flames,
When you toss wide your arms and send the mountains spinning;
As your head flies round and the blaze of rays from your fiery eye
Like a whirling firebrand's circle knits the skies together,
And stars are scattered by the banners which stream at the tip of your lofty club;

*He carries the earth on his back: to Vaishnavites he is an incarnation of Vishṇu.

As the wild applause of ghosts and goblins splits timid Pārvatī's ears,
Driving her into her Lord's delighted embrace:
In your Terror Dance, O Goddess, be our security and joy.

[*They perform a mime.*]

MĀDHAVA Oh dreadful –

In a dress and wreath stained red with lac, 24
A doe at the mercy of two ravening wolves,
Bhūrivasu's daughter faces death from those blasphemers.
Horror of horrors! What cruel trick of Fate is this?

KAPĀLAKUṆḌALĀ

Think, girl, on him whom you have loved – 25
Grim death now speeds you on.

MĀLATĪ Ah, dearest Mādhava, remember me though I am gone. No one is dead whom a loved one remembers.

KAPĀLAKUṆḌALĀ Why, the poor wretch is in love with Mādhava!

AGHORAGHAṆṬA [*raising his sword*]

Blessed Goddess, the offering enjoined 25 cont.
For working of our spells, accept, we pray you.

MĀDHAVA [*suddenly approaching and sheltering Mālatī in his left arm*] Away, villain! Vile sorcerer, you are beaten.

MĀLATĪ [*at the sight of him*] Oh help, sir, help! [*She clings to him.*]

MĀDHAVA Dear lady, have no fear –

The very friend whom in your last extremity 26
You frankly confessed your love for, he is here.

Tremble no more, my fair one: this villain now
Will reap a bitter reward for his ill-judged villainy.

AGHORAGHAṆṬA Who is this rascally intruder?

KAPĀLAKUṆḌALĀ Master, it is the man she is in love with, the son of Kāmandakī's friend. His name is Mādhava, and he is here to sell human flesh.

MĀDHAVA [*with emotion*] Lady, what is this?

MĀLATĪ [*recovering after a while*] Sir, I know nothing – only that I fell asleep on the terrace, and woke up to find myself here. But what of you?

MĀDHAVA [*in embarrassment*]

27 Tormented by my longing
To win your lotus hand,
I was wandering the Burning-ground as a seller of flesh,
When I heard your cries and came here.

MĀLATĪ [*aside, joyfully*] Was he wandering without thought of self, all for my sake?

MĀDHAVA What an extraordinary tale of chance!

28 When my beloved was a crescent moon in the very jaws of the eclipse,
By luck I found her, and snatched her from beneath this ogre's sword.
Will my heart break with fear, melt with love, tremble with amazement,
Blaze up in anger, or open like a flower with joy?

AGHORAGHAṆṬA Brahmin brat!

29 For love of his doe the buck is in the tiger's clutches!
This is the place of sacrifice, and I delight in violence.

You will be my first offering to the Mother of Spirits
With the blood that spurts from your beheaded trunk.

MĀDHAVA Lowest of blaspheming outcasts!

To rob life of its being, the universe of its jewel, 30
The world of its light, a family of its life,
Love of its pride, men's sight of all its purpose,
To make the earth a wilderness – was that what you were planning?

Villain!

Too delicate even for the gently raining blows 31
Of the flowers with which her fond friends laughingly pelt her,
Her body is murderously threatened by your sword –
Let my arm fall like a sentence of death on your neck.

AGHORAGHAṆṬA Strike, scoundrel, strike. This is the end of you!

MĀLATĪ Oh have a care, my Lord – he is a cruel wretch. For my sake don't risk yourself so.

KAPĀLAKUṆḌALĀ Be careful, Master, as you kill the rogue.

MĀDHAVA [*to Mālatī*] AGHORAGHAṆṬA [*to Kapālakuṇḍalā*] Timid creature!

Put courage in your heart – the villain is dead. 32
Who ever talks of risk
When the lion whose paw can fell an elephant
Engages with a deer?

[*Off-stage a commotion. All listen.*]

VOICE OFF-STAGE Listen, all you searching for Mālatī: Minister Bhūrivasu has been heartened by an unfailing assurance from Her Reverence Kāmandakī. These are her orders: surround the Temple of Karālā here –

33 By none other than Aghoraghaṇṭa
Has this fearful sorcery been wrought.
And nothing less than an offering to the Goddess
Is the end he has in view.

KAPĀLAKUṆḌALĀ Master, we are surrounded!

AGHORAGHAṆṬA Now we must show our mettle.

MĀLATĪ Father! Reverence!

MĀDHAVA So be it. I will see Mālatī safe with her family, and then kill off this scoundrel in front of them all.

[*He conducts Mālatī away.*]

MĀDHAVA *and* AGHORAGHAṆṬA [*to each other*] Villain!

34 Noisily scraping through your hard bones,
Pausing for a moment on a tough sinew,
Cutting carelessly through your flesh as if it were mud,
My sword shall hack you to pieces limb by limb.

[*They all withdraw.*]

PRELUDE TO ACT VI

[*Enter Kapālakuṇḍalā.*]

KAPĀLAKUṆḌALĀ Ah, villain who murdered my teacher for the sake of Mālatī, accursed Mādhava! You despised me then as a woman, though I struck at you with all my might. [*Angrily*] Learn then what the anger of Kapālakuṇḍalā can do!

1 How shall the serpent-slayer find rest
While there lurks in unrelenting enmity,
Watchful to bite, and razor-fanged,
Heavy with welling poison, the serpent's mate?

VOICE OFF-STAGE

The elders charge you, my lords, to see to your tasks, 2
And let brahmins delight our ears with their reciting.
Let there be song and dance to bless the occasion.
The coming of the bridegroom's party is close upon us.

And on Her Reverence's advice, the Minister's wife has given orders that before the family of the bridegroom arrives, Mālatī should visit the city temple to make a good luck offering – and wait there for her attendants to bring special ornaments.

KAPĀLAKUṆḌALĀ Enough, the place teems with porters preparing for Mālatī's wedding. I shall withdraw and work towards Mādhava's ruin. [*She withdraws.*]

Act VI

[*Enter Kalahamsaka.*]

KALAHAMSAKA I have had orders from Mādhava my master, who is with Makaranda in the shrine of the city temple, to find out whether Mālatī is on her way. So I can now make him happy.

[*Enter Mādhava and Makaranda.*]

MĀDHAVA

Growing ever since the day I set eyes on her, 3
Brought to fever-pitch by herself when she showed that
  she cared for me,
This endless agony of love must be resolved today

Whether Her Reverence's plan succeeds or goes awry.

MAKARANDA Friend, how could the plan of so wise a person go awry?

KALAHAMSAKA [*coming up to them*] Good news, master – Mālatī is on her way.

MĀDHAVA Are you sure?

MAKARANDA Why ask as if you can't believe it, friend? Not only is she on her way, she is nearly here. Listen –

4 All at once a deep roar,
Like the thundering of wind-torn clouds,
From a thousand ceremonial drums
Deafens our ears to other sounds.

Come, we will watch through the lattice.

[*They all do so.*]

KALAHAMSAKA Look, master, look. Like soaring geese creating ripples in a lake of lotuses with the wind of their flight, yaktail fans are fluttering the banners in the parasol-crowded sky. And I see flocks of beautiful concubines, round cheeks elegantly engaged in the chewing of betel, filling the air with the sweet clamour of their stumbled songs and the rainbow gleam of their jewelled ornaments, mounted on elephants chinking in caparisons of golden bells.

[*Mādhava and Makaranda gaze eagerly.*]

MAKARANDA [*in admiration*] The wealth of Minister Bhūrivasu is certainly breathtaking –

5 Like peacocks' tails massed in a glittering array
Or the flashing lustre of bluejays' wings,
The radiated gleam of jewels fills the sky to the horizon
As with a rainbow or a veil of figured silk.

KALAHAMSAKA Look, a crowd of footmen have hurriedly lowered their bright canes of gold and silver leaf to form a line, and the attendants have halted in a circle some way off. And here, mounted on an elephant dark as the night, with a constellation of pearls against the sunset of its thickly vermilioned face, Mālatī advances a little further, while all look up at her in curiosity, and gaze with admiration at her frailly beautiful body that is like the first pale streak of the new moon.

MAKARANDA Look, friend, look:

Her adornments are lent more grace by limbs pale and exhausted. 6
She is like a flowering vine that withers within.
Through all the splendour of her wedding finery
Shines a deep, wasting melancholy.

Oh, the elephant is kneeling.

MĀDHAVA [*in delight*] She has dismounted, and is coming this way with Her Reverence and Lavangikā!

[*Enter Mālatī, Kāmandakī and Lavangikā.*]

KĀMANDAKĪ [*joyfully aside*]

Let destiny prosper these rites, 7
And the gods smile upon their outcome.
Success attend my aim of uniting my friends' two children.
May all my work be fruitful and well blessed.

MĀLATĪ [*to herself*] How can I win the release of death? Even death can be elusive when an unhappy person longs for it.

LAVANGIKĀ [*to herself*] Poor Mālatī is wasting away under our benevolent deception.

[*Enter a porteress with a casket.*]

PORTERESS Your Reverence, the Minister says: let Mālatī be robed at the shrine in this wedding-dress sent by the King.

KĀMANDAKĪ He speaks well. The place is auspicious. Show what you have.

PORTERESS Here is a white silk bodice, a coloured robe, sets of ornaments for the whole body, pearl necklace, sandalwood, and a chaplet of white flowers.

KĀMANDAKĪ [*aside*] Dear Makaranda will look most attractive when Madayantikā sees him! [*Aloud, accepting them*] Tell the Minister that they will be used.

[*The porteress withdraws.*]

KĀMANDAKĪ Lavangikā, take the dear child within.

LAVANGIKĀ But where will you be, Reverence?

KĀMANDAKĪ I want to be by myself to make a thorough examination of the value of the gems in these settings. [*She withdraws.*]

MĀLATĪ [*to herself*] Now I have nobody with me except Lavangikā!

LAVANGIKĀ Here is the door of the temple. Let's go in.

[*They enter.*]

MAKARANDA Friend, let's hide behind the pillar over here.

[*They do so.*]

LAVANGIKĀ Here are the cosmetics, my dear, and here are the garlands of flowers.

MĀLATĪ What of it?

LAVANGIKĀ My dear, your mother has sent you here at the beginning of your marriage rites to worship the gods for good fortune.

MĀLATĪ [*in despair*] Why do you keep tormenting and lacerating me when I am consumed with misery at this cruel prank of fate?

LAVANGIKĀ Oh, what do you mean?

MĀLATĪ I mean what anyone means who wants what cannot be had, and has what could never be wanted.

MAKARANDA Did you hear that, friend?

MĀDHAVA Yes, but I am not satisfied.

MĀLATĪ [*embracing Lavangikā*] And therefore, dearest Lavangikā, my sister in the truest sense – your friend Mālatī, bereft and near to death, embraces you with the perfect trust of one whom you have never failed to help from the moment she was born – and asks you this. If you will agree to what I say, then remember me in your heart, and look with joy and tenderness upon the noble Mādhava's lotus face, where beauty and splendour find their only happiness – [*She begins to weep.*]

MĀDHAVA Makaranda,

Thank god I was granted the nectar of those words, 8
For they revive the fading flower of life.
They are a bliss to make the senses swoon
And an elixir to gladden the heart.

MĀLATĪ And make sure that the news of my decline does not so torment my rescuer that his lovely body wastes away; make sure that in days to come he does not simply fritter away his life, even after I have left this world, in thinking and talking of me. That is what you must do to make me happy.

MAKARANDA What a heart-rending conversation!

MĀDHAVA

As I hear this lovely creature's despairing cry, 9
Both so pitiful and so enthralling,
So compounded of love and distraction, I feel at once
Alarm, and horror, and exhilaration.

LAVANGIKĀ Ah! I avert your ill omen! I will listen no further.

MĀLATĪ Dear friend, you love my life more than you love me.

LAVANGIKĀ How can you say that?

MĀLATĪ [*indicating her appearance*] Because by keeping me alive with your clever speeches full of hopes about another, you have made me endure this nightmare for so long. But now there is only one thing I still hope for – to give up my life before I sin against him by belonging to someone else. In that, dear friend, do not try to hinder me. [*She falls at her feet.*]

MAKARANDA This is the very height of love.

[*Lavangikā beckons to Mādhava.*]

Friend, go and stand in Lavangikā's place.

MĀDHAVA Friend, I am beside myself with fright.

MAKARANDA One always is, when success is near.

[*Mādhava cautiously takes Lavangikā's place.*]

MĀLATĪ Dear Lavangikā, for love of me agree.

MĀDHAVA*

10 Simpleton, curb these rash longings,
Give up such recklessness, fair child.
The pain of losing you
Is something I could not bear.

MĀLATĪ You cannot slight my act of supplication!

MĀDHAVA

11 What can I say to you,
You who would torment me with separation?

*By a *tour de force* the original of the following two stanzas may be interpreted as being either in the Sanskrit spoken by Mādhava or in the Prakrit (see Introduction) spoken by Lavangikā.

Loveliest girl, do as you will –
And grant me an embrace.

MĀLATĪ [*in delight*] You consent? [*Rising*] I embrace you – though flooding tears prevent my one last sight of you, dear friend. [*Embracing him, with pleasure*] My dear, the touch of your body feels refreshingly different today – as downy as the inside of a ripened lotus. [*Weeping*] And something else: salute him respectfully and deliver this message from me. 'Unhappy that I am, it is long since I feasted my eyes upon your face, that fair moon which robs the day lotus of its beauty. With foolish hopes I sustained a heart that grew increasingly anguished. Ever and again some crisis in my fever meant agony to my friends. Somehow I have survived the blazing rays of the moon, the breeze from the south, a whole succession of afflictions. Now at last I have lost all hope.' And dearest Lavangikā, you too remember me always. Here is that bakula, dear to me because he wove it with his own hands. Look upon it, dear friend, as if it were Mālatī herself, and always wear it at your heart. [*She takes it from about her own neck and is placing it on Mādhava's breast, when she suddenly starts back in fear and trembling.*]

MĀDHAVA [*aside*] Ah!

As she pressed against me, flattening her swelling 12
breasts,
I seemed to feel a drenching of my skin,
Compounded of camphor and pearls and liquid moon-
stone,
Sandal and lotus-fibre and moss and snow.

MĀLATĪ Lavangikā has deceived me!

MĀDHAVA Oh, you who feel only your own heart's pain and know nothing of another's suffering, I rebuke you –

13 Those days of burning feverish torment of body
When nothing but thoughts of our union could ease the pain
And life was sustained by knowing the other's love –
Can you suppose that I did not pass them too?

LAVANGIKĀ The rebuke is well deserved, my dear.

KALAHAMSAKA What a beautiful, tender twist to the plot!

MAKARANDA Lady, it is true.

14 He really has passed all these many days
Kept just alive by thinking of his love for you.
By granting the favour of your hand in marriage
Let him at last find the happiness that he longs for.

LAVANGIKĀ Sir, when her heart has not rejected the thought of being won by force, will her hand hesitate before a wedding-ring?

MĀLATĪ Oh heavens, she is suggesting things that no young girl may contemplate!

[*Enter Kāmandakī.*]

KĀMANDAKĪ Dear timid daughter, what is this?

[*Mālatī, trembling, embraces Kāmandakī.*]

[*Raising Mālatī's chin*]

15 The young man you loved at first sight, as he did you,
Who then filled the whole of your thoughts, as you did his,
Who like you wasted away, and for the same reason,
Is here, sweet girl. Do not be cold, but let Love have his way.

LAVANGIKĀ Reverence, the man is a desperado – on the last day of the dark fortnight when he was roaming the Burning-ground he boldly struck down a blaspheming villain at the height of his murderous activities. No wonder my dear friend is frightened.

MAKARANDA Well done, Lavangikā – just the moment to mention the strength of his love and the greatness of his service!

MĀLATĪ Oh my father, oh my father!

KĀMANDAKĪ Mādhava, dearest child.

MĀDHAVA Command me.

KĀMANDAKĪ Here is the treasured offspring of Minister Bhūrivasu whose feet never lose the stain of pollen from the chaplets of his feudatory lords – Mālatī, his only child, whom the Creator, in his fondness for the union of like with like, and whom the God of Love, and whom I bestow on you. [*She weeps.*]

MAKARANDA Then, by Your Reverence's favour, we have won our desires.

MĀDHAVA Why is your face wet with tears, Reverence?

KĀMANDAKĪ [*wiping her eyes with the corner of her robe*] Sir, I beg of you –

MĀDHAVA No, command of me –

KĀMANDAKĪ

As you grow older, you are one whose love will be 16
  prized,
And I for one reason and another deserve your respect.
And so towards this fair creature do not fail, dear son,
When I am not there, in love or understanding.

[*She makes to fall at his feet.*]

MĀDHAVA [*checking her*] Oh, you are carried away by your love.

MAKARANDA Reverence,

17 That she is well-born, that she is beautiful,
That she has proved great love, that her goodness shines,
Any one of these would be a strong assurance:
When she is this to you, what need be said?

KĀMANDAKĪ Dear Mādhava.
MĀDHAVA Command me.
KĀMANDAKĪ Dear Mālatī.
LAVANGIKĀ Command us, Reverence.
KĀMANDAKĪ

18 Like a dear friend, like all one's kin,
Like all desires, like a fortune, like life itself,
Is her husband to a woman, and his wedded wife to a man:
That is the truth I would have you learn in each other.

MAKARANDA Of course.
LAVANGIKĀ It is as Your Reverence says.
KĀMANDAKĪ Makaranda, dear child, take this wedding-dress of Mālatī's, and disguise yourself in readiness for marriage. [*She hands him the casket.*]
MAKARANDA As you command, Reverence. I'll go behind this picture-curtain and change. [*He does so.*]
MĀDHAVA Reverence, the whole affair bristles with dangers for him.
KĀMANDAKĪ Who are you to worry about that?
MĀDHAVA Truly, Reverence, you know best.
[*Makaranda returns.*]
MAKARANDA [*laughing*] Friend, I am Mālatī!
[*All examine him with interest and amusement.*]

MĀDHAVA [*embracing him*] Reverence! Nandana's a lucky man to be getting such a sweetheart!

KĀMANDAKĪ Dear Mālatī and Mādhava, go from here through the wood to the stretch of garden behind our convent for your wedding. Avalokitā will be there with all that is needed for the ceremony. And most abundantly

With its fruited areca palms bowed down and skeined with betel vines, 19
The vine-leaves pale as the cheek of a lovelorn Kerala maiden,
And its chatter of artless fowl pecking the jujube berries,
And its hedges of swaying lime-trees, that ground will be prosperous to your love.

And there you may stay until Makaranda and Madayantikā come to you.

MĀDHAVA [*in delight*] You have told us that one happiness is to be crowned with another!

KALAHAMSAKA Hurrah, more good news for us!

KĀMANDAKĪ Did you doubt it, then?

LAVANGIKĀ Did you hear that, my dear?

KĀMANDAKĪ Makaranda, dear child, and you my dear Lavangikā, let us be off.

MĀLATĪ Dearest Lavangikā, are you going too?

LAVANGIKĀ [*with a smile*] We are quite superfluous here now!

[*Kāmandakī, Lavangikā and Makaranda withdraw.*]

MĀDHAVA And now

The sweet lotus of her hand with its fresh petal fingers 20

And the downy stem of the arm thrilling all along its
length,
Being scorched by the summer of my love I will take in
mine,
As the fevered elephant catches at a blossom in the lake.

[*They both withdraw.*]

PRELUDE TO ACT VII

[*Enter Buddharakshitā.*]

BUDDHARAKSHITĀ Well! Nandana was taken in by the beautiful and well-fitting wedding dress meant for Mālatī, and married Makaranda: and Makaranda stayed safely hidden in Minister Bhūrivasu's house, thanks to some clever covering up by Her Reverence. And then today we all came here to Nandana's own house – after which Her Reverence took leave of Nandana and returned to the convent. And with the whole household in confusion because of the celebrations marking the bride's entry into her home, tonight will be the ideal time for our enterprise. Just now the bridegroom, in the eagerness of his passion, attempted to claim his beloved – first by means of humble supplications, and thereafter by a violent assault – and received a vigorous rebuff from Makaranda. Whereupon angrily drying his tear-stained face, his voice breaking with embarrassment and fury, he swore on oath that he would have no more to do with the deceitful little whore,* and left the bedchamber. Which gives me an opportunity of fetching Madayantikā and bringing her and Makaranda together. [*She withdraws.*]

*He assumes, of course, that the reluctance is due to a previous loss of her virginity.

Act VII

[*Enter Makaranda in bed, with Lavangikā seated.*]

MAKARANDA Lavangikā, do you think that Her Reverence's scheme, which she has now entrusted to Buddharakshitā, will work?

LAVANGIKĀ How can you doubt it, sir? In fact, from that sound of anklets, I should say that Buddharakshitā has seized the excuse to fetch Madayantikā. Cover yourself with your robe and pretend to be asleep.

[*Makaranda complies.*]

[*Enter Madayantikā and Buddharakshitā.*]

MADAYANTIKĀ My dear, is my brother really furious with Mālatī?

BUDDHARAKSHITĀ Yes, he is.

MADAYANTIKĀ Oh, this is terrible. Come, we must rebuke the girl for being so obstinate.

[*They walk about.*]

BUDDHARAKSHITĀ Here is the bedchamber.

[*They go in.*]

MADAYANTIKĀ Lavangikā, my dear, is your friend asleep, do you think?

LAVANGIKĀ Hush, my dear, don't wake her. She was very upset for a long time and she has only just calmed down a little and gone to sleep: so come and sit very quietly here at the end of the bed.

MADAYANTIKĀ [*doing so*] So the perverse creature is upset!

LAVANGIKĀ Upset? When she has your brother for a husband, with his skill in reassuring shy young brides, and his good looks, and his tactful conversation, and his calm and gentle manner, you think she could be upset?

MADAYANTIKĀ There, Buddharakshitā – *they* are blaming *us*, when it should be the other way round.

BUDDHARAKSHITĀ Well, yes and no.

MADAYANTIKĀ What do you mean?

BUDDHARAKSHITĀ Well, for not respecting her husband's wishes when he threw himself at her feet, the girl must certainly be blamed for her shyness. And on the other hand, seeing that when he failed in those violent advances which were quite out of place towards a young bride, your brother in his chagrin so far forgot himself as to express himself in the most outrageous terms – there, the blame is on our side. And remember: 'Women are of a like nature to flowers, and must be approached gently. But if they are violently approached by one who has not won their confidence, at once they conceive a hatred for the act of love' – that, I think, is how the *Kāma Sūtra* puts it.

LAVANGIKĀ [*tearfully*] In every household men take girls for their wives, yet none of them takes advantage of his power over a simple, sweet-natured and innocent girl, a maiden of good family whose shyness should be an ornament to her, to use hateful, scorching words. These are the rankling darts, bitterly remembered till life's end, which make living in another's house so hateful – the fearful indignities which make a family dread the birth of a girl.

MADAYANTIKĀ Buddharakshitā, Lavangikā seems terribly upset. Did my brother say something really dreadful?

BUDDHARAKSHITĀ Yes, he did: he said, 'I'll have no more to do with you, you deceitful little whore!'

MADAYANTIKĀ [*stopping her ears*] Oh horrible! Oh how awful! Lavangikā, my dear, I don't know how to look you in the face. But even so there is something you must allow me to say to you.

LAVANGIKĀ I am at your service.

MADAYANTIKĀ Forget for the moment my brother's unpleasant and outrageous behaviour. Whatever he is like, you will have to comply with his whims, because he is the husband. And you can't fail to know what lay at the root of his vulgar abuse.

LAVANGIKĀ You expect me to know something, even when it is not true?

MADAYANTIKĀ It has been a matter of common gossip that Mālatī has formed a romantic attachment for that young nobleman Mādhava. And this is what has come of it. And so, my dear, you must make sure that this inclination towards another man is completely wiped out from her mind. You must see that anything else would be a dreadful sin. A girl can cruelly torment a man's heart by a perverse attachment of this kind. Don't tell her it was me that said so.

LAVANGIKĀ Oh, away with you and your false rumours, you foolish, deluded creature. I am not going to talk to you.

MADAYANTIKĀ Please, my dear, please. Or perhaps I haven't spoken plainly enough. Don't I know for a fact that Mādhava means the whole world to Mālatī? Who hasn't seen them? – Mālatī, prettier than ever, with her limbs in their weakness as palely beautiful as the inside of a blossoming ketaka flower, and nothing to live for but the bakula garland which *he* wove, hanging on her bosom; and Mādhava, looking as pale and worn and handsome as the orb of the moon at daybreak. And what of that day when we were at the end of the road near the Flower Garden? – *I* saw the looks they exchanged, so charmingly eager with eyes open wide and pupils softly stirring, taught to perfection by the ravishingly skilful dancing-master Love. And another thing: when they heard that she was engaged to my brother, couldn't I see how their hearts stopped beating and nearly burst asunder, in the agony of what they felt at that moment, and their beauty faded away? And there is something else I was forgetting.

LAVANGIKĀ What?

MADAYANTIKĀ When that young nobleman who saved my life recovered consciousness and Mālatī gave the good news to Mādhava, he, on a sly hint from Her Reverence, as a gift of gratitude pledged her his heart and life to do with as she would. And you, Lavangikā, *you* said, 'My friend accepts the kind offer'!

LAVANGIKĀ Young nobleman? Who was that? I've forgotten.

MADAYANTIKĀ My dear, you remember – the one who risked his life to save mine on that very same day, when I was helpless and felt the hot breath of that threatening beast upon me, the one who with only his strong arms to help him, as an act of disinterested kindness, recklessly sacrificed his own person, which is the glory of the world, and rescued me. The one whose broad muscled chest looked like a cruelly torn garland of hibiscus flowers where the tiger's fangs had rent it, and who for my sake, in the strength of his compassion, endured a hail of thunderbolts from the claws of that murderous beast, and then slew the ferocious monster.

LAVANGIKĀ Oh! – Makaranda!

MADAYANTIKĀ [*happily*] What was that, my dear?

LAVANGIKĀ I said, Makaranda! [*Smilingly touching her body*]

What you say of us is true – I have no answer. 1
But how is it that quite suddenly, as we are talking,
A pure and simple girl of good family
Becomes unnerved and thrills like a blossoming
kadamba?

MADAYANTIKĀ [*in confusion*] Why are you laughing at me, my dear? Naturally my body would feel the sudden effect of mentioning and remembering such a man, who showed courage with no thought of self and laid me under the deepest of obligations by forcibly restoring the life of one who was at the very jaws of death. And you saw him yourself, the sweat pouring from him unnoticed in the pain of his wounds, his eyes closing like dark waterlilies in his swoon, his slender sword sinking into the ground beneath the weight of his body – giving up this precious world, and all for Madayantikā. [*She acts sweating and other signs of emotion.*]

BUDDHARAKSHITĀ Your body seems to have no doubts!

MADAYANTIKĀ [*in confusion*] Oh, get away with you, Buddharakshitā! I was affected by the intimate way this girl here was talking.

LAVANGIKĀ Madayantikā, my dear, I know all there is to know. So please, no more pretending. Come on, let's settle down comfortably to a long exchange of confidences.

BUDDHARAKSHITĀ She is right.

MADAYANTIKĀ The two of you are now my closest friends!

LAVANGIKĀ In that case, tell us how you pass your days.

MADAYANTIKĀ Listen, my dear. Trusting as I did in

Buddharakshitā's judgement, I was already beside myself with curiosity and longing and love. And now that fate has decreed that I should actually have got a sight of him, my mind seethes with such torments of relentless and irresistible passion that my life hangs on a thread! Never have I known such a fire as blazes in me from head to toe, pangs so cruelly fierce that my servants are dreadfully alarmed. It is nothing but hope that keeps me from the blissful ease of death – which Buddharakshitā argues against, so increasing my emotional turmoil. The whole world seems upside down.

And in my thoughts and dreams, in the mad hallucination of love, I seem to see *him*! And oh my dear, his beautiful eyes fly open wide in momentary surprise, and dance, and with a brilliant glance, wavering a little with intoxication, he gazes long at me. And as if it were the note of the sweet-singing goose when its throat is hoarse with lotus pollen, he whispers huskily in my ear, 'Madayantikā, darling!'

And then as my robe slips from my trembling breasts, he affronts me by catching at the end of it and strikes terror in my frightened and fast-beating heart. As I abandon my garment and escape, at once covering my exposed bosom with arms that thrill like lotus stems, I find that my disarranged girdle has come loose and slipped down around my thighs, preventing my retreat. Though I speak severely to him, making every effort to harden my heart to the pain of feeling a moment's anger against him, my eyes that gaze lovingly and needlessly upon him declare everything of what I really feel. He laughs, wraps me in his arms and holds me quite helpless, my dear, and his broad chest with its frightful decoration of scars where the tiger's claws had raked him presses me so close that I cannot even tremble. I shake my head in consternation, and my braid of hair flies about. When I reach up to steady it, he catches hold of my hand: the movement jerks up his head, and he gazes at me unwaveringly, a deliberate suggestion in his eyes. Beneath my left cheek he places the hollow bowl of his pursed and throbbing lips, and I melt at the delicious contact. As my limbs show their agitation and a dreadful swooning giddiness makes my gaze slowly wander, he (with a brazenness in keeping with his unmannerly violence) makes a certain request to me – and when all this has happened to me, my dear, I suddenly wake again to the desolate wilderness of this life.

LAVANGIKĀ [*laughing*] Madayantikā dear, go on with the story – then Buddharakshitā, eyes wide with love and mirth, notices that the mattress you have been lying on is in no fit state to be shown to the servants, and so it is hidden beneath the bedclothes. Am I right?

MADAYANTIKĀ Oh, stop your nonsensical jokes!

BUDDHARAKSHITĀ My dear, she's Mālatī's friend – that's why such comments come naturally to her.

MADAYANTIKĀ Don't make fun of Mālatī in that way.

BUDDHARAKSHITĀ Dear Madayantikā, I'd like to ask you something, if you won't betray my confidence.

MADAYANTIKĀ Have I ever let you down before, that you say such a thing? You and Lavangikā, my dear, have grown as close to me as my own heart.

BUDDHARAKSHITĀ If you could somehow see Makaranda again, what would you do?

MADAYANTIKĀ I should feast my eyes unblinkingly on every inch of him.

BUDDHARAKSHITĀ And suppose he, driven by love, were to act towards you as Krishṇa did towards Rukmiṇī,* and imperiously take you to be his lawful wedded wife – what then?

MADAYANTIKĀ [*with a sigh*] Why feed me with such hopes?

BUDDHARAKSHITĀ Answer me, my dear.

LAVANGIKĀ She has, my dear – with long sighs that betray how much she is affected.

MADAYANTIKĀ Dear Lavangikā, what rights have I over this body of mine, which he at the risk of his own life snatched from the jaws of a tiger, and which now belongs to him?

LAVANGIKĀ That reply is in keeping with the nobility of your nature.

BUDDHARAKSHITĀ Remember what you have said.

MADAYANTIKĀ Heavens, there is the drum for the second half of the hour! I must go and either scold my brother or else plead humbly with him, and bring about a reconciliation with Mālatī. [*She prepares to rise.*]

[*Makaranda uncovers his face and grasps her by the hand.*]

Mālatī, my dear, are you awake? [*Seeing him, in delight and consternation*] Oh! This is something quite different!

MAKARANDA

2 Fair creature, check your fear – your waist will not bear
The burden of your trembling breasts.
See, the one you yourself confess to have favoured with your love,
The subject of those dreams, stands before you as your slave.

*Betrothed to another despite her love for Krishṇa, because of her brother's opposition to the match: on her wedding-day Krishṇa appeared and carried her off in his chariot.

LAVANGIKĀ [*raising Madayantikā's face*]

Here is the lover your heart has a thousand times wished for, 3
And here is a house where all are drowsy or asleep.
The night is dark. From simple gratitude, be kind to him.
With our anklets raised and muffled let us now go forth.

MADAYANTIKĀ But Buddharakshitā, where are we to go?

BUDDHARAKSHITĀ Where Mālatī has gone.

MADAYANTIKĀ Has Mālatī taken the bold step?

BUDDHARAKSHITĀ Indeed she has. And remember your own words – 'What rights have I over this body of mine, which he at the risk of his own life snatched from the jaws of a tiger, and which now belongs to him?'

[*Madayantikā sheds tears.*]

Sir, my friend has given herself to you.

MAKARANDA

Now is my greatest victory won, 4
And the years of my youth are fruitful.
For the Love God has shown himself my friend
And smiled with favour on me.

Come then, let us leave by this side-entrance, and be on our way.

[*They move quietly.*]

How beautifully calm the highway is at night! And now

Returning charged with a lingering fragrance of wine 5
From playing about the turret-windows of mansions,
Scented with garlands and the sudden sharp odour of camphor,

The breeze declares that men are keeping company with their brides.

[*They all withdraw.*]

Act VIII

[*Enter Avalokitā.*]

AVALOKITĀ I have greeted Her Reverence on her return from Nandana's house, and now I am going to join Mālatī and Mādhava. [*Walking about*] Here they are, gracing the stone margin of the pond, after a summer evening's bathe. [*She withdraws.*]

[*Enter Mālatī and Mādhava, seated, with Avalokitā.*]

MĀDHAVA [*happily*] Now night, the friend of Love's maturing, is in its youthful glory –

1 The darkness is split by the rising moonlight in the east,
Pale as a grown and withered palm,
As if a thick nectarous pollen from ketaka flowers
Were stirred and lifted skywards by the blowing wind.

[*To himself*] How shall I win over my wilful sweetheart? Like this, perhaps. [*Aloud*] Beloved Mālatī, I have appealed to you to allay the heat of summer for me, while you are still fresh and cool from your evening bathe. Why needlessly misinterpret me? –

2 While the drops are still trickling from your hair, fair one,
And the cleft of your breasts has not lost its wetness,
And your damp flesh is still thrilled and hard,
Grant me one close embrace, I beg of you.

Unrelenting creature,

Restore me to life by placing about my neck 3
Your arm with its beads of nervous sweat,
Lovely as a chain of cool moonstones
Flowing when the moonbeam has kissed them.

But if that is too much, will you not even grant me some share of your conversation?

If there can be no embrace to refresh my body 4
For all the torment of moon-rays and southern breezes,
Yet let my ear, afflicted by the cuckoo's impassioned
call,
Drink in the beauty of your angel-throated voice.

AVALOKITĀ [*approaching*] Irresolute girl! It was not long ago that you were upset because Mādhava was away for a while, and I heard you say, 'He is late! If only I can see him soon, I shan't be at all nervous, I shan't take my eyes off him, I'll say this to him and I'll say that, and fold him into my arms and cherish him!' Is this all that has come of all that?

[*Mālatī looks at her indignantly.*]

MĀDHAVA [*to himself*] Her Reverence's chief pupil has every kind of skill – how resourcefully she speaks! [*Aloud*] Beloved, is it true what Avalokitā says?

[*Mālatī moves her head from side to side.*]

I conjure you upon the lives of Lavangikā and Avalokitā to answer me in words.

MĀLATĪ I don't – [*She breaks off in confusion.*]

MĀDHAVA How beautiful are her stumbling words! [*Suddenly, looking closer*] Avalokitā, what is this?

A flood of tears has suddenly bathed 5

Her lovely cheek, on which there shines the moon,
Directing there the lotus filaments of his rays
As if he hoped to drink in the nectar of her beauty.

AVALOKITĀ My dear, why are you weeping and choked with tears?

MĀLATĪ Avalokitā, how much longer must I bear the pain of dearest Lavangikā's absence? I cannot even learn what is happening to her.

MĀDHAVA Avalokitā, what is it?

AVALOKITĀ It was your mention of Lavangikā. Now that she is reminded, she is worried about what is happening to her.

MĀDHAVA Why, I have just sent Kalahamsaka there, to Nandana's house, to find out quietly what is happening. [*Anxiously*] Avalokitā, I hope all goes well with Buddharakshitā's efforts for Madayantikā.

AVALOKITĀ Once, sir, at Her Reverence's prompting you made Mālatī a gift of your heart and your life – it was when she gave you the good news that Makaranda had recovered consciousness after his clawing by the tiger. If someone should now congratulate you on his winning Madayantikā, what would be that person's reward?

MĀDHAVA That is an excellent question. [*Looking down at his breast*] I have this, the garland of flowers from the lucky bakula tree in the park of the temple, the tree which witnessed the love I felt the first time I saw Mālatī.

6 For love of me, that I had woven it, she accepted it from her friend,
Wore it upon her rounded breasts and cherished it,
But then when her wedding was at hand and all hope of me was lost,

Supposing me Lavangikā, she gave it me as the dearest thing she owned.

AVALOKITĀ Mālatī, my dear, you are fond of this bakula garland. So watch out that it doesn't suddenly fall into someone else's hands.

MĀLATĪ That is welcome advice, my dear.

AVALOKITĀ Oh, I think I hear footsteps.

MĀDHAVA [*looking off-stage*] Ah! Kalahamsaka has arrived!

MĀLATĪ I congratulate you that Madayantikā is won!

MĀDHAVA [*embracing her delightedly*] Dearest one, I welcome the news! [*He places the bakula garland round her neck.*]

AVALOKITĀ Buddharakshitā has justified Her Reverence's confidence.

MĀLATĪ [*in delight*] Oh, I can see dearest Lavangikā too! [*She gets up.*]

[*Enter in agitation Kalahamsaka, Madayantikā, Buddharakshitā and Lavangikā.*]

LAVANGIKĀ Help us, sir, help us! On our way here Makaranda was attacked by some louts of policemen, and when Kalahamsaka turned up he sent us on with him.

KALAHAMSAKA As we were coming here, we heard such an uproar behind us that I think reinforcements must have appeared.

MĀLATĪ *and* AVALOKITĀ Oh heavens, joy and disaster all at once!

MĀDHAVA Come Madayantikā, my dear, you are welcome; you bring favour on our house. Remember that he is who he is. Why feel uneasy that he is one against many? That means nothing to my friend.

7 The lion needs only one stout comrade in his battle –
The claw whose grating nails strike terror in the foe,
Which unaided splits the skull of the lordly elephant
And makes his face gleam with ichor from his shattered
temples.

I will go and fight at the side of my valiant friend.

[*He walks about fiercely, and goes out with Kalahamsaka.*]

AVALOKITĀ, LAVANGIKĀ *and* BUDDHARAKSHITĀ Pray God they return unharmed!

MĀLATĪ Buddharakshitā and Avalokitā, you must go at once to Her Reverence and tell her what has happened. And Lavangikā, hurry and tell my noble Lord that if he has any pity on me he will not be over-reckless.

[*They withdraw.*]

MĀLATĪ Oh, I cannot understand why Lavangikā is taking so long. Madayantikā, my dear, I will go and meet Lavangikā as she returns. [*She walks about.*]

MADAYANTIKĀ [*apprehensively*] There is an unlucky throbbing in my right eye! [*She sits down.*]

[*Enter Kapālakuṇḍalā.*]

KAPĀLAKUṆḌALĀ Stay, wretched girl, stay!

MĀLATĪ [*with a start of fear*] Ah, my Lord! – [*She is struck dumb.*]

KAPĀLAKUṆḌALĀ [*with an angry laugh*] Why, scream, scream!

8 Where is that sweetheart of yours who murders ascetics?
Let that debaucher of girls, your husband, protect you.
Why play the quail that fears the swooping hawk?
Now at long last I have found and gobbled you.

So off to the Holy Mountain I shall take her, and shredding her piece by piece contrive for her a painful death!

[*She goes out with Mālatī.*]

MADAYANTIKĀ I will go and look for Mālatī. [*Walking about*] Mālatī, my dear!

[*Enter Lavangikā.*]

LAVANGIKĀ Madayantikā, dear, this is Lavangikā.

MADAYANTIKĀ Did you speak with the noble youth?

LAVANGIKĀ No, I didn't. The moment he left the garden he could hear the uproar, and he rushed forward, shouting a challenge, as fast as his long legs could carry him, and plunged into the fight. So I turned back disconsolately. And from every house I heard the people lamenting Mādhava and Makaranda and their rashness, in despair that such merit was in danger. And it seems that the King himself was so incensed to hear that two daughters of his ministers had been seduced that he at once despatched a strong detachment of infantry, and he is said to be watching things himself by the light of the moon from the palace roof.

MADAYANTIKĀ Oh dreadful!

LAVANGIKĀ But my dear, where is Mālatī?

MADAYANTIKĀ Why, she went on earlier to meet you. Then I did the same, but I haven't seen her. Do you think she can have got lost in the wood?

LAVANGIKĀ My dear, we must search for her at once. She is very timid, and there is no knowing what might suddenly have happened to her.

[*They walk about in haste, calling:* 'Mālatī, my dear! Hallo, Mālatī!' *They move about in various directions.*]

[*Enter a delighted Kalahamsaka.*]

KALAHAMSAKA Thank goodness, we're safely out of the

fray! Lord, I feel as if I can still see all the enemy, with the moonlight glinting brightly on their dense array of brandished swords, looking as if Balarāma* in his drunken frolic were whirling up the waters of the Yamunā with his plough, as Makaranda descended upon them with merciless energy, clashing with them and putting them to flight, drawing a clamour from them that rang to the high heavens. And then I remember Mādhava my master sending the soldiers reeling with blows of his powerful arms, snatching from them any weapon that came to hand, confronting and routing all that was left of the enemy and striding heroically down the deserted road.

Ah, the King can appreciate merit: from his vantage-point in the palace he sent down footmen to reason with the contestants and calm the dispute. And when Mādhava and Makaranda were brought before him, he gazed at them long and affectionately, and when he learnt who their families were treated them with the deepest courtesy. To Bhūrivasu and Nandana, whose faces were inky-black with annoyance and chagrin, he remarked with gentle reasonableness, 'Can you have any objection to such noble sons-in-law, who are an ornament to the world, and pleasing alike for their family, their good looks, and their merit?' With which admonishment he withdrew.

And here come Mādhava and Makaranda. Now I must tell Her Reverence the news. [*He withdraws.*]

[*Enter Mādhava and Makaranda.*]

*Elder brother of Krishṇa, renowned for his drunkenness. Once in his cups, annoyed that the Yamunā river would not come to him so that he could bathe, he plunged his ploughshare into its waters and drew them after him till he got an apology.

MAKARANDA Oh, my friend has shone with a heroism that was superhuman!

When the blows of his arm had shattered his adversaries, 9
He would snatch their weapons and show his courage elsewhere.
Through the ocean of battle with its heaving mass of broken bodies
He cut a fearful path, lined with unstirring warriors.

MĀDHAVA But must we not feel regret? Consider –

Those who this very night gaily shared the moon-sparkling wine 10
With sweethearts who fondly granted their embraces,
Now that your arm has wrought its havoc on their limbs,
Are corpses proclaiming the frailty of man's existence.

But think of the King's generosity in treating us so courteously, as if we had committed no offence! Well, come and let's give Mālatī a leisurely account of the whole story of Madayantikā's abduction –

As you are telling it, Mālatī will smile 11
And discreetly turn her gaze towards her friend,
Who will be forced to avert her lotus face
And whose eyes will grow fixed in embarrassment.

There's the garden.

[*They go in.*]

MĀDHAVA Why, the place seems deserted.

MAKARANDA I expect they were so worried about us that they couldn't stay still, and are distracting themselves by a stroll in the wood here. Come, let's see.

[*They walk about.*]

LAVANGIKĀ *and* MADAYANTIKĀ Mālatī, Mālatī! [*Suddenly catching sight of the others*] Oh, thank heavens, sirs, that we see you safe again.

MĀDHAVA *and* MAKARANDA Ladies, where is Mālatī?

THE TWO GIRLS Mālatī? We've no idea. I'm afraid the sound of your footsteps misled us.

MĀDHAVA My heart is in a thousand pieces. Speak clearly –

12 I can think of nothing but some danger to the fair creature.
My heart turns to water and my brain fails.
My eye has an unlucky throbbing, and your words
Presage disaster – alas, I am destroyed.

MADAYANTIKĀ When you left us, sir, she sent Avalokitā and Buddharakshitā to Her Reverence, and Lavangikā to you to ask you to be careful. Then she grew restless and went to watch for Lavangikā's return. I went after her, but I couldn't see her. And so we were searching among the trees here when we saw you.

MĀDHAVA Ah, dearest Mālatī!

13 I fear something, something evil.
Don't joke, cruel one, for I am worried.
Are you testing me? I am tested. Beloved, speak.
My mind is in a whirl – you have no pity.

THE TWO GIRLS Oh, dearest Mālatī, what has happened to you?

MAKARANDA Why so despairing, friend, when you know nothing for certain?

MĀDHAVA Don't you realize yourself what unhappiness might drive her to, in her love for me?

MAKARANDA True enough. But I also think that she may

have gone to see Her Reverence. Come, we will go and find out.

THE TWO GIRLS That must be what has happened.

MĀDHAVA Pray god it's so.

[*They walk about.*]

MAKARANDA [*reflectively, to himself*]

Whether she can have gone to Her Reverence 14
And whether she is yet alive, I very much wonder.
For the joys of union with family, friends and loved ones
Are joys as fickle as a flash of summer lightning.

[*They all withdraw.*]

PRELUDE TO ACT IX

[*Enter Saudāmanī.**]

SAUDĀMANĪ Here am I, Saudāmanī: after flying to Padmāvatī from the Holy Mountain, I am on my way to find Mādhava, for now that he has lost Mālatī he can no longer bear familiar scenes and places, and has left his home to wander with his friends among this vastness of valleys and mountains and forests. Ah, I have flown so high my eye encompasses the whole extent of hills, towns, villages, rivers and woods. [*Looking westwards*] Superb!

The limpid waters of the Sindhu and the Pārā 1
Put a broad girdle round Padmāvatī,
As if the city's lofty houses, towers and temples
Had scraped and rent the sky and brought it tumbling.

*Her arrival is presaged by the mention of her name ('summer lightning') at the end of the previous act.

And

2 There glints the gently rippling Lavaṇā,
The delight of countryfolk when the rains arrive,
For cows in calf love the tender strain of grass
In the pasturage of the woods with which its banks are lined.

[*Looking in another direction*] There is the Sindhu's cataract that splits the earth,

3 From which there comes this roar, as deep and wild
As the thunder of water-swollen clouds,
Reverberating in the mountain caves around
Until it might be the trumpeting of Gaṇeśa.

These forest mountains, fragrant with ripened citrus, with their thickets of sandalwood, sal, karanja, bakula, plantain and trumpet flower, recall the mountains in the jungles of the south, where woods of kadamba and rose-apple shade the dark echoing caves, as the deep roar of the Godāvarī makes the broad mountainslopes resound.

And there, purifying the confluence of the Sindhu and the Madhumatī, is the holy one, Bhavānī's Lord, established here by no human agency, given the title 'Suvarṇabindu'.* [*Making obeisance*]

4 Hail God, creator of the world,
Granter of all desires, holy treasury of scripture,
Whose diadem is the shining moon,
Hail slayer of the Love-god, hail most ancient of teachers.

*'God of the Golden Seed' – a title of Śiva, but one which links him with Agni, god of fire. Fire may have been a particular feature of this shrine: cf. Act X, verse 9, page 415.

[*Acting flight through the air*]

Here, its peak newly darkening with rain-cloud, 5
Loud with the peacocks' impassioned calling,
Its height close-packed with trees whose nests are ashimmer with birds,
The mountain of Brihadaśman gives pleasure to my eye.

The growling here of bear-cubs in their caves 6
Grows dense and heavy with re-echoing
And dense grows the cool, astringent scent of gum trees
Whose branches elephants have ripped and scattered.

Why, it is noon already, for I see that

From the vervain the lapwing trips to the cassia's fresh shade, 7
And bluejays make for the water, beaks brushing the pods of aśmantaka on the bank.
Moorhens settle in the hollow trunk of the blackwood,
While jungle-fowl answer from below the cooing of nesting doves.

Now, then, I must search out Mādhava and Makaranda, and bring all to a due conclusion. [*She withdraws.*]

Act IX

[*Enter Makaranda, supporting Mādhava.*]

MAKARANDA [*sighing tenderly*]

With no way of finding hope or of losing it, 8
The restless mind moves in a blind darkness of delusion.
Our creator has set his face against us,
And ours is the plight of helpless animals.

MĀDHAVA Mālatī, my beloved, where are you? How can you have vanished so suddenly and so mysteriously? Cruel one, I beg you, take notice of me.

9 You who loved me, why are you so unkind?
Am I not the same as the one your hand once gladdened
When it moved, like the marriage-rite made flesh,
To take the wedding-ring of its own accord.

[*After long weeping*] Makaranda, dear friend, where will the like of her love be found in this world?

10 With a body as fresh as a flower, she endured a fever of love
That tortured her long and unceasingly, every moment an agony.
She was ready to give up life as if it were a straw,
And, this above all, dared to give herself to me.

And

11 Before the wedding, when she had given up hope of me,
Those weak and piteous cries, like the last extremity of pain,
Do you remember them? – when she so revealed her love
That my heart too was drowned in waves of agony.

[*In distress*] Oh, oh!

12 My heart is split with pain, but does not fall asunder,
Darkness invades my soul, and yet I stay conscious.
My body is ablaze within, yet never burns to ashes.
Fate wounds me mortally, but does not take my life.

MAKARANDA Friend, the sun is as burningly cruel as

fate itself, and you are ill. Come and sit for a while by this lotus-pool. For

The breeze here, charged with a heady odour of nectar 13
From the masses of tall and newly blossoming lotuses,
And cool with drops of spray from the rippling pond,
Will revive you as it plays about your face.

[*They walk about and then seat themselves.*]
[*To himself*] Let me try something to distract him. [*Aloud*] Mādhava, my friend,

In this moment between the falling and the welling of 14
your tears,
See the undying beauty of this place,
Where, stirred by the wings of the impassioned singing-
geese,
The lotuses on their broad stalks are quivering.

[*Mādhava rises in agitation.*]
Oh, in his distraction he has risen and moved away. [*Sighing and getting up*] Dear friend, I beg of you, do look –

The blossoming cane has perfumed the mountain 15
streams,
And a profusion of jasmine blooms along their banks,
While there, above slopes that are white with the smiles
of kuṭaja flowers,
The massing clouds form a canopy for the peacocks'
dance.

With a dense splendour of opening buds, kadamba 16
trees
Adorn the mountainside, as the horizon grows dark with
cloud.

Growing shoots of ketaka throng the banks of the flowing streams,
And the woods stretch smiling with fresh-scented lodhra and śilindra.

MĀDHAVA I am looking, friend. But a beautiful haze is now upon this landscape of forest and mountain. Why should that be? [*In tears*] But why else? –

17 They have come, the days between summer and monsoon,
Days smelling of rain-soaked earth,
When eastern gales fragrant with arjuna and sal
Toss and fragment the banks of sapphire cloud.

Oh Mālatī, beloved!

18 When the clouds roll thick and dark as tamāla trees,
And cool winds blow fresh drops of rain towards me,
And the air is filled with the peacock's passionate note,
And a rainbow arches in the sky, how can I look about me?

[*He is overcome with grief.*]

MAKARANDA This is a fearful state my poor friend has fallen into. [*Sadly*] And I was so unfeeling that I tried to be cheerful. [*With a sigh*] After this I have little hope left for Mādhava. [*Looking in alarm*] What, has he fainted? [*Into the air*] Mālatī, Mālatī, are you still so heartless?

19 You rejected your family
And dared everything for love of him.
When he has done you no wrong, dear friend,
How can you act so cruelly?

Still he has not revived. Oh, I am robbed –

Alas, alas, my heart breaks and my body shatters, 20
The world is empty, I burn with a ceaseless fire.
My desolate soul drowns in blackest night.
Delusion veils my senses. What can I do in my wretchedness?

Oh dreadful!

The pride of his family, 21
The Moonlight of Mālatī's eyes,
He, my only joy,
Jewel of the world, is dying.

Oh Mādhava, dear friend,

You were sandalwood to my body, the autumn moon to my sight, 22
To my heart you were bliss itself.
If death has snatched you from me.
I am dead, for it has snatched my life away.

Heartless one, grant me your bright smile, 23
Cruel friend, let me hear your voice.
You who love Makaranda,
Why do you doubt your friend's devotion?

[*Mādhava regains consciousness.*]

[*With a sigh of relief*] This fresh rain-cloud as bright and full-bodied as a newly polished diamond has revived him with a shower of spray. Thank god he has recovered!

MĀDHAVA Who in this forest will take a message for me to my beloved? [*Looking*] Ah, good!

To the north of the stream whose ripples break 24
Against groves of rose-apple dark with ripened fruit,

Shaping and reshaping, black as a grown tamāla,
A fresh cloud waits by the mountain's peak.

[*Rising eagerly, looking up and joining his hands in prayer*]

25 Good sir, I trust your dear companion the lightning embraces you,
And that the cloud cuckoos frequent you, delighting in your bounty.
Does the eastern breeze soothe you with its gentle touch,
And the auspicious rainbow curving either side augment your beauty?

[*Listening*] Ah, he shows sympathy with a deep rumbling whose echo fills the caves and draws the cries of the excited peacocks. My request, then. Blessed cloud,

26 If you chance to see my beloved as you wander at will through the earth,
Reassure her first, then tell her of Mādhava's plight.
Tell it in such a way as not to snap the thread of hope,
For that is the only thing that can keep her alive.

[*Joyfully*] Ah, he has set off! I will go elsewhere. [*He walks about.*]

MAKARANDA [*with great emotion*] Alas, an eclipse of insanity is blotting out this moon. Father, mother, Reverence, save us. See the state he is in.

MĀDHAVA Oh dreadful!

27 The fresh lodhra flowers have her loveliness,
The gazelles her glance, the elephants her graceful walk,
The vines have her body's curve – oh it is plain,

My love is slain and shared among the forest.

Oh Mālatī, my dearest one!

MAKARANDA

When my loved friend, my comrade since we played together in the dust, 28
Embodiment of every virtue and lord of my life,
From losing his beloved, is in such agony of soul and body –
Accursed heart of mine, why have you not shattered and fallen apart?

MĀDHAVA But of course, the world is full of imitations of the Creator's handiwork. I will try something else. [*Calling out*] Ho there, I salute you, creatures of mountain and forest, and would humbly ask something of you – for just a moment be gracious and attend to me:

Have you seen a noble girl, a creature of perfect loveliness, 29
While you were here, or have you heard what has become of her?
I will tell you her age, friends: it is the age when Love
Acts boldly on the heart, but is still gentle with the body.

Alas!

My words are drowned by the cries of the peacock, his feathers spread in dancing. 30
Lost in a rapture, the partridge attends soft-eyed upon his beloved.
The ape showers his sweetheart's cheek with pollen.
Whom can I ask? Nowhere is it the moment to heed a suppliant.

And here

31 A monkey raises and kisses his loved one's face
Delicious as a pomegranate split by ripeness,
The teeth reflecting the redness of the lips,
The cheek and temple ruddy as kampila blossom.

Oh, and here is an elephant resting his trunk on his beloved's neck. What, has he too no time for me?

32 To close her eyes in ecstasy by using the point of his tusk to scratch her,
To fan her soothingly by flapping each ear in turn,
To keep up her strength with half-chewed shoots from the gum-tree,
Are all familiarities this lucky jungle-elephant can practise.

[*Glancing elsewhere*] But here is one

33 Who responds with no roar to the thundering clouds,
Gathers no titbits of duckweed from the lake nearby.
His face sadly framed with silent bees that mourn the vanished ichor,
He must certainly be pining the loss of her he loves.

I cannot trouble him. [*Glancing elsewhere*] But here is yet another, the lord of a rutting herd, delighting the ears of his mate with the deep sweet rumble of his voice as he plunges and sports in a lake whose waters he colours with the thick exudation of his cheeks, an ichor as coolly fragrant as fresh-flowering kadamba. His plunge has reduced a bed of lotuses to a chaos of scattered leaves and filaments and fibres and suckers and roots and shoots, and the ceaseless flapping of his ears has whipped the rippling waves into a fine mist, till cranes and ospreys rise up in fright. I'll speak to him. Good sir, lord of elephants, you use your youth well, and your attendance upon your dear consort shows skill: yet it can be faulted.

True that when she had tasted her fill of lotus stalks 34
You offered her mouthfuls of lotus-scented water.
True that you sprayed her refreshingly with your trunk. But after this
You held over her no parasol of straight-stalked lotuses.

Oh, he moves disdainfully away. Alas I am mad to treat a creature of the jungle as if he were my friend Makaranda. Oh my dear friend,

Alas for this wilderness of life away from you, 35
Alas for beauty which you are not here to appreciate.
A curse on any day not spent with you and her,
And on the mirage of pleasure that arises in your absence.

MAKARANDA Ah, despite the veil of madness some reminder of me has awoken his affection and now he thinks I am not here. [*Standing in front of him*] Here is your unhappy Makaranda at your side.

MĀDHAVA Embrace me, friend. As for Mālatī, all hope there is gone. [*He faints.*]

MAKARANDA [*joyfully*] I embrace you, lord of my life. [*Looking with compassion*] Oh alas, he has fainted away without getting beyond the wish to embrace me. No more deluding hopes. My friend is lost to me forever – that is what I must believe. Oh my friend!

Those fears which my love-fevered heart was always feeling 36

Which made me tremble for no apparent reason,
As I counted your sorrows over to myself,
They are all suddenly quietened within me.

Oh friend, I would rather have back those earlier moments when I knew you as one conscious, though you were as you were. But now

37 My body is a burden, my life an iron nail;
Space is empty, and my senses useless;
Time is a woeful thing now you are gone:
Everything in this living world has darkened.

[*Thinking*] Must I live on simply to be a witness of Mādhava's end? No, I will cast myself from this mountain-peak into the Pāṭalāvatī, and precede Mādhava into death. [*Walking on a little, then turning to look tenderly*] Alas!

38 There is the body, dark as a waterlily,
No embrace of which could ever satisfy me,
Which the eyes of Mālatī drank in with obvious wonder,
In a sweet confusion of dawning love.

How can a single body and that so young have held such merit? Oh Mādhava, my friend,

39 A fair moon at its moment of fullness has been swallowed by the demon of eclipse,
A rain-cloud swollen and ripe has been scattered by the blowing wind,
A fine tree ready to fruit has been burnt in a forest fire.
As you became the jewel in the world's crown, you succumbed to death.

I'll embrace him, though he is almost gone from me. It was his last request. [*Embracing him*] Oh my friend, store of bright wisdom, my teacher in virtue, chosen lord of Mālatī, the delight of Kāmandakī and Makaranda, fair Mādhava: here is Makaranda's embrace, the last in this life, which in your last extremity you asked for. Do not suppose, friend, that I could live a moment longer.

Since birth we have lived in one house, 40
And there we were suckled side by side:
Fair youth, I cannot let you drink alone
The water offered in the family oblation.*

[*Releasing him tenderly and walking about*] There is the Pāṭalāvatī below. Holy river –

My next birth be where 41
My beloved friend is born,
And there once again
Let me be his companion.

[*He prepares to jump.*]

[*Enter Saudāmanī.*]

SAUDĀMANĪ [*suddenly checking him*] Child, child! Don't be so rash!

MAKARANDA [*seeing her*] Lady, who are you? Why did you stop me?

SAUDĀMANĪ Sir, are you Makaranda?

MAKARANDA Release me. Yes, I am that unhappy person.

SAUDĀMANĪ I am a yoginī, my child, and I bring a token of Mālatī. [*She shows him the bakula garland.*]

MAKARANDA [*breathing a sigh of relief, tenderly*] Lady, is she alive?

*Deceased relatives were commemorated daily by oblations of water in the rite of *pitr-yajna.*

SAUDĀMANĪ Certainly. But child, your desperate act alarms me: has Mādhava come to harm?

MAKARANDA Lady, he was no more than unconscious when I gave up hope and left him. Let us go quickly and find him.

[*They move rapidly.*]

MĀDHAVA [*reviving*] Ah, something has revived me! [*Considering*] It must have been the work of this breeze bringing drops of rain from the approaching clouds, showing no feeling for the state I am in.

MAKARANDA He has recovered consciousness, thank God.

SAUDĀMANĪ [*regarding them*] They are both as Mālatī described them.

MĀDHAVA Blessed wind from the east,

42 Whirl the water-swollen clouds, delight the cloud cuckoos,
Make the peacocks cry in yearning, ripen the ketakas.
But when a lover finds ease for his pain in oblivion,
Why try to restore to him the agony of feeling?

MAKARANDA Then it must have been this wind, the quickener of all creatures, that revived my friend.

MĀDHAVA Even so, divine wind, it is you I ask –

43 As you carry the pollen of the flowering kadambas,
Waft my life wherever my beloved is.
Or else bring me something cool with her body's fragrance,
For there is none but you to help me.

[*He bows to the cloud with joined hands.*]

SAUDĀMANĪ This is the moment to give him the token.

[*She tosses the bakula garland into Mādhava's joined hands.*]

MĀDHAVA [*seeing it, and overcome with astonishment and joy*] What, can this be the garland of bakula flowers from the courtyard of the Love Temple, woven by me and crushed by my sweetheart's swelling breasts? [*Examining it*] I am certain of it. For

Here is the very part which I wove so badly, 44
Trying to hide my interest in her moon-lovely face,
But which yet gave Lavangikā much pleasure
For all that I had arranged the flowers so clumsily.

[*Rising in a joyful frenzy*] Mālatī, my beloved, I'll find you. [*With a show of anger*] You cannot know the state I am in –

I feel as if life were ebbing, my heart breaking, 45
My body burning, and darkness pressing in.
The matter is urgent, my fairest – no time for jest.
Gladden my sight, do not be cruel to me.

[*Dejectedly, after looking everywhere*] How can Mālatī be here? [*Sitting down, to the bakula garland*] Oh bakula garland, you love her and you have been our friend. And so welcome to you.

Dear friend, when she felt the pangs of love, 46
Irresistible, unbearable, causing grave sickness,
It was caressing you that saved my beautiful mistress,
For she could think that she was clasping me.

[*Examining it tenderly*]

Alas, I remember how you came and went between us, 47
Lying now at my breast, now at hers,
Kindling a joyful fever of desire,
And feelings of deepest passion, and loving fondness.

[*He puts the garland on, and faints away.*]

MAKARANDA [*going to him and fanning him*] It's all right, friend, it's all right.

MĀDHAVA [*recovering*] Don't you see, Makaranda. I've suddenly had this token of Mālatī from somewhere. What do you think, what can it mean?

MAKARANDA Friend, here is the lady, a mistress of yoga, who has brought you this sign of Mālatī.

MĀDHAVA [*looking at her, tenderly and with joined hands*] Lady, tell me, I beg of you – is my beloved alive?

SAUDĀMANĪ Breathe easily, child. She is.

MĀDHAVA *and* MAKARANDA [*with sighs of relief*] Lady, if that is so, tell us everything that has happened.

SAUDĀMANĪ It goes back to the time when Aghoraghaṇṭa, sword drawn and in the very act of sacrificing Mālatī in the temple of Karālā, was killed by Mādhava.

MĀDHAVA [*in consternation*] Stop, stop. I understand the rest.

MAKARANDA What is it, friend?

MĀDHAVA What else can it be? Kapālakuṇḍalā has taken her revenge.

MAKARANDA Is it that, lady?

SAUDĀMANĪ Yes, it is just as your friend supposes.

MAKARANDA Oh horrible!

48 When waterlilies and the light of the autumn moon
Unite for beauty,
It should be well. What can it mean
When clouds out of season try to part them?

MĀDHAVA Ah Mālatī my beloved, what horrors you have undergone!

49 How came Kapālakuṇḍalā
To swallow you, my fairest,

Like an ill-omened comet
Swallowing the moon?

Venerable Kapālakuṇḍalā,

She is a creation to be cherished carefully: 50
Be kindly, do not act the fiend.
When a flower is fragrant, its natural place
Is on the head, not ground beneath the pestle.

SAUDĀMANĪ Do not be alarmed, dear child.

She would have done the crime – 51
She knows no mercy –
If I had not been there
To frustrate her plans.

BOTH [*making obeisance*] Lady, you have been gracious beyond measure. But who are you, you who have been our only friend?

SAUDĀMANĪ You will know in time. [*Rising*] Behold, now

Born of study and penance, 52
Of yoga and the making of spells,
This transporting magic
I use to your good.

[*She goes out with Mādhava.*]

MAKARANDA Oh, a wonder!

Some fearful blend of darkness and lightning, 53
Destroying my sight for a moment, has come and gone.
[*Looking, in fear*]
My friend not here? What has happened?
[*Reflecting*]
But what else?
This mistress of yoga has shown her power.

[*In puzzlement*] Is this good or ill? I am confused –

54 In great astonishment, earlier thoughts forgotten,
But plagued with a new and feverish alarm,
Gloom in a single moment dispersed and intensified,
My mind is streaked with happiness and grief.

I must look for Her Reverence, who is in this wood with the rest of our band, and tell her what has happened. [*He withdraws.*]

Act X

[*Enter Kāmandakī, Madayantikā and Lavangikā.*]

KĀMANDAKĪ Darling Mālatī, child who once graced my lap, where are you? Answer me.

1 Now all the little ways you had,
Which have so delighted me since you were born,
And all your dear sweet turns of speech, remembered,
Torment my body and lacerate my heart.

And oh my daughter,

2 I think of your lotus face when you were small
And your sweet, stumbling mistakes of speech,
And the soft glint of your first few budding teeth,
For then you knew no restraint in smiles or tears.

THE OTHERS Ah dearest, fairest friend, where are you? What sudden cruel disaster overtook your petal-frail body in your loneliness? Oh noble Mādhava, you have already found and lost all your earthly happiness.

KĀMANDAKĪ Dear children,

Your due and joyful union 3
Like the fresh-flowering embrace
Of clove and lavalī vine
Lies blasted by the hurricane.

LAVANGIKĀ [*in distress*] Cursed heart of adamant, are you so cruel? [*She smites her breast and falls.*]

MADAYANTIKĀ Lavangikā my dear, please, revive for just a moment.

LAVANGIKĀ Oh what am I to do? Life is cemented to me and will not go.

KĀMANDAKĪ Darling Mālatī, you have loved Lavangikā since birth. Have you no pity for her when her life hangs in the balance? See her now –

Losing your radiance 4
She can no longer shine,
Like an inky wick
Abandoned by its flame.

And have you deserted Kāmandakī? Why, cruel girl, it was the warmth of my robes that nourished you.

From the moment you left the breast, pretty as an ivory doll, 5
In your games and then more seriously I trained and reared you.
I found you a husband, the best in all the world.
Do I not deserve of you more even than a mother's love?

[*Dejectedly*] Beautiful one, I have lost all hope –

Ill-starred that I am, it is not given me to see 6

A son on your lap, sucking at your breast,
His face wreathed in smiles that have no cause,
White mustard-seed upon his head and forehead.

LAVANGIKĀ Reverence, please, I can bear this life no longer, and I shall seek release by casting myself from this cliff. Favour my prayers, Reverence, so that I shall see my dearest Mālatī in my life to come.

KĀMANDAKĪ Why Lavangikā, I cannot live any more than you without that sweet child, and we have but one longing between us. Besides –

7 If union is not to be, because our deeds in life were different,
Then it is not to be.
At least the quitting of life
Will mean an end to torment.

LAVANGIKĀ As you say, Reverence. [*She rises.*]

KĀMANDAKĪ [*with compassion, looking at Madayantikā*] Madayantikā, my dear child.

MADAYANTIKĀ What is your command? To be the first? I am ready.

LAVANGIKĀ My dear, I beg of you, do not kill yourself. Think of me.

MADAYANTIKĀ [*with a show of anger*] Away with you, I am not your slave.

KĀMANDAKĪ The poor girl is determined, I fear.

MADAYANTIKĀ [*to herself*] Makaranda, my lord, salutation to you.

LAVANGIKĀ Reverence, here is the cliff-top with the sacred girdle of the Madhumatī about its base.

KĀMANDAKĪ Then let nothing now prevent us.

[*All prepare to jump.*]

MĀDHAVA'S VOICE OFF-STAGE Oh a wonder!

Some fearful blend of darkness and lightning, 8
Destroying my sight for a moment, has come and gone.

KĀMANDAKĪ [*looking, in amazement and joy*]

What, my dear child here? What has happened? 8 cont.

[*Enter Makaranda.*]

MAKARANDA What else?

This mistress of yoga has shown her power. 8 cont.

A FOREST-DWELLER'S VOICE OFF-STAGE Alas, here is a dreadful gathering!

Knowing Mālatī gone, and losing all taste 9
For life's pleasures and for life itself,
Bhūrivasu is come to Suvarṇabindu
Resolved, oh horror, to cast himself into the flames.

MADAYANTIKĀ *and* LAVANGIKĀ So suddenly the joy of seeing Mālatī and Mādhava, and so suddenly this calamity!

KĀMANDAKĪ *and* MAKARANDA Happiness! Disaster!

Can sharp knives and cool sandalwood 10
Fall together upon us?
Can nectar rain from a cloudless sky
And spit sparks of fire?

Today fate shows itself 11
As a mixture of poison and healing draught,
A union of light and darkness,
A blending of the rays of sun and moon.

MĀLATĪ'S VOICE OFF-STAGE Stop, father, stop! I long to see your dear face. Embrace me, I beg you. You, the only light of a family which is the mainstay of this world, are you sacrificing yourself for me? And I in my shamelessness called you unkind!

KĀMANDAKĪ Ah, dear child,

12 When, as from another life,
You have been somehow restored to us,
Comes this new calamity
Like an eclipse to swallow you.

THE OTHERS Oh dearest Mālatī!

[*Enter Mādhava, supporting Mālatī in a faint.*]

MĀDHAVA Oh dreadful!

13 Surviving one danger,
She meets another of a different kind.
When fate's fulfilment is at hand,
Who can close the gates against it?

MAKARANDA But friend, where is the yoginī?

MĀDHAVA

14 In haste from the Holy Mountain
I flew here together with her,
But after the forest-dweller's dreadful words,
She suddenly vanished.

KĀMANDAKĪ *and* MAKARANDA Noble lady, save us again. Why have you disappeared?

LAVANGIKĀ *and* MADAYANTIKĀ Mālatī, my dear, Mālatī! [*In alarm*] Help, Reverence, help! She is no longer breathing and her heart has stopped beating. Ah, Minister Bhūrivasu and dearest Mālatī, each of you has killed the other!

KĀMANDAKĪ Oh Mālati, my child!

MĀDHAVA Oh beloved!

MAKARANDA Oh, dear Mālatī!

[*All faint away and then revive.*]

KĀMANDAKĪ What is happening? Suddenly, as if a cloud had parted, a shower of rain plays upon us and revives us.

MĀDHAVA [*with a sigh of relief*] Ah, Mālatī is recovering! Look –

Her bosom is beginning to heave with deep-drawn 15
breaths,
And her moist eye has regained its natural look.
And now her face brightens as the swoon leaves her,
Like a lotus growing beautiful as the dawn breaks.

SAUDĀMANĪ'S VOICE OFF-STAGE

Ignoring the King and Nandana prostrate before him, 16
And preparing to cast himself into the flames,
Bhūrivasu was suddenly checked by hearing my voice,
His joy and astonishment intense.

MĀDHAVA *and* MAKARANDA [*in delight, looking up*] Reverence, all is well.

Here with a parting of the clouds, 17
Comes that yoginī herself,
Her shower of nectarous words
More welcome than a shower of rain.

KĀMANDAKĪ Glad news!

MĀLATĪ At last I live again!

KĀMANDAKĪ [*in joy and tears*] Come to me, my daughter.

MĀLATĪ What, Your Reverence here? [*She falls at her feet.*]

KĀMANDAKĪ [*raising and embracing her, and kissing her on the forehead*]

18 Live, and give life to him who is your life,
And let your friends live.
And with your limbs as cool as snow, my daughter,
Restore life to me and to your dear companions here.

MĀDHAVA Makaranda, dear friend, the world is bearable to me again!

MAKARANDA [*in delight*] Yes, indeed it is.

MADAYANTIKĀ *and* LAVANGIKĀ Beloved Mālatī, whom we dared not hope to see again, grant us an embrace.

MĀLATĪ Oh my dearest ones! [*She embraces them.*]

KĀMANDAKĪ My dear children, what has been happening?

MĀDHAVA *and* MAKARANDA Reverence,

19 The wrath of Kapālakuṇḍalā
Involved us in suffering,
And from our plight this noble lady
Has been at pains to rescue us.

KĀMANDAKĪ What, was it the killing of Aghoraghaṇṭa that brought this upon us?

LAVANGIKĀ *and* MADAYANTIKĀ Oh strange that fate should have been so often cruel and then should end in such happiness for us!

[*Enter Saudāmanī.*]

SAUDĀMANĪ Reverend Kāmandakī, your disciple of old salutes you.

KĀMANDAKĪ Ah, it is my dear Saudāmanī!

MĀDHAVA *and* MAKARANDA What, is this Her Reverence's earliest pupil, Saudāmanī, of whom she was so fond? Then all is plain.

KĀMANDAKĪ

Come to me, you who have amassed such merit 20
By restoring so many to life – come, it is long since I saw you.
Though my body is filled with bliss, delight it further
By embracing me, dearest of friends – give up this salutation.

It is you the world must salute, whose miraculous power 21
Is shown in such deeds beyond even a bodhisattva's encompassing.*
The seed which was always there in our former acquaintance
Has borne us now a most abundant harvest.

MADAYANTIKĀ *and* LAVANGIKĀ Is this lady Saudāmanī?

MĀLATĪ Indeed she is. Being the friend of all who are connected with Her Reverence, she rebuked Kapālakuṇḍalā, took me to her home and tended me as carefully as Her Reverence would have done. And then she took the bakula garland as a token and came here to save all of you as well.

THE OTHERS This second Kāmandakī has been most gracious to us.

MĀDHAVA *and* MAKARANDA Oh, wonderful!

*The Buddhist term *bodhisattva*, 'one whose essence is enlightenment', refers to one who, though capable of entering nirvāṇa, holds back out of compassion for his fellow creatures, so as to guide them too along the path.

22 Even the wishing-jewel
Requires the exertion of wishing.
But this noble lady needed no prompting
To work her miracle.

SAUDĀMANĪ [*to herself*] Oh, such extreme kindness causes me confusion. [*Aloud*] Your Reverence, here is a letter written in Bhūrivasu's presence, and with the glad consent of Nandana, which His Majesty the King of Padmāvatī sends to the noble Mādhava. [*She hands over a letter.*]

KĀMANDAKĪ [*takes it and reads it*]

23 'With you who stand first among men of merit and are of excellent family,
A noble and blameless son-in-law, we are highly pleased.
Therefore for your delight we do this day upon your beloved friend
Hereby bestow Madayantikā, already joined to him in love.'

[*To Mādhava, joyfully*] Do you hear, dear child?

MĀDHAVA I hear. Now I have all I want.

MĀLATĪ Thank heaven, my heart is free of that rankling anxiety.

LAVANGIKĀ Now every one of Mādhava's wishes has come to pass.

KĀMANDAKĪ Why, there are Avalokitā, Buddharakshitā and Kalahamsaka in the distance! They have seen that we are all reunited, and they are dancing with sheer joy.

[*All smilingly look.*]

LAVANGIKĀ Who would not dance, in this festival of satisfied wishes?

KĀMANDAKĪ Yes, you are right. Was there ever a tale so marvellous, so full of charm, so brilliant?

SAUDĀMANĪ What is most delightful is that at last the cherished desire of the ministers Bhūrivasu and Devarāta for a union of their two children is fulfilled.

MĀLATI [*to herself*] What is this?

MĀDHAVA *and* MAKARANDA [*in wonder*] Your Reverence, what Her Honour says is at variance with the facts!

LAVANGIKĀ [*aside*] Your Reverence, what is to be done?

KĀMANDAKĪ [*to herself*] Now Nandana is won over by Madayantikā's marriage, we have no more anxieties. [*Aloud*] No, dear children, it is not at variance with the facts. For when they were students, they took an oath before Saudāmanī and myself to arrange a marriage between their children. But this was how we avoided the anger of the King's minister.

MĀLATĪ What secrecy!

MĀDHAVA *and* MAKARANDA Extraordinary! We salute the unswerving strategy of the mighty.

KĀMANDAKĪ Mādhava, dear child,

The joyful union of you both which had been longed for 24
Has come to pass, through your merit, my plans, and my pupils' labours;
The wedding of your dear friend with his loved one has been assured;
The King and Nandana approve. Tell me what else should be done.

MĀDHAVA [*in joy*] Can there be blessings beyond these? But let this be –

Let the good be flawlessly happy, all evil dispelled. 25

Let kings safeguard the earth, abiding always in
  righteousness.
Let the people's merit ensure abundant rain in season,
And let them enjoy the close and happy fellowship of
  friends and family.

[*They all withdraw.*]

Glossary of Names and Unfamiliar Terms

This glossary is intended to supplement the footnotes in the text, especially by explaining those allusions which are merely incidental or are common to more than one context. Readers anxious for a more systematic or more detailed exposition of the cultural background to the plays are referred to A. L. Basham's *The Wonder That Was India* (Sidgwick & Jackson, 1954) and the bibliographies contained therein. Those specifically interested in the mythology, imagery and conventions of Classical Sanskrit literature are referred to D. H. H. Ingalls, *An Anthology of Sanskrit Court Poetry* (abridged edition for the general reader, Harvard University Press, 1968).

Angiras a legendary sage, author of a lawbook.
arjuna *Terminalia arjuna:* a large pale-barked forest tree.
arka *Calotropis gigantea:* see note on *Śakuntalā*, Act II, p. 64.
ascetic one who practises austerities, esp. in a hermitage.
aśmantaka a plant of uncertain identity.
aśoka *Jonesia aśoka* or *Saraca indica:* a small evergreen tree with spreading branches which bloom red in springtime.
austerities self-discipline, including mental exercises and mortification of the flesh, for the sake of spiritual emancipation or the attainment of supernatural power.
bakula *Mimusops elengi:* a large evergreen tree with extremely fragrant flowers.
betel a plant whose aromatic leaves are made into a preparation with the nut of the areca palm and other ingredients for chewing, esp. after meals.
Bhavānī name of Pārvatī, wife of Śiva.

Brahmā the creator god, forming a trinity with (but in practice of less importance than) Śiva and Vishṇu.

brahmin belonging to the caste or class charged with guardianship of learning and religion.

caste The four great classes (*varṇa*) of Hindu society were Brahmin, Warrior (*kshatriya*), Merchant (*vaiśya*) and Serf (*śūdra*). Below these existed a large body of outcastes or untouchables, contact with whom was polluting. (Scholars now usually prefer to restrict the term 'caste' to the much smaller endogamous subdivisions [*jāti*] of comparatively recent times, of which there are 3,000 or so in present-day India.)

Clerk of Death Chitragupta, recorder of good and bad deeds on behalf of Yama, the God of Death.

cloud cuckoo the *chātaka* (*Cuculus melanoleucus*), supposed to live on the water of rain-clouds.

convent (in *Mālatī and Mādhava*) a community of Buddhist mendicant nuns.

darbha *Poa cynosuroides:* a type of grass with sharp pointed stalks, used in sacrificial ritual.

dark fortnight half of month from full to new moon.

Demon of Eclipse Rāhu, who causes eclipses by swallowing the moon. He is the head, and Ketu the trunk, of a single demon cut in two by Vishṇu. In astronomy they are the ascending and descending nodes of the moon.

dūrvā *Panicum dactylon:* a type of grass, 'panic grass'.

Fierce Goddess see note on *Mālatī and Mādhava*, Act I, p. 313.

Five-arrowed God Love.

Flower City Pāṭaliputra.

Ganeśa an elephant-headed god, the elder son of Śiva and Pārvatī.

Gangā the sacred river Ganges.

Godāvarī a river of southern India.

Greek (Skt *yavana*, i.e. Ionian) Literary references indicate that Greek girls were employed by Indian kings as archery attendants.

Hastināpura Dushyanta's capital city.
hermitage a community of ascetics, frequently in some remote forest area. It was the Indian ideal that once the duties of household and family were at an end, a couple should retire to a hermitage for peace of mind and spiritual salvation.
holy earth earth taken from a place of pilgrimage.
Holy Mountain Śrīparvata in southern India, a centre of Śaivite asceticism.
ichor a sweet fluid secreted on the temples of a rutting male elephant.
Indra war-god and thunder god – the chief deity of Vedic times and comparable with Zeus, but later eclipsed in religious importance by Vishṇu and Śiva. His weapon is the thunderbolt.
Indra's Ford name of a place of pilgrimage.
ingudī *Terminalia catappa:* see note on *Śakuntalā*, Act I, p. 46.
Jain adherent of a religion which, like Buddhism, rejects the authority of the Vedas.
kadamba *Nauclea cadamba:* a tree which flowers immediately in response to the coming of the monsoon.
Kālanemi name of a demon.
Kali age in Hindu cosmology, the last and lowest of the four ages through which the world passes before returning to the start of an aeon. The present Kali age began over 5,000 years ago and has some 427,000 years still to run. (N.B.: there is no connection with Kālī, name of the Fierce Goddess.)
Kāma the God of Love. He has a bow with a string of black bees and five flowers for arrows, of which the most used is the mango blossom. He once aimed his bow at Śiva to make him fall in love with Pārvatī, and Śiva in anger burnt him to ashes with the flame from his third eye; but since Śiva ended by marrying Pārvatī, Kāma's defeat was no more than temporary.
Kāma Sūtra 'Aphorisms of Love', a famous textbook attributed to the sage Vātsyāyana.
kampila *Rottleria tinctoria.*
Karālā a form of the Fierce Goddess.

karanja *Pongamia glabra:* a hardy deciduous tree.

kāśa *Saccharum spontaneum:* a species of grass.

Kaśyapa a primeval sage, son of Marīchi and father of Indra.

ketaka *Pardanus odoratissimus:* a tree which blooms in the rainy season, with white, spiky, sweet-smelling blossoms.

Ketu the other half of the Demon of Eclipse.

Kimpurusha sprites a race of horse-headed beings, celestial singers.

Krishṇa the most important incarnation of Vishṇu – both a god who imparts the highest religious teaching and a hero famed in youth for his amorous exploits.

kubjaka *Rosa moschata:* musk rose.

Kumāra 'The Prince', Skanda, son of Śiva and Pārvatī.

kuṭaja *Wrightia antidysenterica:* a tree which blooms white in the rainy season.

lac a scarlet dye. Among other uses, it was applied cosmetically to the soles of the feet.

Lakshmī goddess of beauty and good fortune, the consort of Vishṇu.

lavalī *Averrhoa acida:* a vine that bears a round white fruit.

lodhra *Symplocos racemosa:* a red-barked tree which blossoms white in the rainy season.

Lord of the Universe Śiva.

Love see Kāma.

lute the *vīṇā.*

Mālinī the river which ran past Kaṇva's hermitage.

Marīchi one of the seven great seers, father of Kaśyapa.

Meru a mythical mountain, north of the Himālayas, the centre and axis of the earth.

Mind-god Kāma.

moonstone a gem supposed to liquefy beneath the moon's rays.

Mother of Spirits the Fierce Goddess.

mustard seed White mustard seed was placed on the head and forehead of a new-born baby to ward off evil influences.

outcaste see caste.

Pārvatī (lit., 'Daughter of the Mountain') wife of Śiva and daughter of the Mountain God Himālaya.

penance the practising of austerities.

poison-girl a secret agent trained to seduce the enemy and administer poison to which she herself had been made immune.

prakaraṇa 'invented drama' (see Introduction).

Puru ancestor of King Dushyanta, founder of the Paurava branch of the Lunar Dynasty.

Purūravas a mythical king, hero of Kālidāsa's drama *Urvaśī.*

Rati 'Pleasure', the wife of Kāma. She mourned bitterly when he was annihilated by Śiva.

River Palace the principal royal palace of Pāṭaliputra, on the bank of the Ganges.

Rohiṇī the ninth lunar asterism (containing the star Aldebaran), pictured as the favourite wife of the moon.

Sacred River the Ganges.

sacred thread the thread with which males of the three highest castes are invested on initiation, and which is worn continuously thereafter.

Śaivite adept The *kāpālikas* were devotees who emulated the asceticism of Śiva himself. They went about naked and smeared with ashes, wearing a garland of skulls and carrying a club or staff with streamers and bells attached to it. The nature and purpose of their asceticism might be benevolent (as with Saudāmanī) or sinister (as with Aghoraghaṇṭa).

sal (Skt *sarja*) *Vatica robusta* or *Shorea robusta:* a resinous forest tree.

sandal, sandalwood a fragrant wood, often made into a cooling paste.

Śankara 'The Beneficent One', name of Śiva.

sānkhya one of the six recognized philosophical systems of Hinduism.

saptaparṇa *Alstonia scholaris* or *Echites scholaris:* a large shady tree.

Serpent Śesha the Serpent King, who supports the world, provides a couch for Vishṇu and is worn by Śiva about his person.

Śibi see note on *Rākshasa's Ring*, Act I, p. 196.

śilindra a plant of uncertain identity.

Śiva one of the two chief gods of Hinduism from Classical times onwards (the other being Vishṇu). Of his three main aspects, two are complementary: the beneficent (Śiva, Śankara, Śambhu) and the destructive (Bhairava, Hara). The third aspect intersects with the other two, that of the supreme ascetic (Sthāṇu, 'The Immovable One'), who performs austerities of unbelievable rigour and duration – for reasons which surpass human understanding, since he is already omnipotent.

Six Strands The six strands of policy are: agreement, conflict, attack, (masterly) inactivity, alliance and double policy (peace with one enemy combined with war with another).

soma a plant from which a hallucinogenic drink was prepared and consumed during the Vedic sacrifice. A recent theory identifies the plant in question as the mushroom Fly Agaric.

Somatīrtha a place of pilgrimage, possibly to be identified with modern Somnath.

Taittirīya recension a particular school of interpretation (ascribed to the ancient scholar Tittiri) of a Vedic text, the 'Black Yajurveda'.

tamāla *Xanthochymus pictorius:* a tree with white flowers but a very dark bark.

Terror Dance the wild *tāṇḍava* dance of Śiva and his worshippers (and so of the Fierce Goddess also), normally danced at twilight.

top-knot the lock of hair untouched when the rest of the head is shaved in the tonsure ceremony of a male child, and left to grow indefinitely thereafter.

Triple City's Victor Śiva, who shot the flaming arrow which destroyed the Triple City of the demons.

Udayana King of the Vaisas, a popular hero of romantic stories.

Upanishads works interpreting the mystical essence of the Vedas; in effect, the earliest Hindu metaphysical texts.
Urvaśī a celestial nymph, heroine of a drama by Kālidāsa.
Vāsavadattā Chief Queen of Udayana.
Vedas the earliest Hindu scriptures, written in a pre-Classical form of Sanskrit. The most ancient, the Ṛg Veda, dates back to about 1,000 B.C.
Vindhyas a range of hills across central India.
Vishṇu a god who in his cosmic form reclines with his consort Lakshmī upon a couch formed by the Serpent King. Central to Vishṇu mythology are his worldly incarnations (*avatāras*, 'descents'), of which ten are regularly mentioned, the most important being his incarnation as Krishṇa. Three others are referred to in these plays. **The Dwarf:** Vishṇu had himself born as the dwarf offspring of Aditi and Kaśyapa, and tricked the demon Bali, who had conquered the Universe, into promising him as much land as he could cover in three strides. He then transformed himself into his cosmic form, and with his first stride covered the earth, with his second the atmosphere, and with his third heaven. **The Boar:** The demon Hiraṇyāksha seized the earth and plunged it into the sea. Vishṇu turned himself into a huge boar and raised the earth up from the water on the tip of his tusk. **The Man-Lion:** Hiraṇyāksha's brother Hiraṇya-kaśipu was immune to assassination 'by night or by day, and by god, man or beast'. Vishṇu took the hybrid form of a man with the head and claws of a lion, and ripped him apart at the moment between day and night.
Vishṇu's mid realm the sky or atmosphere (a reference to the Dwarf incarnation).
warrior belonging to the *kshatriya* caste.
water offering daily ritual oblation to deceased relatives.
wishing-jewel a jewel granting its possessor all his wishes.
wishing-tree a tree granting all desires, one of the five legendary trees of paradise.
without ceremony see note on *Śakuntalā*, Act IV, p. 92.
Yayāti father of Puru.

yellow orpiment a bright yellow dye made from the bile of cattle.

yoga spiritual discipline, asceticism. Used more narrowly, the term yoga refers to one of the six recognized philosophical systems – like sāṅkhya, with which it has certain affinities.

yogī practitioner of yoga.

yoginī female practitioner of yoga.

zone imaginary division of the stage (see Introduction).